LESSER BREEDS

PRAISE FOR NAYANTARA SAHGAL

A TIME TO BE HAPPY

'Mrs Sahgal has put her story, written with high literary accomplishment, into the mouth of a young man...this is a most polished entertainment... presenting her carefully selected gallery of characters with almost Austenian detachment and humour.'

The Times

THIS TIME OF MORNING

'Immensely intelligent microcosmic picture of India today...Mrs Sahgal, like Jane Austen, never gets out of her social depth.'

Sunday Telegraph

'At last something really new in novels by an author who knows her subject and her background thoroughly.'

Manchester Evening News

STORM IN CHANDIGARH

'Mrs Sahgal handles the interweaving of political mission with personal involvement with great skill and finesse...This is a quiet novel which nevertheless never eschews problems of violence...altogether a fine piece of writing.'

The Scotsman

At last what we have all waited for - a real novel about a real India. A credit, not only to Mrs Sahgal's brilliance as a writer, but to Indian letters as a whole.'

The Village Voice

A SITUATION IN NEW DELHI

'This is the story of a woman Cabinet Minister...struggling to preserve cherished ideals under pressure from looming violence and venal compromise. It's a moving, even inspiring novel: an affirmation that ideals are always worth fighting for.'

The Sunday Times

'Recent events in India have lent a peculiar interest and topicality to Nayantara Sahgal's novel...a brilliant and provocative piece of fact-based fiction.'

The Financial Times

THE DAY IN SHADOW

'Mrs Sahgal traces two parallel courses that come together at last ... an important writer and her work deserves wide recognition.'

The Chicago Sun-Times Book Week

RICH LIKE US

'The novel is wonderfully set apart by a fine, clear, disenchanted eye and an acerbic moral intelligence that is devastating without ever raising its voice.'

Publisher's Weekly

'Sahgal's novel ... winner of this year's Sinclair Award, examines the Indo-British cultural inheritance and its links with contemporary events in India ... some of the ignominious aspects of this time form the background to parts of *Midnight's Children*.'

Times Literary Supplement

PLANS FOR DEPARTURE

'Mrs Sahgal handles her ingredients – love, compromise, anguish, serenity, the writing on the wall – with lucent sincerity and a feeling for both kinds of history, outward and inward.'

The Guardian

'The mention of revolution or religion can clear a book-shop fiction aisle faster than a fire alarm ... but with a chilly wit and a metaphysical calm, India's prize-winning Nayantara Sahgal has mastered the difficult art.'

Time Magazine

MISTAKEN IDENTITY

'With subtle irony, adroit wit and accruing suspense, Mrs Sahgal skillfully reveals a personal moral quandary and India's cultural and historical triumphs in the face of grave political turmoil.'

New York Times

'This is an elegant, adroitly constructed, mordantly written book, in which the general image and particular manifestation of our glamorous Raj is a garrulously over-tenanted prison cell.'

The Guardian

LESSER BREEDS

Nayantara Sahgal

HarperCollins *Publishers* India
a joint venture with

New Delhi

First Published in India in 2003 by
HarperCollins *Publishers* India
a joint venture with
The India Today Group
B-315 Okhla Phase-I, New Delhi-110 020

HarperCollins *Publishers*
B-315 Okhla Phase-I, New Delhi-110 020, India
77-85 Fulham Palace Road, London W6 8JB, United Kingdom
Hazelton Lanes, 55 Avenue Road, Suite 2900, Toronto, Ontario M5R 3L2
and 1995 Markham Road, Scarborough, Ontario M1B 5M8, Canada
25 Ryde Road, Pymble, Sydney, NSW 2073, Australia
31 View Road, Glenfield, Auckland 10, New Zealand
10 East 53rd Street, New York NY 10022, USA

Typeset in 11/14 Classical Garamond by

Printed and bound at
Thomson Press (India) Ltd.

With love to
Gamma, Getto, Kabir and Zum

Who are otherwise known as
Gautam and Giorgio Sahgal
Kabir and Ayan Joshi

If, drunk with sight of power, we loose
wild tongues that have not Thee in awe
Such boastings as the Gentiles use,
Or lesser breeds without the Law.

—Recessional
Rudyard Kipling

*Vaishnava jan t'o tehne re kahiye je
piid parayi jaaney re*

(Him we call a Vaishnav who knows the
pain of others)

I

Company Bagh

'... two hundred thousand men for the regular army, voluntarism if possible, conscription if necessary.'

Sir Michael O'Dwyer, Lt Governor of the Punjab,
4 May 1918

'What is required is some façade which will leave the essential mechanism of power in our hands.'

Viceroy Lord Irwin, July 1929

'The British in India ... have lived their life apart, relying on their vast and intricate organization and the force behind it.'

Jawaharlal Nehru, 1934

'The disturbances were crushed with all the weight of the Government ... Larger reinforcements have reached India and the number of white troops in that country is larger than at any time in the British connection.'

Prime Minister Winston Churchill, 1942

One

The tongawala's whip landed a vicious lash on the horse's scraggy rump. The startled animal reared violently on its hindlegs, jolting Nurullah downward on his seat as they turned into the compound. He righted himself when the creature dropped its legs disjointedly to the gravel and stumbled into a clumsy canter up the circular drive. The lawn they were skirting was scorched yellow where it had not gone dead brown. A hawk hovered high above, suspended in the brutal blaze.

Nurullah twisted round to look over his shoulder at the sun-struck two-tiered mansion ballooning out shiningly in the heat like an illustration in a child's storybook. Its third less lofty tier of roof terrace was crowned by, of all things, a dome! He had the feeling he was approaching a monument.

The tongawala jerked to a stop under the columned portico to let Nurullah down and flicked his horse mechanically toward some tree shade further on where other tongas and a car or two waited. Wide shallow steps led to the verandah encircling the mansion. On the lawn side a steeper flight went down to a dry fountain baking in the sun. Stone fish stood on their tails around the rim of its cement basin with their mouths gaping open. A grizzled old mali with a wet rag on his head was inching along on his haunches down there, uprooting weeds and tufts of wizened grass with deft digs of his khurpi and flinging his dug-up waste into a bamboo basket. Nurullah watched a trail of loose dark earth lengthen behind him until the mali stood up on buckling bow legs, hitched his loincloth higher on his fleshless thighs, wound his headrag tighter and hoisted the basket onto it. Before Nurullah remembered to call after him he had clumped off like a rider astride a sagging sway-backed mare.

There was no other servant in sight. Once there had been an army of them and there must still be a chowkidar to show sightseers around. The place had been every patriot's Mecca for the last eleven years, ever since the family and a couple of hundred other Akbarabadis had stood their ground when they were cavalry-charged outside the gates for demonstrating against the Prince of Wales' visit in 1921. A trampled mess the horses' hooves and club-swinging mounted police had made of them as they went down unresisting in obedience to the new creed: If blood must be shed in this battle, let it be your own.

Nurullah had joined the University of Akbarabad as a lecturer in English to First Years only six months ago and had never come here sightseeing. But he had been here once before, to a reception in the garden with his mentor, Professor Bhattacharya. His clearest recollection of that evening was of being prodded through the throng of guests by the professor's sharp-knuckled little fist in his spine and halting every time Robin-da halted to socialize, as garrulously with once-met acquaintances as with his lifelong friends. Without the slightest warning Robin-da had propelled him into the host's presence and introduced him with unnecessary flourish as 'an impoverished but immensely promising young man'. To his own utter astonishment Nurullah had then behaved worse than the smitten sightseers who came here gaping like the fountain fish, expecting an encounter with celestial beings. He had stood there witless as an imbecile, forgetting even to do adab. He didn't know what he had expected of the mansion's owner, a condescending nod perhaps, the self-importance of one who has been present at great events and knows that none can take place without him. But instead the host, a bronze-haired man some years older and slightly taller than himself, with eyes of the light brown colour known as hazel, had taken Nurullah's hand between both of his and given him a radiant smile.

He went up the verandah steps to a rose-reddish white-flecked floor. A closer look revealed an odd mosaic of roses sprinkled with rice grains. The front door being open and no servant in sight, he lifted the chik and walked in, to a big antechamber as bare as a bone. There was not a sign of the luxury he had heard so much about. It must have gone with the queer turn human behaviour had taken since the new creed. He looked about him for some remnant of the cushioned extravagances of the rich but there was none. An uncarpeted staircase angled sharply at a landing and went on up to a higher landing open to the fierce flooding heat of the upper verandah. A copper-bound globe light of dusty turquoise glass studded with glass rubies hung over the stairwell on a long ornamental chain, but not long enough to reach when the bulb needed changing. One of the army of servants must have had to heft a step ladder to the first landing and risk his neck leaning out sideways to do the job and that must have been when the globe got dusted. Every fixture in the house must have been designed for a regiment of servants in their muscular prime.

The bench beside the tall black telephone in the stairwell was the businesslike sort whose seat lifts up to provide storage space. Only the mirrored hatstand aflower with curly brass hooks looked like a piece of family furniture and it must have been out of use since the family's callers took to wearing Gandhi caps. The door to the next room was open a crack and he could hear voices in conference. He sat down on the hard bench to wait, fanning himself with the envelope he was carrying, and wondered what had thrown him into confusion on his previous visit.

A portrait of the late master framed in sandalwood hung opposite him. Nurullah had seen gaudy replicas of it garlanded with marigolds in paan shops in the bazaar. There was a thread of wilting jasmine on this one, too frail and wispy for the proud grey head and commanding features. Incense smoke had already overpowered its fading scent on its own perfumed spiral into the high vaulted ceiling.

The portrait's painted eyes held whoever's was looking into them from wherever the viewer sat. The whole effect left one in no doubt about the magnetic pull of the lawyer's personality. He was best remembered for the treason trial after the Great War and his defence of the sole survivor of the bloodbath below Victoria's statue in Company Bagh that had killed his three co-conspirators. The survivor had had to die too, on the gallows, but his lawyer's chilling argument — a far cry from the emotional oratory of his contemporaries — had whipped the mask off a ruling power whose law courts condemned men to death for following its own example. 'For the crime', he had famously declared, 'of putting their words to your music.' Nurullah could not believe he of all Indians had submitted to a martyr's death, standing his ground and being trampled under horses' hooves outside the gate. The arts of war must have been more his style as cold accuracy had been his hallmark at the trial. No one would ever forget his description of the 1919 slaughter in Company Bagh. One body, blown apart against Victoria's pedestal, had died propped up by it with its chest ripped open and its legs flung wide. The second youth had caught the bullets in his back halfway up her marble skirts and fallen backward in a broken heap. The third had been gunned headfirst into the red, white and blue flower border, all three mown down for rising against the invader, what any Englishman would have considered his sacred duty. Then at a signal from the bandmaster the military band had played on.

The statue had escaped without a cracked chin or a chipped diadem. Very few had heard the actual shots and the screams of the nearest invitees had sunk into '*Send him victorious, happy and glorious,*' so triumphantly had the band played on, brooking no more delay, for the diamond jubilee celebration to mark the anniversary of the day the Queen took over from the Company had already been delayed a year because of the war. News of the drama travelled sedately by beat of drum proclaiming martial law in the city.

In Company Bagh an officer read out the proclamation. Then he had a row of iron sheets lined up on a mound behind him machine-gunned in a deafening display of fire power. Ordering the machine guns turned around to face the thunderstruck assembled citizens he informed them they would likewise be riddled with holes if they ever again rose against the Sarkar. Nurullah had a newcomer's interest in the sights, sounds and stories of this, his first city. Leaning on the iron railing put up that day in 1919 to fence off the bloodied marble he had thought that thus casually observed, years after the event, what one knew as history did not grow claws and tear into one's flesh.

The antechamber was becoming a furnace. He edged into the adjoining room and stood pressed against the wall, invisible as a fly in the half-dark, revelling in the breeze of the two fast ceiling fans. Tinted skylights bathed the shuttered room in a light like cool green bottled water. The furniture had been pushed to the walls and people sat on a white floor sheet lounging against bolsters. A roar of laughter greeted his arrival making him break into a sweat again. He was about to start explaining his presence when he realized they hadn't even seen him. They were enjoying an Urdu sher recited by a plump man in a sherwani who was shaking with laughter himself. A delayed boisterous shout came from a woman in thick white khadi like the rest of them after the couplet was translated for her. As his eyes got used to the gloom he saw she was wearing an enormous red canna behind one ear. The greybeard next to her drew his dhoti up to his knee to scratch his hairy shin, making a scraping rasping sound in a room that must once have heard nothing coarser than the whisper and rustle of silk. He seemed to be presiding because he called on the master of the house for an account of his tour of the province.

The master apologized for his dust-choked throat and started to speak but Nurullah, recalling that this was a son who at nineteen had stood distraught over his father's trampled corpse on a road of trampled corpses, missed his opening remarks. Could a son forget the sight of a father done to death before his eyes? The thought sent a feverish spasm through Nurullah. A hundred hows and whys laid siege to his mind for he was unable to connect the atmosphere in this cool calm room, its spirited exchanges and its humour with atrocities seen and suffered. Many of those present must also have been there on that road, holding their ground when two lines of mounted police galloped upon them and horses reared up on their hind legs with their hoofs trembling high in the air before they came pounding down. To be sure the plump-cheeked man in the sherwani had referred to the new District Magistrate as one reputed to be a haramzada, and a younger dhoti-clad party member had roundly abused the police, calling them the bastard sons of foreign swine, but it was evidently just their way of talking.

He listened to the master describing his tour as a deeply moving experience of withering crops, dying cattle and famished shadows of men and women who had been driven into the fields when the rent collectors had seized their goods, grain and animals to recover the raised rents they could not pay. He had sat with them around their cooking fires and been impressed by their determination not to be cowed. Not so long ago their kin had been conscripted for the Great War as soldiers and as labour and rushed to relieve the British at Ypres and Flanders. The heirs of many who were killed were evicted from their holdings and those who survived the trenches came home to another war, against raised rents and impoverishing cesses. Remember the carbuncle cess a zamindar had levied to finance month-long temple prayers for his recovery from a septic carbuncle on his buttock? This raised a laugh but the master held up his hand.

'In no free country could anyone force them to pay,' he said, his anger straining to be heard. 'They're ready to organize a No Tax campaign with our help.'

There was an instant babble of alarm. It was abnormally loud and assertive after the husk of a voice but the bitter-sweet reminder that some in this world are born free made Nurullah lose the thread of the argument.

'Not so fast, Nikhil,' spoke someone agitatedly above the rest. 'Already we're outlawed. Our public meetings and processions are banned. Our bank accounts, our property, our cars are up for grabs. At this rate we'll lose our zamindar supporters.'

Nurullah made himself comfortable on the floor, resigned to a long wait. The greybeard intervened to say raised rents and rapacious extractions were nothing new. The robber Company had started them and the Crown had reduced kisans to serfdom by making zamindars outright owners of all cultivable land and revenue collectors for the Crown. There were no poorer peasants in the country but the question right now was whether the party could risk losing its zamindar supporters.

'Every move we make is a risk,' agreed the husk when it could be heard again, 'but all our supporters know that estates will go to the cultivators the day we come to power.'

For some strange reason this statement had a magically silencing effect. Nurullah supposed it must be because that mythical day need not concern them this afternoon. The next thing he knew they were getting down to arrangements for a kisan conference here in Akbarabad to flag off a No Tax campaign.

'I'm telling you from now it'll be a dismal failure,' the boisterous woman warned, 'the authorities will see to it that the kisans don't get here.'

'There's bound to be some show of force to discourage them,' the master agreed, 'but the Government won't want another kisan uprising on its hands like they had ten years ago.'

A date was set and details discussed, disagreed, agreed. There was no end to their talk. Finally, it was noted that party workers who volunteered their help at meetings, boycotts and pickets must be instructed to keep the kisan delegates from turning violent no matter what the provocation, especially now that there were orders to shoot agrarian agitators. Nurullah had seen those puny volunteers at a meeting Robin-da had taken him to, mere chokras some of them, in their flapping khadi shorts, who wouldn't be able to control a flea much less a roused kisan. But on that note of fantasy the worthy citizens who had argued every other issue threadbare got up to go, bland as butter and in complete accord. Nurullah found himself alone.

He looked about him at sofas and chairs upholstered in a fabric of green dragons and blue butterflies. Little round black-lacquered tables were wedged in among them. A blue-patterned pitcher glimmered in a wall niche. Scrolls of bamboos-and-willows hung on either side of it. A glass-shelved cabinet was empty but for the top shelf. He went over to admire two prancing green horses, a translucent stag with delicately branched antlers and a fat white seated goddess. These must be all that was left of the jade collection which had been confiscated in a sweep on valuables after the cavalry charge when the family had refused to pay the fines imposed for civil disobedience. In all his travels over Europe, the late master was said to have collected only Chinese things.

The master came back after seeing his colleagues off and before Nurullah could clear his throat to introduce himself, a smile of charmed surprise illumined a face both younger and older than thirty.

'So, Nurullah! At last!' spoke the husky voice, 'I keep hearing about you from Robin-da!'

Nurullah who had been rehearsing what to say had the words ready on his tongue and he was acutely aware of the man waiting for him to respond. But the warmth of the hand resting on his shoulder, the eyes smiling into his, the sheer sweetness of this heart-stirring welcome to a stranger so bewildered him that he could only deliver the professor's letter with a mumble and would have blundered out had it not been for the restraining hand. He heard himself replying to remarks he could not afterwards recall and was then seen off with the same courtesy and ceremony as the others before him. He had never known such civility, or met such a man — one who, in Sa'adi's words, would by his honey-tongued gentleness 'manage to guide an elephant with a hair.'

A week later he began to come and go. Robin-da's letter had arranged for him to help Bhai (as he now called the master of the house) with his correspondence during his free time from teaching. Once he had to stay overnight to work late over the backlog that had piled up during Bhai's tour of the province, and Bhai had suggested he move in.

∿

'Should I move in, Robin-da?' he asked his mentor doubtfully after tea and samosas at the philosophy professor's house when the other guests had gone.

Nurullah should have known the reply would be an astounded outburst from the tiny grasshopper frame.

'Move in? Naturally, move in! What is there to ask? Why are you wasting time asking? Does an invitation like this come every day? Well, well, what an oddfellow you are, Nurullah, this obstructive attitude will be the curse of you. Why are you always putting obstructions? Put away this tendency. Move in, move in. Where will you get another such opportunity to study the Movement firsthand?'

Nurullah carried a tray of used cups and chutney-smeared plates to the kitchen for time to think up a tactful reply. He wished he'd asked Eknath's advice earlier that evening, but Robin-da's tea sessions were too lively for private exchange. Even that old bore, Matul, whose philosophy students slept soundly through his droning monotone, got witty here. And Matul's wife, Hashi — Robin-da's precious chatterbox niece — hung though she was with Matul and her bunch of clanking household keys, listened for a change, her eyes shining like fresh black ink in her much admired wax-white face.

'Well?' demanded Robin-da impatiently, 'don't dawdle about. Be quick and speak your mind.'

How could he mortally offend his mentor by saying there was nothing to study in a Movement that had never so much as sent a shiver through the Raj — except once when a furious mob had burned a police thana with constables inside it. But even that had come to nothing when the Mahatma had called the Movement off and said the violence had run a rapier through his body so let us pray.

'How old may you be?' asked Robin-da sarcastically, as if he didn't know.

'Twenty-three, of course, Robin-da.'

'Of course. And clogged with ideas from everywhere but here. Ask yourself what country your brain lives in, Nurullah, and why from morning to night you are passing on a meaningless mass of harks, yonders, skylarks and daffodils to your First Years. If you cannot produce something from the mysterious mechanism of your own mind, learn from those who can. Observe what is going on around you. Cultivate another way of seeing.'

This second scathing outburst was only the tea session winding down and needed no response. Not that Nurullah could have explained why dead English poets' words of joy and sorrow, love and battle sang in his ears, or why what had begun as a livelihood — teaching mere print on a page — had entered his veins to drug and infatuate him. The dead poets echoed and re-echoed in him. 'Forget it, yaar,' Eknath had jibed, cutting into one of Nurullah's favourite quotes, 'at this rate you'll never have a thought of your own.' But if it had been forgettable it would not have been the poetry it was. Nurullah only knew that a world he had never seen loomed up around him, now ominous, now light and luminous. He was alive to its presence as one is to danger, or to an ache one cannot ignore. But what in any case, did it have to do with his dilemma?

He had a proper sense of his own worth and didn't want to be taken for a hanger-on. Still less did he fancy living in a monument on public display. Since the cavalry charge in 1921 sightseers had been coming in hordes and not just peasants from this rack-rented province. Only this morning a patriarch from the distant south had sauntered up the drive ahead of his womenfolk, his hands clasped on his portly stomach. Behind them hulked an eagle-nosed Pathan from the far northwest. What was he, whose tribe provided the savage abusive prison guards at Port Blair, doing here? One and all they behaved like pilgrims to a shrine. Nurullah had seen them stroke the rice and roses of the verandah mosaic, follow Binda the chowkidar's tottering tread around the house and stand gazing through open windows in a trance. He had seen worshippers like that, submerged waist-deep in the Ganga at daybreak lifting their arms and faces to the first ray of light, oblivious of the rubbish bobbing around them or the half-cremated corpses of paupers floating sluggishly past them on the turgid brown Ganga of the ghats. But there was that touch of trance about the town's notables, too, when they came to call, though less like the Ganga and more like Romeo's 'Soft! What light through yonder window breaks!'

'Too much literature addles the brain,' said the professor shrewdly, and pleased with his little parting shot he advised Nurullah to hurry up and move in.

But Nurullah was comfortably settled in the room Robin-da had found for him at a nominal rent at Mrs Shona Tiwari and Tiwariji's house. They were an amiable dreadfully untidy couple, uncannily lookalike, even to the gaps in their front teeth. He had a key to the side entrance and came and went as he pleased. He hardly ever saw them or their other lodger, the immaculate

Misraji, who sat fanning himself on the front verandah with his frilled Orissa hand fan. Living with the family in the domed monument would be another matter, though Bhai's was not a family in the usual sense, just his spry widowed mother, his six-year-old daughter and an ancient relative.

Ammaji spent a ritual hour spinning thread on her charkha every day, fulfilling her party pledge to spin two thousand yards of khadi thread a month. She kept her unwieldy Mahabharata on its stand beside her open to one of its blinding blue and orange illustrations of Krishna Bhagvan's heroic exploits. When there was enough handspun thread she sent it to the Khadi Bhandar in the Chowk to one Gosiben, the Bhandar in-charge, who sent it somewhere else to be woven into cloth. Nurullah had not seen Gosiben but her penetrating nasal wail pierced the dawn on Sundays when she did her rounds with party workers singing national songs. It was a relief when the wail for martyrdom gave way to robust shouts of *Bolo Bharat Mata ki jai!* as the procession passed his rented room and turned the corner.

The child, Shān, brooded menacingly over her convent homework. The relative appeared in the scorched garden before sundown to lift and lower a lionheaded cane, languidly directing the mali's hose and watering can to patches of weeded soil, potted plants and newly dug beds. Between lifting and lowering, Pyare Chacha stood surveying the scene with immense dignity, one pointed jooti planted slightly forward and outward of its pair, one narrow crinkled hand placed over the other on the lion's head, looking like a lifesize portrait of himself in shades of weak tea and tarnished silver.

Two days later Nurullah, still only half decided, crossed the reddish-pink verandah mosaic carrying his small trunk on his head, his bedroll under one arm and his tiffin carrier. He waved Ramdin, the mali, away when he came hurrying on his buckling bow legs to help. His luggage deposited upstairs, he was taken to an outhouse to cyclostyle notices of the kisan conference. Bhai looked in when he was stacking the cyclostyled sheets and tying them into bundles, and Nurullah assured him he would smuggle the bundles out for distribution after dark with three of his trusted students. Bhai was vastly amused.

'No need for all that rigmarole, just distribute them,' he said. 'We don't work in the dark, Nurullah, because we have nothing to hide. I've already informed the District Magistrate about our plans.'

He added warmly, 'I hope you're going to be at the public meeting on the last day.'

Nurullah, who had had no intention of being there, had felt dutybound to attend and was caught in the middle of the crowded shamiana when the furor began. The speeches had scarcely ended when he heard the sickening thud of lathis on both sides of the packed gathering. Cursing his own stupidity he willed the kisan crowd to break up its solid seated ranks and get out of this death trap. In rising panic he realized no one was getting up. A reedy voice behind him called 'Eeeen-kalab' in a wierdly unlikely longdrawn out summons to revolution, and 'Zindabad' rose roaring in his ears, but the only movement he could see was flailing arms and legs being dragged out of the shamiana. He searched frantically for an exit but trapped as they all were in a monster's snapping jaws, there was no escape. In horrifying minutes the monster came battering its way through. Nurullah was struggling to his feet when a blow between his shoulder blades sent him sprawling face down on the coir matting where he lay winded till he was booted over on his back, seized by his arms and dragged out of the shamiana. Outside was a welter of bodies painfully disentangling in a fog of dust. Some lay writhing on their backs, others folded knees to chest like crumpled question marks on mud that was scoured by the trails of dragged bodies. He rolled onto his hands and knees and crawled his way out of the welter. On the main road the speakers, Bhai among them, were getting into a barred police van in orderly single file.

Nurullah spent the next hour helping to lift and carry the worst injured on durries making do for stretchers, for removal by the volunteers. Dazedly following their directions he learned that some were being taken back to the mansion where a dispensary had been set up in one wing after the Prince of Wales' visit. The volunteers were marvelling at the moderation of the police. What a change, said the old ones, from the murderous assault that time, or the well-aimed brutality on the Salt Marchers on Dandi beach two years ago. Nurullah shudderingly recalled a foreign journalist's account of the carnage on Dandi beach. Rods had descended on unprotected heads, leaving fractured skulls and broken shoulders on the sand. Then the police had borne down on the inert bloodied bundles and savage kicking had begun.

'They aren't used to non-violence,' he heard a volunteer say regretfully, 'ahimsa turns them into mad dogs.'

Nurullah unlocked his bicycle from the jungle of machinery at the entrance and reached home as Ammaji and Shān were getting into a car. He was beckoned in beside the driver to go with them to Akbarabad Jail in case Bhai had any instructions for him, but when they got there he was not allowed into the jail office. He tramped back down the road to a tree stump in the shade. A burning breeze blew his sweat dry. He felt filthy, disordered and disgraced. His kurta was torn, the skin of his back was raw, his face was gashed and bleeding and his arms had nearly been wrenched out of their sockets. Anger flamed through him on a tide of delayed reaction. Rigid on the tree stump he relived the shame of crawling on all fours among other kicked and beaten crawlers. The misbegotten order forbidding them to return blow for blow had reduced men to this craven condition.

A hundred yards distant two convicts yoked together like oxen were hauling water from a well in a leather bucket and emptying it into a trough. He watched them plodding back and forth until their dreary dementing drill swam out of focus. It was a relief to hear the grate and clang of rusted iron as the massive jail gate was pulled shut, bolted and padlocked. Bhai's solitary figure stood behind it gripping the bars and Ammaji was coming down the road holding Shān by the hand.

Suddenly snatching her hand from Ammaji's, Shān went storming, stumbling back. Nurullah raced after her but she was there before him, her arms wrapped round her father's legs through the bars, screaming frenziedly. The noise was harrowing. Nothing like a child sobbing her heart out, it was all the furies unleashed, and she kept at it with the stamina of a mourner at Mohurrum. Nurullah stood by helpless, as did Bhai on the other side, his face contorted with anguish, his hands nailed to the bars far above her. When at last she slackened her convulsive grip on his legs and hiccoughed to a stop, Nurullah picked her up and carried her to the car where Ammaji took charge, saying she should have been prepared, it happened every time. At home he tried to lift Shān out but she shoved him aside with both fists and darted into the house without a backward glance. Like an arrow to its mark, thought Nurullah, noting that today had set the girl's rebellious spirit apart from her surroundings in some impressive way.

Old Mrs Framjee whose car it was waited on the front steps with her son, Nusli. The aged lady was wearing one of her lace-edged saris pinned about with brooches. Her stately height, her hump and her drooping cheeks gave her the noble look of a sorrowful camel. She received Ammaji into her open arms as Nurullah had seen her do every time they met or parted, and held the smaller woman to her aged bosom in a close customary embrace. Short neat sixty-year-old Nusli in his round black topi looked on. They went indoors where a roomful of callers greeted Ammaji's entry into the Chinese room. A dishevelled man came out, glanced approvingly at Nurullah's torn kurta and gashed face and requested him to send in drinking water.

Dying of thirst himself Nurullah poured two glassfuls from the surahi in the pantry, drained them and hollered for Kallu. He left the cook filling glasses on a tray and started up the stairs to take a bath. He would take formal leave of Ammaji in the morning. Shān's lung-bursting farewell had allowed no talk with Bhai and nothing had been said on the way home but for the driver's cryptic comment on the sky, as they drove home under its livid sagging load of unshed rain.

He was halfway up the stairs when Robin-da emerged from the Chinese room guturally intoning a complicated alaap in his tuneless voice, a sure sign in him of suppressed excitement. He caught sight of Nurullah and twirled an imperious finger toward the door without interrupting his alaap. Nurullah reluctantly accompanied him across the burnt-out grass to the neglected tennis court where, screened from the house by a trellis draped with some bedraggled creeper, more time was wasted ambling to the far end of the red gravel till the alaap vibrated to a growl and Robin-da spoke, suddenly brisk.

'There's a message for you. Nikhil wants you to tutor Shān until his release. Of course I told Ammaji you would.'

Nurullah fought down his irritation — minor compared with the day's earlier punishment — and dismissed the message from his mind. Robin-da now chatty and mellow, explained that the Sacred Heart Convent did not suit Shān's temperament and what school fed children on anything but *Elsewhere*? He had seen the child scowling into space trying to conjure a dog for a composition titled My Dog. The venerable pundit who taught her Hindi at home was no better. He and his kind picked out titles from old Board Examination papers. This one's 1919 favourite was The Moonlight of Winter. All this must alas continue. What Nikhil had in mind was its correction.

'Counter-teaching is required, Nurullah. Cast your mind about for ways to correct what she is taught. Cultivate in her another way of seeing.'

Taking Nurullah's baffled silence for consent he began his tuneless humming again. Thunder rumbled and subsided as they headed back to the portico where Robin-da had parked his bicycle. He raised each tiny foot methodically against the opposite kneecap to examine the soles of his chappals and knock red grit off them with fastidious flicks of his thumb and middle finger. Nurullah stood holding the cycle while the professor tucked up his gauzy dhoti with a metal clip, mounted and trundled off, wobbling over a bump.

Upstairs he made for the white-tiled bathroom. Furnished with a long tub on curved brass claws and a flush toilet instead of a common commode it had dazzled Nurullah when he first saw it. With rare delight he had pulled the chain and watched the flood it released. But for his bath he had stuck to the less daunting brass pail. The water gushed out lukewarm but two pailfuls revived him.

No other room he had lived in had had a dressing table. He towelled his head dry at its tilting oval mirror. The mirror stand had two toy drawers (for what miniature belongings he could not imagine) resting on a table with two regular drawers. He had had nothing to put in any of them. The deep mirror-doored almirah was empty too but for his few pyjama-kurtas. Now he wished he had made use of all that shelf and hanging space for his books. He took them out of his trunk, wiped their spines on the khadi bedspread and lined up history, poetry and his carefully chosen collection of Lives on the shelves. The pointlessness of it struck him as he was laying his world atlas on the hanging side with his teaching notes, textbooks, pens, ink bottle and blotting paper, but he decided to leave them there till morning.

It was his first meal in the dining room. Dim bulbs (for economy) made every room shadowy after dark but here the elaborately carved black table and purplish-red walls intensified the gloom. Chinese scrolls hung here too, Mountain and Water behind him, Tiger and Rushing Waterfall on the opposite wall behind Bhai's empty chair at the head of the table. Some callers had stayed for dinner. The Framjees, needless to say, and a Dr Bihari who had vowed not to cut his hair until swaraj. It was thinning and hung in limp grey strings to his jaws. The boisterous woman had stayed on too. Miss Basappa was stout at close quarters. The yellow canna bobby-pinned behind her ear had withered and collapsed long since but Miss Basappa herself was all energy. 'You were there!' she shouted triumphantly down the table, 'I saw you!'

Nurullah was thankful he had seated himself at the bottom of the table, leaving empty chairs between himself and the others. Doing as they did he clutched his fork in his left fist, pronged a slithering kidney and sawed at it with the knife in his right. This left right left right made no sense when one right hand was all one needed.

Fortunately no one noticed a sawed slice flying off his plate. They were going over the day's events with subdued satisfaction. In their opinion it had all been quite perfect. Word came during dinner that Bhai and his cellmates had been permitted to sleep in the cellyard because of the heatwave, chained to their iron cots to prevent them from escaping over the wall.

'Like dangerous criminals,' said Miss Basappa, making them all laugh.

Head down to prevent another mishap, Nurullah grappled as tensely with their bizarre acceptance of being kicked and beaten as with the slippery innards on his plate. Old Zenobia Framjee was assuring Ammaji she would make her Nusli speak severely to Kallu about serving up a mixed grill on the hottest night of the year just because no one had remembered to give him an order and when he should know by now there was no Lea and Perrins Worcester Sauce or anything English in the house to flavour English cooking. It was not as if the old black rascal had nothing to fall back on but the British army's diet he had cooked before being fired from the army Mess.

'He wasn't a c-c-c-cook,' Nusli reminded his mother, 'only a m-m-m-masalchi.'

'Never mind that. Any cook's mate learns cooking. And haven't I taught him Bhaji-ma Bheja and Frenchbeans-ma-Gosh?'

Kallu reappeared with the grill, rocked backward a step into the pantry and out again. He flashed the aged lady a grin and salaamed her with a reckless flourish of his right hand, dangerously tilting the grill in his left. Mrs

Framjee gave him a curt nod and ordered her Nusli out of the side of her mouth to find out if the old rascal was still getting a rum ration from the army. She and Ammaji began to commiserate the loss of the family's beloved Hafiz Ali, who had had to go when economies began and boycott put an end to buying British goods. Now he came to Government House, Akbarabad from Government House, Lucknow with the Governor's staff for two weeks every winter and called here without fail bearing marvels he had specially prepared in the Governor's kitchen. Nothing to beat these Mohammedans for loyalty, grumbled old Zenobia Framjee, glaring after Kallu's unsteadily departing back, and no one had known how to smoke river fish as Hafiz Ali had. Nurullah heard about Hafiz Ali's artistry with mutton, his versatility with vegetables, his crystallized cherries and sugared violets, whatever those might be. All the talk of food whetted Miss Basappa's appetite and she demanded more about the old days with the enthusiasm of a hefty toddler at story time. Pyare Chacha gladly obliged, starting with a quick survey of the family's migration from the Kashmir valley to the plains, and going on to the late master's father's narrow escape from crossfire in Delhi in 1857.

A stylish chronicler Pyare Chacha turned out to be. After Father's father's providential escape during the Mutiny he resurrected a genealogy brimful of vanished bhabhis, chachas and diddas and breathed life into the trivial doings of these remote extinct relatives, be it Basso Masi's perilous journey to Kashmir by tonga with only a one-eyed servant in attendance or Kishen Chacha's art of peeling fruit all in one strip. Fluid gestures of his crinkled ivory hands unravelled generations of relationship over the table's carved black surface, his fingers as fluent as his tongue. But to what purpose, marvelled Nurullah, or was this pastime normal to people who had ancestors? The saga of ancestry and pedigree made him, a kith-and-kinless upstart in their midst, feel like an unhammered nail jutting out of a masterpiece of wood carving.

He laid his knife and fork carefully side by side on his empty plate as he saw the others doing. He was finding it hard to keep awake but Shãn was drinking it all in, as enthralled by the saga as her elders.

'We're too wound up to go to bed mark my words,' observed old Zenobia Framjee from the other side of her mouth to Ammaji, 'we've had too much excitement today.'

After the hot meaty blast of fried innards a scent of saffron drifted deliciously to Nurullah from the sweet being served by the shuffling bearer, Beni, in the Framjees' own silver dish. He had just finished helping himself to golden strands of sewain when Nusli, leaning forward to catch his eye, told him to s-s-s-see to the jammed f-f-f-flush of the t-t-t-toilet adjoining the late master's study. It was a hideous shock. If Nusli Framjee had casually assumed he was a lackey here, so would other people. Nusli looked puzzled but nodded when Ammaji murmured that the Christian Workshop was sending a plumber.

Pyare Chacha's chronicle had moved from the dead to the living. Nurullah learned perforce about talented cousins who had grown up here and gone away to futures in government service and British companies — what other futures *were* there, as he charitably put it. Naturally they hadn't wanted to be a burden on a household that was selling its cars and carriages, cutting down staff and starting strict economies in response to the Mahatma's clarion call from his hut 'to enter a dynamic condition of conscious suffering.' Nurullah thought it more likely the cousins had bolted like bats at daylight at the sound of the clarion call, but Pyare Chacha was halo-ing and garlanding them in memory the same as Basso Masi, Kishen Chacha and the rest. Family bonds were notoriously sticky but he had never seen anything like this glue. You couldn't pry them apart. The leg of one of them could have been the arm of another, as legend had it Krishna Bhagvan's feet, enthroned in Radha's heart, blistered when she drank scalding milk.

Zenobia had rightly predicted that Shān would not go to bed but the girl stopped her tantrums when she was persuaded to choose a record from a box in the Chinese room and the gramophone was wound up. Nurullah recognized the jhik-jhik rhythm of the moomphally song, an arresting contrast to the insipid ailing noises of their other records. The sprightly old Parsi dame jabbed a loose hairpin back into her sparse grey bun, pinned her sari more securely to her hair and took Shān's hands in hers. Leaning over the child she guided her forward, back and sideways along an invisible square, the pale crumpled skin of her upper arms swaying to the call of The Peanut Vendor.

'Remember, Shāndarling,' she instructed, 'if the lady treads on her partner's toes it's the gentleman who has to say "My fault". And when the dance is over he says "Lovely".'

This glimpse of life on the moon brought a gleam of animation to Shāndarling's obstinate face. Nurullah who could not imagine the lives the cousins had fled to pictured them shod in patent leather, jhik-jhikking talentedly to the moomphally song along invisible squares murmuring 'My fault' and 'Lovely'.

When he got into bed at last the welts and bruises on his back shrieked protest making him turn cautiously to one side. He was wide awake. His thoughts marched backward over the past week to the kisans' arrival, sixteen hundred of them. Some had come uneventfully by bullock cart but the train travellers had had stories to tell of armed police blocking off wayside stations and beating back kisan delegations to prevent them from boarding. Nurullah could see them hoisting themselves up by the handrails of third class railway carriages, hauling up their staffs and bundles and clambering aboard with the dogged defiance of men possessed as he had seen them staying obdurately seated in the shamiana waiting to be battered, though Allah knows even a goat doesn't willingly stay put to perish.

In the dark he relived the nightmare. Hundreds of eyes around him had flashed defiance and he had sensed a mammoth crouching force. Let go it would have torn like a cyclone through fields of sugarcane. By any reckoning this should have happened as it had ten years ago when drought and destitution had driven them to rampage in their thousands from one zamindar's estate to another, breaking open godowns of grain, and when the police opened fire, fighting them with axes, spears and stones.

Hatchet blows penetrated Nurullah's doze, landing on the leaves below his window. An answering hiss steamed up from the soil and cool earth-scented air gusted through his mosquito net. He drowsed on his other side to the sound of steady soothing rain falling straight down from an overburdened sky and dreamed of Chinese tapestries, of Hafiz Ali fashioning myriad-leaved pastries, sugaring violets, rendering choice cuts of meat into choicest silk, of Ramdin in langot and headrag on his bent bow legs in the portico holding a rose like a beggared parody of a Moghul emperor to welcome absconding cousins home. Nurullah reminded himself to take leave of Ammaji first thing in the morning and drifted in half-sleep to an Akbarabad story of a woman weeping wildly over a dead body outside the gates within earshot of receding horses' hooves. On the deserted untarred road outside the jail today her arm held out to Shān had fallen weakly to her side. What if he had not been there to fetch the hysterical girl back to the car? Had there been an able body around since the flight of the cousins, jhik-jhikking talentedly to the moomphally song wherever they were with their patent leather toes polished to a glare they could see their faces in? He was not aware of reversing a decision before he fell fathoms deep into sleep, only of the mesmerising radiance of a smile and a voice exclaiming huskily, 'So, Nurullah! At last!'

Nevertheless, Nurullah knew himself to be a man of the twentieth century who lived by reason and this was his first thought on waking. This, not some spell cast at midnight, had decided him to stay. It was a service he owed Bhai, along with the fact that an able body was a dire necessity here with the cousins fled. But if spell it was, it was the first he had encountered outside the printed page and daylight made common sense of it. Bhai was one of the privileged who had seen the world, crossed oceans and set foot in the free countries of Nurullah's world atlas. This alone could explain his attraction for one who had never left his province or even been near the towering mountain reaches of it where snow reared gigantically for miles. The Indian Ocean halfway down the peninsula was harder to imagine, and then only to reflect sombrely on how different history would have been if Akbar the Great had secured the sea around his empire as he had the land he ruled. Skilled strategist that he had been, why had the Great been stoneblind to the sea?

Ammaji was at her charkha early as usual. Her outsize Mahabharata was open to a bright blue Krishna grown huge, trampling the 101-headed orange serpent Kaliya Nag to death in a poisoned pool of the Yamuna. Pyare Chacha was down by the fountain getting the creeper at its base thinned out. He lifted his cane in languid salute as Nurullah pedalled past after breakfast. The sun was mild, the air was humid. It was the day, the last of July 1932, that Nurullah began counting his stay in the house.

Two

The rain worked its wonders. The garden sprang to turbulent life. Ramdin's swinging scythe slashed jungle growths of grass. Nurullah cycled to the university for his classes and back, and to King and Co. in the Civil Lines on errands for Ammaji where he bought iodine, cotton wool, disinfectant, bandages and other dispensary items under blown-up cardboard cutouts of mem cinema stars advertising powder and paint. His turn at the counter came after Angrez customers had been served. Old mems in ankle-length flowered frocks and broad-brimmed straw hats or floppy cloth ones shading their soft creased faces saying, 'The Scotts Emulsion, I think, don't you, Mr King?' in their wavering voices. Young muscled mems in tennis gear. Other Angrezes, some with dogs. Then him. In his room at night he thought about ways and means to correct the education Shãn was receiving at school, with no great sense of urgency, but nevertheless the matter was urgent since he was being paid for it.

On Makar Sankranti he took Ammaji by tonga to the Ganga for her pre-dawn purefying dip in the river under the prescribed constellation of stars. With practice he loosened his wrestler's grip on knife and fork, and taught himself to hold them as he would two pens. While he was mastering knifing and forking he learned the difference between the meat and fish ones, relying on Kallu's second-hand knowledge of regimental dinners. Nurullah had a mind that harried detail. It made him curious as to what primitive European taboo accounted for the notches in fish cutlery, and what had prompted Europeans to devise an armoury of implements for conveying food to mouth in the first place. Whatever the reason, it had joined the imposing paraphernalia of conquest their ships had brought out: guns, gunpowder and cannons alongside soup and pudding spoons, carving knives and ridged wooden spatulas to roll butter prettily into curls and balls. Kallu described tables laid with serried ranks of newly shone spoons, forks and knives reflecting and returning the sword-and-dagger sparkle on the walls. Teak sideboards displayed trophies of wars Indian soldiers had fought and won for the goras up and down India, Afghanistan and Burma.

In Kallu's nostalgic memories of the 'Cantt' the Mess reigned supreme. How those goras relished flesh, he reported. Not only was mutton 'cutlis', mutton 'chamnp' or pig served for every meal from waking on, but so were their 'puteens' made of goat kidney fat or the loin fat of oxen. Dreamily he recalled the maunds of mutton, ice and butter the military had commandeered in the days of martial law with a snap of a sergeant's fingers. Kallu transformed the city of Akbar into a formidable Cantt with the rest of Akbarabad no more than a harmless little frill sprung up around it. Nurullah would not have known the Cantt existed but for the occasional military lorry rumbling through the Civil Lines or the red-faced tommies at the Picture Palace. Invisible as the nerves in your body was the army of occupation until a hint of trouble sent the troops scrambling for their guns and pouring into Company Bagh.

Once a month Nurullah accompanied Ammaji and Shān to the jail for their twenty-minute interview with Bhai, to be on hand outside when Shān let loose her fury against the bars. The only time he was allowed entry was the day he was sent between interviews with quinine and citronella for Bhai. It was eleven o'clock of a sultry morning and he was let into the fetid malarial air of the walled yard where convicts were having their three-monthly interview with their families. Herded on either side of the bars they were all yelling to be heard before their time was up. For Bhai, whom Nurullah saw being taken past to the jail infirmary, the bedlam must have sounded like an extension of his own raging fever. Nurullah pushed through to the bars but his shout joined the delirium and he was pinioned in the suffocating crush of convicts' families until he could struggle out to space and air. The terror of a vice-like grip on his body was harder to throw off. His feet dragged on the verandah steps at home and lifted with manacled slowness up the stairs once he got inside. He was soaked through with sweat.

'Are you all right, Nur Sahib?'

His upper half, arms outstretched, was laid along the bannister like a wet garment. He lifted his face from his arm and nodded when he heard Beni's anxious upturned enquiry.

Friends of the family called in the evenings and he got to know the regulars. Dr Bihari looked in twice a week on his dispensary days, the faithful Framjees more often. A gaunt Angrez, Mr Harvey, came in pyjama-kurta and spoke Hindustani to Ammaji in an effort of concentration that lowered his eyelids and jerked up his chin. Nawab Sahib Vazirabad and his Begum Jahanara, known as Bibijan, arrived in their smoky topaz Chevrolet. He stepped out first, slender to emaciation in a sherwani moulded to his perfectly symmetrical skeleton, she after him, all abundant billowing flesh, trailing her voluminous gharara up the verandah steps. Two of the three Vazirabad brats, Barkat and Salim, whined for attention when they were not gouging flowers out of their beds and spreading a trail of destruction. The youngest, Murad, was Shān's age and followed her about doing her bidding. Nurullah had once seen them pasted against a pillar out front like arrow-pierced saints, posing for a column of pilgrims filing past. Sometimes, to keep them quiet, they were all bundled into the Chevrolet and sent out for a drive. They shoved and quarrelled noisily getting in but were quiet as soon as the car moved, letting their faces hang peacefully out of the windows and their hair blow back like dogs tranquillized by the breeze.

Miss Basappa was a frequent favourite visitor. Sport was the breath of life to Miss Basappa. Nurullah had heard her tell of the swimming event she had won in her college sports down south, strongly breast-stroking the length of the pool and back in record time and climbing out with her head still covered and every fold of her sopping sari in place. A lot less weighty she must have been in her student days. Disdaining tongas she pedalled vigorously about town on her bicycle, never minding the sun blazing down on her. She butted into Pyare Chacha's stories, thought nothing of hailing Nurullah if he happened to be passing through the courtyard where they all sat and her laugh was like a dig in the ribs. Woman was the last word he would have applied to Miss Basappa, a word that, for Nurullah, conjured the bleakest images. A maggot-ridden pi-dog flattened by a thundering lorry on Warren Hastings Road and left there to decay brought 'woman' to mind, raw red carcasses fresh from the slaughterer swinging from hooks at Jalaluddin butcher's in Colonelgunj, a mongrel bitch being pelted with stones outside the butcher's where she sat waiting for scraps. He had picked up a stone and hurled it at the bitch's tormentors, scattering them. She had limped painfully to a mess of rotting garbage, sunk her pregnant belly to it as if onto a blessedly soft pillow, and crossed her injured paw delicately over the other. Nurullah had squatted and cautiously felt the paw for broken bones. After one agonized yelp she had feebly palpitated her tail and smiled into his eyes. He had heard her heave a small canine sigh as he stroked both sides of her patient pointed face. Compared with the bitch Miss Basappa's flag of a flower, her manly laugh and her outrageous vitality gave

Nurullah tantalizing glimpses of a female future he would never have believed possible.

Nusli Framjee pored over accounts at the end of every month, paid the servants their salaries and Nurullah his. With Beni and the chowkidar shuffling behind him he made sure everything was in order and the light bulbs were weak. Sometimes he sent for Joseph of the Christian Workshop to make repairs.

At tea and samosas one afternoon a couple of months after the arrests, the talk at Robin-da's was about the Viceroy's new ordinances to bring newspapers and printing presses under stricter control, seize the bank accounts of offenders and saboteurs and tamper with mail. Blowing on his steaming tea and swallowing a mouthful of it Robin-da said every ordinance gave the people one more reason for protest and strengthened the Movement. Matul said no such thing would happen. It was the kisans who were in control, not the Movement. He had seen them massed outside the courthouse wearing headshawls and sharing umbrellas a month ago, and they were still there. Hundreds of them were camped under makeshift tarpaulin shelters on the jail road when he had gone to the jail for an interview with his invalid grand-uncle. Jail gossip had it that officials were afraid the kisan mood was going to turn ugly and endanger European lives. The town was under siege by them and they would keep coming till their leaders were released. Robin-da was nodding sagely when Eknath who had no inhibitions about arguing with his elders interrupted to say the peasants would get quicker results if they stormed the jail.

'You, Eknath,' said Robin-da witheringly, 'will not rest until you see severed heads dropping into baskets.'

'Why not? It's a European example and isn't Europe our example?' enquired Eknath needlingly, thoroughly enjoying himself.

They got embroiled in one of their wordy duels. To hear Robin-da who would have guessed he had once had fierier ideas himself? Hashi served her husband another cup of tea and did her duty as hostess by calling sing-songly for hot samosas. She caught Nurullah's eye, her mouth twitched and she suppressed a violent giggle, her way of being friendly. He smiled vaguely back, his attention on the life he was leading, King and Co., knives and forks, and how to start re-educating Shān when he should have been expanding his horizons, cultivating useful contacts at the university, getting on.

Matul was both right and wrong. The kisans' leaders were released but for the party's leaders — the ringleaders, according to the Sarkar — there was no release. The Movement far from winding down as Matul had predicted surpassed all expectations, delivering a hundred thousand willing prisoners to the country's jails by the end of the year, Miss Basappa and Gosiben among the thirty thousand women.

Akbarabad was in the grip of processions. Who were those people, who came out of nowhere in their hundreds, wage-earners all, who had everything to lose by marching along banned thoroughfares, singing banned national songs, waving the banned national tricolour and landing in jail? Nurullah saw the tricolour snatched back and forth in

grim struggles with the police. He could soon foretell the
unwatchable sequence of events as he stood on the
barricaded road outside the house where the police waited
armed with clubs and rods to tear through the marchers
when they refused to disperse. The procession's leaders
were manhandled into barred vans, the youngsters in the
crowd were kicked and cuffed, and the obstreperous flag-
wavers among them were pulled off the road and flogged.
Nurullah picked up Sitaram, a boy volunteer he recognized,
blubbering like a baby from his whipping and took him
to the dispensary. Dr Bihari had been arrested but his
compounder, helped by Khurram who had been the family's
chauffeur before the car was confiscated, washed and
dressed the wounds, where the whip had lacerated the
flesh of the boy's cheeks and back.

The house wore a deserted look. Nawab Sahib
Vazirabad thought it better not to come with Bibijan and
the children in view of the 'disturbances' and Mr Harvey's
visit could have brought little comfort to the two old
people, Ammaji and Pyare Chacha. He was back from
Peshawar with news of persecution, travelling there and
back in Pathan clothes though he was a Quaker and
concealment was against his principles.

He had not seen the Movement dealt with so
ferociously anywhere else, he said. It had been war against
the Frontier since 1930. In Peshawar he had seen Pathans
paraded through the city stripped of their turbans, shirts
and shoes and ordered to salute the Europeans they passed.
In Charsadda protestors who had picketed the law courts
were stripped naked and made to run for their lives

carrying headloads of earth, chased by a mounted officer. Their villages were surrounded and raided in the night by troops who beat them unconscious and threw them into icy water. Those who raised Gandhi slogans had their testicles twisted with loops of rope.

Pyare Chacha leaned forward and asked tensely, 'But did they retaliate?'

Mr Harvey replied that the Red Shirts, as Gandhi's Pathan followers were called, had sworn oaths on the Koran never to surrender and in no circumstances to turn violent. Their leader was a non-violent giant of a man, known as the Frontier Gandhi. Such large numbers of his people had offered themselves for arrest that the military were finding it simpler to beat them unconscious than to arrest them, but those who had been jailed were being kept on short rations and whipped for insubordination.

This whole terrible recital had the effect of releasing Pyare Chacha and Ammaji from unbearable tension. They were visibly relaxed even as Mr Harvey reported the army's troop marches through towns and villages on the Frontier and said the Royal Air Force too was overflying remote villages. In fact, said he, the British delegation at the Air Disarmament Conference in Geneva had rejected a proposal to abolish bombing from the air. Anthony Eden had said bombing became necessary for keeping law and order 'in certain parts of the world'.

'The point of view,' said Pyare Chacha philosophically, 'makes all the difference, does it not?' unintentionally alerting Nurullah and providing him with what he needed, the key to re-educating Shãn.

'It certainly does that,' agreed Mr Harvey ruefully. He repeated for them what Mr Winston Churchill had said about the Mahatma's meeting with the Viceroy:

> the nauseating and humiliating spectacle of this onetime Inner Temple lawyer, now seditious fakir, striding half-naked up the steps of the Viceroy's palace there to negotiate and parley on equal terms with the representative of the King-Emperor.

'Bichara Churchill,' said Ammaji. 'What does the poor man know about langots and how we revere fakirs that he calls them nauseating? No one is insulting his King Emperor. He just upsets himself needlessly.'

'Good Lord!' exclaimed Mr Harvey, jumping up, 'we're forgetting all about the chrysanthemums. We should have seen to them before I went away.'

He and Pyare Chacha got up to walk around the garden discussing where to plant them. Arms akimbo, big bony hands on his hips, the Angrez called Nurullah over.

'What about chalking out a badminton court on that tennis court, Nurullah? No one's played tennis there for years by the look of it. Give badminton a thought, eh?'

The friendly suggestion in no way resembled Nusli's peremptory stuttered order to fix the jammed toilet — Mr Harvey was a courteous man — but it did assume as they all did that he was a permanent fixture here. They took him for one of them, wedded to their creed, not realizing that commandments such as 'Love will disarm the enemy' made his hair stand on end.

'"If the enemy realized you have not the remotest thought in your mind of raising your hand against him even for the sake of your life, he will lack the zest to kill you,"' he quoted to Eknath one night at Mehfil, a favourite haunt of theirs near the railway station where they went for kebab-roti.

It was impossible to ignore ahimsa, unreal though it was, since it was happening around them. Eknath who was a historian put the question into its historical perspective, saying it was violence that made a mark which accounted for all history being Europe's and Europe being master of the world. For savagery as a way of life the Europeans took the prize. Witness their tribal wars of succession, their ferocious religious persecution, their global plunder, their cannibal appetite for flesh to subdue, their avarice for land and gold. Observe their bloodthirst when they didn't get their way, their arrogance when they did. They couldn't even take to religion without making it an excuse for a jehad and packing it off to holy war with their Pope's Christian blessing. Moral: If you want a place in history, do as Europe does.

Nurullah was a good listener and Eknath did have a flair for these succinct masterly résumés. His subject lent itself to them. Literature didn't seem to.

'What about other greedy savage people?' asked Nurullah, not sure what other people he meant.

'Who else has been so greedy or so savage?' retorted Eknath, 'which is why no one else counts. Who rules the world? Whose history were you taught? Whose literature are you teaching? Wake up, yaar!'

Eknath was right, if one put aside (for the moment) other violences by other races including — since mercy was not meant for man alone — suffering horseflesh and the torments of the bitch in Colonelgunj. The subject was confusing. So was the undeniable fact that whether they were violent or non-violent, heroes were heroes. The wall facing their table had calendar pictures tacked to its flaking yellow plaster. Between the guileless appeal of Leela Chitnis and the wilier allure of Sarita Devi was the proud grey head, its stern commanding features garishly lit by the room's unshaded bulb. Below it hung an artist's conception of the Company Bagh martyrs exploded into grotesque postures by British bullets. They had been young, the oldest a schoolmaster the same age as Eknath and Nurullah himself. What anxieties must have assailed these plotters before they went out to do their daring deed — one of them to target the Governor, the others to blow up Victoria — and got massacred themselves instead? A passage he had underlined in his *Life of Mazzini* came poignantly back to him:

> 'Here we are,' said Jacopo Ruffini to his fellow
> conspirators at Genoa, 'five very young men with
> but very limited means, called on to do nothing
> less than overthrow an established Government.'

He got up to join Eknath at the grimy washbasin, rinsed out his mouth, washed mango pickle oil off his fingers with the sliver of soap and dried them one by one on the cleaner side of the towel.

'Non-violence is a great experiment,' conceded Eknath. 'So was that fellow's who flew too near the sun and crashed down in cinders. But since time began every mother's son has gone to war armed with something, sticks and stones, bows and arrows, whatever. The Company Bagh martyrs found weapons. A regular armoury was discovered in the house where they used to meet. We need to get ourselves some military training. For one thing it would leave the loafers less time to stand around picking their noses, scratching their crotches, and hooting and screeching at matinees.'

Eknath could be categorical because he didn't live in the domed monument, didn't see sightseers coming like pilgrims to look at what wasn't there — blanks where pictures had hung, holes and hollows in carpets where heirloom furniture had stood. The old peasants among them had skins as cracked and wrinkled as bark, their bark shoes made walking trees of them on the gravel and when they came in droves they beat upon the path like rain. Eknath didn't go up the spiral stair to the roof terrace and lie on his back under the stars to puzzle out why 'soul force' had possessed the country and sent a hundred thousand people to jail. Up there, close to the spinning planets, the voice from the hut saying 'Non-violence is not submission, it is the soul's unvanquishable strength and power' or 'I want India to recognize she has a soul that cannot perish and that can rise triumphant above any physical weakness' or 'Strength comes from an indomitable will' rang in Nurullah's ears with absolute reality. He went down to his room convinced of their truth and settled down in this frame of mind one night to mark a poem in a textbook for his class next day:

And if then the tyrants dare
Let them ride among you there,
Slash, and stab, and maim and hew —
What they like, that let them do.
With folded arms and steady eyes,
And little fear and less surprise,
Look upon them as they slay
Till their rage has died away.

A thrill of horror and revulsion rippled through him. Words like these had been converted to blood and gore during the cavalry charge outside the gates when the voice from the hut, eerily like the English poet's, had instructed: 'If we are to stand the final heat of the battle we must learn to stand our ground in the face of cavalry or baton charges and allow ourselves to be trampled under horses' hooves.' He dropped Shelley's *Mask of Anarchy* as if it had been a flaring match and searched through class texts for something less dangerous, something with verve and jingle that would appeal to fifteen- and sixteen-year-olds. He needed images of true and tried conventional combat, war as it had always been fought, in which both sides shouldered arms and risked their lives.

He read his choices through in a quick mutter, then got up and recited each one out loud using his hands for flourish. But other teachers he had known had done this with little result. He tried repeating each line twice, three times, like an Urdu sher, pausing between lines for their meaning to sink in, and felt an interior prickle of excitement. If it worked it would revive the most moribund or nitwit student in his class. Wonderful how it did next morning! His elation knew no bounds. The pure delight on faces told him teaching had to be this kind of give and take and a teacher without a trick or two might as well not teach.

As a pupil Shān was proving more of a problem and the fault was his. He knew nothing about any child but the child he had been, a snotty creature caked in dried dirt who had spent his seven years between the servants' quarter and the backyard of the big house. He could precisely recall the deadness of hours unpunctuated by events except the journey across the stony backyard to the kitchen door for a slice of buttered sugared double roti. There had been nothing else to divert him from his solitary dust-kicking idleness, no task needing his concentration except squatting to empty his bowels and be rewarded by the turds coiling neatly in the dirt under him.

He was kicking pebbles with his bare toes at the edge of the yard when he saw someone at the back door of the house watching him. He had birdbright eyes on a grasshopper frame, not the grandchildren's mustachioed master sahib but some smaller important city person wearing a wristwatch. The stranger came out, picked up a stick and drew lines in the dust with it. Nurullah sat down on his heels and stared at the scratches with passionate concentration, waiting to learn what they meant but instead of explaining the man scooped up handfuls of pebbles. He divided these into twos and threes and made Nurullah count them.

He was back a little later with a hard green tablet in a metal dish. He put pebbles under the tablet and asked

Nurullah why. Answer! Answer! He commanded exuberantly but Nurullah's mind was infuriatingly blank. His body baulked like a calf on stiff front legs. He looked up at the stranger in quiet desperation.

'To keep the soap from melting, of course!' the stranger cried.

Seeing that Nurullah did not know 'soap' he pressed the hard green tablet into his grubby hand and lifted it by the wrist to his nose. Nurullah dragged short eager sniffs from it and let his hand be guided, tablet held fast, under the municipal tap. Water flooded the thing he held and washed a stream of filth off his hand. Nurullah gasped, every fibre of his being thrilling to 'soap'. It shot out of his grasp and the man cried, 'See? Just like a fish it has slipped and gone!'

A silent pleading despair came over Nurullah. He did not know 'fish'. The strange man turned the tap off and sat back on his heels gazing deeply into Nurullah's eyes. But whether it was sorrow or a sorrowful happiness that brought tears to the man's own Nurullah was never to know. He only knew that the following day — washed and dressed in clean clothes — he started his education with the master sahib in the big house at a desk apart from the grandchildren's.

Leaving Shān at her convent homework he got up to look around the library where they were sitting. The room's three double doors opened onto the encircling verandah but it smelled of seclusion and long settled dust. He climbed a ladder, picked a book at random from the highest shelf and blew on it. Age had brittled the paper and punctured the pages with fishmoth holes. Corners broke off in his fingers when he turned them. The books he lifted from other shelves were as worn and well-handled. He replaced each one with care and stepped down, satisfied that he was not without resources. His glance swept the shelves with the proprietary pride of a peasant viewing the barrels of surplus grain he is keeping stocked against unforeseen disaster. An inspired opening for tomorrow's class came unbidden to his mind. 'In English poetry,' he would tell his First Years, 'an ode to a nightingale is not about a nightingale.'

He came back to where Shān was sitting hunched like an old crone and wondered what lapse of common sense had made him think she was a child.

I don't suppose you know, he found himself telling her, that this province's eastern region where I was born is famous for its buddhus. But slow-witted simpletons though we are called, it was one of us, Mangal Pandey, who started the mutiny against the East India Company. Fools rush in, the English poet truly spoke, where angels fear to tread.

When this mutiny became war another famous Fool of our region was the raja who led his peasant troops in spectacular victories against the Company at the age of eighty.

Mangal Pandey was hanged and other mutineers were more picturesquely dealt with, but so fearful were the Angrez of Fools that no one from this famous region was allowed to join the army any more. After the Mutiny they chose carefully whom they would arm.

Nurullah's future benefactor, another titled zamindar, was still in his mother's womb when the war was being crushed. From her window in the zenana his mother could see mango trees festooned with mutineers' skulls and news kept coming of mutilated sepoy bodies swinging by their necks on the road to Calcutta. In Delhi sepoys had been executed ten at a time, pinioned together, or tied to the mouths of cannons and blown up. And from Akbarabad to Rampur armed Angrez volunteers were out in mobs, burning villages, slaughtering males and stringing them up in fancy figures of eight. Later hanging parties saw pigs feeding on their carcasses.

The babe in his mother's womb was bound to be born an avenger. Deprived of weapons of war he could not start another mutiny but by the time he inherited the estate he was known as a fanatic for justice. As kings of old had gone on shikar, scouring the jungle for boar, buck and game, he thrashed about his domain like a maniac on horseback, his moustaches blowing apart, a red tilak slashed down his forehead, hunting for wrongs to right. Lunging through a clearing in the jungle one day he heard terrible human screams from a hut and galloped back to it with his servants. Gagging on thick acrid smoke they saw a child hung upside down. Her naked body was tied by the ankles to a wooden beam, her face was roasting in a fire of chillies and a sturdy peasant, watched by a boy, was thrashing her pregnant belly with thorn branches. The evildoer stopped at once for the raja's vengeance was unsparing. On pain of instant death he fell cowering to his knees and chattered for mercy: The cow gives no milk,

O Shelter of the Poor, the rain holds off, and last night a cheetah tore the goat from its tether. There is no end to calamity since this accursed witch came under my roof.

The raja had the child cut down, the evildoer stripped, hung upside down and beaten till he bellowed. He took the child home on his own horse and delivered her to the care of the maidservants in the zenana. When she died giving birth soon after, her son was named Nurullah to make certain no one from her vile past would try to reclaim him. The raja was no bigot. Twice he had gone off his head in mystical experiences he could ascribe to no particular religion. Wisely he gave Nurullah the lifelong refuge of Islam. The boy knelt on a prayer mat facing Mecca to do namaz five times a day and studied the Koran. But racing with other children and barking pi-dogs behind the peasant columns passing through to join a fifty-mile march to Akbarabad he shouted *Sitaram* with all the rest. He squirted colours at Holi, whirled firecrackers at Diwali, and fasted during Ramzan. He played hide-and-seek with the grandchildren in the big house forgetting he was a servant and slept in the servant's quarter dreaming a master's dreams. In truth he did not know if he was Hindu or Muslim, lord or vassal. All that mattered was he could read and write. Prompted by the birdbright stranger, the raja had seen to his education to make up for the cruellest wrong he had found in his domain.

Shān had listened avidly. It was a tale of that enthralling subject, ancestry, after all. Nurullah reckoned he had made a beginning. As far as food for thought was concerned it was an improvement on My Dog and The Moonlight of Winter, and even on Kallu's yarn describing his marriage to his 'Jarman' bibi. The wedding day had dawned broiling hot. The sun had shone fiercely on the Mess. The Cantt was bedecked with Union Jacks. Trumpets sounded. Kallu arm-in-arm with his moti-tazi Jarman bibi high-stepped in slow motion under a regimental archway of crossed swords. With their free hands he and his fat German bride tossed gold sovereigns to the cheering throng of Colonelgunj's butchers, ironmongers, beggars and thieves.

Nurullah asked Ammaji's permission to add walks to Shān's correction programme and regretted it as soon as she came running out of the house on her matchstick legs. He had forgotten about those. But after all, horses' unlikely legs had thundered across continents, and he remembered her remarkable lung stamina at the jail gate. They walked all the way to Government House.

'Here is the white-walled palace where Hafiz Ali spends two weeks every winter,' lectured Nurullah, treating Shān like his class. 'He comes by special train from Government House, Lucknow, in his magnificent gold and scarlet livery, looking grand. The Governor comes too.'

The palace stood at the far end of a sloping sunlit acre of new grass. Its grounds were separated from the road by tall spiked iron railings guarded by motionless sentries in black Wellington boots and striped cummerbunds to go with their striped turbans, stiffly holding bayonets in their white-gloved hands. Almost as fine as the guard at Kallu and his Jarman bibi's wedding must have been, commented Shān generously. A uniformed mali was clipping a shrub into a giraffe shape. She glanced indifferently at other animal-shaped shrubs, flower mosaics exact distances apart and a fleet of uniformed gardeners who needed no lionheaded cane to direct them, but whooped excitedly when she saw a peacock through the railings, followed by his harem of five peahens. She began strutting about imitating his raucous shriek.

'This gorgeous polygamous sultan,' continued Nurullah, 'is here because he is a symbol of royalty and this premises fancies itself royal.'

He drew her attention to the horse half of the equestrian statue on its lofty pedestal behind the railing.

'See how the stallion paws the air and how his muscles swell with living breath and ripple in the sun! How wonderfully this statue honours his splendour!'

'Who's the man on the horse?' she asked.

'Some governor or the like,' said Nurullah, not bothering to read the name engraved on the steel plaque.

But what's a governor without a palace and a Hafiz Ali, without sentries and bayonets and peacocks, whereas a horse is always gloriously a horse. Reams had been written about ants and bees yet no one had written the embattled history of the horse. Briefly he acquainted his pupil with horse discipline and horse heroism and the uses men had made of horses in their just and unjust wars.

An ayah was standing at the end of the railing with one hand on the handle of a regal four-wheeled perambulator. Her face was black and haughty above the starched white pleats of her blouse except when she stooped to squeak obsequious pidgin English to her missy baba in the pram. Shān stared. Incredulous with joy she shrieked,

'Jessie-ma, it's my Jessie-ma!' Jessie-ma stood stock still, then alertly wheeled her pram around and strode haughtily away, her nosering and her pleated lehenga swinging. Shān threw herself on the road in front of the motionless sentries and began to howl with her usual frenzied abandon. Nurullah signalled a passing tonga and lifted her to the seat where she slumped sulkily against him.

'Hey, dost,' he said after a while, having decided to call her Friend in neutral fashion, 'look up there. What do you see?'

She squinted at the faint crescent barely visible in the still daylit evening and snapped shrewishly, 'The moon, of course, you buddhu.'

'The crescent moon,' he corrected, discoursing on its voyage from sickle to shield and back.

Shān straightened up, restored to her natural grumpiness, and gruffly demanded more explanation.

∿

Teaching is give and take. The bludgeoned womb and blinded eyes returned to him in sleep. The zenana women had never been able to make sense of his twelve-year-old mother's crazed babble before the hurricane of giving birth killed her. Nurullah could not count the number of times he had re-lived his own birth from their descriptions of it. From stable talk he learned she had been rescued from a sugarcane village and had been brought there from another one nearby. The rest everyone knew. Jungles on estates had been cleared for cane cultivation a hundred years earlier when the Company demanded sugar. Company officials and speculators from Calcutta business houses had come to see that cane was planted for gur-refining mills in Cawnpore. Zamindars had become the Company's agents who must pay it fixed revenues as tribute or forfeit their estates, and hell's cycle had soon set in, mortgaging kisans to estates. Girl children were sold to pay crippling debts as she must have been. Six or seven she would have been, trudging beside her father, crying to be lifted to his shoulder — only the rich had carts — to be delivered, piteously recoiling, to the man and the boy. Servant talk helped Nurullah piece together her life until fragments of it were as clear to him as if he had watched her living it. He saw her huddled in a shocked heap in a corner of the hut, her teeth bared in the silent snarl of an ambushed animal keeping predators at bay. Her live coal eyes picked out fallen scraps of food to snatch and devour when they were finished eating and gone. She scraped the rough iron cooking pot with swift savage licks of her tongue before scouring it with a fistful of hot ash from the dying fire. Nurullah watched her disintegrate from terrified child to dumb tortured beast. He never heard her speak. He heard only the thrusting grunts of the older, then the younger, astride her. The sound drilled holes in his skull and tightened screws in it to exploding. He didn't know he was shouting for help until his hoarse cries forced him out of sleep and he sat up, grief-stricken, dry-eyed and panting for breath.

After the rains Nusli came round to get the spattered skylights washed. Under his watchful eye fluff and dirt were wiped off ceiling fans to drop in lumps on old newspapers spread below them. After getting the skylights and fan blades cleaned to his finicky satisfaction he stood on tiptoe in dark corners locating cobwebs while old Zenobia Framjee in her lace saris and swinging earrings must have been minding the fashionable well-stocked glass shelves of Framjee and Son's liquor shop in the Civil Lines.

At King and Co. Nurullah came across intriguing, unconnected word configurations. Vanishing cream; fruit salt; lime and glycerine.

'Dagget and Ramsdell, is it, madam?' Mr King was asking a mem in the strangled voice he reserved for mems, with even his neck stretched forward to be of service, 'will it be the cold or the vanishing, madam?'

Madam said the vanishing with toneless disinterest in a voice as faded as her pallor. She paid and began tugging without much hope at the lead of her monstrous bulldog, urging it to 'Come along now, Martha.' Martha consented at last to heave her leathery bulk off the floor and the mem went out forgetting her six rupees worth of change on the counter.

'Here!' boomed Mr King agitatedly, 'the lady's forgotten her change.'

Seeing there was no one else to do it Nurullah collected it and went to her car, just in time. He handed it in through the window. The coins were received with a strained nod from the mem and an ominously ugly rumble from the dreadful Martha beside her on the back seat. This mem was obviously one of the nondescript ones whose dogs had a more noticeable personality. Mr King didn't bother with thank you either. Nurullah bought the dispensary items on Ammaji's list. The Movement's battle-scarred had stopped coming but the poor came for free treatment and Dr Bihari's compounder, assisted by Khurram, attended to them.

Every time he went to the Imperial Bank of Akbarabad with Ammaji's cheque — a job Nusli Framjee had foisted on him — Nurullah expected to be told the account had been frozen. So far it hadn't been but his errands to this pleasant double-storeyed building whose verandah was lined with lush greenery and hung with wire baskets of flowering plants always reminded him of the all-powerful invisible hand that controlled the destinies of Akbarabadis — in this case visibly in the person of a stocky broad-boned russet-haired manager. Nurullah dealt only with the teller but he had seen Mr McCracken at his desk one day when the manager's office door happened to be open. He was studying a paper on his desk, figures probably. Quite a flair they must have for figures with all the practice they'd had since the Company's trickery captured Bengal, monopolized its trade, squeezed out the competition from Europe and Asia and beggared the weavers and artisans.

Nusli Framjee was standing on tiptoe on a star-shaped design of ochre mosaic in the stairwell, peering up at the ruby-studded globe light when Nurullah got back from the chemist and the bank.

'J-j-j-just who I was looking for. Where have you b-b-b-been?' he stuttered irritably, 'it's fused.'

His whereabouts being no business of Nusli Framjee's, Nurullah did not reply but since there was no other able body to do the chore, and Nusli was not only old but short, he went out for the ladder, set it up, leaned sideways over the stairwell to detach the bulb and was handed the replacement by Nusli. The chore always made perfectly coordinated partners of them for the few minutes it took. When Nusli switched the light on Nurullah could as usual hardly see the pitifully weak wattage it cast on the ochre design far below. It wasn't the drill Nurullah minded, it was Nusli who assumed he was here to cash cheques and change bulbs. He had seriously considered moving back to his accommodation at the untidy Tiwaris' before Nusli Framjee made a family retainer of him, stuck like flylegs to flypaper. But in all conscience he could not abandon his post until Bhai's release. Not that anyone would blame him if he did. With their maddening charity they would think up some virtuous reason for his desertion. Ammaji would make a Kabir of him, a messenger of love and integration, the only Mussalman she knew who had put on a dhoti and waded into the Ganga with her on Makar Sankranti. Pyare Chacha would add his name to the chronicles of dead and living dear ones.

Once or twice a month he and Eknath went to the cinema, for preference to Hindi films at the Chowk cinema but sometimes to English and American ones at the Picture Palace in Civil Lines. Eknath had a weakness for films featuring gangsters who kept their pockets stuffed with pistols and whipped them out to spray their surroundings with bullets. In one memorable scene, a gangster's car bore down steadily on his victim, forcing him to back up against a wall. The car's blazing headlights skewered the dishevelled old man to the wall in open-mouthed wild-eyed terror. Its screeching engine overpowered his gibbering cries for mercy. Nurullah had to close his eyes. He objected strenuously to spending a rupee of his hard-earned money to watch this thuggish behaviour but he saw Eknath's point that it provided a window into a society they knew nothing of and whose appalling side they should get to know along with its lighter side. Unfortunately, his first glimpse of the lighter side was The Something Follies of 1932. Scene after scene of the Follies showed mems with vacant faces descending endless stairs, or posed in tinsel and spangles on a revolving platform while a man with plastered patent leather hair lowed like a cow at sunset about his love for all of them and clouds went rolling by behind him. Nurullah was quite aghast at its pointlessness.

The gallery of 'stills' from old silent films at the Picture Palace interested him more. In one, a woman's swan neck arched to the man behind her and her naked arms around his head were drawing it down to hers. In others, women in swooning postures had men's mouths pressed to pulsebeats on their throats or in their upper arms or inside their elbows. It was as far removed as it could get from what Nurullah knew of nature's lustful mauling and coupling. These visions were calm and eternal. They might always have been there, heedless of century, clocks, alarms. It was love as love might be made in paradise. Nurullah knew no Sanskrit but an Italian professor of Sanskrit from the University of Venice at one of Robinda's teas had said the fifth century poet Kalidasa had believed true lovers are destined. Supreme love unfolds over many lifetimes through centuries and civilizations until at last the lovers meet again in India Beata to celebrate their arrival in paradise.

∽

Company Bagh had a flowerful profusion of delicate pinks and purples on the mound where machine guns had riddled holes into iron sheeting. Below the mound the grass where Akbarabadis had stood stunned was a floral carpet of ravishing colours shading into each other. On New Year's Day of 1933 the military band played tunes Nurullah now recognized as *Danny You Have A Damn Fine Face* and *Tipperary*. He got Shān to teach him flower names she knew and stowed carnations, petunias, azaleas, phlox and crepe myrtle away in memory along with which cutlery to use when and other superfluous knowledge that the life he had embarked on seemed to need.

His longest walk with Shān took them off the roads named after the Company's lords and generals onto the highway of Akbar the Great's triumphal procession of elephants, camels and horses into the city that still, praise be, bore his name. From here they took a tonga to the river road and got down on the sandbank where the Yamuna's clear blue waters swirled into the Ganga's muddy tide.

'Here we are,' lectured Nurullah conscientiously, 'on the world's most thickly populated sand. The sadhus, vendors, worshippers, cripples you see around you and millions of others come to the Ganga, and were coming long before the Europeans, and will keep coming long after them. Here there is no Company and no Crown —'

'What about Fa Hien?' Shān rudely interrupted.

Nurullah who set great store by rhythm and continuity in a lecture, and respect for a teacher, would have tweaked her ear to teach her manners, as his Koran maulvi had done mercilessly in class. But teaching was give and take. Whether Fa Hien had come to the Ganga or only Hieuen Tsang a couple of hundred years later he decided not to pursue at the moment. She probably knew more about Chinese pilgrims than he did, given the family obsession.

'All right, Fa Hien. It took that Chinese pilgrim six years to travel here through Central Asia on his quest for Buddhist texts. He stayed another six. And he left behind a ninety-two page record on silk and bamboo. Did you ever hear of a European taking a six-year walk to read a few books?'

Shān had never heard of a European. What was it?

'Well, now,' said Nurullah, taking a deep breath, but before he could begin she was off to torment her grandmother's priest, prancing around the paunchy punda, accusing him of guzzling chickens on the sly. She shrieked with laughter when he pinched his earlobes and rolled his eyes in mock horror.

Nurullah sat down where he was. Here Bhai had addressed the kisan rally and they, sixteen hundred strong, had pledged to defy the raised land revenue. On that day the battle hymn of freedom had sounded a new mantra over these ancient enigmatic waters. Falling into a deeper distorted reverie his thoughts drifted miles downriver to the child being raped and tortured and then reprieved only to give tempestuous birth to him and die. He shook off the evil crowding his brain and surfaced from it with difficulty. What was there to connect the kisan rally with the child, yet one had led downriver to the other as if all sufferers were chained to the same block of misery.

Shãn came ploughing barefoot through the sand and flung herself down beside him, ready for the lesson to continue.

'Millions come to the Ganga's banks,' he resumed, 'but once upon a time this plain we're sitting on was a sea.'

Shãn's eyes narrowed in frank skepticism and her rude 'What rot!' obliged him to explain that geological upheavals had driven back the sea and left a miraculous fertility where grain and wisdom had blossomed and those who had barged in as uncouth conquerors had learned better and made Hindustan their home. Even Babur who wrote arrogantly in his diary: 'On Friday the first of Sofar 932, when the sun was in Saggitarius, I set out on my march to invade Hindustan' stayed on and no power on earth could have persuaded his offspring to call any other place home. Everyone surrendered to the spell of Hindustan. Except the Europeans. A subject for another lesson.

'Is this history or geography or what?' She liked her information in tidy compartments, as conveyed by the nuns, he supposed.

'Um — both,' said Nurullah. 'It's like this, dost. History and geography are just long names for the feelings that surge up in us when we sit here on this sand. This plain has whirled all us old and new arrivals together like leaves, then whirled us all conmingled into this river's soil and slime so that nothing can separate us again.'

They jogged home companionably by tonga, eating jalebis. Shān had just the one childlike trait. She could stuff herself with sweets and sit back in a torpor of speechless contentment. He almost liked her when she was in this rare frame of mind. It took his own mind off the responsibility of teaching her and of teaching in general, of whose perils and pitfalls he had never before been remotely aware. Slow-witted perhaps, and certainly not for want of guidance.

'Yes, yes, of course you must stick to the curriculum,' Robin-da had rattled off with his typical lack of forbearance when Nurullah had sought his advice about a course, 'but what do I keep telling you, apply correction to it. *How?* By the tone of your voice, the tricks of your tongue, the look in your eye, how else? Use your cunning, Nurullah. Why else are you a teacher?'

Robin-da had waited, head tilted, for some sign of the bait taken, before telling him to get a move on. The largeness of the agenda was as intimidating and seemed as futile as challenging a machine gun with soul force. It was absurd to think one could shake Europe's unshakeable arrangement of the world by the twist of a lip, the flick of an eyelid, by tone, pause or inflection, using the only weapons left to people who have no weapons. If he did not resort to these it was because literature had no need of these devices. It did the job itself. He was responsible only for selecting the raptures, the rages, the sombre soliloquies with care. He lit the bonfire with the words of others. Igniting it with words of his own could end in summary dismissal. Treason was hunted in many garbs.

Cycling home from the Chowk cinema after the late show one hot April night, Eknath and he wondered how the title song had got past the film censor. They started singing rousing snatches of it. Past the lights, people and animals of the bazaar a friendly darkness fell away on either side of the open road and they cycled far apart, holding hands across the gap. Night rushed exhilaratingly into their faces, trees spun round on their roots and danced past them in the dark. Their lifted voices invented songlines they couldn't remember and when they ran out of invention Eknath who had a monkey's agility and the heart of a clown bounded up off his seat, threw out his legs and made hoops in the air.

'I went to pay my respects to Tiwariji and Mrs Shona Tiwari the other day,' said Nurullah. 'I can't get over them looking like twins even to their missing front teeth and their creaky little cackle.'

'Owl!' exclaimed Eknath, doubling with laughter, 'it's Misraji, the lodger, who is her twin. Tiwariji is the immaculate one who sits fanning himself on the verandah.'

Mrs Shona Tiwari, all Akbarabad knew, had been a firecracker since way back. On her elder sister's wedding night in the 1880s the sister was said to have had hysterics and Mrs Shona had gamely crept into the nuptial bed (just for the night, but who knows?) for her sister's sake. A crisis had been averted. Eknath didn't know how long after her own wedding she had settled down with Misraji. But here they still were, thought Nurullah, an amiable hag and her devoted twin lover, leading a love life as charmed as any in paradise.

Eknath and he parted as usual at St. James Church to go their separate ways. The hour was approaching midnight when night has settled into silence and Nurullah was negotiating a peaceful passage through the dark lane between Cornwallis and Havelock Roads. A roaring hullagulla broke out at ground level a few yards ahead, a menacing mix of human and canine uproar. The solid hedge on his left moved and a man came crashing through it on all fours pursued by a snarling beast. Before he could get to his feet the animal had sunk its fangs into the seat of his shorts. In the light from the main road there was no mistaking Martha. Nurullah leapt off his bicycle and let it fall. Grappling with the deadweight of Martha, a strip of cloth she had ripped off her victim's backside revealed the skin of no common thief or burglar. This was the backside of an Angrez. The beast, furious at being thwarted was digging more savagely in and when at last Nurullah succeeded in wresting her off the Angrez she came away with a slobbering mouthful of his shorts.

'Filthy-tempered bloody bitch,' swore the thoroughly frightened Angrez.

Pouring sweat and out of breath himself, Nurullah uprighted his cycle and swung a leg over it to depart when Martha sprang forward again barking dementedly. Through a gap in the hedge Nurullah saw a lantern swinging toward them and the chowkidar's bloodcurdling *haraharahara* yell of shikar beaters in the jungle. He was nearly pitched sideways as the Angrez took a running leap onto his carrier gasping, 'Faster, man, faster, get on with it.'

A car was parked in shadow a short distance up Havelock Road. 'There!' gasped the Angrez. He dismounted without a word or a wave, got into his car and drove it off at maniacal speed. In quite a state he was and little wonder.

'The wretched dog could have got *you*,' Eknath pointed out at the university next morning, 'and then the chowkidar would have nabbed *you* for an attacker or a thief. You should think of these things. Anything can happen these days. And what was it to do with you anyway?'

But what else could anyone have done? And frankly Nurullah felt sorry for a man having to go through fourteen anti-rabies injections in the stomach to be on the safe side. From what he'd seen of Martha's fangs they would have dug deeper than cloth and from what he knew of her temperament he wouldn't bet on its sanity.

He set out early the following Monday to be first in the queue at the bank to cash Ammaji's cheque. The manager was coming down the outside staircase from his upper floor flat. The stocky burly figure Nurullah had seen at his desk was descending slowly sideways holding onto the stone banister for support. He went into the bank with a careful hobble. Something about him stopped Nurullah in his tracks. In an inexplicable coincidence the man stopped too and twisted his upper half stiffly round to look at Nurullah, in which instant it was plain that this was Martha's ravaged victim. But Mr McCracken showed no sign of recognition.

Nurullah felt a stinging outraging slap of dismissal. An infinitesimal tremor twitched Mr McCracken's facial muscles. Over his shoulder he enquired, 'Er, was it you the other night?' Nurullah nodded. The manager said, 'Good of you', hobbled to his office and went in. The door shut firmly behind him. Nurullah's overwhelming urge to take a running kick at it ebbed out of him. What had he expected? A grateful handshake? Sincere expressions of Mr McCracken's profound relief at his rescue instead of this shadow play at the bank? He cashed his cheque and on his way out what should or should not have happened ceased to matter as the meaning of Mr McCracken's crawl through the hedge at midnight, set upon by the ferocious Martha, dawned on him. If the bank manager's retreat had not been exactly similar to Romeo's in the great love story, here was a passion to rival Romeo's.

He would have liked to swap theories about its romantic and dangerous implications with Eknath but Eknath's marriage had just been arranged and he was busy feigning a tense sort of nonchalance about it. And then his interests were more political than personal. Nurullah himself would have forgotten the episode had he not seen Mr McCracken again one cloudy afternoon during the rains at the skating rink where Nurullah had stopped, thinking of trying the sport. He never did go in. The steady rattle of metal pounding wood told him the rink was full and one look showed there were mostly Angrezes inside, as if some unwritten law had reserved it for them and their families on a Sunday. The smallest learners were being tenderly guided along the rail by their parents, but only slightly older ones who tumbled were helped up, dusted off and rolled on before they could cling to the rail or let out a self-pitying howl. Nurullah was impressed.

Mr McCracken was skating alone, his backside clearly recovered long ago from Martha's mauling. He had the look of a man out for a leisurely stroll on wheels with his hands behind his back in a posture designed for whistling. One stocky leg sailed out, then the other, and in this fashion he rolled around the rink with utmost casual ease, hailing no other skater and immersed, it seemed, in exquisite thoughts of his own.

It was odd that once you had personally encountered an Angrez and could pick him out of the rest he turned up again and again. Nurullah saw him again a few days later coming out of the Picture Palace although God Save the King had just struck up inside. Nurullah and Eknath made it a point to leave the cinema hall before the anthem but it was still playing when Martha's pallid mistress came out to join Mr McCracken. Their fingertips touched and then they went their separate ways, but almost at once Mr McCracken swung round and strode to her car. Nurullah saw him take the limp white hand she let fall out of the window like a flag at half mast and crush it to a deader whiteness down to its fingertips before he let it go. So agonized a parting must be a final one and it recalled to Nurullah a poem in a tattered collection he had bought in the second-hand bookshop:

My most, my most, O my lost!
O my bright, my ineradicable ghost ....

What he himself knew of love and the powerful feelings
it evoked — for the man who had taken him into his home
and his family on trust, for the child who had died in
agony to give him birth — had this tragic intensity, this
texture of pure grief. He waited till she withdrew her
hand, started her car and the small flurry of dust raised
by her tyres subsided. Now he could put a name to her,
having seen it on her gate going past it.

⌁

In Company Bagh formality reigned in keeping with the
showpiece it was, like the Viceroy's palace in Delhi, the
Governor's palace here and imposing imperial structures
such as Victoria Terminus in Bombay. Its flowers and
foliage had been laid out with a purpose, to awe and
impress. In Robin-da's younger days benches here had
been marked Europeans Only and Gandhi cap wearers
had sheltered in Khusrau Bagh, named after the Great's
first grandson, to escape arrest during martial law. Company
Bagh overflowed with children, ayahs and balloon sellers
on Saturdays when the military band played but it had no
lingerers or loiterers on weekday afternoons. Nurullah
had his pick of its benches. He ate Kallu's mutton
sandwiches with a gold and purple blaze at his feet that
he could now identify as pansies. The October scents and
colours around him had a deafening exuberance. He would

have stealthily plucked a posy of pansies to take home
except that a glass of water would have been a meagre
substitute for their joyous cohabitation here. The air was
beginning to be mild with the beauty of winter around
the corner.

He finished his sandwiches, took himself on a lazy
botany trail to see what he could recognize of trees whose
names he had learned from Pyare Chacha and congratulated
himself on the progress he was making. Coming to an
avenue of weeping ashokas he knew them instantly by
their shape, tall narrow cones whose densely layered leaves
pointed sharply earthward. In an encircling girdle of them
he came upon Mr McCracken fallen to his knees. He was
bowed over in the prayerful posture of namaz with his
russet head between the bleak white parted thighs of Mrs
Crik. She lay spread wide open on the grass. Only her eyes
were closed and her pallid features were twisted into an
expression of anguished unendurable pleasure. Nurullah's
hand clamped his mouth shut. He backed noiselessly out
of the glade and trod the path back to the park's sunlit
centre in mortal fear of crackling a leaf or a twig underfoot.
The high keening crescendo rising behind him could have
been a bird in distress in the shrubbery or a message borne
on the breeze had he not divined it came from Mrs Crik.
He collapsed on a bench and breathed deeply to calm his
agitation. He was guiltily aware of the enormity of having
trespassed into paradise, as anyone could so easily have
done. These were reckless lovers who would abandon
themselves beyond recall on what they hoped were hidden
grasses all over Akbarabad, without a thought beyond

making love. They would seek out likely shelters for their trysts and lose touch with the very ground they lay on.

His concern for their predicament brought him a possible practical solution. He still had the key to his room at Mrs Shona Tiwari's where some of his books and belongings were stored. In her toothless beneficence, calling him Son, she had made him keep the key and treat the room as his. For days Nurullah considered approaches that would serve to offer Mr McCracken this simple solution but in circumstances where hardly a word had been spoken between them this was a mountain of a task. Yet total strangers though they were to each other Nurullah was loath to give up trying. He was in the unique position of having been vouchsafed astonishing glimpses into forbidden territory: the human side of an Angrez. Mr McCracken's hedge crawl had shown he was a man like any other. The passion of his parting at the cinema and the namaz in the glade of weeping ashokas elevated his love for Mrs Crik above common lust and revealed in him a higher human quality. Intuition made Nurullah certain that Mr McCracken would not throw an Indian's luggage out of a first class coupé and order him to find himself another berth on the train. Nor would he say to another Angrez, 'Mind if I share your coupé? There's a nigger in mine.' Unproven though this was, Nurullah backed his surmise.

There followed nerve-wracking alternatives of exactly how to deliver the key but there was no getting over the shocked embarrassment it would cause Mr McCracken. Had ordinary conversation been possible as between any man and his well-wisher even this hurdle could have been crossed. Nurullah knew it could not. The past hundred-odd years had not allowed it. The realization revived the soreness of soul that such situations leave behind. Feeling defeated and dejected he kept his key.

Mr McCracken as lover buttressed Nurullah's own evolving philosophy of love. When he heard Bibijan remark to Ammaji that she was on the lookout for a bride for him his mind shied like a nervous horse. Brides had curtained faces and a doomed drowned air. More his idea of a woman's allure was the bold and winsome wench the cackling crack-toothed Mrs Shona Tiwari must have been in the 1880s, and still was, judging by Misraji's lifelong devotion. Recently he had had another example of truly enduring vitality. Nawab Sahib Vazirabad had invited Pyare Chacha and Mr Harvey to the fabled Chhappan Churi's performance at his house and Nurullah had gone with them. Fifty-Six Knives, Pyare Chacha had clarified, was so called because of the fifty-six dagger wounds on her. Flesh wounds only, he explained, the most jealous lover would not have been insane enough to destroy her beauty or put an end to her sublime dancing career.

Now trained in Chinese exquisitries Nurullah had been dismayed by the china dogs — one lifesize one at the entrance to Vazirabad House — fringed lamps, bead curtains and ungainly paintings of mem maidens languishing among ferns in the drawing room, termed Victorian junk by Mr Harvey in a whisper. Led to expect a vision of beauty he saw a mound of flesh waddle in and sink to the cool green marble beyond the carpet. Her smile uncovered paan-blackened teeth as one fleshy hand traced the ritual adab. When the coarse creature began to sing it could have been coarsely lined wool issuing from her fat throat. Ya Allah! Was this the legend? The song completed, Chhappan Churi prepared to heave her bulk to her feet and lo! the mountain rose like a bubble! Extending an arm she arched the hand like a swallow in flight and curved it into the most miraculous shell Nurullah had set eyes on in his dreams of seas and shells. All her unwieldy shapelessness dissolved into the lightning footwork of kathak and the room into a realm of cool green marble bounded by the tabla's hypnotic beat. Chhappan Churi radiated the aura of a battle-scarred fortress recalling heroic unforgettable deeds. Nurullah had seen a photo of one which the evening light had seemed to lift and float above its hilltop in the Rajputana desert. When the great bulk trembled to a stop and sank to the floor he had erupted into applause, making a thunder clap of noise in the murmured appreciation around him.

There was no such transcending sorcery about Eknath's marriage ceremony in November and Eknath had looked so timorous at the reception afterwards that it was to his bride Nurullah handed the flat volume of verse he had been carrying in his kurta pocket, reluctant to leave it among the handsomer presents. He wished them both the lasting joy of literature and a pleased little smile touched her lips. She held the book out to her husband with an un-shy comradely gesture that reminded Nurullah her family came of the clarion call breed.

Eknath looked washed out and anxious when they came round to play badminton but Usha played a good fast game. The badminton court was proving a great success. Nurullah had taught Shān and the Vazirabad brats to play. Robin-da displayed unexpected prowess, leaping high as a gazelle to send the shuttlecock smashing down on his opponent. Kallu and the Framjees' driver tried their hand.

∿

He came down from the roof terrace one night wanting to clear his brain of starlit fancies before going to sleep, and crossed the road to Colonelgunj only to find all the shops, even the tea stall, shut. He was on his way back when a police van stopped and ordered him in. On the drive through deserted night-lit streets one of the men who must have been hauled in like himself kept quarrelsomely demanding to be let out. He got a shower of abuse and a free-swinging backhanded blow across his face that glanced off Nurullah's jawbone with stunning impact. A truncheon prodded them out of the van at the police station and a hostile stare lumped their ill-assorted crew handily together for fast collective questioning. You, you, you, you, you, what were you doing on the road? In the hubbub of voices denying knowledge of the eight p.m. curfew Nurullah remained rigidly silent. His teeth throbbed under his swelling jaw. His brain refused cooperation, belying his flexible approach in civilized situations.

'You! Speak up, what were you doing on the road?'

His arms were forced behind him, his head jerked sharply sideways by a hand bent on slicing it in two. His angry van mate had not stopped demanding his release. He lay curled into a ball, being kicked into silence. They spent the night in the lockup where one of them said the curfew had been clamped because an Angrez had been found dead in suspicious circumstances.

The morning newspaper reported it was the manager of the Imperial Bank of Akbarabad. His body had been found with its neck broken at the bottom of the stone staircase. In view of the politically charged atmosphere an assault on an Englishman had to be taken very seriously and the authorities had taken stern measures for public safety. The editorial informed readers that bank managers had been targets of misguided revolutionary fervour during Martial Law in the Punjab in 1919. At that time, it would be remembered, the population had run amuck after two well-known anti-British agitators were arrested and deported. A mob had sacked the National Bank in Amritsar and murdered both the manager, Mr Stewart, and the accountant, Mr Scott. The manager of the Alliance Bank, Mr Thomson, had confronted the mob and fired revolver shots into it before he, too, was killed and his body burnt when they set fire to the bank. An unsuccessful attempt had also been made on the Chartered Bank.

'That was in 1919,' said Nurullah to Eknath who was reading the item to him, 'what makes them so jumpy now?'

'For the authorities it is always 1919,' said Eknath, 'and in Akbarabad it is still 1857 as far as they're concerned. Once a mutineer, always a mutineer.'

Nurullah's swollen jaw and temple were smarting under the unguents applied by Khurram and the compounder. He said he had never heard such bilge. Bank murders, mobs, mutineers! The stuff of Angrez brain fever. And *of course* it wasn't 1919. They had violence on the brain though they were dealing with ahimsa now.

'Besides,' he said, cupping his painful jaw with one hand, 'why would anybody kill Mr McCracken?'

'Those whom they call "disaffected elements" might. Someone whose account was frozen, maybe. Someone with a political grouse. They'd have to round up likely suspects. They'd probably hang one to be on the safe side.'

Nurullah took strong issue with Eknath on that point. There were law courts. There was the law. The law was sacrosanct.

Eknath raised a cynical eyebrow. 'Aren't you the one who told me a magistrate threatened a kisan with his cane when he came to register a complaint against an Angrez planter?'

It had happened to the kisan ahead of him at the magistrate's outdoor hearing. Nurullah, proudly literate at twelve, had gone with an elderly peasant at his request to do the reading and writing for him if need be and had ducked his head between his knees when he saw the wrathful cane come round the table though it was not meant for him. The Englishman must have been an unusually nervy magistrate, over-sensitive as we all are, to the concerns of our own kind. The chasm between life and law, as between life and literature could be vast. It was because of literature that Nurullah saw the Angrez as they saw themselves, a just and upright breed who ruled even those they subjugated according to the law. If he thought of 'the Englishman' at home in England as a being nobler, finer and more admirable than other Europeans it might well be because he had read the literature of no other. Ultimately there was only literature to know them by since life, as it was constituted, put the most ordinary encounters — let alone love and friendship — out of bounds, and bent the law to shelter them from seen and unseen danger.

Convinced that no one had killed Mr McCracken he became contrarily convinced that someone had when the same newspaper gave it as its editorial opinion that the bank manager, 'a loner by reputation, a night wanderer, a solitary man by choice', had lost his footing in the dark and plunged to his death. McCracken was not the man to lose his footing on stairs he must have known by heart. A nimble, surefooted man, the bank manager, and a supple one, as quick to crouch or bend over double as to glide smoothly upright on roller skates. Whatever the cause of his violent ugly death Nurullah mourned as he would have had Chhappan Churi's iridescent bubble of a performance been brutally terminated or if Mrs Shona Tiwari's hag-magic inexplicably ceased to work. Moreover, what he knew of the dead man had assumed an archival importance for him. The hedge crawl, the desperation of the handclasp, the worshipful namaz in the girdle of weeping ashokas, had thrown light on facets of a character he would never in the cast-iron scheme of things have come to know, and how else except through human acts could one know another human being? Above all, he mourned the lover who had adventured fearlessly at such risk to himself. The state of the bereaved beloved he could hardly bear to imagine. A woman left half alive, her anaemic pallor would fade to transparence in a bereavement she dare not make public. He wished he could call on Mrs Crik and express his sympathy. There being no way, as there had been none with the key, he was oppressed by a sense of waste and loss, of doors that needed forcing open. Denizens of one and the same earth were not meant to live like this.

He was irritably out of tune with Eknath's cut-and-dried analyses these days (never mind how correct they were) and would tell him to shut up and stop blasting off. But Eknath, having overcome whatever conjugal nerves had been ailing him was restored to his categorical self and his withering masterly résumés of national and international affairs. In sheer exasperation after one of these, Nurullah, copying the drawl of gangsterspeak, countered with 'You know your trouble, buster? You ain't got no faith in human nature.' Eknath burst out laughing and patted Nurullah superiorly on the head.

The incursion into gangster style had a tonic effect on Nurullah. He felt enormously refreshed and stimulated. He experimented with another fragment. Looking threateningly at himself in his dressing table's triple mirrors he drawled, employing the salacious softness of toughspeak, 'I just *ast* you nice, didn't I? You want me to ask you not-nice?' Could menace be more sinister? Gangster language came as a revelation to him. Its lack of smokescreen, its unassuming structure, its overpowering honesty gave it a sturdy peasant forthrightness that had never struck him before. It was a way out of the veritable labyrinth of human communication. Invigorated by daily practice, he perfected bloodcurdling gems like 'Come on, worm, squirm!' and the lighter-hearted 'What's cookin', good-lookin'?' in front of his triple mirrors. In the privacy of his room he resorted regularly to gangsterspeak after the death of Mr McCracken. It was healing and consoling, perhaps because it was the antithesis of paradise and carried no desolate reminder of the pain of paradise lost.

Three

One wall of Bhai's study had a horizontally elongated map of the world designed by a cartographer with a disdain for conventional maps. Taking a close look at it for the first time Nurullah saw that spaces showing natural wealth were expanded accordion-like and the same accordion technique had squeezed all other spaces small. Its colours were the cartographer's own too, not the mottled browns and yellow-browns of hills and deserts, the green-browns of rain forests, the reptilianly winding greens and blue-greens of rivers or the established colours of European occupation. These were scarlet, purple, indigo, black, harsh patches whose authority compelled the eye to tin and timber, copper, rubber, lead and oil. To gold and diamonds, too, and other open and buried treasure, all duly labelled with its (mostly Angrez) ownership. An Angrez company controlled oilfields between the Black Sea and the Caspian and a long black arrow traced the oil pipeline being laid across the desert from Upper Iraq to a Mediterranean port. A label between the Red Sea and the Persian Gulf proclaimed it Britain's holy highway to India which must be defended at all cost, because of which Ibn Saud must be watched and Egypt's independence kept under British control.

Italy's share of captured loot seemed to be confined to Africa where Angrez ownership again stretched the formidable length and breadth of that continent and France owned three thousand miles of it from the Mediterranean across the Sahara, as well as Madagascar off the east coast. Tiny Belgium had the rich Congo. Italy was left with just Libya, Eritrea and Somaliland and this last place, read the label, gave her good reason to grab Abyssinia if opportunity arose.

Nurullah noticed an American company owned one million acres of Liberia, and in the Caribbean, what the Angrez didn't own was controlled by American companies and banks.

He had known, of course, in a general way, that Europe owned the world but the map's altered scale and harsh colours gave this dry well-established fact the thrust of a sensational discovery and made a Greater Europe of most of the earth. He had not begun to convey the fact to Shān and had no idea where to get started. Exploring the high shelves of the library he chanced upon *Palashi* by Pyarelal Tussu, published in 1912, and learned that Pyare Chacha had chronicled more than the doings of Basso Masi and Kishen Chacha. The little hundred-page book which he took down and quickly read was a scintillating departure from class texts on the prelude to empire.

'Today we'll talk about Palashi,' he said to Shãn.

'Plassey,' she corrected crossly, 'you can't even pronounce it. It was a famous battle and Clive was its hero.'

'That's the story that got around, dost, but it was no battle, it was a plot. And the place was Palashi where Angrez and Hindustani budmashes — each no better than the other when it came to sharp practice and crooked business — got together and outwitted the Nawab of Bengal.'

'There was fighting,' she objected, 'and the English side won and the Indian side lost.'

'But not because Indians can't fight,' he said sternly, 'Clive had two thousand Indian soldiers fighting on his side and only eight hundred goras. As far as fighting goes it's been done for them by Indians up and down this land and all over the world. Indians won India for the Angrez.'

'Sister Clara says Plassey was a battle and Clive was its hero,' the obstinate girl persisted.

'Sister Clara is very sincere,' said Nurullah who had met and liked the rosy-cheeked woman who looked happy to be a nun, 'do not blame her. There's a conspiracy to keep history books in darkness about what really happened. Here's how it went. First they came as traders to trade, then they got greedy and broke the trading rules, then they armed themselves to protect their ill-begotten profits, then they hired soldiers and built fortresses to defend the loot. Then they grabbed land and called it theirs. The story of empire, dost. It goes from Company to Cantt to Crown.'

Nusli Framjee slaved loyally in preparation for Bhai's homecoming. He got the window glass sponged and wiped with crumpled newspaper and the library shelves turned out with a great beating and banging of books after which they were sunned and returned in their proper shelf order right side up to their shelves. Carpets were severely thrashed. With his usual careful forethought he brought in a consignment of weak bulbs for future use and Nurullah did the needful in the stairwell with one of them, all to no purpose as it happened. Bhai's younger sister, Nina, arrived with her friend Jeroo Ghasvala the day before Bhai's release and lost her temper the minute she walked in, declaring she would not have the house looking like a morgue for her brother's homecoming. Immediately she sent out for sixty and a hundred-watt bulbs. The tedious trek with the ladder had to be repeated and a strong bulb fitted. The star-shaped ochre mosaic far below opened and blossomed under Nurullah's gaze like some wondrous sun-drenched flower. Nina hadn't waited to see it. She was rearranging the Chinese room with her Parsi friend, both of them pushing and pulling furniture and loudly bewailing the plundered jade cabinet instead of attending to their suitcases, bedding rolls and thermoses in the anteroom. Nurullah hollered for Kallu and hefted the luggage upstairs.

It was the first time Nurullah had seen Nina, having been away when she and her husband Sheel came in July. She had the darkly lipsticked mouth and hairless eyebrows of the mem cinema idols on King and Co.'s counter. Her friend, who was new to the family and to Akbarabad, likewise. Dress them in spangles and ostrich feathers and put them on a revolving platform and they would be the

Follies mems. Their pencilled arcs made a startling contrast to Shān's thick black brows so often beetled in a scowl. For the present, however, Shān was all thrilled excitement at the prospect of her father's release and was prancing between aunt and friend with a patter of radiant talk.

On December the first Bhai got out of the Framjees' Nash to receive Ramdin's reddest rose and the mali broke down and wept. Bhai's arm went around his heaving shoulders before he joined the citizens gathered on the lawn to welcome him home. Nurullah hung back during the jubilant family reunion on the verandah but Bhai searched past their faces, found his, and the sweetness of his smile could have been for a blood brother. Then, without a breathing spell, he went to the Chinese room where the press waited, straight into the hub of current affairs.

Nawab Sahib Vazirabad and Bibijan drove in with pomegranates, partridges and grapes. Old Zenobia Framjee took charge along with Miss Basappa who had been released from jail a week earlier, not noticeably slimmer, though Bhai had the sallow drawn look of repeated malaria.

Party members started arriving for a meeting in the afternoon before Nurullah left for the university. He had the impression they were going to assess how the Movement had fared, and new tasks would have to be assigned to the men and women who were being released. He knew how they would go about it, having sat out the longwinded debate in the Chinese room that had launched the No Tax campaign. That every lame and leper soul must have its say and be given the chance to make up whatever Allah had given it for a mind, seemed to be their way of going about urgent business. Quite the opposite of trends in Europe. Italy's popular hero was doing all the talking for his people and had said Italy would be a lot better off if a dozen of its Parliament's deputies were shot in the back. The rising German hero, an excitable fellow in a brown uniform, was of the same bandit disposition. Neither of them would have lasted two minutes at a party meeting in the Chinese room.

Nurullah heard a late arrival bellow on the verandah, 'You still alive, man?' presumably to Ramdin and laugh richly at the reply. The laugh was deceiving. It was a towering scarecrow who walked slowly in, a grey shawl hanging from his spare frame. As soon as he entered the drawing room the others got up from the floor and closed joyfully around him, all talking together, protesting his frailty, while he — obviously a missing thread of their tapestry — waved off their concern saying ancient carcasses didn't need much food. Before the door closed Nurullah heard someone banteringly ask, 'And how are things in the great world?' He replied in the same bantering vein, 'Not very advanced, I fear, bhai sahib. There are countries where everybody is a Christian, and countries where everybody is a Mussalman. The monotony was unbelievable. We, here, are not used to it.'

The meeting was over when Nurullah got back from his class but a few people were still there around Ahmed Zaheer who, Eknath had told him, must just have returned from ten years' banishment.

'What did he do, throw a bomb?'

'People hang for that, yaar. He edited a newspaper. Took up kisan problems. At his trial the prosecution charged him with wanting to turn out the Europeans and his weekly was shut down. They put him in jail but when he got out he was had up again for his part in the kisan uprising, so they exiled him.'

Bhai was upstairs closeted with a podgy retired judge who had come to acquaint him with developments during his absence and they were joined by two barristers, one of whom had shared Bhai's cell. Dinner was delayed and Nina was getting restive, fretfully asking 'Where's Bhai?' every few minutes in the wistful bleat of a lost lamb, unlike her bossy way with bulbs and furniture. When Bhai came in, deeply preoccupied, he said he had asked the judge and the barristers to dine next week.

'We should ask young Sitaram and the other boys, too, Ammaji. There's little we can do to repay those youngsters. Justice Mahabir was telling me how cruelly Sitaram was thrashed when Gosiben's procession was broken up by the police.'

Nina puckered her pencilled arcs. 'The judge and the party workers *together*? We might as well throw in the Christian Workshop man, Bhai darling.'

'Yes, why not?' said Bhai absently, 'Joseph is such a help to us.'

Bright lighting had brought the dining room out of its gloom to reveal its graceful proportions, the intricacies of the table's carving and the majesty of Tiger and Rushing Waterfall. Chrysanthemums filled a yellow crystal boat that Nina had taken out of storage and placed between two tapering yellow candles in ornate silver candlesticks, giving Nurullah a glimmering of what the house must have looked like before the clarion call. Jeroo went into mem-like raptures over the chrysanthemums, reverently fingering a chestnut-crimson one that was gold in reverse, and Nurullah had to admit they made a gorgeous display, rosy purple, bronze, an aristocratic silver pink. With his chronicling skill, Pyare Bhai described a magnificent copper orange one he had yet to grow called Genghis Khan because of course the chrysanthemum was originally a Chinese flower. Indeed the Chinese had worked on the common daisy from 500 BC — a very persevering people, the Chinese — to evolve the glorious garden chrysanthemum.

'No!' exclaimed Jeroo.

'It is a fact,' confirmed Pyare Chacha, 'that Europeans did not set eyes on a chrysanthemum until the last decade of the eighteenth century.'

Ammaji and he beamed hospitably on Jeroo, lovingly on Nina. Two little girls home from school they might have been, with Shān looking positively elderly between them. Nurullah attended with professional ease to his knife and fork, relieved that the time he had spent mastering this superfluous paraphernalia had not been entirely wasted. Bhai, he noticed, had yet to make the wrenching adjustment from prison cell to Nawab Sahib's quail and partridge, roasted for his homecoming candlelit dinner.

'I could weep every time I see what's left of Father's precious jade,' Nina was saying, at which Bhai's withdrawn attention rallied.

'I don't know why they didn't make a clean sweep of it. Justice Mahabir has been telling me some entire properties have been attached this time. Why d'you suppose they spared this house?'

'Really, Bhai!' cried Nina in scandalized protest.

'Nurullah,' said Bhai, singling him out to his intense embarrassment, 'did you hear of any move to sequester this property or any part of it?'

Unprepared for all their eyes on him he managed to lay his knife and fork side by side in the clatterless way he had perfected and, hoping his voice would convey as much confidence, he came out with far more than he had intended.

'No, Bhai. But how could they have done so? Public opinion would have gone against them.'

'That didn't prevent them from giving me a stomach-kicking on Dandi Beach during the Salt Satyagraha and booting my head down into sea water to give me my fill of salt,' recalled Bhai ruefully.

'You know very well why that happened,' said Nina, 'You wouldn't stay with the leaders. You insisted on joining the party workers. How were the police to know the difference? Why can't you stay where you belong?'

'And where's that, my sweet?' her brother teased.

'You know exactly what I mean, Bhai darling.'

Jeroo looked from one to the other of them, her elbows on the table and her hands clasped under her chin like one of the cutout mems at King and Co.'s. But her eyes had a glow Nurullah had never seen in any eyes. She could have been the first human beholding the first sunrise.

'It's all — so — bewildering,' she said haltingly.

'What is, Jeroo?' asked Bhai.

'Well that's just it, I don't know. Being here. The Chinese inventing chrysanthemums, Europe being nowhere on the scene ...' she trailed off.

'Why should that surprise you?' Bhai smiled at her. 'Wouldn't one expect such an achievement from people who conjured a mountain from a single curl on parchment centuries before Europe woke up to abstract art?'

Jeroo, near to tears, held her face in her hands as if to hold it steady and said not a word.

After goodnights were over she and Nina reclined at opposite ends of the sofa in the Chinese room.

'Your uncle Pyare is so *sweet*,' sighed Jeroo.

'But they're all quite cut off from reality and Bhai is a babe in the woods when it comes to practical matters. It's enough to drive one to despair.'

'This brother of yours, this beautiful valiant knight — not the saintly one, I mean the dashing one, Lancelot — could be skiing with royalties in St. Moritz and spending his summers sailing with celebrities in the Mediterranean. But here he is, mixed up with peasants and getting kicked in the stomach. Why didn't you ever tell me the police had treated him like that? It's outrageous.'

'It happens,' said Nina resignedly, 'but it needn't have happened to *him*. Let's face it, class distinctions are a fact of life. And of dinner parties. Bhai just throws everyone in together.'

'I haven't brought anything to wear to a party.'

'It isn't going to be that sort of party. Wear any old thing. Polite society has ostracized us since the family joined the Movement. Even Shān's ayah cut her dead the other day. So it rather put the lid on entertaining. People who would never have fetched up in a drawing room started coming to the house instead and Bhai had the bright idea that parlour games would help them mix. So it's been parlour games ever since.'

Nurullah, playing chess with Shān on the carpet, heard Jeroo say the influence of Gandhi was quite extraordinary as if parlour games were played at Sabarmati Ashram.

'And there'll be no drinks,' Nina warned. 'The family gave up everything foreign with austerity and the boycott. I couldn't even give you a drink before dinner.'

She made up for it by offering her friend a cigarette and lighting one for herself.

Dropping her voice she said, 'I worry so about the infant. The infant's life is being ruined. She's never going to know a normal life. All these weak bulbs in the house and no fridge. D'you realize she practically never hears the telephone ring? Nobody *uses* the telephone. They send chits round. Dire news comes by telegram. And there's hardly a car in Akbarabad. It's a dead bore. Nothing happens. I don't know why I love the wretched place to distraction.'

'I begin to understand Sheel's dilemma,' said Jeroo, 'about whether to throw in his lot with Gandhi and join the Movement or not. If I stayed here long enough I'd probably want to fling myself into jail too, just to follow your beautiful valiant brother's example, he has that effect on one, but just the same I do wish Sheel would stop having rows with Jhangoo about Manchuria.'

Nurullah untangled this thoroughly confused sentence to gather that Sheel had been disagreeing with Jhangoo Ghasvala about Japan's invasion of Manchuria.

'You have to remember how sensitive Sheel is,' said Nina, 'it's hell for a man like him not to take the plunge and join the Movement, or to hear Jhangoo say it's all right for Japan to march into Manchuria. Sheel says he'll never get over China pleading with the League of Nations to stop the aggression.'

'Actually, Nina, there's no Manchurian crisis any more so what's all the fuss about? Jhangoo says it's blown over now that Britain and France have both recognized Japan's right to be there.'

Jeroo's placid observation gave Nurullah the impression that Mr Ghasvala was a man who judged invasions by this ready reckoner.

∿

Everyone who had been invited to the party came, including Joseph of the Christian Workshop who mended furniture and replaced confiscated heirlooms with workaday items like the bench in the anteroom. Joseph's aesthetic sense was nil but there was a great willingness about him. Nurullah had seen him only once when he came to deliver a completed dreary looking order. Ammaji had persuaded him to stop for a glass of her mulberry juice. He had drunk it sitting on the edge of the takht, given short respectful laughs and made his getaway as fast as possible. Now he was no more at ease, sticking close to the wall with the two old and two young party workers, all four of them in their flapping khadi shorts. But like them he got into the spirit of the party when games began with musical chairs. Well-trained by now, Nurullah guessed.

Joseph darted alertly from chair to chair to the sliding strains of 'O Silvery Arizona Moon' on the gramophone. The other players besides the family and the party workers were Robin-da, the Framjees, Mr Harvey, Miss Basappa, two barristers and their wives and Justice Mahabir. Dr Bihari shielded the gramophone from view and Gosiben, the Khadi Bhandar in-charge, who turned out to be a competent flat-chested lady, managed it. Nurullah removed chairs as required. He thought Miss Basappa looked resplendent in a sari of pink and gold Banaras tissue and one of Pyare Chacha's silver-pink chrysanthemums behind her ear. She was stepping nimbly in tennis shoes and white wool socks but laughing so hard at Mr Harvey's deliberate capers ahead of her that she was the first one out. Old Zenobia Framjee in swinging earrings, lacework sari and little skull cap of spidery lace, won the game.

'Jeroo!' Bhai called gaily when the chairs had been cleared, 'you must know a game.'

This lighthearted request seemed to give Jeroo a faint electric shock. Recovering her poise she described a game called How Green You Are from her schooldays. One person was sent out and brought in again to perform some silly little act the others had agreed on. Like switching off a light or plumping up a cushion, any silly little thing. Everyone had to sing How Green You Are to the tune of

'Auld Lang Syne', loudly when the person got near doing the act and *softly* when he got far from it. That was all there was to it.

A devastating silence reigned.

'Oh!' cried Jeroo in a small distressed voice, 'well never mind then.'

'You'll have to sing it, Jeroo,' Bhai encouraged, 'Everyone doesn't know "Auld Lang Syne".'

He joined her along with Nina and Mr Harvey and after a patchy rehearsal Justice Mahabir was sent out and brought in. The judge must have forgotten the rules. Paying no attention to the loud and soft signals he trotted around the room in chuckling good humour, conducting the chorus with one finger. The chorus might well have put him in such a quandary he had decided to ignore it. Gosiben's 'Haaaow green' transformed the lines into a wail of woe. Robin-da, off-key as usual, was guturally alaaping them. Joseph's unexpectedly melodious and triumphant rendering recalled a hearty hymn celebrating the birth of Christ that Nurullah had heard carollers sing last Christmas. Sitaram's voice cracked on the high notes and came forth bass when least expected. Jeroo's game might have gone on all night had Bhai not taken firm hold of the judge, marched him to the designated chair and put him in it.

Nurullah joined in when slips were drawn for Murder. The lights were switched off until the victim was murdered and Miss Basappa's shriek brought them on again. A hundred-watt bulb blazed down on her pink and gold magnificence. She looked even more imposing recumbent

and, biologically speaking, all woman — a fact it was easy
to forget from time to time. The rules obliged her to lie
where she had fallen until Shān who had drawn the
detective slip caught out Nusli Framjee, the murderer. Mr
Harvey then went to the trouble of retrieving her scattered
bobbypins and handing her her squashed chrysanthemum
and she, still prone, resting heavily on one elbow, thanked
him with an upward, frankly feminine flicker through half
closed eyes.

Joseph had provided folding chairs and tables from
the Christian Workshop for the evening and had set them
up in the dining room in place of the dining table. Immersed
as Nurullah had been in his teaching routine here and at
the university, the gradual replacement of the British army's
diet by finer fare had gone unnoticed by him. He paid
prayerful tribute to the skill — clearly Jalaluddin butcher's
— that had carved shin and chest meat from the goat with
such precision and preserved marrow bones in all their
succulence. No breath of onion or garlic marred this or
any other preparation. The peas and cauliflower, the turnips
in the meat, were winter-sweet and tender. Rice bloomed
fragrantly on its own. Robin-da helped himself lavishly,
hum-muttering 'Een the *shar*dows let me *cleeng* to you'
from one of the musical chairs records. Melody did not
come naturally to Robin-da, only a love of it.

Pyare Chacha played benevolent host to the judge and
the Brahmin barrister. A silky pashmina shawl draped his
frail patrician shoulders. His every gesture furnished living
proof that history's whirlwinds had bypassed his own if
no other bloodline on the Ganga's plain, leaving it pristinely

pure. With much the same gracious aloofness the old dame, Zenobia Framjee, inclined her head a fraction when greeted and moved on. Just so had Nurullah seen a camel sway loftily through a herd of milling cattle in the Chowk, sniffing a higher purer air.

He himself ate with Robin-da, the humbler barrister and the two older party workers, listening to them reminisce about Martial Law fourteen years ago. The trickiest part had been keeping up with the notices the military kept posting or be punished for breaking some new instant law. The two party workers had got beaten up, taken unawares by the law that Akbarabadis were not permitted to walk two abreast. A gathering of four was an 'unlawful assembly' to be 'dispersed by force of arms if necessary.' Forty lashes was the penalty for shutting down shop and refusing to serve the army and police. And the richest of the lot was Sarkar Salaam, a punishment Colonel O'Ryan who was running the show (and after whom Colonelgunj was named) must himself have invented. An Akbarabadi 'who came into the presence of gazetted commissioners or the European civil and military officers of His Imperial Majesty' had to get down from horseback or his carriage, *lower his umbrella,* and perform the prescribed salute. Colonel O'Ryan deputed a sergeant to teach offenders how to get it right, drilling their right arms in fixed jerks to his barked orders and whipping them till they performed respectfully.

'I tell you I was practising it in front of the mirror just in case,' said Robin-da and went off to get a huge helping of Ammaji's glistening gold *halwa.*

'Well may you look dazed at our local history, Nurullah,' he said between mouthfuls, 'you were not here when students tore off Martial Law notices at the university and five hundred of them including Nikhil were marched three miles in the burning sun as punishment by the zealous Colonel.'

'But the barristers got the worst of it,' Madan Lal reminded Robin-da, 'or have you forgotten? Ninety-three of us were made to do duty as constables, patrol the city and be in attendance when citizens were flogged.'

He and twenty others had protested and were locked into a cell with one chamber pot for twenty-four hours. Later when a furious mob set fire to the railway station and looted its property, its ringleaders, Jalaluddin butcher, Asghar Ali barber, and Chunnilal halwai, had been charged with sedition. They had had sticks driven up their anuses in public by a havaldar. *Takht lo ya takhta* was the ultimatum they were delivered. *Choose between the throne and the gallows.* Madan Lal and some of his cell-mates had been forced to witness the Colonel's carnival.

'Anyone care to dance?' floated Jeroo's voice from her table amid general laughter and Bhai came round urging Nawab Sahib Vazirabad's grapes and sliced pomegranates on his guests.

The Framjees stayed after the other guests had gone. Nurullah heard Jeroo say in the Chinese room, 'What a *sport* you are, Zinny-bai. I can't for the life of me see Jhangoo's mama or for that matter mine joining in like you did.' The old dame was in a sentimental mood. The late master, she said, had helped her Burjor to set up their now flourishing liquor business in the Civil Lines, thanks to the Cantt being their biggest customer. And this house had been home to her and her Burjor long before khadi, boycott and all that rubbish.

'It's been such fun,' sighed Jeroo with a catch in her voice, 'I can't bear the thought of getting back to normal life.'

'Well, what's the hurry then?' said Nina and made her agree to stay longer.

Nurullah heard no more. Kallu was reported drunk in the kitchen. Nurullah hauled him out of his basket chair and lurched him to his quarter by the light of Binda's lantern. He pulled off his chappals and left him snoring on his charpai. When he got back to help Beni clear the table Jeroo was relaying Bombay gossip. That gnome, Dr Bowmanjee, had been knighted. The little Commissariat girl was engaged to marry daft Jimmy Ginvala and was given the Ginvala diamonds as an engagement present. They were the size of the Gwalior emeralds and every Parsi mama had coveted them for her daughter, never mind poor Jimmy being mental, but Jeroo felt sorry for pretty little Babsy who was just out of school and deserved a better fate.

Old Zenobia sternly reprimanded her.

'The Ginvalas are a solid family, Jeroo. Everyone can't have old money. And the best families can have some far back streak of insanity even among we Parsis. What does it matter?'

Nurullah dried the cutlery Beni had laboriously washed in the pantry and put it away in felt-lined drawers under

Mountain and Water. He heard Jeroo ask who Nurullah was.

'He's a protegé of Robin-da's, the darling old Communist who was singing off-key. He lectures at the university and Bhai's got him tutoring Shān. Bhai won't keep a governess for her and he won't hear of sending her to boarding school. It's the nuns and Nurullah and a queerer mixture there cannot be,' Nina replied.

'I could get her into Rodean, my old school,' offered Jeroo. 'She'd fit in anywhere after a good English schooling.'

'Jeroo dear,' said Nina patiently, 'Bhai doesn't *want* her to fit in. Bhai says there's no point in fitting her into a world that he's spending his whole life changing.'

'I see,' said Jeroo doubtfully, and then with a spark of sunrise in her voice, 'yes, I believe I do.'

'It's more than I can say. It's all rather worrying. I'm thankful she gets *some* normal life with us during her holidays.'

The education of Shān, thus explained, made Nurullah's share of it clearer to him. It put Sister Clara in another light too, as ally and counterpoise to him in a manner of speaking — the good nun in charge of this world, he of the next, in a peculiar reversal of their roles.

'I think Nurullah's rather a pet,' said Jeroo, 'so good-looking and those beautiful eyelashes are wasted on a man — but I've never seen desolation writ so large on a face.'

'My Nusli's training him up,' put in old Zenobia, 'making him useful around the house. We are all very kind to him, goodness knows where-all he comes from.'

The two younger women started choking on the look Miss Basappa had given Mr Harvey when he picked up her bobbypins, and squealing over her tennis shoes and white wool socks. Nurullah had thought them serviceable, sensibly warm on a chilly night and well suited to Miss Basappa. It was the pink and gold Banarsi splendour that had been out of character. He had been sorry to hear her tell Bhai she would be going back to Coorg and then further south to Brahmin strongholds to revive the agitation for Untouchables' entry into temples, but there was no better person than Miss Basappa to confront Brahmins and storm these citadels of caste.

He heard Jeroo say the evening had been marvellously quaint and she was quite fascinated.

'I'd probably want to give up *everything* if I stayed here long enough,' she said in an impetuous burst.

'Fancy a lovely intelligent girl like you talking such utter rubbish,' scolded old Zenobia.

Nurullah smothered a snort of surprise, wondering if the old dame was off her head. He found hairless eyebrows and mindless chatter somewhat off-putting himself.

Later he had reason to revise his opinion of Jeroo. She had an actress' talent for mimicry and gave a wonderfully funny imitation of Pannalal Jeweller whom she had visited to have her broken pearls re-strung.

'There we were, Niki, knee-deep in gold and jewels and Pannalal kept bringing out more. He thought I might be a customer for his most priceless acquisition, a pure green diamond set in gold from one of the royal houses of Kathiwar. Then suddenly the old humbug makes a mournful face' — here Jeroo transformed hers into the mask of a sad old ape — 'casts his eyes to the ceiling and piously asks Nina, "And how is Bhai Sahib? Tireless as ever in his selfless labours for the poor?"'

She had them all laughing another day with her imitation of an English monarch at dinner, tearing meat off a bone with his teeth, from a film she had seen in London last summer.

'I'm glad I saw it in London. That scene won't survive the censor here. Isn't censorship a god-awful bore, Niki? Cutting out that sequence will ruin the scene. And whatever *for*? We all know that was Tudor times. No one's going to mistake lusty Henry for dignified George the Fifth.'

Bhai admitted the ways of censors were hard to fathom. They were zealous guardians of 'face' and who said 'face' was an exclusively eastern obsession? Answering to 'Niki' and to 'Bhai darling' had taken the sallow brooding overlay of jail off him. Nowadays he ran up and down the stairs. He would link arms with the women and take them and Shān off for a walk through the guava orchard behind the house and the fields beyond, or drive the Framjee Nash to the Yamuna for a boatride and a picnic on the sands, or to Company Bagh where he would buy up the vendor's whole stock of balloons for Shān. One evening old Zenobia was doing her mathematical rhumba routine along invisible squares with Shān when Bhai came in. He moved into the enticing beat with snapping fingers, flashing eyes and a fluid irresistible grace that brought Nina and Jeroo to either side of him. The impromptu trio danced to no pattern but all three surrendered to the beat as if born to it, and as if they had its music in their blood.

An atmosphere Nurullah had never known pervaded the house, not altogether explained by the brighter lights, the music, the flower-filled rooms or the new aromas from Kallu's kitchen. All these he had imagined existing somewhere, to some extent, if not in this abundance. He did not know what to call the suffusing tenderness that had come to occupy the rooms. Nina's husband, Sheel, who came for a few days seemed the only outsider — the visitor from normal life — for Nina and Jeroo had succumbed, at least for the time being, to Akbarabad. Sheel dressed in suits and spoke English with the slight simulated stammer of the highborn English Nurullah had seen in films. He would have made more of an impression but for his air of chronic uncertainty due (perhaps) to not being able to make up his mind whether to throw in his lot with Gandhi and go to jail the next time round. He seemed to be waiting for it to be made up for him. Nurullah could have told him the family would be no help, incapable as they were of laying down the law and impossibly democratic in all their dealings. He doubted that Imperial Chemicals were in danger of losing Sheel to lathi charges and jail, but the conflict told on Sheel. Being so sensitive, Nina said, the dilemma was absolute hell for him.

Nurullah would not have guessed Bhai could have anything in common with Jeroo but their conversation revealed shared tastes in food eaten in other parts of the world — oysters, ripe Stilton, rich black Viennese chocolate cake, port-and-lemonade after tennis — and their memories dovetailed in politics as it had once been 'before the Mahatma let the peasants in, Niki.'

'Remember those pearls I had re-strung at Pannalal's, Niki? They were my grandmamma's. She wanted to take them to the party's annual session in Calcutta to wear with her little pearl tiara — what a fashion parade annual sessions used to be! — and my grandpappa had a fit. He forbade her to show off. She could wear either or but not both.'

Zenobia Framjee clucked feelingly of Jeroo's long departed grandfather, '*Evo* sensitive-*ne*-retiring *dikra*. Never one to flaunt his wealth and his position.'

One afternoon of Jeroo's extended stay she asked Bhai what, actually, was wrong with the British being here.

'It's history now. Why not let them stay?'

Nurullah was in the library sorting books that were to be disposed of to make room for new ones. He had stopped work for his mental recital of the day's third prayer, adding his own outpourings to the majestic language of the Koran. Faith is the legacy of upbringing but a mind grows, as Akbar's had, to expand and overflow its frontiers. Bhai and Jeroo were on the terrace protruding from the verandah outside the library where a table had been laid for their tea and from where they had a panoramic view of the circular driveway. It was sunny but a breeze had sprung up. The knot of kisans trudging up the drive were shrouded in headshawls muffling half their faces and falling below their knees, men whose natural climate is heat. Jeroo's was not the infantile question Nurullah would earlier have judged it. She was a person who needed a practical answer for everything.

'Why not let them stay?' Bhai repeated dryly, 'because, my dear, we can't afford them.'

Nurullah heard tea being poured into the glazed pink Gwalior pottery cups that had replaced the family's flower-patterned English china.

'The very first year the East India Company took charge, it raised land revenue by a hundred percent, and by another hundred percent over the next ten years. The famine in the province killed ten million people but Warren Hastings was proud to report that revenue collection in 1771 had gone up even though cultivation had dropped drastically because a third of the population had been wiped out.'

'Oh, Niki, that's ancient history, over and done with. We've already been over those nasty beginnings.'

'It's not over and done with,' said Bhai. 'The Company's enormous profits from the land and from its trading monopoly went back to Britain to finance their spinning jenny and powerloom and steam engine and gave the Bank of England capital to invest in the British Isles. They called it "India's tribute". And when the Crown took over from the Company most of this "tribute" was *lent* back to India and called the Public Debt. When Indian taxpayers — who else? — repaid it, it was used to finance British wars, in Afghanistan, in China, in Ethiopia. And where do you think the money comes from to pay the expenses of Britain's Mediterranean fleet? And who funds their petroleum ventures in Iran and Iraq, Saudi Arabia and Kuwait?'

'The Moghuls must have fleeced India, too. Try this cream roll, Niki, Nina and I taught Kallu to make it today. What's the difference between one invader and another?'

'The Moghuls had their extravagances but the money stayed here. From Turk to Moghul, through the Muslim kingdoms, the money stayed here. Now it drains out, while here no national industry of ours is allowed to grow so that theirs aren't threatened.'

'I had no idea you had such a head for finance, Niki. Looking at you one doesn't.'

'Others have made that mistake. I don't know why anyone thinks nationalism is some kind of misty romantic upsurge. No wonder the kisan uprising shook the Government as nothing had done since the Mutiny. A tax rebellion is dead serious business.'

'And now you are saying you'll give the land to the peasants who till it, *if* you ever come to power. Have a heart, Niki. What on earth are the landlords going to do without their zamindaris?'

'Earn a living, naturally, like everyone else.'

Jeroo gave a disbelieving gurgle and said she couldn't see it happening. She sounded vibrant and confident, with none of the spell-struck hesitation of the first night here and for days afterwards. But her voice was much less certain when she spoke again.

'All this leaves you no time for yourself. There's so much more to life ...'

Nurullah had thought so himself the day he had watched the trio dancing, when Nina had spun off on her own, laughing, and sat down, leaving her brother and her friend shiningly partnered. He had pictured this man, so favoured by fortune, in other wonderfully carefree settings, with every door of the world open to him.

'You could,' suggested Jeroo, 'do other useful things for the country, write articles for the press, lecture, campaign for other worthwhile causes besides the kisans.'

'Years and years went by, Jeroo, with the country's best brains doing just those things. They sat in the Government's mock councils and legislatures making stirring speeches. They passed Resolutions petitioning for more Indians to be allowed into the imperial service, into the commissioned ranks of the Royal Artillery, the Royal Engineers and the Royal Air Force. Whether their Resolutions were adopted or defeated made not a jot of difference to policy, though they *wanted* to cooperate to the fullest. It's only since the talk-show ended and we took up civil disobedience that our rulers have had to sit up and take notice.'

Nurullah separated the children's books from the tomes for donation to the university library and started making lists. It was peaceful in the book-filled room and all around him the house basked serenely in the last of the day's sunshine. Its calm was curious for a house where no day was like another and no one knew what would happen next. The two voices outside argued more lazily back and forth over their tea, traversing the century and three-quarters of British occupation. As if the subject was of prime importance. To their knowledge of each other perhaps. In his attendance on Bhai's correspondence, Nurullah had dealt with some letters from women. A reigning beauty of the Hindi cinema had sent him, unasked, her photograph and Bhai had hung it obligingly in his study. It was back-lit, making her face and figure stand out from a lighted pool and startle with their perfection. One langorous hand held her gold-bordered sari palla over her black hair, of which a single tendril kiss-curled on her forehead. The other hand rested on the curve of her hip from where her sari clung down her body until it swirled its gold border around her ankles. Another woman, a half-European artist whose exhibition of paintings was to open in Calcutta, had sent him an invitation to it. Her picture on it, full-lipped, bold-breasted and intense of gaze, had stunned Nurullah with its sheer physical impact. How well Bhai knew these women he had no idea but the photograph and the invitation were clearly messages of admiration, no less for his cause and creed than for his manhood, coming as they did from an India apart from his, where life was content to imitate (but never quite achieve) the life of free countries. Some instinct told Nurullah these (and who knows how many other) women would claim intimate, passionate acquaintance with Bhai whether or not anything more than their eyes had met, and their minds not at all. Outside, the talk had lapsed into occasional restful comment. Who would have thought it would be like this between them?

Jeroo's sole acquaintance in Akbarabad was the District Magistrate who had been at Oxford with Jhangoo Ghasvala. She asked if the family would mind awfully if she accepted his invitation to dine. He had been transferred at short notice and was having a farewell. No one minded. Pyare

Chacha said the last time he had dined with a District Magistrate, circa 1919, pre-Jallianwala Bagh, had been most pleasant. The English host had been enlightening about the flora, fauna and birdsong of the lower Himalayas, a true lover of the region, so loath to leave it that he had eventually retired there, divorced his wife and married a hill woman, grown apples till the day he died and was buried in the village that like Colonelgunj here, still bore his name. The chronicle completed, Pyare Chacha wished Jeroo an enlightening evening.

She told them about it at dinner the day after the Magistrate's party. Willie Crik was a dear, she said, Jhangoo and he had been chums at Oxford so it had been nice meeting him after many years. Nurullah's fork clattered to the floor. He had had no idea Crik was the DM, an office he associated with the assault on the public meeting last year, the chaos of dragged bodies dumped outside the shamiana and the attacks on processions.

'Lavinia Crik looks like an alabaster angel,' reported Jeroo, 'but she gorges like lusty Henry. More delicately, of course, but I swear she polished off half the duck last night. Willie is besotted with her. It's indecent the lecherous looks he was giving her right in front of everybody and she was lapping him up along with the duck.'

⌣

On his way up to the roof terrace these nights it warmed Nurullah to see the lights on in Bhai's room and Bhai at his desk. Tonight he was filling his fountain pen and winding up his wristwatch — cheap of choice, with a common cloth strap — and lining these up beside the expensive green leather of his father's princely gold-initialled wallet. Nurullah knew a prisoner's personal belongings are taken from him at the jail gate. It gave him a pang to see them arranged in the lamplight near the brass mould of Abraham Lincoln's hand, as if the prisoner had only just found the time to reclaim them. Bhai saw him at the window and called him in.

'I don't think I've thanked you for taking on Shān's tuition, Nurullah.'

'It's not proper tuition,' confessed Nurullah abashed, 'I improvise. I should have some proper plan.'

Bhai spoke meditatively. 'We belong to a league of nations that was not schooled in Hellas. We have our foundations in an antiquer antiquity and our spires beyond the stars. The world we live in and all its arrangements have been designed by other people for their convenience, not ours. It should appeal to your poetic instincts to 'remould it nearer to the heart's desire'. You will know how to go about it. Robin-da tells me you are a born teacher, with a heart as well as a mind.'

In the peace of this rewarding moment, Nurullah would have liked to make the most of it, to receive answers to troubling questions such as how was time prevailed upon to pass in jail? How — in the words of the same poet — did a prisoner cope with time 'in a Box whose Candle is the Sun'? Above all, why oh why, in a universe of possibilities, choose prison as a way of life?

But the somewhat heartbreaking nature of these questions kept him from asking them.

He did ask an impersonal one.

'Bhai, one thing bothers — some of us. Is ahimsa going to change anything? What use is non-violence?'

The answer came swift and curt. 'What else have unarmed people got?'

Nurullah's misgivings about it fell dramatically into place. It was a way, then, of marking time until something better offered.

'But since you ask,' continued Bhai, 'it has been a great education for us and a greater human experience. Already it has changed *us*. Other changes will come.'

When? How? We know how change comes. Earth was once a molten mass. Stars are born and die. Let scientists rejoice in epic changes. Let saints and martyrs wait for them, holding up their tattered black skins and forgiving their flayers. What have they to do with *us*? It angered Nurullah to picture the greyer, gaunter men and women every prison term would release in their punishing war without violence. Nurullah's eyes went to the map. Meanwhile, that would be the order the sun rose and set on.

The moon was high and full. The stone floor of the roof terrace chilled him through his warm sherwani. Most nights this was an interlude when his mind chased possibilities. He contemplated his postponed life and how soon he should resume it, but the dinner party the other night had shown up ambition for the farce it was in a world whose map set iron limits to it. One could aspire, within the limits, rising just so high. One could scintillate where one was, on a revolving platform like the Follies mems, going nowhere. A stupid dangerous idea, ambition, in this Follies setup. Transgress the limits and you lay dead in Company Bagh, or alive in stinking confinement, or tied to a whipping tripod or suffering rods up your anus — and if you were lucky, only a spectator to the sport.

The childlike games and glee of that evening broke into shattering howls of pain as Asghar Ali barber, Jalaluddin butcher, Chunnilal halwai and three other Akbarabadis writhed naked-bottomed in the mud. Filthy with blood and excrement they scrabbled to their feet and shambled round and round ankle-deep in shit, like blind circus bears roped through their nostrils.

Nurullah thought of the man, his mentor, who had made him literate and lured him into teaching. Painstakingly he had nurtured the teacher in Nurullah. To what purpose? In answer, Eknath's derisive 'Wake up, yaar!' pounded in his ears. He heard Eknath cutting comic capers through Europe's history at Robin-da's teas, making comedy of Europe's treaties: "'I'm hanging on to this half of Asia but you, my cousin-brother-king, can have the other half. And my royal in-law-king gets extra African highland to make up for losing all the jungle he had before." Property agents at heart, these Europeans!' At Robin-da's that droning bore, Matul, rose wittily to the occasion too, swivelling Descartes around into a colonial gem: 'We think, therefore you are.' A rollicking irreverence that could not run riot in class put them in the frame of mind for teaching what otherwise could not be taught.

'Use your cunning, Nurullah. Why else are you a teacher?' Robin-da had said.

And Nurullah had used his cunning, but as a teacher does, longing with all his teacher's ardour to see his charges lean toward him, eyes alight, intent on his every word while he strove to recreate the miracle of soap made real by living water which had started his own ascent from illiteracy. Now, it seemed something more was demanded of a teacher. These were times when Law and Order itself was the attacker and left a chaos of dragged, dumped, murdered bodies in its wake, one of them — it came shockingly to him — Mr McCracken's at the bottom of his stairs. Who but the District Magistrate, consumed with lust for his wife, would have wanted the bank manager dead?

If he shared this conclusion with Eknath tomorrow he knew what his friend would say.

'Where do you get your melodramatic ideas about jealousy? Jealous husbands fan themselves with frilled fans on their verandahs like Tiwariji. And others go about their business pretending they don't know. What do you know about jealousy anyway?'

Nurullah's slightly pompous reply would have to be that it wasn't given to every one of us to experience the whole gamut of human emotions. Literature did that for us. Othello had told us all we needed to know about jealousy.

Eknath: 'That was complicated by colour. Europeans never kill each other, except on their own soil.'

But Nurullah now saw that if one of them *had* killed another here in Akbarabad it would be a scene that Law and Order itself would censor out of existence. This would explain why the magistrate was being transferred at short notice. A killer who cannot be seen to be punished is best quietly transferred. The anguishing part of it was not that Mr McCracken's murderer should not be convicted like any other murderer. Law and Order's crimes were in any case too numerous for any but the trial court of Allahmian. The tragedy was the elimination of Mr McCracken of all Angrezes. In a last gesture to the dead man he inwardly saluted the lover he had been. Not so the woman Mrs Crik who far from being bereaved had devoured half a duck at dinner and revelled in her husband's indecent advances over the bank manager's dead body in full view of the guests at her table.

After the brightness of the roof terrace the spiral stair going down plunged Nurullah into darkness, but rounding the corner to pass Bhai's rooms moonlight flooded the verandah again making a daylit public domain of it. It streamed into Bhai's open bedroom window. His and Jeroo's laughter rang out in the stillness. They were in full view, sitting side by side on his bed, their arms about each other, their heads bent over something they were reading. In the split second of Nurullah's passing the book fell as they lay themselves down luxuriously entwined, with a thorough disdain for the theatrical brilliance bathing their naked bodies.

'We don't work in the dark, Nurullah. We have nothing to hide.'

ʃ

'Imagine if you can,' I tell the young researcher, *'the texture of a time very different from today's in 1980.'*

His half smile informs me he wouldn't be here if he didn't know this much. He is an immensely tall, round-shouldered American. I suspect he could hold himself straight if he chose and that his stoop is a polite concession to shorter people, for he is excessively polite. His eyes have a searching sincerity through his thick-lensed gold-rimmed spectacles. There is something touching about his appearance which had I seen it decades ago I would have discounted as a mirage, since no white man in Asia in those days had this troubled tentativeness. He is not sure when to allow himself a smile, whether or not to come out with what he has in mind and how to put it when he does. These brakes on his behaviour appear to be self-imposed because he does not come of hesitant stock. He is disciplining himself to be what his own experience could not have taught him and so his restraint is rather touching. After all the even pattern of his life has never ended uproariously in a night, sending long lines of his people trudging with bundles on their backs. The hand of the destroyer has not whimsically redrawn his boundaries or his destiny. The fate of his countrymen for generations before him was not ordained by arbiters overseas. Such crudities have been committed on other people, not on him. Therefore his halting efforts to join the human race interest me.

He is a student of politics *'researching'*, as he puts it, non-violence and its use of soul force. He knows the history of the period. What he wants is impressions from players on the scene and someone has suggested me. He *has the romantic idea that ahimsa is an underground Indian river, now hidden, now surfacing, but always present in our culture and our consciousness. He sees it as a leitmotiv. I tell him it is nothing of the sort. It was a time cut out of time, cut off from before and after. It was just that once. It was hard to believe even while it was happening. Every bystander asked himself, Can it be true? Am I seeing this happen?*

The researcher nods. Unbelievability, he confirms, is the authentic hallmark of every remarkable phenomenon. He digs out a ringed notebook from his over-stuffed shoulder bag and hunts through its copious ballpoint jottings for what Einstein wrote about Gandhi in 1944:

> *Generations to come, it may be, will scarce believe that such a one as this ever in flesh and blood walked upon this earth.*

Maybe so but ahimsa, I assure him, made no difference at the time to the occupying power. True, the odd jailer who dealt with political prisoners stepped back a pace and felt a shiver down his spine as in the presence of apparitions walking on water, for what ordinary mortal chooses jail? One anguished judge faltered while sentencing the illustrious prisoner in the dock. He had to resort to the Bhagvad Gita to describe his own, not the prisoner's plight: 'My limbs give way, my mouth has become parched, my body shivers ...' It was Arjuna's incomparable cry on the battlefield before the vision of the Supreme Being, the one we fall back on when the furthest reaches of our being cry out for expression. But don't count that jailer or that judge for whom, in the language of your Bible, 'glory shone around'. The political prisoner was singled out for vengeance. In prison the common man bore the brunt.

Nor did ahimsa put an end to violence, I point out. It even spurred it on, aroused savage instincts bred from time immemorial to expect resistance, savager when deprived of the familiar fighting adversary or fleeing quarry. Good old-fashioned war was waged against ahimsa and ahimsa did not escape war's legacies and tragedies, war's prisoners, its wounded and its killed. The war on ahimsa wreaked havoc. It left orphans and widows like any other war. No lethal weapon-wielder stood back and said this man before me is unarmed so I will not strike.

'It was not like any other war,' the young giant corrects me, 'only one side suffered war's legacies. When there's no retaliation the sum total of suffering gets halved.'

This nice little academic point is a shade too fine for me. Does he not see it was the one-sidedness that made the war against non-violence the only war intolerable to watch?

He is wide of the mark too in considering me an actor on the scene of his researches. Like most, I was a bystander, merely Nurullah, a newcomer to flowers, caught in twists and traps of history I had had no hand in shaping. However, he only wants an hour of my time and is anxious not to tax my strength or memory, both of which are in good repair. Come to think of it his allegiance to non-violence — for he is a pacifist — reminds me of the Movement he is researching, when people committed their lives to an idea whose time will never come.

There was no need for Nurullah to accompany Ammaji to the Magh Mela in January for her ritual dip in the Ganga. Miss Basappa was going with her and was spending the night in the upstairs guest room so that they could make an early start. The room, like all the outer circle of rooms, opened to a garden view. It was furnished with thick printed khadi chair covers and curtains from Gosiben's Bhandar like the rest of the house but Ammaji had had plain khadi embroidered for its bedspreads and dressing table cover, the one in cherry clusters, the other in chains of forget-me-nots along its borders. She had shown the embroidery to Gosiben who had passed an appraising thumb over a bunch of cherries to get the smooth raised feel of it and wagged her head in appreciation. Jeroo had approved of it too when the room had been hers. Miss Basappa's taste tending more toward flamboyance she was not the person to notice prettiness. Nurullah pictured her moving about the oval room with the slow heavy deliberation and trunk-swinging gait of an elephant in captivity.

It was the night his nightmare chose to return. He shouted himself awake, sat up struggling for breath and toppled forward to slump over his raised knees. He was too drained to move a muscle or to care that the door to his room was opening. A great long-robed shadow with streaming hair filled the doorway. He had no time to pull himself together before Miss Basappa came in. She poured a glass of water from his bedside jug, sat down on his bed and held it to his lips while he drank. The cold trickle eased his dry throat and calmed him. Her familiar benign presence made him want to sob out his nightmare and rid himself of it once and for all but he had never felt less inclined to talk. He thanked her groggily, lay down and fell asleep.

Almost at once the queer notion that she had covered him with something warmer and heavier than the razai that had slipped off him plucked him out of sleep and it was she herself laid along the length of him. He felt his buttocks grasped in strong capable hands and thought he was about to die of a riot of unnameable unmanageable sensations. After that he had no further thought. He was imprisoned under a triumphal arch, performing to its command. He might have been drugged or blindfolded, so little did he know or care where he was being taken. He only knew a purdah had been parted, the deliverer had come in, and like the women of harems and ghazals, ravenous for a touch, he was being rescued from death by starvation.

Under the sheltering, victorious arch the night became a banquet. In one torrential release after another Nurullah knew what had befallen Arjuna on the battlefield when Krishna Bhagvan appeared to him in the light of a million suns with mouths and eyes and faces turning everywhere, innumerable arms and thighs and jaws expanded to contain the universe, a vision to stun a seasoned warrior. At some moonlit hour their conjoined bodies reversed position, not of his volition because he had none, but in obedience to the epoch of change she had initiated. Before he fell into the soundest sleep of his entire life his gratitude knew no bounds. He opened his eyes much later than usual to a morning he knew would never come again.

All his life he thought of it as an awesome historical event or an upheaval of nature that transforms a landscape forever. A century of progress had taken place far into the night. Things had irrevocably changed. His very brain cells had grown and multiplied. The respect he had had for Miss Basappa grew into the regard that pupils recall till the end of their days for a unique teacher. In spite of all this no trace of Miss Basappa lingered on his inner eye though every surface of his body leapt with reminders of her.

His lectures to his First Years gained authority. A subtle extra dimension empowered him to convert English literature into the stuff of their own times. He could look back tolerantly on his early earnest experiments in teaching. Now the distant words of dead poets rose like swords from the prescribed texts when he read them to his class. They needed only the emotive steel of his voice to make unsheathed weapons of them. Every call to war, each lyric to the motherland might have been written for this beloved India, and so nakedly did every verse he chose cry treason — for which the penalty was deportation, life imprisonment or death — that Nurullah marvelled no canny censor had struck Sir Walter Scott, Shelley and others off the curriculum.

Correcting Shãn's education was systematically broadening his own. He was finding history puzzlingly unconnected with geography. Going through his atlas, which he liked to do partly for the pleasure of discovering sonorous city names or following a mountain river's path from its glacier to infinity, he came across primordial continental expanses that had no histories to speak of in history books or none but meagre mentions. He tried to visualize the forests, prairies and sierras of the Americas as petrified vistas waiting tens of thousands of years in static epic silence for Europeans to come sailing and their history to begin — for textbooks began with Europe's arrival — but he doubted that this could be. It made him wonder (with genuine alarm) what scant and threadbare treatment Europe's textbooks must be giving to the likes of us, fears that were realized when Shān brought hers home.

Nurullah was conscious of a feeling of suffocating confinement wherever he turned for knowledge since all knowledge was Europe-ordained. Surely, he thought, no mullah intoning There is no God but Allah from his muezzin in a bazaar had crammed all creation into one formula as had the tribe known as European. In their heyday successive bursts of conquest had made them masters of the world and in this respect they resembled all slaughterers and occupiers since time began. But the White Peril alone had scoured land masses clean of previous habitation and started dating history from that day forward.

Introducing Shān to the Americas he had to inform her he had not been able to trace its BC. Everything began After Columbus. In AC the Spaniards fell upon gold, silver, precious stones, heathens and land, limitless land. The good news reached Europe. The Portuguese, French and English came sailing to claim their shares. Their white hordes swarmed over two continents for the treasures of ancient cities, for acres to occupy, their eyes unwaveringly on someone else's horizon. Nurullah's large loose gestures sketched wave upon wave of armed white horsemen, their men of business and their priests. Imagine one of their ships nearing land, dost, its sails fluttering in a breeze wafting nutmeg, pepper, cloves and the perfume of unknown flowers, reviving tales of gold, stirring appetites to frenzy on board for shrines to plunder and booty to load on galleons sailing home to Europe. Great stalwarts, these Europeans After Columbus, for whom no strait was too narrow, no sea too wide.

Nurullah had a literal mind and he took his task of correction seriously so he was not given to inventing his own versions of texts, only to examining what they offered, presenting it from a different perspective and being amazed by what this new eye view revealed. A rewarding flush, more rarely a flood, of intuition then came upon him, illuminating the scene before his eyes in microscopic detail. Sometimes he was able to supplement this method with the discoveries he made on the library shelves, using only dependable eyewitness material. One of these was an eyewitness account of the Columbus era by a historian named Bertelome de Las Cascas who gave awesome details of how previous inhabitants had been exterminated from the Americas. The Spanish and Portuguese had roasted them on spits, hunted them with dogs, hanged and then hacked their bodies to pieces for dog meat, killed them with forced labour, and infected them with germs from Europe of smallpox, measles and flu. The English had gone in for simple massacre by their armies but as their frontier advanced west and south they had broken treaties with tribes and forced them to migrate at gunpoint, paid hired killers to scalp them and distributed gifts of smallpox-infected blankets among them. In quite another book Nurullah came across the nineteenth century US General William Sherman's comment, 'The more Indians we kill this year, the less we will have to kill next year.' Strange how the texts had nothing about Africa except mention of a Dark Continent, but so tidally had the White Peril engulfed that vast continent's length and breadth that it could hardly be left out of Shān's world awareness. Drawing on information gleaned from the library he instructed Shān that the Europeans had carved it out among themselves in the second half of the nineteenth century. Like vultures they had descended on it, divided and devoured it, with Britain and France, Mr Ghasvala's messiahs, claiming the lion's share. The Germans, Belgians, Portuguese and Italians gobbled what remained until only little Abyssinia was left independent and gave the Italians a sound thrashing when Italy invaded it in 1896. But now Italy was at it again.

Shān could not have cared less about Abyssinia. She had been to Bombay as usual for her winter holiday at Nina and Sheel's and come back from her spell of normal life full of useless information and an irritating air of condescension. Sheel had a new car whose roof slid back. Nina wore striped beach pyjamas on Juhu beach and puffed sleeve blouses with her silk saris. The sleeves had a tiny slit down the middle of the puff. Like puff sleeves tap dancing was the fashion. So were Ginger Rogers and Fred Astaire. The last item at least made sense. The lissome dancing pair had enchanted Nurullah in a film at the Picture Palace. Shān had started a Notebook to record these and her other significant findings and had written down the words of a song that was also in fashion.

'Here,' she offered grandly, 'You may read it.'

To oblige, Nurullah did, making nothing of it until he came to a name or two he recognized in one of the verses:

'You're the nimble tread of
the feet of Fred Astaire
You're Mussolini,
You're Mrs Sweeny,
You're Camembert ...'

'Who,' he enquired, 'is Camembert?'
'Cam-em-*bare*,' said Shān severely, 'it's a cheese.'
'And who might Mrs Sweeny be?'
'She's a Beauty.'

None of which explained the connection of the Beauty and the cheese with the fascist hero admired by Mr Ghasvala's messiahs. He wondered if the excitable German hero whom they also admired would be figuring in a popular song soon, although Hitler would be a nuisance to rhyme.

More was heard of the Italian brigand when his armies invaded Abyssinia, supported by poison gas and bombardment from the air. Nurullah took down a message Bhai was dictating:

On behalf of our party we send Ethiopians, our brothers in distress, our deep sympathy in this hour of their trial.

We stand with them today in their sorrow as
we hope to stand together when better days
come ...

Nurullah waited, pen poised, for Bhai to continue but he
stopped there, jaw clenched, frowning. He had never
looked so angry.

'I'll finish it later today,' he said, 'we must get busy
immediately organizing an Abyssinia Day.'

Nurullah did not know it then but it was the first of
the Days he helped organize to condemn invasions that
left Mr Ghasvala's two messiahs supremely unconcerned.
Petruchios, the pair of them. How aptly the lines from
Shrew described them:

Petruchio: Good Lord, how bright and goodly
shines the moon!
Katherina: The Moon? The sun! It is not midnight
now.
Petruchio: *I* say it is the moon ...

'What is Mr Ghasvala's opinion of the invasion of
Abyssinia?' he asked Shān.

'He says the League of Nations' rules don't apply to
savages,' said Shān, 'so what's all the fuss about.'

When her brush with normal life wore off Nurullah
gave her a lesson on Abyssinia, little realizing it would
become a serial. In the second instalment he was describing
the Abyssinians fiercely fighting back under a fiery hail
of Italian bombs when Shān flopped over the table with
her head on one arm and broke out into her intemperate
bawling. It was a weeping rage of the jail-gate variety or

the one brought on by Jessie-ma's betrayal, and it was a long time since it had happened. Nurullah was shaken by the effect his vivid picturization of current events had produced. A shudder of regret passed through him. He had an overwhelming desire to console her with some shred of hope, just for balance. But what hope was there for Abyssinia and how could he concoct a false ending to cheer her? He did not even say, 'That's enough now, dost' but let her weep herself to a hiccoughing halt, sitting beside her in grim sympathetic accord.

They made Haile Selassie's message to the League of Nations an occasion for solemn mourning. 'Apart from the Kingdom of God,' it ended, 'there is not on this earth any nation that is higher than any other.'

Shãn sat up and scowled accusingly at Nurullah.

'You never told me Haile Selassie was a *Christian!*' she flung at him. 'Don't Europeans only occupy *heathen* countries?'

'They do what they like, dost,' said Nurullah resignedly. 'If they feel like it they call the sun the moon. Like Petruchio.'

She waited, sharply attentive.

'It's like this, dost. Once there was a woman called Katharina who was labelled Shrew because of her independent unbowed spirit. A man called Petruchio made her captive and broke her spirit. She had to start calling the sun the moon because he said so. That is what happens when Petruchios rule the roost. Anything goes.'

It did not surprise either of them when Mr Ghasvala's messiahs recognized the invasion that made Abyssinia part of the Italian empire.

Four

Hashi was outside her gate haggling with a guava seller. She hailed Nurullah from across the road, beckoning him over with her usual exaggerated high spirits. He was on his way home from an afternoon class but he walked his cycle over, only to be kept waiting, listening to her haggle, shushing her s's and rounding her a's into o's, Bengali style. Her bunch of clanking keys had pulled her sari palla off her head or she had left it off her washed dripping hair. It hung loose smelling of soap. In a final singsong rush of aggression that had not allowed the vendor a word she inveigled him into selling her his basketful four annas cheaper and made Nurullah carry it into the house for her. The palla back over her head, she directed her servant Kirti to make tea and banished him to his quarter as soon as he had set the tray down in the enclosed verandah. Nurullah, at Robin-da's request, had engaged Joseph to enclose the long verandah with wire-netting but no one had told Joseph to knock a wilderness of windows into it. The wire-netted ones opened out, the glass-paned ones in, the whole length of the verandah. It gave Nurullah a splitting headache to look at the abomination which, however, had not troubled Hashi.

Pyare Chacha had a theory that prolonged colonial occupation had done much worse than drain resources to enrich the occupier and to finance his industrial revolution at home and his wars abroad. It had killed off good taste. His monograph on the subject, printed by the same obscure defunct press that had published *Palashi*, argued that China had only been buggered (to use Eknath's word) on the fringes, though thoroughly, by the infamous treaty ports, but India right through her navel (Eknath's measure of the furious tireless foreign thrust). The Company becoming zamindar of Bengal had bled it dry. Quoting an English contemporary of Clive, Pyare Chacha had chronicled that 'a gold-lust unequalled since the hysteria that took hold of the Spaniards of Cortes' and Pizarro's age filled the English mind', and the conquest of the rest of India had legalized buggery, but would that this had not come to pass in the frumpish age of Victoria was Pyare Chacha's lament. The mere furnishing of a room in passable good taste would take a century of freedom to achieve. He thanked God that India's cuisines at least had survived, but for decoration in all its refinement India must fall back on China, Cambodia, Siam and other less corrupted heritages until she could reclaim her own. Joseph's windows gave Pyare Chacha's thesis a frightful validity and other houses and furnishings Nurullah had seen were as deplorable. On this ugly urban scene the domed monument could have been lifted from the Arabian Nights and each of its few remaining treasures was a delight, which, he realized, was why they had chosen Chinese.

In spite of everything, the windowed enclosure was an improvement on Hashi's square drawing room where rows of chairs faced each other. Here at least he could sit cross-legged on the takht beside her and feel comfortably at home, relapsed into an earlier easier self, the man he had been at Mrs Shona Tiwari's before he took up residence in the monument. He blew steam off the tea in his saucer and took hot reviving sips of it. Hashi skipped blithely from topic to topic requiring no comment.

'*So?*' she demanded, abruptly signalling it was his turn to talk.

It was typical of Hashi but he was unprepared. He spluttered into laughter, spilling tea on himself.

'Now look at you,' she scolded, drying his wrist with a corner of her sari.

After his second cup he uncrossed his legs saying he must be going but Hashi stopped him with more than her usual impulsive warmth, forgetting to take her hand off his. Nurullah looked down at it. His skin was leaping under it, but mildly, nothing like at Miss Basappa's touch. The hand slipped up his arm under his kurta sleeve leaving him in no doubt what would be happening next in gangsterland. But his every instinct warned him against the consequences of gangsterland tactics in Akbarabad. Joseph's frenzy of windows was another infuriating obstacle to progress. Alone in his room at night under Miss Basappa had been another matter.

Hashi's hand came sliding down and slipped into his. Her palm was as voluptuously cushioned as her vowels and so faintly crisscrossed with so few lines that nothing of the slightest importance could have happened to her or ever be going to happen. It was the first hand he had held not counting children's games and occasional hand-swinging and trick-cycling with Eknath. He turned it over carefully and the customs of the ages (plus the windows) rose up to prevent him crushing it and pulling her close. Men had been maimed or killed for less and, remembering Desdemona, so had women.

Hashi, innocent of history or literature, knew no such caution. She settled herself adroitly against him and began training his mouth to perform kisses he knew nothing of and had not known existed. The night with Miss Basappa for all its roving abandon had glossed over kissing much as an earthshaking cataclysm makes one forget minor happenings on that day. Hashi eased herself and him down on the takht where they lay glued open-mouthed in a drowsy deepening stupor. He would presently have forgotten where he was had a nerve in his brain not stayed strung taut for a sound signifying Kirti's return.

Not Kirti but the piercing agony of a stab wound sat him upright to find Hashi's bunch of brass and steel gouging his belly. She quickly unknotted it from her sari and threw it on the floor and Nurullah's fractional alertness evaporated during the next dizzying sequence of his training. Hashi heard before he did her name being called on Matul's rising-falling note of complaint. She whipped her sari into place and knotted her keys while he was still groping for his second chappal under the takht. At her hissed command he grabbed both chappals and lowered a leg out of the nearest window where it sank into a hose-flooded zinnia bed. He pulled it out with frantic speed and duck-waddled through squelching mud below the mile-long window ledge cursing Joseph for a sister-fucker. His cycle was where he had left it, blessedly hidden from the path to the gate.

'Nikhil,' Pyare Chacha was saying gravely when he got home, 'Vazirabad is beside himself with anxiety. I had lunch with him today. He thinks we might win this coming election.'

'I thought he was with us.'

'That's just it, Nikhil. He wants to know where you stand on zamindari.'

Bhai was astounded.

'He knows exactly where we stand. We've been shouting it from the housetops for years. Zamindari will be abolished if we come to power in this province.'

'Yes, yes,' said Pyare Chacha soothingly, 'of course he knows. Everyone knows. But who *believes* it? Vazirabad realizes you have to say these things. Naturally he doesn't expect you to *do* them, you who were born and bred to refinement. I have given him my word as a gentleman, Nikhil, that all will be well.'

'You've done *what*?'

Then seeing Pyare Chacha without meaning to had dispensed wisdom, Bhai put a loving arm around him and thanked him.

'Can you come up to my study, Nurullah,' said Bhai, and glancing at the state of his feet and mud-soaked pyjama, 'after you've had a wash.'

'This is not an election we want to take part in,' he explained when Nurullah reappeared. 'The government is calling it a great step forward but in fact the elected provincial assemblies will have very little power. We thought of boycotting it but the general consensus is we should take part, if only because it gives us an opportunity to test our strength. Khurram is going to be our candidate here from the Yamuna constituency and I'd like you to look after his campaign.'

If Bhai had said Kallu, Nurullah could not have been more flabbergasted. Khurram had been deprived of chauffeuring when the car was confiscated after the Prince of Wales' visit and had refused to leave for a lucrative job. He helped in the dispensary and was a reliable man-of-all-work whom Nusli Framjee bossed into painting, plastering, polishing and other chores. When disobedient hotheads in Gosiben's liquor boycott demonstration had yelled slogans in front of Framjee and Son against her express orders and then smashed the fancy-lettered glass front, Khurram had personally boxed their ears and expertly replaced the sheet glass. He could mend fuses and had learned to turn a hand at carpentry. Joseph gave him jobs whenever he needed extra workmen. He was an excellent trusted servant of whom Bhai said he would have gone far in a free country but the party had taken leave of its senses putting up a servant as candidate in the first test of its political strength.

Nurullah said, 'If by any chance Khurram does win, Bhai, what is he going to do in an assembly of nawabs and other bigwigs?'

'He'll have plenty of ordinary company if we win.'

'But what about transport?' the constituency being miles away.

'Transport will be no problem. Everyone will pitch in and there's the old party bus. It's fitted with a loudspeaker and carries a full load of workers.'

The fantasy of the enterprise put it beyond further argument but when Nurullah heard Nawab Sahib himself would oppose Khurram in the constituency which, after all, was on his estate, he envisaged a cavalcade of gleaming Chevrolets transporting the Nawab's tenants and labourers to drop their thumb-impressed voting scraps into his boxes and thence to feasts of roasting sheep. Nawab Sahib and Bibijan came to call as before, bearing the season's fruits, venison and biryanis. Barkat and Salim ran wild in the garden and Murad remained a slave of Shān. Bibijan was conferring with Ammaji about the fourth daughter of the Vazirabad estate manager for Nurullah. Everything was as usual. Love and affection and cherished family bonds had nothing to do with politics which could change direction, as Nawab Sahib's had. Life among us, thought Nurullah, is damnably confusing, and he speculated whether the same was true of all ancient Asian societies, for Europe and America in contrast were much more cut-the-cackle and arithmetical: I'm right, you're wrong (and here's my gun to prove it); This is mine, that's yours (and keep your arse out of my prairie); In short, it was what gangsters learned at their mothers' knee, and how else could you usurp the world? All this dallying with biryanis and affectionate teasing and mutual admiration hardly seemed the proper climate for a crucial political contest. And when Pyare Chacha announced he would campaign for Khurram who had remained faithful to the family, Nurullah was thrown into a panic. There was enough to cope with without the addition of Pyare Chacha to a losing proposition.

The fact that he was deep in deceit with Hashi did not help matters. Never again such idiocy, he had vowed as he leapt out of Joseph's window, but naturally they had resumed where they left off. She had selected Thursday afternoons during Matul's Descartes to Kant philosophy class. There was no danger of Matul barging in on a Thursday. He invariably tonga-ed to One Bailey Road after his class for tea with his invalid granduncle. The habits of bores like Matul are cast in iron and sealed in cement.

Gosiben seemed to take Pyare Chacha's announcement in her stride. A born in-charge, she had taken command of the campaign and Nurullah found himself one more body in the band of 'sisters' and 'brothers' she had loaded into the ramshackle party bus. Where had she found all these women? She solved the problem of remembering the new ones' names by calling them all 'ben'. The ban on the national flag had been lifted and the orange and green tricolour with a charkha on its white middle band fluttered from the bonnet of the bus. The loudspeaker blared patriotic songs. Led by Gosiben, the party workers raised slogans calling for victory to peasants and workers and long life to the revolution as they escorted Pyare Chacha, a spotless misfit, to rickety makeshift daises where he sat sublimely disregarding the racket, looking like a vision descended from the sky, from his hair of antique tarnished silver and his cream sherwani to the tapered toes of his juttis. Tsa! What elegance! Gosiben remarked admiringly, listening to the courtly Persianized Urdu of his speeches as if she understood it. Nurullah who conversed with the constituents in the dialect he had in common with them doubted if the squatting peasantry knew or cared what Pyare Chacha said as they gazed up at him agog, shielding their eyes as much from his pearly dazzle as from the sun's.

Gosiben brought a harmonium to every meeting. It was carried to the dais and back to the bus by Sitaram. Accompanying herself on this whining instrument she and a few 'bens' opened proceedings with a shrill nasal Vande Mataram. If other speakers were late she and the 'bens' kept up a heartening dialogue with the kisan 'bens', Gosiben believing no opportunity to communicate with the masses must be missed. The communication consisted of enemas, poultices, urine therapy and other tips of a medical nature. Cautionary information about days of the month was entrusted to the married 'bens'. All this took care of the waiting time. The brothers in her team educated their kisan brothers.

'O-mi-gawd Nurullah, why are you dawdling about, you who are a teacher by profession? *Teach*!' she ordered, busily apportioning duties.

Nurullah was launched into a novel phase of his career, unexpectedly tongue-tied now that he had to stumble along unaided by the written words of others. As he became conversant with carbolic acid, dung, neem and the burial of shit in pits dug six feet deep, it needed an effort to make the mental shift back to skylarks, daffodils and swordplay for an afternoon class.

Once a week Hashi reduced him to an instrument on which she honed her skills to his and her excruciating delight. Grateful for this manna from heaven it was months before he had the ungrateful thought that it was becoming a circle of hell. They were getting no further forward. To be sure Hashi looked gorged and glutted but she had old Matul to finish the job while he was left to his own clammy clumsy devices. Sinking softness was Hashi, a cat who pounced and played. He thought of the light years he had travelled in a single night with Miss Basappa. He dreamed of Mrs Shona Tiwari sportingly adventuring into her sister's nuptial bed undaunted by the weight of winter bedclothes, to electrify a bridegroom laid low by celebration. Hashi indignantly drew the line at copulation because how could she do that to Matul?

She was a sexual cheat and pirate, a Mrs Lavinia Crik. Mrs Crik's every crack and crevice had been titillated to ecstasy, from her bloodless fingers to her bleak white parted thighs and the high keening crescendo they had given birth to. In memoriam Mrs Crik had devoured half a duck and welcomed the District Magistrate's lecherous advances over her lover's dead body, so gluttonously that a guest at her dinner table had recoiled from the heat. Yet

Hashi lacked Mrs Crik's brazen appetite and her native daring. Far from flinging her arms and legs wide in Company Bagh she could not even be persuaded away from the plague of windows to the privacy of her bedroom because how could she do that to Matul? Nurullah bled unappeased while Hashi's joyful jewel eyes sparkled in her wax-white face like a cat's tormenting its prey. Had he been split and felled by forked lightning and left to die his condition could not have been more critical.

'Looking a bit peaky, aren't you?' commented Mr Harvey, just back from a trip to Europe where he had seen and heard the two reigning heroes.

Bhai had a firsthand account from him of the situation on that continent where the Germans and Italians appeared to be clicking and jerking in European versions of Sarkar Salaam in stadiums and amphitheatres packed with enthusiastic Sarkar Salaamers. These military galas sounded like an operetta he had also seen, all dashing uniforms, barked orders and helpless rapture in time to martial music. To give Shān an idea of what was going on Mr Harvey got into an athletic half-crouch, balled his fists and his biceps and set up an unearthly howling tattoo of 'Du-chay! *Du-chay!* DU-CHAY!' he had seen roadside spectators give vent to in Rome as that great dictator's motorcade sped past. The excitement in Akbarabad was as high, without the clicks and jerks, when Bhai's party won the election, and the spontaneous emotional upsurge that greeted Khurram's victory would have been the envy of Europe's dictators. But for Nurullah, who went to Lucknow with Bhai to see Khurram installed in the provincial capital's imposing imperial edifice as an elected legislator, there was nothing to equal the emotion of that solemn occasion. Khurram himself was the soul of dignified calm. Cleaner than Nurullah had ever seen him, in starched white khadi and Gandhi cap, he looked as if nothing could be more natural than to add parliamentary skills to his already impressive list of accomplishments, thus giving Nurullah the kind of uncanny foretaste Miss Basappa had given him of a future he would not have believed possible.

Hashi alone of his acquaintances seemed impervious to what was going on around her. Lying on top of the seductive cushion she was, well armoured by layers and underlayers of clothing and smug in her ban on copulation, he missed the generosity, the beauty, the bravery of the times. Leaving aside Chhappan Churi who had aroused and unforgettably appeased the desires of two generations of Akbarabadis, there was Gosiben. He saw her surrounded by the 'bens' she had led on marches through Akbarabad when marches had been forbidden, Gosiben's tenacious tricolour-snatching furies with the police, the townsmen's wives and daughters she had organized for militant boycotts of foreign cloth and liquor (avoiding Framjee and Son), the jobs she had assigned the 'bens' in Khurram's constituency, the months and years many of them had spent in jail. They had the strength of flying cranes arrayed across the sky in fearless formation. The haze of pilgrims Nurullah had watched trekking up the drive by day had drifted far and wide throughout the land in his dreams. It, too, had been women indistinguishable from the men in their uniting blur of white. What manner of anachronism was Hashi with a soul steeped in the price of guavas and thighs that no pitch of ecstasy could pry apart? If he stayed addicted to Thursdays it was because Akbarabadis could not be choosers. For the fastidious it was this or nothing, and he was too far gone to be his own master. Hashi had ensnared him with rites like drugs and potions that left him ragged as a row of bats electrocuted on a high wire but which he could not do without. If he kept telling himself things would get a move on it was not because he believed it, despite the fact that nature intended copulation and Allah had so designed us. Meanwhile, he consoled himself that experience from the Buddha to Blake had not been bought 'for a song, or wisdom for a dance in the street'.

It was not a subject he could discuss with Eknath, Hashi being Robin-da's niece and Eknath no expert in these matters until recently. More to the point Eknath would call him a donkey to stay stuck in a rut of Hashi's choosing, no better than a dhobi's hopping donkey whose forelegs are tied together to prevent it getting away. He would have told Nurullah to stop dithering. In his marital bliss he would also have pressured Nurullah to agree to Bibijan's estate manager's fourth daughter although Nurullah had clearly told him he had something else in mind.

'What "thing" else? What moonshine has got you now?'

Eknath was resigned to his quotes so Nurullah resorted to one he hoped would serve as an answer.

'My most!' he quiped raffishly to avoid making heavy weather of it, 'My most, O my lost! O my bright, my ineradicable ghost.'

Eknath had shaken his head like a doctor making a dismal diagnosis and told him not to be a unmitigated ass.

'Marriage, yaar,' he had advised, thumping Nurullah's shoulder, 'let Bibijan arrange it.'

✧

A number of foreign visitors were coming to the house. The CID informer posted incognito outside the gate made notes on them. He was a miserable looking sunken-chested specimen whom Ramdin supplied with glasses of water and Binda the chowkidar with the odd bidi. (The authorities used the smarter CID fellow to rustle up the occasional communal riot in Colonelgunj.) Ammaji would have made the poor wretch sit comfortably on the verandah where he could have snooped at his ease — after all, what was there to hide? — but that would have blown his incognito. Nurullah wondered what the Criminal Investigation Department made of the assortment of people who came and went. The ones he himself had shown into Bhai's study were a shaven-headed Austrian lady in a renunciant's orange sari who called herself Suhashini Devi, an American missionary who told Nurullah that Gandhi was the Christ of the Indian road, a fez-hatted delegation from Egypt, a venerable black-robed Chinese with a young Chinese interpreter, a small soft-spoken man who looked Chinese but wasn't, two men from Indonesia, an Afghan and an Iranian.

He was not sorry to have a break from Thursdays and Hashi's cat-and-cotton-wool games when Bhai sent him to Bombay with a letter he wanted delivered by hand to escape the censor. He alighted at Victoria Terminus after the longest journey he had ever taken. A coolie streaked ahead of him on wiry legs with his trunk and bedding, clearing his path with rapid bursts of Marathi. Nurullah had planned to look around the vast terminus built in celebration of Victoria's golden jubilee but the speed and energy of the coolie had him hurrying to keep up. Outside the Terminus lay Bombay. Competing crowded impressions of its past and present jumbled his mind as Nina drove him through ordered lines of motor traffic past huge hoardings advertising food and drink and films of British manufacture, and then along the curving sea front where the Arabian Sea rolled endlessly away from land to further seas. Unbelievable that Akbar-e-Azam had left it undefended for Europe to drop anchor in search of fast fabulous wealth, and come ashore, and stay. And so to Nina and Sheel's flat on Malabar Hill. Suffice it to say that what he had seen of Bombay was a foreign place and he would not be here long enough to delve deeper.

That night Nina and Sheel took him to a party at the Ghasvalas' whose acres bordered the ocean and included a private beach. A theatrical company from England was going to stage a play in the garden before dinner. Its trim tall cypresses made it a natural setting for an outdoor production of *A Midsummer Night's Dream*, not a favourite of Nurullah's but he was fairly keyed up waiting for it to begin, it being his first play apart from student productions at the university.

What had never struck him before as he watched the silly fairy farce was its amazing resemblance to life. Mortals running around in a fog. Immortals leading them a dance. The wrong lovers meeting. Confusion, frustration, woe, all contained in a misleading deceptive harmony. Life! But the real revelation of the evening was the donkey Titania made of Bottom.

> Come sit thee down upon
> this flow'ry bed,
> While I thy amiable cheeks do coy,
> And stick musk-roses in thy
> sleek-smooth head,
> And kiss thy fair large ears,
> my gentle joy.

'*Allah!*' swore Nurullah in pent-up inner fury.

After the play he retreated to the low stone parapet dividing the grounds from the billowing black ocean, made luminous by invisible rays since the moon had not risen. He sat down, self-consciously separate from the other guests in black and white Angrezi evening dress. From here he could watch the party, a splendid affair of scale and management, as much a stage setting as *A Midsummer Night's Dream* had been. Nurullah had never seen so many of the strangers who ran the country gathered together. Their clothes, their talk, their manner were absolutely brilliant in their scorn for their surroundings. A man not far from him greeted another, introducing himself as Wheelock, Imperial Jute. The other replied Jackson, Shell. Imperial Tobacco and Imperial Chemicals joined them. Clues to a larger identity, obviously, as maharajas considered themselves Mysore or Baroda. His own momentous journey from a servants' quarter to teaching English at Akbarabad University dwindled to nothing compared with the seafarers who had dropped anchor as traders to live in humble huts of thatch and mud and wattle until the Company's machinations made it master of Bengal and avarice its way of life. Some way off Nurullah heard Sheel who was in black and white like the rest diffidently suggest it was a pity molasses from sugar factories was going waste because power alcohol was not allowed to be an Indian industry. One of the imperials pointed out there was no logic in duplicating effort, was there, when Britain had the manufacturing capacity to meet all India's needs? Much the most imposing of them all were the liveried servants bearing trays, like mobile replicas of the trim dark cypresses, recalling the 'forest close and mute' of the Gandhi-Shelley poem he was now using in class.

He looked up. The stars were pinpricks in a dark expressionless sky. Down here was the turbulence. The ocean sprayed his skin with salt, the breeze off it reprieved him temporarily from Bombay's overpowering humidity. He could not have endured living in this climate. The Company's eighteenth century adventurers had kept dying of it but they had kept on coming, as likely as not to end in closely packed cemeteries when two monsoons were said to be the life of a white man. Never would Nurullah have suspected that to make a fortune — not love, lust, jealousy or hate — was man's highest, most death-defying passion. Would that Shakespeare had lived to unravel this obsession as he had every other of the human heart.

Mr Ghasvala had the all-seeing eyes of a seasoned host. He came up to his lone guest at the parapet to say in his mellifluous lipless English, 'But my dear chap, hasn't anyone given you a drink?' and crooked a finger for a bearer, asking, 'What will you have?' Jeroo appeared out of the semi-dark and lifted a coconut shell off the tray for Nurullah. She supplied him with a straw and sat down beside him leaving Mr Ghasvala free to resume his duties. Nurullah didn't know if this was a good time to deliver the second letter he was carrying but there might be no other time. She took it eagerly, slit it open with one long pointed fingernail and laughed at her own haste since it was too dark out here to read it. She folded the envelope and tucked it carelessly into the front of her choli-blouse. The blouse had no back, only two silk strings tied together. Her sari being diaphanous and only half covering her dipping front Nurullah could not help noticing a stiff corner of the envelope sticking out. After all, he could hear her thinking, everyone knows.

'I've got to go and mingle, Nurullah,' she said regretfully after hearing his Akbarabad news, 'but if you get hungry or frightened just give me a shout. Dinner will be late.'

Sipping his second coconut water Nurullah saw an Angrez arrive not wearing black and white. He wore no jacket either and no tie and his shirt was open at the neck. He did up his top shirt button, fished a tight wad out of his trouser pocket and shook it loose revealing a crumpled necktie which he knotted loosely around his neck. Running a hand through his tousled hair he walked into the party like an actor into a scene. Mr Ghasvala was with him in a trice. Jeroo was sent for and one on each side of the newcomer they escorted him into the gathering.

Edgar Knox was uncomfortably aware of being a collector's item but even had he not been, an American was a quaint rare species here. Rumour had it Americans were backward. They took hiking instead of arithmetic at school and couldn't spell. Practically the only American here was the Consul, or was it Trade Commissioner, whose chief social attraction was his accent and his latest model record player which dropped records automatically on the turntable. Piloted and introduced through the throng he discovered soon enough no one here was collecting the item he was said to be. He met with a vaguely solicitous concern at his appearance and restrained smiles before they turned to each other again and their backs to him. A few had heard his name, in some connection they couldn't recall. Edgar relaxed.

'You look awfully pleased that no one's heard of you,' said his hostess, a bewitching person in a see-through sari.

'One woman back there almost remembered where she'd heard it,' protested Edgar.

'Probably in the nursery rhyme we all learned at school,' she said wickedly, 'do they have it in America?'

> Mr Knox
> Keeps his sox
> In a pale pink chocolate box

Edgar didn't think they had that nursery rhyme in America.

'The messenger who has your letter is over by the garden wall,' she said.

Edgar had already seen the solitary guest in Indian dress, as quirky as himself among the penguins. Drink in hand he crossed the garden resolutely, feeling like Stanley approaching Livingstone, and took delivery of the missive. With such letter deliveries in mind he asked the man if he had to travel much. Nurullah said hardly at all and this was his first trip to Bombay. An unspoiled original, Edgar marvelled, even less travelled than his great uncle Desmond, only Desmond made a boast of it and Nurullah sounded wistful.

'How does Bombay impress you?' Edgar asked, quite curious.

With his regard for accuracy, Nurullah replied what he had seen of it so far — the Ghasvalas' garden — impressed him as being the Company in bursting bloom again. The East India Company, he explained, multiplied and magnified. Bombay could well be one big Company Bagh. Edgar wanted him to go on but Nurullah was more interested in where he came from.

'America,' said Edgar.

'North?'

'No, I'm from the east coast,' said Edgar before he belatedly understood the question and corrected his answer, 'Yes, from North not South America.'

If this is how we trip up in our own hemisphere, claiming we alone are America, he thought, small wonder we're in the Stone Age when it comes to other hemispheres.

Nurullah sat on when Edgar Knox was led away. Music drifted through the drawing room's open windows to join the sea sound in his ears. A stranger settled softly on the wall. Looking out on the luminous expanse of water she sighed, 'How wonderful it all is! I can't believe I'm really here!' and lifted her shining eyes to his. A beauteous butterfly of a girl, fairer-skinned and fairer-haired than any he had seen or imagined. He had only read of her. But what entranced him most was her innocence of caste and code. So guilelessly had she settled here next to him, she must be brand new to India. He wanted to reciprocate with the same natural warmth, in words that would touch some common ground between them, and memory supplied his need.

'It is the fairy Peaseblossom, isn't it?'

'How *clever* of you!' rejoiced the fairy in her lilting voice, 'especially when I only had *five* words to say!'

She stretched a slim leg out and slipped off a silver slipper. The fragile stuff of her dress floated about her slender calf in a breath of salt breeze from the sea. All five words of her tiny part were vividly with him. He had absorbed every detail of the performance with a first-timer's rapt concentration. He explained this to her, saying a first time was in a class by itself. That first thrill never came again. The fairy denied this absolutely.

'It's not like that in theatre. Every time is the first time, for everyone, on stage or in the audience. There's simply nothing to compare with the thrill of the curtain going up.'

Under a late-rising moon she told him how lucky she was to have landed this tiny part with India thrown in, how excited she was to be going to Calcutta from here and then to Madras.

'And then back to school?' asked Nurullah only half in jest.

Peaseblossom laughed delightedly. She was not quite as young as that, she said, but she would be going back to drama school when she got home.

'Suzy!' came a loud proprietal summons and Lysander emerged from an animated threesome on the lawn. '*There you are!*'

With a breathless goodbye and 'Lovely talking to you' she was up and flown to join the three. He heard loud unfairy like explosions of laughter. An hour later he saw her in the dining room surrounded by her friends of the cast. She was helping herself from giant silver dishes, reclaimed by the rhythms of expected behaviour, no longer new to India. He took his own plate into a book-lined room off the dining room where Mr Ghasvala soon came looking for him.

'I thought I'd find you here,' he said. 'Jeroo tells me you're keen on the mystic poets. I'm afraid we don't have anything in that line but you'll find other books to interest you.'

Mr Ghasvala located a few on their immaculately arrayed shelves and laid them out for Nurullah's inspection, handling them with a book lover's familiarity and spending an unhurried quarter hour telling Nurullah about each one while they both ate. His intelligent Oxford-educated eyes regarded his guest with a genuine, very personal interest, and lit up with real pleasure when Nurullah said, meaning it, that the magnificence of Parsi cooking had quite taken his mind off books. He went away leaving his guest among friends as it were. His attitude to Abyssinia had not prepared Nurullah for such kindness and grace of manner.

Instead of glancing through Mr Ghasvala's choices after he had finished eating he explored the shelves and found the German hero's *Mein Kampf* among the Lives. A random sentence — 'I believe that I am acting today in accordance with the intention of the Almighty Creator' — caught Nurullah's attention. He had helped organize two more Days last year in Akbarabad, one for Austria, one for Czechoslovakia, to condemn this mad mullah's invasions.

Europe! reflected Nurullah. What a saga of kinship gone wrong was Europe — of brother against brother, of cousinly betrayals, of rampaging rivalries and ferocious bloodletting such as had never before been caused to flow across the earth's expanse. A word that invoked terror. Where had Europe ever gone in peace? If there had been a Fa Hien among Europeans, braving a six-year pilgrimage to shrines honouring non-injury to man or beast, he must have died unsung. And now that a master race had risen from the master race itself, what infernal arts of destruction would it invoke, what heights and primitive depths of monstrousness would befall earth's hapless people?

Mr Ghasvala who was as faithful to his messiahs as Katharina to her lord, had like the two of them, not condemned the latest invasions. It could be that his relaxed attitude toward invasions in general kept him goodnaturedly unconcerned about the love affair Jeroo had made fashionably famous. It struck Nurullah that of the cuckolded husbands he knew the only barbarian had been Mr Crik. Tiwariji and Mr Ghasvala had stayed peaceful charming cuckolds. And he rather doubted Othello would ever have turned assassin but for European interference and instigation.

Five

Nawab Sahib Vazirabad had nothing to worry about. The new legislators in Lucknow did not have time to abolish zamindari because six thousand miles away Europeans plunged the world into war again, the Viceroy ordered Indian troops to battlefronts abroad without consulting the elected assemblies and they resigned in protest. So much for self-government and the great step forward was their bitter reaction. It had been reduced to ashes at the bugle call to the Viceroy's war.

Nurullah had never heard tempers run so high at a party meeting in the Chinese room as the day the lantern-jawed British aristocrat drafted India into Europe's war with Mussolini-style contempt for elected legislators, but feelings ran higher when he rejected the party's offer of cooperation in the war and said all decisions, above all those concerning the defence of India and her participation in the war, would be taken by himself.

What amnesia drove us to make an offer he could kick us in the teeth with? went Zaheer Sahib's incredulous, angry argument. Did a Viceroy who had already shipped our men out like cattle, started conscription and made free with our money and materials need our cooperation? Would such a Viceroy give us charge of war decisions or even our own defence? What if we decide to bring our fighting men home from foreign battlefields to defend us here instead of the British empire in the Middle East and North Africa? What if we don't agree to scorched earth against the Japanese? What if we should negotiate our separate peace?

His attack on the party's rejected offer made stark unarguable sense and no one in the room argued back. What had cooperation in their last war got us but bullets and belly-crawling and jail, he continued. Had everyone in this room forgotten the foreign power's priority first and last was men and money for its wars? The crash order last time had been for two hundred thousand men from these parts, voluntarily if possible, by conscription if necessary; fixed quotas for every district, tehsil or village; compulsory contributions of half to a quarter of an income tax assessee's income to the war loan; failure of His Majesty's subjects to do their duty to be taken into account. Zaheer Sahib spat out information he had published in his short-lived weekly after Europe's Great War as if its acrid taste still soured his tongue. He had not spoken seated as others before him had done. He was on his feet, arms outstretched, a scarecrow towering over them. He looked like an omen of disaster in a field already strewn with skulls. The silence he commanded was profound. It was a measure of the room's respect for a comrade who has done battle to the limit of his strength and capacity. *When will we stop laying down our lives for their wars?* he demanded. We captured Khartoum for them, defeated the rebellion of Arabi Pasha in Egypt for them, dethroned King Thebaw and conquered Burma for them. They used Indian troops to crush the Boxers who were Chinese patriots trying to stop the sale of opium. They forced us into duties which, had we been independent, we would have refused to perform. Indian soldiers were rushed to the Front at Ypres and Flanders to relieve the British. Yet after the victory the King Emperor adamantly refused to give Indians command of the army because no British officer must serve under an Indian. The only war they did not send us to fight for them was the Boer War because they were shit-scared that fighting goras there would give us ideas here, though that did not prevent them from packing us off to the Front in 1914 — for fifteen rupees a month — to relieve them in their desperate situation.

'So what was this deluded juvenile offer you made of *partnership*, Nikhil?' he finished in bitter scorn glaring straight at Bhai. '*It*, and *you*, have been kicked aside, as you should have known you would be.'

And that looked like being the end of all argument. Nurullah was not sure how the next thing happened. The change of mood and direction was so subtle he missed the moment of its arrival as Bhai began to speak. Nor could he explain what accounted for it. Words could only express so much, after all, and every emotion words aroused had worn thin with overuse. He only knew that within a minute or two the Nazi terror overrunning Europe was taking possession of the room. It was there in the room with us, he told Eknath afterwards, it had us by the gut. There was no escape from it, and the struggle of Britain's people fighting for their lives and liberty had become our struggle — as had been the Ethiopians' and the Czechs' and all others who had been set upon by barbarians in this our century, whose cry for freedom we had heard and responded to as if it had been our own, whose lost freedom was as precious to us as our own. For if freedom itself dies, Bhai asked, what will be left for us to claim our share of? Is there any history, he persisted, that is not the history of us all? This was why we had made our offer. Yet the Viceroy, Lord Linlithgow, who is no barbarian but an Englishman, who well knows that only the free can fight for the freedom of others, has arrogantly rejected it. Hence the need now to protest being dragged to war in harness like animals without our consent.

ᶴ

'What would have happened if war hadn't broken out just then?' the researcher whose name is Pete Ryder asks me. 'Would those elected assemblies have been granted greater powers in due course, and so on gradually to self-government?'

'Unlikely,' I say, 'in fact, impossible, given the conundrum.'

I spell it out for him.

Master: You have my solemn word you will be granted self-government as soon as you are capable of defending your country.

Slave: But how can I defend my country when you forbid me to bear arms and even those who do are not trusted to hold command?

Master: Very true. Therefore self-government must wait.

'What do you mean not trusted?' asks Pete Ryder. 'Why wouldn't they trust an army that had done them proud?'

Because the occupier is doomed to dream mutiny, I tell him. The ground beneath the tyrant's feet rumbles after dark, the walls around him cry mutiny. It matters little that he has native allies — the princes and the titled landlords — who swear loyalty and pay tribute in return for their privileges or that native soldiers patrol his worldwide empire and fight his enemies. What makes his flesh crawl in the night is the frightening tenuousness of a design that only British bayonets make possible.

It was the Bengal army, recruited up and down this countryside, that had mutinied so this region was disbarred from the army and branded militarily worthless and a new army was recruited — from Gurkhas and Dogras, and Muslims and Sikhs from the Punjab. These were named the martial classes. All the same, to guard against future mutiny regiments had to be composed of mixed communities. Only in 1918 were Indians allotted a quota of ten a year at Sandhurst and made eligible for King's Commissions. The quota went up a little but at that rate it would have taken another hundred years for the army to be officered by Indians. An Indian Military Academy was not set up till 1934, and when the Viceroy's war broke out in 1939, of the thousand majors in the Indian army, only eight were Indians. So, given the conundrum, how could the question of self-government arise in any forseeable future?

You see, I repeat, an armed Indian was a fearsome risk, combustible material that had to be wired to European control and command. When at the end of the Second World War there were two point seven million Indians in the army who had fought on every battlefield of modern war, there were too many armed Indians, and a rebel Indian army besides. That was when the British left. An armed Indian was a fearsome risk.

'If we could please get back to non-violence,' says Pete Ryder gently, 'it must have made some impact.'

'You must understand the kind of world it was, made up of Europe and the lesser breeds whom Europe had a right to rule. Armed or unarmed revolt made no difference to that right. Only war and its fortunes drove Europe out.'

A staleness creeps over me as I re-live the airless confinement of an era when ambition and aspiration could not take wing. The Persian poet's words best describe it: a Box whose Candle is the Sun. Prison, for those who suffered it, I see now, was the only way out of the mimic lives we of non-Europe were assigned.

∽

Civil disobedience was to start again in the New Year, but differently this time. The voice from the hut had forbidden crowds to take to the streets. There must be no processions, no demonstrations, nothing that would harass the Sarkar at a time when the British people and their freedom were in peril. The command said party members could volunteer to court arrest singly, by protesting against the Viceroy's dictatorial action and India's compulsory participation in the war.

Bhai was to catch a train for a brief holiday on the Ghasvala beach in Bombay. The people who had come to see him off had swelled into a public sendoff that took up the entire platform. Nurullah had to wrestle his way through jostling, shoving party supporters to steer Bhai's luggage coolie to a third class compartment. The station master was having a table carried above the crowd's heads to the middle of the platform for Bhai to stand on and be seen. Nurullah saw a policeman pull him roughly down by the arm no sooner had he stood on it. He made desperate efforts to attract Bhai, waved both arms and hollered, sent a messenger running out through the station master's office but all too late. The stampede after Bhai to the police car left Nurullah alone but for the luggage coolie on the platform. A rough peremptory arrest for no offence — since Bhai was to make his anti-war speech in Khurram's constituency on his return from Bombay — it was an ominous portent of worse to come. This then was war.

He arrived too early for his class next day. Turning his back on the empty rows of desks he erased yesterday's markings from the blackboard and stood facing it with a stick of chalk gripped convulsively in his fingers until the chalk snapped. He ground the stumps to gritty particles and let them fall. The class was assembled when he turned around, every seat filled.

'Love,' he announced harshly without preamble, 'for friend or country, is a faithfulness unto death that every lout and loafer among you may one day be privileged to discover.'

He opened the prescribed text armed with their attention and began to read from it in the compelling style he had made peculiarly his own. He sensed them being consumed by the pain, seared by the slow fire of a dirge that kindled their defiance and empowered them with the will to act.

Time spent with Eknath and Usha did nothing to alleviate his wretchedness or allay his anxiety. A dullness pervaded his spirit that he could not shake off even in their stimulating company. Civil disobedience was not the drama it had been. The grand law of love decreed that the British people's ordeal and their heroic resistance to the Nazi hordes of the air must be respected and no additional burden placed on the Sarkar. Instead of a mass movement, lone men and women were volunteering to make anti-war speeches and were being thrown behind bars, locked into a few square feet of space, out of sight for a year or more. It was making no more impact than one sacrificial goat at a time on an indifferent altar, a pathetic contrast to the herd drama it had been. In May 1940, Norway, Holland and Belgium fell to the Nazis. France surrendered in June. But the grand law of love did not allow political advantage to be taken of these catastrophic defeats.

Dr Bihari's grey hair lay in lank strips on his balding scalp and hung limply to his shoulders. He was a mild methodical man of medicine, not given to oratory or harangue as the party's trade unionists were in orations to workers to down their tools and call a halt to defence production. He made a calm sort of anti-war statement at a public meeting in Mohammed Ali Park and was promptly arrested. Nurullah went to his trial with Gosiben who had placed herself next in line for arrest and wanted to know what to expect by way of a sentence when her turn came. The City Magistrate accused Dr Bihari of 'bringing the Government established by Law and Order into hatred and contempt and influencing the attitude of the public in a manner prejudicial to the efficient conduct of the war'. Two years' rigorous, Gosiben bet Nurullah in a mutter, but the magistrate sentenced him to fifteen months which meant that much less hard labour too. Not so bad. Gosiben wagged her head with satisfaction and came out calculating how many days she should allow herself to make arrangements for a long absence from the Khadi Bhandar before getting herself arrested.

'Nurullah, you are very down in the mouth these days,' was her comment as they watched Dr Bihari driven away to jail, 'what is the reason for this?'

Ya Allah! they're all mad, thought Nurullah. Gosiben was showing wrinkles, her skin had slackened and the veins stood out on her hands. She had grown old selling bales of khadi and going to jail. She and Nurullah hung around under the shade of a gnarled peepul saying nothing much while she made her calculations in her head. Crows raised a croaking clatter in the dusty branches above them.

There was not even Hashi for diversion. He had got out of that rat maze by telling her his benefactor's family (who no longer knew he existed) were trying to finalize a match for him. Hashi took matrimony seriously. She understood the solemn purpose for which he must mentally re-orient himself. Afterwards, maybe. Avoiding her had meant missing Robin-da's teas for he was afraid of being sucked into the maze again. He knew he had no resistance at all to whatever miserly bait she offered. At home he avoided the family too, going straight up to his room after his university class but old Zenobia Framjee waylaid him on arrival one day to make use of his arm up the steps and clutched it until the side verandah where Ammaji was giving tea to Lily Hulbert who sometimes delivered the embroidery her mother did on tea napkins and tablecloths. This time it was a set of hand towels embroidered with chinar leaves, Ammaji's favourite leaf.

Lily was complaining cheerily about 'this awful khaddar' pronouncing it like udder. Nurullah suspected it was her policy to mispronounce Hindustani. It set her apart, made her feel a cut above, more dignified. (And did no one else any harm.) Today he found it refreshingly funny. It cut through the bog of a depressing day and an unsuccessful class. She gave his grin a look of ladylike surprise.

'Compliments of the season men! Where've you'll been, hiding somewhere? Haven't seen you in ages. Been back to Bombay?'

'Come, sit, Nurullah,' invited Ammaji, pouring him a cup of tea and passing him a hand towel to admire.

The conversation, about hand towels, chain stitch, English lawn and fine French chiffon, and then what was on at the flicks, had a cartoon's breezy bounce. Lily Hulbert could have been Minnie Mouse from the neat bow in her hair to her shoes which always looked a size too large strapped to her fragile Minnie Mouse ankles. Minnie's and Donna Duck's oversized high-heeled shoes or cork-soled clogs and their demure behaviour were an endearing contrast to British Movietone News: The Eyes and Ears of the World before the main feature at the cinema. Nurullah had grown fond of these bright spirits. Lily Hulbert also had Minnie Mouse's friendly personality but her looks were her own. Her high bald forehead tapered to fingerwidth at the temples. Wide cheekbones and a pointed chin completed the odd triangle. She kept her small mouth primly pursed, for dignity like her memsahib Hindustani, a habit that would crepe her upper lip like an old woman's if she kept it up.

Nurullah said he had not been back to Bombay but she asked enviously as if his trip had been yesterday, 'What all did you do men?'

He thought back to a year ago and gave her the highlights. The Ghasvala garden, the Shakespeare play, a three-layered ice cream sundae at the Parisian Dairy with Mr Ghasvala's nine-year-old nephew.

'Didn't you see any flicks?'

'One. *Tarzan the Ape Man*.' Chosen for its suitability for Mr Ghasvala's nephew.

Lily made a face. 'Childish, ain? What a waste. When we go to Cal we go to the flicks every evening. There are so many cinemas. I'd love to go to Bombay.'

'Go, then, beti,' Ammaji coaxed.

She explained to Zenobia Framjee that Mr Hulbert's younger sister whose married name was Doreen Salamat Ali was the famous Bombay Talkies film star, Sarita Devi. (Nurullah had seen her last in *Yeh Pyar Hai*) Lily's bua, Aunty Dor, wanted Lily to come and try her luck in the films.

'Well, what are you waiting for, *dikri*?' urged old Zenobia.

'No men,' Lily firmly ruled it out — 'No Bombay Talkies for me. I'm going to try my luck at *home*.'

Nurullah had heard this before but Lily's fervent ambition was not likely to be realized in this life. Home was Number Eleven, Clive Road, Akbarabad but her obsession with going 'home' to England prevented her from learning shorthand or taking nurse's or teacher's training. Pining for a homeland that had never been home seemed to be all the rage. Lily's at least existed. Jinnah Sahib who should have known better at his advanced age was hankering for a non-existent one, and that too For Mussalmans Only when his home had always been a luxurious villa in cosmopolitan Bombay. What on earth would he do among Mussalmans Only? The more imaginary a homeland, the more fanatic it made its hankerer. It could be that as a Khoja disciple of the Aga Khan, a wealthy gentleman who spent his time on the French Riviera and married foreign wives, Jinnah Sahib needed to prove himself more of a proper Mussalman. History had others like him whose hankering for more identity than they were born with had endangered life and limb on a colossal scale. Napoleon had been born Corsican and Hitler Austrian. Nearer at hand Nawab Sahib Vazirabad had become an ardent supporter of Jinnah Sahib's hankering.

'He's talking like an owl's tail,' Ammaji had admonished Bibijan, 'what's all this about some new "stan"?'

Bibijan took her husband's side from habit and duty but having disposed of that formality she said she for one wasn't going anywhere.

'But Ammi,' she appealed, 'it's just that himself is worried sick about zamindari being abolished. The Angrez war saved us this time but who knows when we'll be threatened again?'

'If you won't have a zamindari in this new "stan" either, why not stay put? If I know you, Bibi, you'll be bored stiff among Mussalmans Only. Variety is the spice of life.'

Lily's was an innocent hankering, unlike those of the heroes of history. She nursed it by buying Picturegoer, collecting Stars of the Silver Screen from Nestlés chocolate wrappers and, according to Ammaji, practising film star poses in front of her mirror.

'Take her back on your bicycle, Nurullah,' said Ammaji, 'it's too late for bichari Lily to go alone by tonga.'

It was daylight but Ammaji who had led thirty women from Akbarabad to walk with the Mahatma for a segment of his marathon Salt March in 1930 and had a neck tremor from a lathi blow that year, had her own rules about girls going about alone. She also knew that riding the bar or carrier of a man's bicycle was not forbidden to girls of Lily's community and her parents would not object. Lily said 'Ta for the tea', gave Ammaji a kiss, and chose the carrier. As usual her shoes looked enormous strapped to her dainty ankles. She directed him to what he already knew as the Christian mohalla.

Mr Hulbert in socks and braces opened the door and seeing he had given Lily a lift home, asked him in and hospitably offered him a peg. Nurullah declined saying he did not touch alcohol.

'Touch it, man, it's good for you,' Mr Hulbert urged genially.

Their neighbours, Mr and Mrs Colbury, were there too with their shoes off and their feet on footstools. The wives called each other Mrs Hul and Mrs Col and were eating toast spread with a masala paste. It had a nose-tingling mouth-watering pungency. He took the slice Mrs Hul, a buxom body on bony legs, handed him.

The room had an upright piano with a photo of the Huls on their wedding day, she in the long white frock and veil of a Christian bride and he as he must have been then with all his hair and his own teeth in the prime of his railway career. A framed magazine picture of the Angrezi princesses, Elizabeth and Margaret Rose, hung on a wall. Nurullah studied them and his surroundings. Flowered curtains, loose flowered covers on the chairs which Jeroo had seen at the Criks' and called 'chintz'. At the same time there was this tingling un-Angrezi masala paste. Another Akbarabad. He was intrigued by what they would be eating for dinner, what after-dinner pastime would fill their evenings. Long and leisured these would be with Mr Hul and Mr Col both retired. The Huls must have been quite old when they had Lily.

He was invited to join them on Christmas Eve as they were not going to Cal this year.

'We get around the piano and sing. You'll must come. You'll are looking so mopey men,' said Lily, worry and concern writ large on her small triangular face.

Nurullah went. It would have been churlish to refuse their kindness but he was not in the mood for festivity even of a subdued hymn-singing variety around the piano. The Huls and Cols, however, sang no hymns. They belted out songs from a songbook on the piano stand that had been popular at 'home' before the last war.

She pushed me into the parlour,
    pushed the parlour door,
Pushed herself upon my knee,
    pushed her kisser in front of me,
She pushed me round to the jeweller
    near the Hippodrome,
She pushed me in front of a clergyman,
    and then she pushed me home.

Mrs Hul played the piano. Her husband stood behind her with his hands on her shoulders. Mrs Col held her hands interlocked between her baggy breasts. She had taught Shān singing at the convent till she retired and her voice had a high professional quaver better suited to

'Hark, hark the lark at heaven's gate sings' than to all this pushing. Mr Col kept an arm around her. Gran, the white-haired light-skinned one among them sang from her chair.

'Sing!' Lily jogged his elbow, pointing to the line they were on in a rollicking encore and Nurullah joined in. Shot out of every rhythm he had hitherto known he *pushed* with gusto as they were doing.

The Huls and Cols went to the flicks regularly and once he went with them. There was a Viennese actress of great beauty in this love story and her French leading man's deep resonant voice bidding her 'Com wiz me to ze Casbah' gave a profound and fateful significance to his invitation to the Arab bazaar.

'You see why I don't want to join Bombay Talkies,' whispered Lily during a passionate love scene, 'this is more like real life man.'

The love scenes in *Yeh Pyar Hai* had had Aunty Dor and her leading man romping around hairpin bends on a Kulu mountainside singing a duet and swinging from a deodar during one refrain. In Nurullah's recent experience things didn't get much further along in real life.

Getting to know the Huls and Cols was like walking out of bruising winds into a small safe shelter composed of potato cakes and curry, vindaloo paste on toast, the Angrezi princesses and now a picture of their low-bellied dogs beside them on the wall. The outside was neat and manageable too. No massive overhanging trees to cast shadows, no ariel roots descending from their ancient branches to strangulate their trunks, only cropped grass, flowers in pots and a fence. Nurullah still did not touch alcohol, disliking the taste when he tried it, but he was getting uprooted from such roots as he could lay claim to, and from the domed house that had adopted him. The melancholy associated with his nightmarish origin and the clinging present sorrow he could not define were slipping from him as though in a fit of absentmindedness. They would enfold him to suffocation later, he supposed, but for now he had the distinct sensation of being liberated from his present and his past and buoyed by a lightness that was entirely alien to his nature. Anxiety gnawed at him when he thought of Bhai's vicious three-year sentence for an offence as yet uncommitted, but with the war going disastrously for the Allies, the Sarkar would need the nationalists' cooperation and would have to release political prisoners. It was part of his new optimism to believe this would happen.

He automatically stood up for God Save the King when a film he went to with the Huls ended, instead of making a hurried exit on principle over a row of legs before the English anthem struck up and a portrait of the King Emperor and Empress lit up the screen. Lily beside him was standing very straight, her eyes on their Majesties. The ceiling fan blew a strand of her black hair across her high forehead as Long toooo rei-ei-n over us vibrated thrillingly through the hall. Lily's profile had the awesome incandescence of one whose soul is rising to the stars. The chords died but not their mystical echo or the loyal light in her eye as she said a hushed goodbye to him outside. Nurullah remembered reading the Huls' community leader's statement to the press that no matter if they had only *one* drop of English blood in their veins, it was the drop that mattered. Lily liked to be called Lilibet which she had read in *Woman and Home* was what Princess Margaret Rose called her elder sister.

He took a present of Ponds Vanishing Cream (on Lilibet's advice) for her mother's birthday. When she had cut her cake and they had sung Happy Birthday, Mr Hul kissed his wife in front of them all, pressing his false teeth long and lovingly against her lips. Nurullah politely averted his eyes. It was strangely moving, this placid way of life he had strayed into, devoid of yearning, unburdened by soaring unattainable dreams. What circumstances of history or character had produced this contentment, or was contentment only possible to people who accepted the world as they found it? Nurullah would have thought Anglo mixed with Indian would churn up scarred psyches and throw identities into turmoil but not a bit of it. The psyche problem may have been solved by their leaders' one-drop theory, but whatever accounted for the sanity of the Huls and Cols, they were proof positive of the wisdom of mixing races and bastardizing blood. Incredible that this was a crime in some countries and transgressors were killed for it. Still more untenable when it was pure breeds who caused grief and raised hell, from poor daft Jimmy Ginvala to dreadful thoroughbred Martha, and now the master race's master race in its most murderous new manifestation. How fortunate that we of Hindustan are blended and bastardized beyond unravelling. Thinking about it, this seemed to him infallible insurance against the streaks and outbursts of insanity, the ailments of soul and body, that afflicted the racially pure. In an illuminating moment that included Lilibet's incandescence in the presence of her King and Queen, he saw Hindustan as the whole human race, incomparably rich and blessed in its variety. It was how he was feeling these days.

The reliable magic of Nurullah's cherished poets was receding alarmingly leaving the foreground of his mind unencumbered by poetry. Simpler word formations dallied in it. He sang She *pushed* me into the parlour and Inky-pinky parlez-vous and Tipperary while he shaved or had his balti bath. Com wiz me to ze Casbah interrupted his preparations for class. He abandoned the balti and tried the shower above the tub. One day he filled the long enamel tub and lay chin-deep in it for the novelty of the experience, after soaping and scrubbing himself at the balti first. To please Lilibet he had shirts and pants made at Ahmed Gents and Ladies Tailor in the Civil Lines where she had her frocks made. He got into a needless rage with Keats' ode about fever and fret and groaning palsied men. Uttering an oath he slammed the book shut and sent it crashing across the room. Enough was enough.

The iron railings put up around Victoria after the massacre in Company Bagh had been replaced by a low stone balustrade festooned with honeysuckle creeper. It made a perfect enclosure for him and Lilibet on their folded blanket. They could hear the frenetic barking of stray dogs and a jackal's howl in the distance but here there was peace. The sky too was peacefully remote. It did not have the disturbing dazzling closeness the heavens had on the roof terrace at home. He could lie on his back in blank bliss after love with Lilibet. If he thought about anything it was about what a historian had called the palimpsest of India's history, the writing and re-writing on it that had brought us to where we were, and to marvel at the living layer the stars were looking down upon these nights. His and Lilibet's lives and limbs lay love-tangled where the blood of martyrs had soaked the marble under the folds of their blanket. History's wrongdoings could not be undone nor the dead brought back to life but memory — the unforgiving unforgetting begetter of future wrongs — could be given better things to remember: a slip of a girl who weighed a feather, her hipbones his handspan apart, a face whose sharp outlines had been etched with a knife. For the mysterious alignment of its bones no word had yet been invented.

She spoke a mincing stilted English she thought was English English. She mourned her beautiful black hair and longed for it to be a colour called ash blond through which she would have worn a narrow black velvet band. She lamented her smooth off-white skin and carried a flowery parasol to protect it from darkening. Her winsomeness could shift at will into old feminine wiles when she played at being a film star and practised a future steaming love scene on him that left them both breathless. Clinging together they rolled off the blanket to the shivering cold crescent-lit marble, hitting the sharp edge of Victoria's pedestal just where one body had died propped with its chest blown open. Nurullah picked up the blanket and carried it folded on his shoulder. They strolled hand-in-hand up the mound where Colonel Ponsonby had machine-gunned bullet holes through iron sheets, promising Akbarabadis a dose of the same, and came tearing headlong down it. Night-blooming shrubs perfumed the inner pathways of Company Bagh. On a night when they had a waxing moon for light and time to explore they strayed into the girdle of weeping ashokas and into paradise.

'I saw you with that chee-chee girl on the bar of your cycle,' said Hashi knowingly one teatime at Robin-da's.

Nurullah nodded and told several lies. There were situations that made liars of men. Plans had to be made, secrecy ensured until hurdles were crossed. He knew they would be. Aunty Dor who had been Doreen Hulbert had become Sarita Devi who had become Begun Salamat Ali. Hindustan, thought Nurullah, a magician's conmingled brew from the Ganga's frozen source to the Bay of Bengal, a plain on which Nurullah's beloved answers to the ridiculous nickname of England's future queen.

Six

Edgar Knox was aware of the irony of writing about a subject that did not exist in its own right, but as a British, French or Dutch handout. He did what he could to penetrate the colonial curtain. He searched out incipient situations not yet in the news and not likely to be if the slant and the censors had their way. He met the least as well as the best known actors on the scene. He forecast prodigiously, undeterred by being in a minority of one. He ignored the presiding western presence by never using western yardsticks for comparison, never writing 'The United Provinces of Agra and Oudh are roughly the size of France.' It was an approach that made him better appreciated in Asia than in some command centres of the West whose bosses devoutly wished him back reporting Europe — though one self-confessed admirer he had in his own country was Franklin D. Roosevelt. The President, open to ideas and approaches his embassies failed to bring to his attention, had once helped Edgar out of a difficulty and had said on the telephone, 'If there's anything more I can do, Edgar, let me know.'

When he had been reporting the run-up to war in Europe, Europe had been remote enough for his fellow American islanders. Asia was over the rim of imagination, out in space. Newsreels of the war were making a difference between no knowledge and some but the knowledge gained was of Europe. Americans watched European cities fierily alight under bombardment like birthday cakes shimmering with countless candles and were shaken by the sight of people like themselves trapped in those infernos. Japan's war might as well have been Attila the Hun's. No telling if those formless huddles on the screen driving their pigs and buffalos, pushing everything they owned in boxes on wheels, with the newborn strapped to their chests and the decrepit to their backs, fleeing to a safer scrap of interior over a hill, had human lives at all, let alone continuous ones. The horrors of war granted them a minute's reality before 'Asia' disappeared in a trick of the camera as soon as the lights came on. He put the speculative point to his editor, an observer of high professional standing. They were in Edgar's apartment on East Seventy-First street, not an ideal location from which to visualize war in Asia. Sam Sullivan was scrutinizing the label on a bottle of Bourbon he had taken out of the Javanese chest Edgar used as a cocktail cabinet. He proceeded to mix himself a Scotch Old Fashioned and gave the emaciated ashwood Balinese dancer on the chest his concentrated attention before he sat down with his drink.

'All that may be so, Edgar. I still don't think you need to include India in your tour this time. Nothing's happening in India. India isn't news.'

'The Bengal famine wasn't news either when I first reported food riots. The Government of India was calling it a false rumour.'

Sam shrugged.

'So corpses will out and half a million corpses is news,' he said.

'But not an act of God,' said Edgar. 'The Government had been shipping grain out recklessly to war areas and they've shipped hundreds of locomotives and railway carriages out to the Middle East. There would have been no transport mess if they had allowed India to manufacture locomotives and automobiles.'

Sam sighed peacefully and reached for an olive.

'That's your say-so, nobody else's. And as far as news value is concerned you're talking about a country sixty percent Americans wouldn't be able to identify on an outline map. Gandhi may be a household word out there but here he's a word for a loony bag of bones. *And* Great Britain happens to be our ally. There's a point beyond which carping and criticizing shouldn't go at this time. I am not about to print anything that will embarrass our Allies. The line you're taking — independence right now — will. Do you really expect the British, French and Dutch to walk out of their possessions in the middle of a war?'

Edgar lounging drinkless against the wall with his hands in his pockets gave an incredulous laugh.

'They're not walking, they're running out of Asia. If they had pledged independence to those countries they would have had their support and wouldn't be surrendering them to the enemy without a fight. The British have retreated from Burma, surrendered the Andamans and Singapore. The Vichy has dumped Indo-China without a shot fired. But not a single statesman of our "Free World," believes the Asian leaders assurances of their support if popular governments are set up right away.'

'Somebody besides you has got to be convinced of their intentions,' said Sam. 'When Gandhi makes the front pages here the *New York Times* calls him an appeaser of Japan and a dabbler in international intrigue with a moral stature equal to Franz von Papen. The *Chicago Tribune* calls him a stooge mahatma and the *Washington Post* says the Indian leaders are traitors to civilization, giving aid to the enemies of mankind.'

'And how could those high priests be wrong?' murmured Edgar, sitting down. 'Listen to me, Sam. This stooge Mahatma owns nothing but a loincloth, his eyeglasses and his wooden clogs. The Vietnamese chose Ho Chi Minh their leader because *he* owns practically nothing.'

'Now you're telling me they've got fruitcakes for leaders.'

'I'm saying these are unusual men. Freedom is the most romantic necessity men ever dreamed up and while they're after that Holy Grail they're more dedicated and self-denying than it is humanly possible to be. That particular conjunction of days and nights never comes again. We should know. It's quite a while since the day George Washington couldn't tell a lie. In time we all rejoin the human race and become the same old lying cheating bastards. I tell you these are legendary times in Asia and these men are living legends, heroes to their people. *Now* is the time to befriend them.'

The telephone beside Sam's chair rang. He picked it up. 'It was Leda to say she's just leaving her office.' Edgar hit the table with the flat of his hand.

'Those people are *on our side,* Sam. They put us on a pedestal. They quote English poets and American philosophers. They revere western law. Ho Chi Minh's League for Independence is only asking for what the French take for granted for themselves: education, hospitals, a decent wage, justice. I've already shown you a draft of their Proclamation. It's haunting the way it beseeches — that's the word — the United States to support their demand for freedom, and for arms and advisers to help fight the Japanese.'

He picked it up from the coffee table and began to read:

We believe in the sanctity of the principle
for which the world is shedding so much blood ...
We beseech the Great Powers, and particularly
the United States, to give aid and assistance
in our fight for national liberation ... We
will back the Allied cause, welcome Allied arms,
give all needed aid ... This we will swear to do
in our struggle against the Japanese and for our
own liberation ...

'Are you sure you didn't help them draft it?' said Sam dryly, 'and what's stopping them from fighting the Japanese, or for their own liberation as you put it?'

'Sam,' said Edgar keeping his temper, 'the people of countries known as imperial "possessions" are not armed.'

'All right, you had a chance to talk to FDR at the White House lunch. What did he say? Or did he just listen pleasantly?'

'The President has already taken some initiatives. The Philippines wouldn't be with us if they hadn't been promised independence. He's ready to help Britain lose her empire but a little press support might speed the process. What do Indians have to do to get our backing? Become Generalissimos? Convert to Methodism? Eat hotdogs?'

'Nothing wrong with any of that,' agreed Sam affably.

'India is supplying men and materials to the Middle East. It's also our supply line to China. Calcutta is only twelve hours from Chungking. We have thousands of American soldiers in India. Indian news — not British handouts — has got to be news for us. It's time we made assessments of our own and got to know those people.'

'So we're out there getting to know them. It takes a while to learn about new places.'

'*New!*' exploded Edgar wrathfully.

'New to us for Christ's sake. Not so long ago we didn't know where China was either. China used to be bucktoothed little yellow men in pigtails pulling rickshaws. Now we know they're flying jet planes. And incidentally, Edgar, keep the Communists out of dispatches. We have it on the authority of the Kuomintang officials here that there is no Communist party. It surrendered to Chiang Kai Shek long ago. The Communists are not news. It's news we're after.'

'Which as you know is, the British navy has been driven out of the Bay of Bengal and most of the Indian Ocean, and they've been outmatched in the air.'

'We can't keep harping on Allied defeats, Edgar. It's lousy for morale. Save your stories for your next book.'

The doorbell rang and Edgar let his sister in. Leda reminded Sam of lavender water, smelling salts and fainting Victorians. It made him want to smack her wrists to speed up her circulation.

'Good to see you, Leda,' he greeted her, 'at least *you* know the difference between news and fairy tales if Edgar doesn't.'

'Not any more, Sam,' said Leda with unexpected vigour. 'Who does, now that blue-eyed blonds have a divine right to rule the world and are destroying the world to prove it. How about that for a Teutonic fairy tale that's making front page news every day?'

Edgar gave a shout of approval as if a slow-witted dog he had been trying to train for years had finally jumped through a hoop and invited Sam to join them for dinner at the Russian Tea Room, Leda's Bohemian choice. Over borscht and blinis Sam said Edgar's books were doing so well, why didn't he stay home and write instead of bumming around the world and coming back touched in the head. Edgar had described Angkor Vat to him a few years ago as a sight hundreds of travellers before him had seen yet his had been the first eye, woefully unprepared for that revelation of human faces on pinnacles rearing out of primeval jungle under a wondrous red early morning sky.

'Such sights brand you forever, Sam,' Edgar had said. 'Never can your dreams be untroubled dreams again.'

It was the kind of reaction that could throw months of businesslike calculation into a tailspin. On the other hand, it could plant a scene in memory as only Edgar could and his was now too important a voice to be ignored.

⌇

The Governor of the United Provinces and his lady obviously kept to the tradition of making an entrance, announced by an ADC, after their guests were assembled. Edgar was the only guest, a privilege he assumed he had been accorded as a courtesy to his high connections and not his controversial reputation as a journalist but protocol was going to be observed nonetheless. He saw the point of the delayed entrance — time allotted to taking in the power and the glory. The room had a lofty ceiling, rich furnishings, extravagant portraiture. The sweep of emerald lawn outside the window was as extravagant, sloping to a slender dancing river. The Yamuna then, a clean clear blue. What he had seen of the holy river was muddier with its weight of sin and sorrow.

Edgar pondered protocol. He had met it in monarchies and dictatorships besides other empirelands. It made its pithy point. Less so when history's clowns made a farce of it. In Louis Fourteenth's Versailles Princes of the

Blood had bowed before the royal napkin, salt cellar and carvers when these were carried through the palace. In Louis' bedroom, one courtier took the royal nightcap, another handed the dressing gown, a third combed the royal hair. The Master of Wardrobe took the royal nightgown by its right sleeve, the First Valet de Chambre by its left sleeve. Yet it had taken two more Louis for all hell to break loose.

Two tall erect Excellencies walked in escorted (but not announced) by an ADC in naval uniform. Greetings were cordially exchanged. Gin and tonic was offered on monogrammed silver by a turbaned liveried attendant. They drank it standing in twos, the Governor mutedly amiable with Edgar, his lady with the cheerful ADC, and went in to lunch, not in the dining room but what must be the breakfast-lunch room they preferred when they were alone. Maybe because of Edgar an elaborate correctness prevailed here, too. The fall and fold of damask, the soldierly array of knives, forks, spoons recalled sacred inviolable traditions of silver and linen ritually arranged through war and peace down the ages. Chairs were drawn out for them to be seated by splendidly dressed minions round a table laid for four with sweetpeas in a silver vase at its centre. Apples, oranges and guavas adorned a bowl on the sideboard, blue and purple grapes another. From his chair, Edgar could see more well-watered green sloping to the river. The printed menu at each place said Lady Curzon soup.

'You know the country well, I understand, Mr Knox,' said his Excellency Sir Humphrey Hartley.

'No, I don't actually. I've only been here a couple of times. But who can claim to know India well?'

'I believe we can make that claim. We've been here long enough,' said Sir Humphrey with a pleasant civilized assurance.

'That's very true,' Edgar acknowledged.

'What brought you here originally?'

'It was the Salt March, in 1930. That command of Gandhi's to "Let the fist holding salt be broken but let there be no voluntary surrender of salt" sounded like something new under the sun. I was intrigued. I have been ever since.'

'I remember now. You wrote about police action on the beach at Dandi to stop Gandhi's followers from raiding the salt depot. A gory description you gave of it as I recall,' said Sir Humphrey good-humouredly. 'It didn't spare us.'

The temperature that day had been 116 in the shade but the quilt of bloodied bodies on the battlefield had lain broiling in the sun. No sooner had the first contingent fallen, the next had marched doggedly forward to receive the same treatment without an arm uplifted to ward off blows. No cheers from the sidelines to keep them going. No witnesses but a handful like himself. No sign that Edgar could see of healthy human cowardice. Edgar had turned aside and vomited violently on the sand. Afterwards in a temporary hospital set up nearby he had counted broken bones, gashed scalps and fractured skulls among the 320 casualties taken there. The better off among them had been kicked in the stomach and testicles. Evidence surely, if any were needed, that it is madness to go unarmed into battle.

The Governor was saying there had been no civil disobedience since the early thirties.

'The trickle we had of it recently was a considerable comedown from mass agitation. I don't know what purpose it served.'

'Their way of objecting to being drafted into the war without consultation?' suggested Edgar.

'It was the Viceroy's prerogative to declare India at war.'

'I saw an example of that individual protest,' said Edgar.

Lady Hartley, showing much more than diplomatic interest, asked him to please do tell us about it, you see we never see this sort of thing ourselves, and Edgar obliged. He had been on a train packed with GIs going to Calcutta. The night had been blisteringly hot and they were being chewed up by monsoon insects. The GIs in his compartment were cursing the China-India-Burma theatre of war and wishing they could get out of — if Their Excellencies would pardon the expression — this stinkhole of a country. The train ground to a clanking halt at some station during the night and Edgar happened to sit up and look out of the window. There was this elderly villager in white on the platform, standing in that bucklekneed posture of feeble old men. A grimy lightbulb over his head had him illuminated from the surrounding dark and people had come with garlands to see him off, on the next train presumably since this was a troop train. Edgar couldn't hear and wouldn't have understood what they were saying but it looked like a queer mixture of formal ceremony and spontaneous jubilation. The send-off committee took turns touching the old man's feet. His hand hovered over their bent heads except when he hugged two little boys clamouring for his attention. And in the end he didn't catch any train. A policeman strode out of the shadows, clamped a hand on his arm and marched him back out of the station. The old man went laughing soundlessly into the dark.

After a pause Lady Hartley said, 'You make it seem quite like a Rembrandt painting,' with a smile that had escaped entombment in official graciousness.

She must once have been the quintessential cream-petalled English rose and still had the sensibilities to match.

'It would certainly have been a fit subject for the great man,' admitted Edgar. 'It was a scene from a vanished century, an Age of Innocence set apart from the slaughterhouse we're making of the world. It made me wonder if my entire life would be worth one day of that old man's. It was all over in a minute but it left me with the impression that stamping out a resistance movement of people like him must be like trying to lasso the Holy Ghost.'

Everyone laughed, the ADC loudest, at the cowboy similie.

'As I said earlier,' Sir Humphrey pointed out, 'the resistance seems to have died a natural death. It was reduced to such episodes as the one you describe. Even so it was not harmless. An anti-war speech in an industrial centre could incite a strike that would cripple defence production and there were other ways of obstructing the war effort. As you know we've released the political prisoners we took then. We hoped they would respond and pledge their cooperation but nothing of the sort has happened. Obviously the Government can't bow to their conditions.'

Edgar's tastebuds were revelling in the most delectable fish he had ever eaten. Smoked bekti on the menu. He complimented her lovely Ladyship on it.

'It's local river fish,' explained Lady Hartley, pink with pleasure. 'I'm told our head cook prepares it on a charcoal brazier over a bed of burning straw and smokes it very gently through jaggery — that's the molasses they use in the countryside.'

'There's a Chinese proverb,' said Edgar, '"Govern a family as you would cook a small fish — very gently."'

He hoped this would not be misconstrued as unsolicited political interference but Lady Hartley received it thoughtfully, said how wise, and that she must remember it. Edgar turned to the Governor, noticing that she and the ADC broke into inconsequential chit-chat at once as if on cue.

'Then, as law and order problems go,' ventured Edgar 'the scene is pretty quiet these days?'

'This is not a province of which that can ever be said with certainty, Mr Knox. It has a violent history. Places around here were battlegrounds during the Mutiny. Akbarabad itself fell into the mutineers' hands. They were joined by a mob that plundered and burned European residences and butchered Europeans. They even set up a city government in the Delhi emperor's name with a petty schoolteacher in charge, and the main police station flew the green flag of Islam. European women and children had to be moved into the Fort for safety. Then we — I am referring to my predecessors — had serious agrarian disturbances here soon after the last war. The peasants refused to pay rents and demanded an end to what they called feudal dues. They were put up to it, of course, by political agitators. One publication in particular wrote treason in issue after issue. It was edited by a seditious scoundrel whom we had no alternative but to jail and finally to deport for ten years. He was attacking the land tenure system we had put in place and promoting straightforward rebellion to cut off revenue to the government.'

'When was this land tenure system put in place?'

'By the Company, and carried on under the Crown with some changes. After the Mutiny there was naturally a mistrust of the native population in these parts. Much thought was given to conciliating the classes we could rely on to be loyal so the zamindars were given proprietary rights subject to their loyalty to the British Government.'

'I read a sympathetic write up in *The Times* back in 1922 about the peasants' agrarian demands,' said Edgar. 'It said the tenants had been crushed by requisitions of all kinds, but now because of the political awakening they had begun to fight for their rights.'

'Judgement from London is easy, Mr Knox. The Government here bears the brunt. Agrarian militancy was so widespread we had to use military intervention. At one time a thousand villages were flying what they called the "national flag" and the peasants had taken to hand spinning, a clear symbol of revolt. As you know the "national flag" has a spinning wheel in the centre. We keep a close watch on agricultural developments since Gandhi brought the lower classes into agitation. As I said, in this province we're dealing with a seditious mentality. Some years ago the Manager of the Imperial Bank was found mysteriously dead. They never got to the bottom of it. I might add that the man you're going to meet is the architect of much of the agrarian trouble in the past decade. He's no run-of-the-mill troublemaker and all the more dangerous on that account. Good family. Culture. Money. Enormous influence. But educated here entirely without the leavening of western influences. Before his last arrest we had reports of a conference he was planning. The man is fanning the ambitions of every Asiatic who wants to damage the West. The house is under watch. We never underestimate the Bolshevist influence.'

Lady Hartley turned the talk to pleasantries during the undistinguished meat course. Cook number two probably. It lacked the artistry. Then, surprising Edgar again, she asked him what had intrigued him about the nonviolent movement.

'Well,' said Edgar, 'I have a sister who collects fairy tales.'

Lady Hartley raised her eyebrows enquiringly and said with positively youthful enjoyment, 'All very mysterious, but what does it have to do with my question, Mr Knox?'

'Let me explain. She has one that must be Persian or Central Asian in origin. It reads like a prototype of the genre, with all the classic ingredients of a fairy tale including an impossibly long journey — this one is to the Caucasus — and cryptic signposts along the way. "Go along this road until it forks into three; take neither the right nor the left but the middle path; follow it for five days and six nights until you see a column on which are inscribed Cufic characters. Do what is written there ...'"

'And so?'

'And so the Movement as I see it is very much like that endless journey, following coded signposts of its own. A conventional battle is based on known weapons and strategies, on the experience one has gained from other battles. This one does without true and tried weapons. It has no guns to arm it, only its language, and a bizarre language it is. It might as well be Cufic characters. How's this for a command barked out to the troops: "The tyrant has power over your body, he can have no power over your soul!" Or "Hate the deed, not the doer." It's the stuff of fairy tales. I'm only afraid it'll end up with a classic happy ending.'

'Now I *am* mystified, Mr Knox. What could possibly be wrong with that?'

'In this tale the Causer of Causes rewards the prince with three more beautiful wives and punishes the Negro slave for his perfidy by chaining his arms and legs to four swift horses and whipping them off smartly to the earth's four corners.'

Lady Hartley shuddered.

'Fairy tales do have some pretty ghastly endings. My sister says their most horrific punishments are designed for those whom Kipling called the lesser breeds,' said Edgar.

In the silence that followed, custard apple ice cream was served. Edgar had never heard of the fruit or tasted so superb an ice cream. The head cook again. He gestured his inarticulate praise of the dessert. Lady Hartley said yes indeed, the head cook's confections were quite Cordon Bleu. She would have ordered one of his patisseries had it not been too heavy for lunch. But Mr Knox must try the crystallized ginger from the glass dish in front of him. Violets and cherries were a specialty of his too. And now she would leave Mr Knox and her husband to their deliberations.

Edgar stood up regretting his lack of Versailles manners. He would have liked to bow over her long white English ladyship's hand but she seemed just as pleased with his firm handshake. The ADC went with her, and Edgar with his host to another garden and river view from the Governor's study where coffee was served. Grateful for the valuable time put at his disposal and for his host's plainspeaking he dispensed with *pas de deux* himself and went to the heart of the matter, seeking this outspoken conservative's opinion on 'the Indian question'. Was self-government for India on the agenda? he asked. If not now, then after the war? Or after the war's aftermath? Edgar hoped the leisurely scope and span of his phrasing would take the sting out of what Sir Humphrey might consider a naïve and meddlesome American question. Sir Humphrey being nobody's fool decided to treat it as precisely that.

'Self-government is always on the agenda but it is not possible to set a date for it.'

He added that the Atlantic Charter's wording of freedom for 'all nations' and 'all peoples' naturally referred to the Nazi-occupied countries of Europe.

'Would that position be true of the French and Dutch governments too? Back in 1936 the Dutch Governor General of Indonesia said "We have ruled here for three hundred years with the whip and the club and we shall be doing it another three hundred years."

'I can't speak for other governments,' said Sir Humphrey smoothly, 'but it would be fantasy for any forecaster to assume that the old sovereign ties will not be re-established in South and Southeast Asia after Japan's maniacal Co-prosperity Sphere has been destroyed. Malaya will be restored to the British, the East Indies to the Dutch and Indo-China to the French. We have to think of the best interests of the millions whose destinies Europe holds in trust. So there are going to be no speedy transfers of power. Nor is our authority in these areas going to be diluted by any form of international control. In fact the war has made it necessary to reinforce our presence in Asia. We've had to occupy Iran to prevent oil from falling into Nazi hands.'

Edgar said President Roosevelt would be greatly disappointed. The President was taking a personal interest in 'the Indian question'. He would have liked to see a provisional Indian government set up immediately.

'Notwithstanding the enemy at the gates,' nodded Sir Humphrey. 'It is a romantic view, is it not, and rather as if this were 1776 with the thirteen colonies fighting George the Third. The question is a good deal more complicated. I gather you're writing a book about this region.'

'I'm calling it Empire, trying to understand the why and wherefore of it.'

Sir Humphrey chuckled.

'As for ourselves we came as merchants but British trade faced a severe crisis in Bengal from native and French competition and from part of Asia. We would have been driven out had we not taken action. Of course once we had Bengal we had no choice but to expand. Great empires have always needed to control a fringe of surrounding states and that has meant wars. With Russia an aggressive power we've had to make our presence felt in Afghanistan, and Burma forced hostilities on us. They imposed a disgraceful and unjustifiable fine on our major trading company, the Bombay Burmah Trading Corporation which held the concession for extraction of teak. The British Resident there and the manager of the Irrawaddy Florilla Company, a fine Scotsman, were treated with insolence and required to prostrate themselves in the reception hall before the Burmese throne. There are limits to patience, Mr Knox.'

In a reminiscent mood Sir Humphrey said the annexation of Upper Burma (which had completed the occupation) had been agreed after a leisurely breakfast on the Viceroy Lord Dufferin's verandah. Sir Mortimer Durand's diary noted it had been a Sunday in October 1885 with 'a sweet sunny breeze and the hum of bees round us'. The decision was quickly made as the War

Department in Calcutta had had a plan for the invasion of Upper Burma ready for ten years. Once it was over Sir Mortimer noted: 'I could not but feel the pride of the power of the sword.'

'Empires are not built in sanitized conditions, Mr Knox,' he said with a thin smile, 'it took time to overcome Burmese resistance but British energy and justice succeeded in establishing peace where there had been lawlessness for centuries.'

What, indeed, is out of bounds or beyond the pale for a deed that should never have been done, thought Edgar and he warned himself against pursuing that line of questioning. Nor did he quote Marco Polo's finding that Burmese temples were 'covered with gold a full finger thick'.

'Earlier you mentioned Afghanistan, Sir Humphrey. That would be why India's northwest frontier is a sensitive area for you.'

And it would remain so. If the day ever came that the British thought fit to lay aside their responsibility for India, the frontier must be secured in reliable hands, friendly to us, Sir Humphrey assured him. He had been Governor of the Frontier Province during the Salt stir in 1930. He was unlikely to forget Gandhi's dangerous influence there.

'The Pathans are men who kill before they think. Some of those Frontier tribes are barbarian nomads. For them to become non-violent and revel in martyrdom, and for their leader to be known as the Frontier Gandhi, was so uncharacteristic as to be macabre. And when men of the Garhwal Rifles refused to fire on their "unarmed brothers" as they put it, we might have had a full-fledged mutiny on our hands. We were faced with an extraordinary situation up there. Had to take serious note. Can't risk trouble on the frontier.'

'There wasn't much about it in our press. It's hard to come by material on India,' said Edgar.

'I should have thought there's an abundance of material. Kipling. Forster. Orwell.'

Edgar agreed there was that. He thanked Sir Humphrey for being so generous with his time.

'With your credentials we could scarcely do less,' the Governor replied cordially. 'The car will take you to your next appointment. It should be interesting. I gather the war has put the Asiatic or Asian conference he was planning into abeyance. Asiatic. Asian. Whatever the word, what does it signify? What is the binding factor? Not race obviously, nor culture, nor religion. What then?'

They've all been buggered, Edgar silently supplied.

In the hall where the ADC hovered to see him into the waiting Government House car, the Governor pursued his thesis.

'Western civilization on the other hand is a distinct biological and cultural unit so "Europe" has a meaning within those terms.'

Edgar shook hands, repeated his sincere thanks and got into the car. He loosened his tie and sat back reflecting on the pleasure it always was to hear high British officialdom articulate. Impeccable diction carried its own unassailable authority. If Sir Humphrey Hartley had said western civilization is a condition others enter when their time is ripe, the proposition would have been as sacramentally received as Louis Fourteenth's nightgown at Versailles. The alchemy of diction! It could bestow consequence on Jemima Puddleduck and make a boy scout of Adolf Hitler. Hitler's self-confessed ambition was to retire to the hills of Berchtesgaden and paint, the British ambassador had said in Berlin one week before war broke out. Too bad there had been no one in the gathering to guffaw a ribald Cockney 'Go'orn!'

A few nights later he was having dinner in the gloomy dining room of the Imperial Hotel in Delhi. Formally attired couples, some few Indian among them, foxtrotted a sedate six inches apart to a doleful Dorothy Lamour love song from the movie *Moon Over Burma*. It would have looked like sleep-walking even if jitterbugs weren't doing acrobatics on dance floors at home. *They say that you-ooo are the wonderful goddess of love,* moaned the singer. Edgar could almost hear his great uncle Desmond — a man given to bellowing his approval and snorting his disgust — react to the Imperial with 'Call this *dancing?* Looks like dead meat out cold.'

Dead meat out cold aptly fitted Sir Humphrey Hartley's postwar scenario. Edgar knew better. The war had ended Pax Britannica. Wherever he had been in Asia he had had insistent warnings of change. What Edgar knew of Asia's mind convinced him no Japanese-occupied territory would return docilely to its former imperial master after the war. The signs were there and the Governor had seen them but maybe a spinning wheel and the Sermon on the Mount looked like containable trouble, as did the odd seditious scoundrel. He went over his meeting in Akbarabad with the trouble maker the Governor had described.

Edgar walked into a bare anteroom. A man about his own age and height came quickly down the stairs. His hands took both of Edgar's in a lingering clasp more like an embrace and Edgar, long wandering, was home. He knew this was the discovery he had journeyed miles to make. Such a complete reaction seldom overwhelms an experienced observer at first sight. It is wise to heed it when it does. He had the curious sensation of continuing, not starting, a conversation. This was followed by shock. He had — of course — seen this man before — that unusual bronze hair and light eyes — among the battered casualties in the temporary hospital near Dandi beach.

Voices from the next room filtered through to him from the meeting about to begin, reminding him he was here to collect what is known as news. He went in with his host, leaving his shoes at the door, and took his place on one of the cushions on the floor sheet. Long open windows let in the afternoon light. He saw Chinese scrolls, chairs and sofas upholstered in fading Chinese brocade, and women among the men, all in the same coarse white handspun. Where he came from women did not figure in such numbers, if at all, in decision-making, and in Europe the Führer had locked, barred and bedded them down to breed for the Fatherland. Hoping his legs would last out he listened carefully to the proceedings, understanding not a word. This had its uses. What he heard was a conversational tone and timbre, often forceful but lacking strident pitch. The tension that marks meetings of this kind was missing. Strategies for the capture of power had a different rhythm. His host had told him they would be discussing the British Government's latest offer: independence for India after the war on condition that every British province and Indian prince's state would then have the right to declare its own independence if it so wished! Edgar's very entrails revolted. This merited *discussion?* On similar provocation Abraham Lincoln had gone to war.

Several people came up to him as they left the room to praise his book on Southeast Asia. One woman hoped he would inform the world about 'our struggle'. After seeing his colleagues off Nikhil led the way upstairs to his study, apologizing for the delay but a decision had had to be taken to convey to the party's national executive. A servant brought tea in glazed pink pottery. Made in Gwalior, Nikhil explained. The household did not buy British and since there was only British to buy, the house had been somewhat bare since the boycott.

Edgar had no desire to talk business. He wanted to sit there, sipping companionably, indulging in idle chitchat about books, music, the Chinese art downstairs and what's your favourite dessert. Making an effort he asked about the aborted Asian conference.

'Sir Humphrey Hartley says it has a subversive sound.'

'So it has,' laughed Nikhil, 'we are, after all, pledged to subversion. I had in mind an exchange of ideas with other national movements and a script of some sort to deal with common problems once we're in charge of our own affairs.'

'What sort?' asked Edgar.

'For a new world order, of course,' said Nikhil, mildly surprised at the question.

'Don't you ever miss a plain ordinary life?'

'I long for it,' said Nikhil fervently. 'What is it like? Tell me, I've quite forgotten.'

'During my last jail term,' he continued, 'I asked for pen and paper and was allowed it. When it came I was so overcome I put the stack of paper on the window ledge of my cell and my eyes must have wandered to it every hour. I sat on my iron bed a couple of feet from the window and my fancy made spiralling white flowers of it, or a plant whose powdered petals were stirred into wine to perfume it in Sanskrit times. When the jailer came round a few days later and saw it lying there unopened he thought it was because I had no table to write on, which I hadn't noticed! He said he was authorized to provide items of this kind. So finally I began to write. I must be an advanced case of yearning.'

There being no clock in the room to interrupt a train of thought, Edgar had no sense of time passing and no professional urge to fill the minutes.

'The last time I went to the cinema,' said Nikhil, a while later, 'the scene that affected me powerfully showed two people gently gossiping over a cup of tea! Our deepest longings are for such very ordinary things.'

Edgar asked about the Chinese furnishings downstairs.

'Father's. He opted out of the environment the times had thrust on him. "There's enough around us of British manufacture," he used to say, "including ourselves". I'm glad you're here at last, Edgar. We need your ideas.'

'They're at your disposal,' said Edgar, 'for what they're worth.'

'As I wrote in the letter I sent you to Bombay before my arrest, Asia hasn't the West's long experience in protecting its interests, and we're in no position to at the moment. But we need to work out a way of keeping control of our own resources when the time comes.'

Nikhil pointed to the wall map over his shoulder and Edgar got up to take a look. Let independence come, he wanted to say, and the rest will take care of itself. It was an observation that had nothing much to do with who stayed in charge of resources as he looked across the map.

'We would want trade to be a bargain that benefits both sides,' Nikhil was saying, 'and an ancient and honourable profession should not need guns to protect it, should it?'

'Since when?' demanded Edgar. 'These here are sacred arrangements known as free trade which need control of the world's oceans and waterways to carry that trade. You wouldn't be wanting to tamper with them, would you?'

'Wouldn't you, if you were me?'

I *am* you, spoke an idiotic prompting in Edgar, why else do you think I am here?

'Asia will have a better chance with a collective approach,' reasoned Nikhil.

An Asian blueprint for an era yet to come. It was a proposition amounting, at this point, to a castle in the air. Since university Edgar's mind had not grappled with the abstract, and journalism did not provide reckless freewheeling opportunities for crystal-gazing. He was attracted and stimulated.

'I'll tell you what an American President did for strategy,' he said on an impulse. 'He told Europe to bugger off and cordoned off his hemisphere.'

'That was all? I haven't read American history. What happened then?'

'Consternation. Uproar. The wrath of Metternich. The mighty Metternich thundered at the temerity of "these United States" which had astonished Europe by another act of revolt. He swore Europe would frustrate their criminal plans.'

'And did Europe do so?'

'I can't remember the follow-up,' admitted Edgar, 'but it couldn't have mattered much. The Monroe Doctrine stays sacrosanct. Its principles were approved by a nearly unanimous vote in both Houses of Congress a couple of years ago in the summer of 1940.'

'Remarkable. What do you say to an Asia Doctrine on somewhat the same lines?'

Edgar's imagination pulled up sharp at the images this conjured, the future Metternichs who would have no truck with continental insolence and intransigence, who would cause tempests to arise where they willed and strike down whom they willed with distant lightning. Or disdaining drama, they would simply re-order the universe one Sunday morning in a sweet sunny breeze on a hum of bees. But for now, and some time to come, Edgar reasoned there would be no such Doctrine. It would only be a thought in the mind of Asia, and there was no law yet against dangerous thoughts. Penalties there were from whipping to death, for acts listed as sabotage under the wartime code. He didn't have to say any of this aloud and Nikhil understood what had not been said. They understood each other like partners in crime getting ready to nail down a crate of explosives and parcel it in festive Christmas wrapping to wait for Christmas.

Nikhil called Nurullah in, the man Edgar had met in Bombay and asked him to take notes while they charted a course for the region. Edgar provided names and addresses and promised to keep as closely in touch as the war allowed.

Nurullah had read Edgar Knox after meeting him in Bombay. His spoken language matched his written word. Its tongues of flame were well suited to the fires of freedom he was stoking, this witness whose terrifying prophecies about Europe had come true. His was no vague visionary Asian blueprint. It bore Edgar Knox's practical stamp. Bhai had done well to seek his advice and to add his own battle-hardened experience to it. Nurullah who had no shorthand could hardly keep up with the pace of their dialogue until it suddenly shifted into another key and was gone, into a shimmering other substance that a trick of light could lift and float as it had the massive medieval fortress above its hilltop. They had forgotten he was there. They were opening new highways into Afghanistan and further north, reopening long forsaken waterways linking India and Burma with Laos, Cambodia, Thailand and Vietnam. They were reviving lost harmonies. Inspired by each other they were looking back from some

far distant future on the Age known as European when
civilizations dating from antiquity who between them had
invented most things from glass and gunpowder to the
zero, had been labelled Europe's 'possessions', and Europe's
seizure of these lands and impoverishment of their people
had been called 'the mission of Christendom'. Once upon
a time this had been the natural order of things! The
future fantasy of it bound them in high humour. Theirs
was the intoxicated laughter of reincarnated lovers met
once again in India Beata.

Nurullah felt his hands and feet grow cold. It was the
glow of passion in their talk. The most reckless adventurers
so far had only set out to change the world's shape from
flat to round, not to rock its foundations. More tragedy
had been wrought by unbridled hopes and aspirations
than by anything else on earth. In the end, earth's stunted
ruins remained. Only a Persian poet, already safely dead,
could get away with declaiming,

> Ah, Love! could thou and I with Fate conspire
> To grasp this sorry Scheme of Things entire,
> Would not we shatter it to bits — and then
> Re-mould it nearer to the Heart's Desire!

Winter's early dusk was in the room when Bhai started
talking about Shān. With the future so uncertain, both the
country's and his own, he wished he could be sure at least
of Shān's. He would have liked to send her to university
abroad, to breathe the air of a free country, but England
was under bombardment and he had no contacts anywhere
else in the West.

'Can you still say that?' Edgar accused, and asked Bhai to leave the arrangements for her education to him.

As they said goodbye downstairs he warned, 'You will be careful, won't you, Nikhil? You said you couldn't count on civil liberties in wartime.'

'Or in peacetime either if one stepped outside the limits of His Majesty's loyal opposition.'

'Then be extra careful.'

'And you?'

Why me? I'm free to come and go as I please, figured Edgar that day. Their handclasp was the last thing he remembered. In the car he raised a hand in sombre farewell to the figure in white. The livery of freedom, Gandhi had called it. The devil's own choice of colour. Muddied easily. Bloodied easily. Great patches of blood came back to Edgar along with the 1930 refrain:

With dear old Gandhi
We'll all march to Dandi
And break all the salt laws
That a white man ever made.

Hour after hour they had borne the consequences of that march. No marcher had raised an arm in self-defence to ward off a blinding blow as he was viciously, methodically beaten to the ground. Column after column had walked steadily forward to crumple in blood-sodden heaps on the sands at Dandi. It was the no-holds-barred deadly treatment reserved for the Movement's rank and file, stripped of the pretence of legality they used in dealing with its leaders.

Seven

Nurullah would never forget the fiendish heat of 1942. The very sun rose scarlet and twisted branchloads of red dhak blossom shouted Southeast Asia's new imperial colours as Japan, star pupil of Europe, advanced with deadly aim. Trains were bringing fleeing migrant workers home from Calcutta and Jamshedpur. Their stories of famine and panic left a stench of rotting carcasses on the air. In the open, where Nurullah slept, a burnt-out firmament drove its scorching black rays through his mosquito net, making dry crackling of his freshly dampened sheets.

Army trucks full of British and American soldiers rumbled through the Civil Lines. Uniformed men straddled the chairs at Framjee and Son's newly opened ice cream parlour adjoining the liquor shop and bought up evening shows at the Picture Palace. The wooden floor of the skating rink groaned with them. At the European Club they danced to the music of two wars with women of their kind and, this being wartime, making do with those who passed muster, Lilibet among them. Lilibet had met a sergeant at Ahmed Gents and Ladies Tailor. He had been trying to tell Ahmed what he wanted done about his torn khaki satchel. She was translating for him in her carefully mispronounced Hindustani when Nurullah came to fetch her. The sergeant's lively glance on her face, down past her boyish figure to her ankles in their preposterous shoes, was forming some satisfying judgement of his own.

The effort of summoning his self-control put Nurullah into a seething, barely suppressed fury that Lilibet did not or pretended not to notice, either then or later when she was dancing the Beer Barrell Polka and other war dances with Sergeant Ronnie Mason at the European Club. Her stories of evenings at the Club slipped from her thrilled I to a restrained casual we in the telling, but under the casualness she was possessed of a ruthless new stature that took its own presence as sovereign and expected others to do the same. The Huls and Cols rejoiced in her miraculous good fortune. It was remarkable how swiftly Nurullah ceased to be. His logic told him hard facts could not be as easily discarded as he had been. There was Lilibet's odd face, her squeals of excitement, her prickly elbows and knuckles digging into him in fright at the cinema. Lilibet was all sharp corners, by far not the voluptuous doll of wartime entertainment. She would need comfort when she was as humiliatingly abandoned by the sergeant after he got his marching orders. How he himself would then respond he could not foretell. He only knew his dreams were of deserts from which the seasons had been expelled and the air had lost its power to carry sound. A stranger walked through them in a rage that tore the living heart to pieces and in an extremity of dream suffering cried out on bended knees for the merest touch of a hand upon his face.

He took to walking in the fields behind the house as a discipline, extended his walks through a goatherds' village beyond the fields and further on until the rains came leaving the soil too soggy underfoot for the extra uninhabited stretch. Then came August, recalling him abruptly to his life before Lilibet. Bhai's party held a meeting in Bombay. Done with appeals and offers it resolved to quit India of the British. Before the news was out, its leaders had been arrested and taken in the night to a secret destination 'somewhere in India'. Bhai and others at the meeting disappeared into hiding to escape arrest. Nurullah's first fearful reaction — *what do people like him know about hiding?* — became calmer as he thought about it. People learn what they have to. And he had enough cause for anxiety in Akbarabad when students took to the streets. Class attendance was so lean that the Vice Chancellor closed the university for a week.

It had been closed for two days when a policeman came to the house at first light to take Nurullah to Government House where three students had got past the sentries during the night. The great empty palace was locked and they had not broken in. That, Nurullah suspected, had never been their intention. They had climbed to the roof, burned the Union Jack and been bayoneted into the hollyhocks. One of them had a note in his pocket from Nurullah referring to a rehearsal for a play. It was his sickening task to identify their Shakespeare and Shelley-loving corpses.

Gorge rose in him. He drove it down his gullet to keep it from erupting wrenchingly into the hollyhocks and turned his back, unable to bear the sight of staring eyes and rigid open jaws that no one had thought to close. They had died of English literature, lines he had fed them, as surely as they had of bayonets. He had sent them to their horrifying deaths, these three who had been gifts from a teacher's gods, to whom he had directed the poet's impassioned call above the heads of the plodders and swatters. He knew the lines they had died of:

Shake your chains to earth like dew
Which in sleep had fallen on you
Ye are many — they are few

A lesson he had taught them had been too well learned. Nurullah gave the police their names and the names of their parents in neighbouring towns. He claimed responsibility for the bodies until they were collected. Having done so he took practical note of the fact that they would not need coffins. These bodies would require cremation. At home in the dispensary he ordered blocks of ice to lay over and under them and kept the fans going full blast. Dr Bihari came to look at them. He bent over the grimacing darkening corpses, straightened, and his lips moved in some muttered incantation Nurullah hardly heard. All his energies locked fiercely into preventing further putrefaction, he did not take in the doctor's presence even when he pressed Nurullah's hand and gripped and shook his elbow as though testing a reflex. When he had gone Nurullah sent word to Ammaji for Ganga-jal. Uncovering the faces of the dead he dripped the holy water on their foreheads. He did not know their prayers for the dead. Khurram looked up at him from the floor he was wiping before replacing a bucketful of melted ice with an empty one and spoke urgently. Something about taking over the vigil. Nurullah, unwashed, unslept, and tearless, kept ordering and administering ice until two of the rigid corpses were claimed for cremation by sunset and the third the following day, and his own numb ritual condolences were conveyed.

It was days before he learned that he alone was not responsible for their deaths. The Bombay arrests had unloosed revolt across the province. Two of his students had been killed in police firing on the streets. From Akbarabad to Ballia mobs had torn down telegraph poles and set fire to railroad stations. Kisans had removed fishplates from rails to use as ploughshares and an army supply train had been looted while he kept his sightless sleepless vigil in the dispensary. In Ballia, a crowd had surrounded the jail and released prisoners, marched to the district headquarters and declared the district independent. Fools rush in, no matter that uprisings were being brutally militarily aborted. In Ballia too, revolt ended bloodily when the army moved in.

He was in the goatherds' village sitting on a charpai with Murli, the old headman, when they saw an army patrol in the distance, approaching from the wasteland on the other side. What did they want, Murli demanded of Nurullah. A patrol doing the rounds it looked like, he said, the army was everywhere. Murli put down his hookah and peered through the dusk at the approaching column. If it be recruits they're after for their war, they won't find them here, he promised. Getting up he fetched his horn and began blowing on it to sound an alert. The patrol which would have gone past changed direction and tramped straight toward them. The captain, an Angrez, strode up and ordered the old man to stop but Murli kept blowing as villagers came running. Nurullah's chest contracted in ghastly anticipation of horror foretold. The captain put his revolver to Murli's head. Blood and brains flew, sprayed Nurullah and splattered the ground. A glutinous shred hit Nurullah's cheek and stuck. The patrol closed in to beat the dying man to death with their rifle butts and screaming madness broke loose as the villagers fought their way through the assaulting rifles to drag the body out.

ʃ

'Such happy news,' Ammaji was saying to old Zenobia Framjee.

It could not be about Bhai, Nurullah knew. To their relief he remained well hidden.

'Lily is getting married. Come, Nurullah, she has brought us invitations.'

It was then he saw Lilibet. The window behind her was turning sunset pink and transforming her in its brief extraordinary light. There were sights he would never be rid of. Bodies bayoneted into flowers. Half of a shattered human head at his feet, its thick dark human blood and brains upon him. Such sights were everlastingly branded on soul and body. Nothing whatever could be done to erase them at any future time. The face before him now was one of these. It told him she was not fickle, not unfeeling. She had passed into her hankering and was gone. She gave Ammaji a smacking kiss of joy and begged her to come to the wedding.

'*You* will, won't you?' Her eyes beseeched Nurullah, setting him apart, relying on him to rise above the devastation that seemed to have ground itself into his features. The shaky appeal, the quiver of her lips told him she was not devoid of emotion or of its memory herself. She looked as if she was going to cry. The same appeal showing the same earnest concern a lifetime ago had been *You'll must come, you'll are looking so mopey, men.* Its transformation into a wedding invitation was a measure of the distance she had travelled. So, too had he. Every angle of his own face was now at his command, learned from the many mirrors in his room.

Ten days later he sat in St. James Church watching Lilibet make her vows to her sergeant, with Shān beside him representing the family. It was one more act he would never in sanity have chosen to do, use knives and forks to lift food to mouth, immerse his body in a tub, witness barbaric murder in cold blood and be powerless to bear witness against it. And now this. He answered Shān's whispered queries about the service. He rested his glance above it himself, upon the stained glass angels and saints of the church he had cycled past so often in that other life. It's lucky for her the sergeant Lily's marrying is British, Zenobia Framjee had remarked. She had heard the American army had stricter requirements concerning evidence of whiteness.

∽

Eknath had heard the Allied forces were recruiting in the region to train men in guerilla tactics for the border.

'Only armed rebellion can turn the tide for us now and we can turn this guerilla training to our own advantage,' he said.

Eknath was an admirer of the patriot who had escaped the British authorities and flown out of India to seek German and Japanese help against the British to raise an Indian army abroad. Eknath said Robin-da must arrange for him to meet Bhai as soon as there was word of his return. Bhai only had to say so and recruitment could get going.

They had heard from Bhai that he had been close to the Burma border when the military had cornered grain supplies and shipped them out, confiscated cattle and imposed collective fines as reprisal for revolt. Soldiers were now the law and their orders were to shoot when in doubt. A market crowd taken for a rebel mob had been gunned down and the survivors marched fourteen miles to the nearest police station with their arms roped to their sides to be interrogated, fined or shot. He himself was safe in his disguise and being of what use he could to villagers who were fighting for their grain, their cattle and their lives. But how long, thought Nurullah, was a stranger to subterfuge safe in any disguise? Even children knew more about conspiracy. *We don't work in the dark, Nurullah, we have nothing to hide.*

Two months later Nurullah had to admit he would not have known the ash-smeared sadhu in his soiled orange robe, looking years older than Bhai, who joined him, Eknath and Robin-da in the backroom of Framjee and Son which Nusli used as a godown for storing crates and cartons of army rum and whisky. Robin-da embraced him emotionally, ignoring the train soot and dirt on him. The windowless room was rank with the sweat of their bodies and they strained to see each others' faces under the single dim bulb. A flimsy network of cobwebs attached to the ceiling fan revolved slowly with it, barely stirring the air. Any faster and its creak would have been heard in the shop, a chance they could not take although Nusli had closed shop for the day. There was no time to waste and Eknath briefly explained the need for recruitment to arms which Zaheer Sahib and some others had already approved. Trained recruits would join the armed camp they had set up in the jungle on the Indo-Nepal border.

'They're counting on you to give the signal, Bhai.'

'*I?*'

The baffled whispered word, his only response to Eknath's terse message, had a peculiar force.

Robin-da interposed with unusual reluctance.

'It is a possibility you should consider, Nikhil. Those who are out of jail must move in some direction. You galvanized the Ganga for your No Tax campaign. You made Manchuria, Abyssinia, Czechoslovakia, Spain causes for people who had never heard of them. If you agree, you can convince this territory to volunteer for training in arms.'

'I'm the wrong man,' said Bhai shortly, 'I've been delivering another message too long.'

Robin-da leaned forward and put a hand on Bhai's knee.

'We have all been delivering the same message, Nikhil. It may be time to change it. You taught the kisans of this province all they know of revolt. Turn your influence to advantage now.'

They could not see Bhai's face clearly but he sat in the posture of exhaustion, his hands hanging loose between his knees, as if he would have liked nothing better than to lay his weary head down somewhere and sleep. But there was no trace of this in his sharp rejoinder.

'*Teach. Grant. Hand out.* What has imperialism's vocabulary to do with us? I taught them nothing. I happened to speak their minds. You are using the language of those who tell us we are their creation. From a formless void they created us a nation and trained us like good dogs to bark and beg for freedom. Democracy, they tell us, is Athenian. Love is Christian. Freedom is a bargain. We must go on passing tests till we are Greek enough to merit it. Now *you* are telling me we must turn our backs on the Movement that galvanized us in the first place and order our people to resort to violent struggle.'

This made Eknath speak up, his eyes blazing.

'They have left us no alternative, Bhai. But we should have taken up arms long ago. Only Japan in all Asia learned Europe's lesson that military power comes first.'

'And now puts Asia on the rack as Europe has done,' retorted Bhai in growing anger, 'with invasion, occupation, empire. Japan will modernize as Europe did, by bleeding Asia. We have been watching Japan's Europeanization since their slaughter in Manchuria.'

'Nikhil,' Robin-da reminded him, 'if the Government had accepted our offer of partnership in the war, it would have meant general mobilization.'

'But they threw our offer in the gutter,' said Bhai bitterly. 'Now, even as they flee Asia, leaving it to the Japanese, their evacuation arrangements are For Europeans Only. Our people are straggling out of Burma in their thousands, dying of hunger, sickness and wounds. It's a six-hundred mile march through jungle and hills. Those who survive it are in desperate need of food, help, shelter when they reach the frontier. We are doing what we can there. I have to go back. The pass that Europe has brought us to now, Europe must resolve.'

Eknath's question was unanswered.

'As to your question, Eknath, let military might deal with military might. What they brought on, let them bring to an end. This is no time for amateurs to enter the game.'

Robin-da nodded, wiping the sweat streaking down his nose and the tears from his eyes. He reached both hands out to Bhai who took them.

'Besides,' confessed Bhai with a small apologetic smile, 'there's such a thing as habit, twenty-one years of it. I find it hard to break. Killing needs a frame of mind I don't have any more.'

He spoke as if apologizing for a fault he couldn't help. Not even Europe's callous indifference to Asia's fate could return him to the world's old hatreds and its violent ways.

'I'm sorry,' he said gently to them all.

He and Robin-da both got up and embraced. Robin-da left in tears. Someone had to go first. Eknath left a few minutes later, unusually becalmed.

'Well, Nurullah, who goes next?'

'You, Bhai. I must lock up afterwards.' Nurullah had a sudden dread of Bhai's permanent disappearance into the night and added foolishly, 'you will be careful, won't you?'

Bhai brushed a flying insect from his face. He pointed to his mendicant's robe, the grey, matted hair that had no hint of tell-tale bronze, and his two-month stubbly growth of beard.

'You don't trust my disguise then?' and he laughed as freely as caution would allow. 'Tell me the truth, would you know me if you saw me on the road?'

He slapped the insect from his face again, the curiously innocent face of an amateur at subterfuge, wiped of fatigue by its radiant smile. Nurullah was afraid to speak for fear of diverting precious time to unimportant matters. He listened while Bhai went over the plans he had made with Edgar Knox for Shān's education in America and stood up when Bhai did. His heart was heavy, his legs felt unsteady. There was much he wanted to say.

'Bhai, there's something I've been wanting to say —'

'I have to go now but we'll find time when I come back.'

Clasped to each other under the flurrying cobwebs neither said another word. Nurullah wept unrestrainedly, was comforted by the arms around him and then tenderly unclasped. He opened his eyes to find his brother gone. His absence filled the stale darkness as overpoweringly as his presence had. Nurullah heard Nina's pathetic parasitic bleat, 'Where's Bhai?' His own was no less craven for not being uttered. A wandering giddiness seized him and he sat down on a crate of rum.

Episodes of the kisan rally, at railway stations, at the river bank, and other venues of the war without violence, hovered over him tenacious as the rotating cobwebs on the fan until it seemed to him these had not been just chance reversals of normal human behaviour but a new code of behaviour. *Behold I bring you glad tidings of great joy,* as in Shãn's convent Bible, tidings that would spread and survive as the spider's abdominal ooze becomes the tough gossamer gauze combed out to lie over fields through wind and calm. They would live, those uncanny images of kisans hoisting themselves up on trains by the handrails, deaf to the guns jittering behind them, the goatherds risking death to drag out a body already dead.

He made sure the crates were back in their places, the fan and light switched off. He opened the outer door of the godown, locked it behind him and hid the key where Nusli had told him to before taking a circuitous unpatrolled route home, moving stealthily through the night-lit streets of his own city in his own country like a skulking criminal instead of a citizen on his way home.

In December he went to the railway station to collect a parcel Nina had sent for her mother from Bombay. A train had come in and he watched travellers disembark and stream past the police patrolling the platform as he had done before, scanning the crowd on the slim chance that there might be a message carrier from Bhai but careful to give no sign of recognition or make contact. The tattered bearded fakir carrying a staff and a lota, one more face in the crowd, would have gone past him had he not sighted Nurullah, had his face — amateur at subterfuge, unversed in deceit — not lit up spontaneously at Nurullah's presence on the platform, and had he not in sheer unguarded delight taken a step toward him. Nurullah turned to stone as the fakir was brusquely waylaid, handcuffed and marched away.

In sleep he saw the deed repeated. Every night Bhai stepped off the train and came up the platform. Night after night he was robbed of his safe impenetrable disguise and betrayed by his glad acknowledgement of Nurullah. Adorned and embellished, the scene re-rose afresh each night, intolerably bright, driving hot needles into Nurullah's eyes. He would sit up wild with pain and press his eyelids to relieve their torture only to see Bhai again behind his closed eyes, resplendent and all shining in his rags, saying, Dry your tears, Nurullah. Rejoice for you have come of age! At last you know how we are all joined, why the arm of one is the leg of another and every history is the history of us all. This is the love that makes us one in joy and keeps us shackled to each other's pain.

ᔪ

The chapel was a part of the convent he had never seen but he knew it was in the same building as the junior classrooms. The door was open so presumably they did not mind if one went in to sit on a bench at the back for a while. He drooped his head thankfully like a weight abandoned, sank his chin to his chest and sat in soporific silence, cut off from associations past and present. The only sounds from the verandah were the lowered voices of passing nuns and the swish of their habits. In here were incense, idols, candles, flowers, the congregation of items that places of prayer see fit to surround themselves with, which produce the intensity of concentration known as prayer, in words that childhood training brings expeditiously to mind. The sun is setting and it is the hour for the day's fourth prayer. But in this foreign place it is a line of Shan's school prayer — *forgive us our trespasses* — that floats like a thread through memory. He doesn't know any more of it but he thinks he must be praying.

I don't know when we'll meet again, he prays, so hear me now. I did not plan my father's suffering, only his death. My part was swift. I was at the ghat before dawn on Makar Sankranti when he, like other worshippers was waist-deep in the river. His arms and eyes like theirs were raised skyward, facing east. In that trance they do not see the refuse around them or even paupers' half-cremated corpses moving sluggishly downriver, where a man squats on the bank and uses a forked branch to keep them from being washed ashore. Underwater they rot, and fish and turtle consume them as worms do Christian corpses underground, leaving no trace that here was a body. The river has crocodiles too, hunted for sport. I have heard a small child wailing maa-maa-maa and seen it is a crocodile's, not a human child, shot while sunning itself on the sand.

I know my father well from stable talk at home. His right hand has two middle fingers missing from a scythe accident in the field. Whether he or his father is my parent does not matter. The older is dead and the remaining one must die. I am strong enough at fourteen, though half his age, to overpower him by stealth in his trance, topple him forward head down in the water and hold him under till he expires. But when I push his body further out, the water moves tumultuously. A snout lifts out of the river. My father's body is caught by the waist in monstrous jaws and he is screaming to be saved. The reptile raises its long narrow head higher till I see the bony plate of armour on its neck. Its catch is too large to swallow whole and it thrashes about with huge twisting turning motions, breaking the body in two, tearing my father to pieces.

The worshippers and other villagers gather round. One holds shoe leather to my nose to revive me from my faint. They say crocodiles have taken bodies before. In the heat of the sun the reptiles lie on the sand like parched grey logs, the largest of them five times the size of man, and the maneaters among them give furious chase to their prey, killing with their powerful lashing tails. But there is no sun. It is not yet dawn.

I am not remanded to custody to await jail or hanging, but to a boarding school by my mentor before murmur becomes talk, to the study of English literature and love everlasting of the English tongue, and thereafter, years after, to you who took me in. Only you did not know the man you took in. No longer can I keep the truth from you.

He does not expect an answer to prayer and there is no answer. The Catholic version of the Divine Mother stands silent in her plaster draperies of blue. Her head tilts forward in humility. Her eyes are cast down. When the answer comes he should have realized long ago what it would be: We took you in, knowing. That this must be true Nurullah is now certain, knowing them as well as he does. Yet why had they done so? The forgotten thread of Shan's school prayer comes haltingly back: *That – we – may – learn – to – forgive – those – that – trespass – against – us.*

∿

Pete Ryder regrets the violent uprisings in 1942. They were a setback to non-violence.

'But a great step forward otherwise if we look at the effect they had on the Raj, which non-violence never did,' I assure him and I show him the Viceroy Lord Linlithgow's message to Churchill on 31 August 1942.

I am engaged here in meeting by far the most serious rebellion since 1857, the gravity and extent of which we have so far concealed from the world for reasons of military security. Mob violence remains rampant over large tracts of the countryside and I am by no means confident that we may not see in September a formidable attempt to renew this widespread sabotage of our war effort. The lives of Europeans in outlying places are in jeopardy.

Pete Ryder looks at me with old wise eyes.

'Maybe they concealed the gravity and extent of the non-violent rebellion, too, for reasons of security. Will we ever know? Why would they make a dangerous new weapon public knowledge?'

II

An Island Called America

'Necking still applied to action that took place above the neck; petting involved enthusiastic probing, short of intercourse, from the neck down ...'

'Society continued to accept the notion that young men would do all they could to encourage their dates towards intimacy, and it was up to the girl to say no.'

America 1941, Ross Gregory

When your heart goes bumpety-bump
It's love, love, love.

Popular song, 1940s

Eight

In her eleven years as translator of French and German manuscripts for Mr Jenner's family firm, Leda had come to be respected as an artist who worked on her own schedule. She and Mr Melville Jenner had a mutually accommodating relationship. He tactfully ignored her on judgements involving dollars and cents but he was in no doubt about her value to his business. Few people had her concentration. She had appeared in his office a girl not yet twenty with fine brown moleskin hair, fine pale skin and finely formed features, no one you would notice but for her air of permanent panic. It had never stopped reminding him of wildlife fleeing for cover. During her first year at Jenner's he had frequently found her at work during the lunch hour, her unwrapped uneaten sandwich reposing on a pile of manuscript pages beside her. He had insisted she take the afternoon off, spend it in Central Park. Once he had advised fish liver capsules.

Mr Jenner was a silver-haired Bostonian who cultivated a manner to match and Leda felt rested in his company. He was a graceful sight when he turned his revolving chair a quarter sideways, extended his elegant legs and held his tapering fingers tip to tip beneath his chin. In this ruminating posture he inhabited the timeless zone of the books he published. He specialized in journeys to the far unknown that were no better known at the end of the journey. One she had translated before the war narrated a Bavarian countess' progress through undulating vistas of desert accompanied by hawk-eyed hawk-nosed servants, camels, tents and cooking gear that materialized goat paprika and green almond mousse for moonlit repasts on the sands. At Leda's suggestion that the journey be more fact specific, Mr Jenner had demurred over his fingertips. The harsher sights, and indeed sites, need a softer lens, he had said. That aura of dream-like progress through a desert would dissolve at a heavier touch and would lose the special stamp of a Jenner book. Readers did not want to confuse *there* with *here*. The Map of the World facing his satin-wood desk admirably preserved the distinction. Early medieval Europe floated in unnamed seas surrounded by blank lands lettered Peopled by Monsters.

For the mood of romance, Mr Jenner maintained, a formality had to be preserved. And come to think of it, Leda, didn't that rule apply to our modern lives here as well? Europe's pastmasters at it had understood its worth. Verdi, for example, used to kiss his wife's hand even if he was taking leave of her for no more than an hour's stroll. Had it not been for the touch of Boston ice in Mr

Jenner's veins when it came to finance, and the hearty mid-western wife she couldn't imagine putting up with hand-kissing, Leda might well have concluded he was a man for whom the day does not end, it takes blue-grey flight.

His grandfather, Jeremiah Jenner, a ruggeder character to judge by his high colour and black-whiskered jowls, had established the printing and publishing works some sixty years after the first American clipper set sail from New England to the China coast in 1784. He had been so intrigued by the images it brought thronging to his mind that he had adopted it as his logo and made a name for himself with harrowing, harrowingly illustrated sagas of bygone land and ocean travels. The only one Leda had read had been a sea voyage recording the unspeakable trials and terrors of navigating an uncharted sea by the path of a star. Its awesome veracity included a fairy tale ending: the dungeon and starvation for the navigator, treasure for the king.

After Jeremiah's death and the firm's relocation from Boston to New York, the thirst for exploration and raw adventure had got watered down and the present Mr Jenner had recast the travel genre to specialize in allure. His infallible instinct told him this was the surefire prescription for our own day and age. Leda knew it was illogical of her to harp on realism when the lack of it had made Jenner's the sanctuary it had proved to be, enabling her, among other blessings, to shelter from English. For a year after cutting short her university career Leda had recoiled from the sound of English, whatever its accent or inflection. Her tongue had stumbled over it. English had been a mouthful of stones, the savage tongue of savages, made tolerable only by the presence beside it of the language she was translating.

Her problem once she settled into Jenner's was how to spend the time outside work in ways that would lead her as surely into some form of oblivion. She joined a cooking class she had seen advertised, conducted by a White Russian with courtly credentials. It proved ideally suited to Leda's requirement. In the calm of her cathedral-windowed kitchen Madame Ivanovna's introductory lesson called for an attitude of devotion as the ambience vital to the preparation of memorable food. She asked her class to consider what this could do for the humble egg. What it had done was inspire the great and only sauce, invented by the Order of St. Benedict founded in the year 530, whose monks had vowed to abstain from laughter and the natural appetites. Their cloistered dedication had created a succession of soul-melting flavours in their monasteries crowned by Benedictine, the supreme liqueur. Madame then proceeded prayerfully to Eggs Benedict.

In a simpler second lesson, she broke twelve eggs into an enormous pottery bowl. Patiently whipped to a foaming haze and folded into a pound of powdered walnuts they baked into a traditional Græco-Russian festival cake. A syrup of fresh lemons, confectioner's sugar and a light sprinkling of brandy had then to be concocted and drizzled drop by drop into it when it cooled.

Leda's new friend and neighbour in Greenwich Village, Rosa Mongini, who was a terrible cook and had hoped to improve her skills for the doting Mr Mongini, had given up and quit the course after Gateau Marie Louise. But Leda stayed on, learning to sauté oysters in fresh roasted butter, to disguise the potato with clotted cream and cognac and to fashion the myriad papery leaves of millefeuilles. To her Græco-Russian and French repertoire Madame Ivanovna added her own ingenious innovations, introducing her class to seaweed and saffron, juniper, stem ginger and coriander, infant lamb and aromatic broths.

The course banished anxiety from Leda's conscious mind. The foaming castles of Madame Ivanovna's egg yolks, the apricot and aniseed liqueurs, the oils of rare nuts and unidentifiable ambrosial ingredients of her creations removed them from any connection with food on earth to the stratosphere of what a diva and her lover might enjoy at midnight after a taxing Aïda. And not long after the course ended Leda had the good fortune to hear about a lecture series that served the same drugging purpose.

'The extra-natural force called astral light is said to be responsible for magic and thaumaturgy and is the agent for mystical experience,' spoke Dr Zoerner through the pitch dark, directing his pointer and his trim pointed beard to the bluish blur emanating from the skull on the coloured slide. His illustrated presentations on the new orientation that would now be required of human thought if it was to comprehend works of wonder and the phenomenon of miracles, released Leda from herself as effectively as the egg yolks and liqueurs.

'In the religion of ancient Egypt,' lectured Dr Zoerner, always in the half-dark, 'the heart is weighed in the Hall

of Osiris and if the soul is found worthy it is conducted
to the meadows of Paradise ...'

She could find nothing to replace the slumbrous peace
of the lectures but a visit to the Metropolitan Museum
one holiday proved unexpectedly soothing. After that she
kept in touch with the Metropolitan, moving idly through
rooms of bland blonde madonnas, flowery grasses and
sun-dappled water.

Coming downstairs one day she took a wrong turning
into a dim corridor lined with monolithic statuary, massive
sarcophagi and winged human-headed bulls. At its far end,
a flat-headed colossus crouched with its long stone arms
draped around its knees. Terror threatened to engulf and
paralyse Leda. She got through the corridor with her eyes
glued to the ground only to come out into a vast high
room of towering Pharoahs and their catfaced queens. She
never knew what effort of will propelled her through it
to arrive at last at the top of the Metropolitan's steps.
Taxis, buses and pedestrians moved reassuringly up and
down Fifth Avenue. Go home, voices counselled, as though
she had any other thought or destination in her head.
There are safe precise limits set by the skin-cages we live
within. Don't venture.

Later she had seen no need to give up her art education
which she was enjoying. Mentally marking the frontiers
on the room diagrams beyond which she must not stray,
she had continued her occasional visits.

With fewer manuscripts coming in since the war Leda
was using the time to learn Russian at the Berlitz School.
Her adaptability to yet another language came as no

surprise, nor the ease with which the glottal Slavic felt at home in her gullet. Edgar's Czech friend Milo's comings and goings gave her practice in both French and Russian. This time he was here from London for talks in Washington about American defence equipment being earmarked for the Czech and Polish armies in Russia and he had grumbled on the telephone in a voice that fitted his size about the strategists' catastrophic slowness to move on Europe's bloodily embattled eastern front.

'So what would you like to do this evening, sweet Leda?'

'Let's go to *Oklahoma*,' she suggested, knowing he would have no trouble getting tickets.

'A charming musical, I hear. Farm boys and girls leap through the air scattering the chickens and the ducks and sing upliftingly of wheat and corn in the best Soviet style. Forget these entertainments for children, Leda. They take a toll of the nerves. You need an evening out. Allow me.'

On his last trip he had taken her to the midnight-blue gold-curtained dining room of the Stork Club where they had eaten pheasant, the most expensive item on the menu at an exorbitant seven dollars fifty a serving. The ladies' room, too, was Never Land. The toilet seat was said to be sanitized and sterilized by violet ray attachments. The mirror light had given Leda the chalky face of Chen Yu lipstick ads. She had re-reddened her mouth, printed it on lavender tisssue and taken thankful leave of her reflection.

This time his choice was the Copacabana where they were ushered to a privileged table customarily reserved for him. Apparently he was a habitué. But so, he explained, was he at the Diamond Horseshoe and El Morocco. He relaxed in nightclubs. His mother had got him used to the cosy smoky dark, the rosy lights, the bow trailing off violin strings, when he was a small boy. Fashionable night life in Prague had been the perfect setting for his gay irresistible mother and the gallants who escorted her ....

'How many men at a time did your mother date?'

Milo shrugged his powerful shoulders.

'As the spirit moved her, sweet Leda. Two by two is sacred only here in these United States. A hangover from the Ark. In Czechoslovakia we were not so regimented. My father was a very busy man and a woman must have adorers. Now let us have the national drink,' he said and ordered lethal cocktails.

The floor show had a Latin singer whose volatile hips were swathed in layered ruffles. She had a pile of tropical fruit for a headdress. She joined them after her act minus the fruit. Lean, brown and lustrous at close quarters she kept throwing her head back in a lioness' laugh to match her leonine slenderness and her gilded terracotta skin, crying 'Oh that is droll!' at Milo's pedantic remarks. Her brown fingers absently stroked the pink puckered skin of Milo's right hand while her dark eyes regarded Leda with astonished pity. Then she forgot Leda and laughed herself into streaming tears at his stories of the hostesses he had suffered as a junior diplomat in Washington between the wars. Instead of introducing him as Third Secretary they had hailed him as Thomas C. Masaryk's uncle's second cousin's son, at the end of which scarlet embarrassment he hadn't known whether he was his own uncle or his mother's second cousin. When Czechoslovakia began to be overrun by brute force he had refused to indulge the American insistence on information, retreating into 'As matters stand, I do not know precisely who I am.' But this had only captivated hostesses and brought him still more invitations. Leda knew from Edgar that Milo's smashed fingers were the bequest of Sudetenlander Brown Shirts who had plundered and set fire to the houses of the Prague government's supporters in 1938, rounded up resisters at bayonet point and beaten them up. Milo himself never referred to the incident and a hostess who pressed for facts had been told with a dismissive wave of his mutilated hand that a nod here triggered a bullet there. 'I want you to meet this man, Senator,' he heard her say to her guest of honour, 'he surely is a living saint.'

Milo's and the lioness' knives sliced sharply into noisettes of lamb, leaving pools of pale pink grease in their plates. Leda's went slower.

'She's a dreamer, our Leda,' Milo told the lioness with the tenderness of a man whose patron saints, if he had had any, would have been ill-treated women and neglected children, 'she collects fairy tales. Myself, I do not care for the genre. I have spent too many years disentangling Czechoslovakia from fairy tale castles, aristocratic ancestors, chandeliered feasts and horse-drawn sleighs bearing aristocrats to the next chandeliered feast.'

It had been incredibly difficult, he said, getting hostesses to see a foreigner as an ordinary person who might be closer to horse than ancestor.

Leda bestirred herself to seem alive. It was the least she could do by way of return for love of Edgar and for Milo's loving munificence.

'I don't know why we Americans treat foreigners like freaks,' she mustered.

But the hilarious lioness and Milo were well into a joke she had missed while she was still surfacing from fierce plum brandy.

ʃ

She set about understanding abstract art, its dots and dashes, cubes and hexagons, entire canvases of curlicues. With no idea how to decipher its hieroglyphics she surveyed it from far back and close. She was alone in the roomful of abstractions squinting at what looked like spilled pink paint, except for the man on the circular seat in the middle of the room, when his stifled laugh made her swing round. He was greying-haired, immensely at his lounging ease and no longer able to control his mirth. He apologised for his rudeness and to make up for it invited her to join him for refreshment — his formal way of putting it — in the museum's caféteria. Over glasses of iced tea he said she had reminded him of a tourist he had seen in Mexico trying to samba. The lady believed she was achieving the authentic Latin touch by jerking her head like a marionette over her left, then her right shoulder with every backward kick.

'She looked a bit like you. Was it you?'

'Certainly not,' said Leda tartly, 'I've never even been to Mexico. And I was just trying to figure out those paintings.'

'The process need not be so acrobatic,' he assured her. 'You can survey art comfortably from a chair.'

His amused clinical detachment put her at her ease. So did the fact that he was an artist, a species she had never yet encountered and therefore could have hopes of. He lived, like herself, in the Village and they took the bus downtown together, getting off at Eighth Street where he had a studio at the end of Macdougall Alley. They crossed a raised ledge into a walled garden strewn with sculpture, walked up a paved path into a straw-matted, sparsely-furnished interior and out again to sit on stone stools with lemonade, talking until dark. Leda confessed the Pharoahs and their tombs had reduced her to craven terror. He said stone could do that. He knew an Inca staircase whose steps weighed a hundred pounds each. But why go far or far back for an example when there were street corners in New York where if one made the mistake of looking up, one's eyes collided with a mile of menacing architecture poised as if to strike.

Leda took to dropping in at his studio. She liked to sit and watch him folded into deep abstraction as he contemplated a slab of stone, while she worked on a translation. When she began modelling for him they were closeted for hours at a time within the priestlike discipline of his art. No newcomer to solitude herself she had never dreamed it could be shared. She slipped painlessly into his circle of friends whose assorted nationalities — French, Austrian, Chilean, Mexican and others — were the setting she would have chosen, but had never yet found for herself. It was a company the war had flung together, invigorating in its disregard of breed or border. These were people whose religion was line and mass and colour, whose curious untaintedness in this regard made the freedom of their talk a discourse between the civilized and the civilized. The fact that she spoke some of their languages and her acute ear picked up smatterings of others gave her a status of her own in their enchanted circle. She had never heard herself so uninhibitedly articulate in all her tongues. After a time she knew this was where she belonged and must stay.

Desmond called from Brookham — another planet — and groused goodnaturedly about how long it was since she had been home for a weekend.

∿

Desmond stood back to admire the wooden steps he had fitted to his back porch and dipped his brush in paint, mellow in anticipation of Leda's visit. Mellow, too, in his lobster count, ninety succulent beauties this season. He had distributed them among his friends and given a record number of lobster suppers. Same menu. Martinis. Lobster. Best food there was, seafood. Best brainfood, too, if Leda's aptitude for languages was any indication. Her high school French teacher had asked if Leda had any French blood. Desmond had guaranteed there was no French blood in his older brother's grandchildren whom he had brought up because their mother (his niece) had died at Leda's birth and their father in 1917, saving the Italians from the

Germans. He had boasted about her linguistic ability until she went to university down south and majored in French and German. It didn't seem natural for a born and bred New Englander. He didn't have any idea why she didn't go back to university after her first year but she joined a language school nearby. That was when he began to be plagued by nightmares in which Leda went crazy. It was what a traffic block of languages could do to a brain. Leda had assured him Europeans took several languages for granted. And there was no bigger mess than the one Europeans had made out of Europe, Desmond had wanted to say, and now were making it all over again.

He had to admit Leda was earning a living out of her languages. Edgar was making healthy money too but neither of his brother's grandchildren were like other people. Edgar roamed the world, restless as a drunken monkey. Leda, a spinster past thirty, looked like translating manuscripts and collecting fairy tales for the rest of her life. Edgar's smitten brand of politics got translated into Leda's fairy tales and vice versa. But Edgar was a man and would look after himself. It was Leda he worried about, fearing she would go manless to her grave. There was no man around her that he could see except the Czechoslovakian who was more absent than present. Desmond dropped his nagging remarks about her spinsterhood more out of habit than conviction, and as time passed, with the diminishing certitude of the court of the Virgin Queen. But hell, the court at least had known the feisty Virgin enjoyed a slap and a tickle on into her dotage, hired and fired her boyfriends, and had so many of 'em she could afford to behead the boys who barged in and caught her bald-headed without her wig or makeup. Hey, Leda, he would call over the noise of the lawn mower, why didn't you bring that Checko-slo-vakian frienda yours and Edgar's down again. Dammit, he would shake his handsome white head in utter perplexity, Leda's not getting any *fun* out of life, and he would fix his bewildered gaze on his ageing child, his sleeping spinster. Leda's manless status was acquiring, for him, the pedestal and propriety of Queen Victoria's endless widowhood instead of the sexy bawdy Virgin Queen he would have much preferred her to be.

Leda and Edgar had come here together before Edgar went abroad again on an assignment, and as usual he had called on Florence Burns, the old divorcée across the road, come home and carried on about her mysterious aura — aided and abetted by a devoutly attentive Leda. Desmond was plainly staggered.

'You talkin' about that antiquated Peter Pan? I don't know what you're going on about.'

'Of course, you don't Des,' Leda soothed, helping him to lay the table for supper on the porch.

Edgar said Florence Burns had told him she attributed her chiselled beauty to having been conceived in a hand-carved bed in Florence, Italy, and that was how she got her name. Why this ageless enchantress had decided to settle in this dull little suburb of Boston Edgar couldn't imagine but Desmond should rejoice he had Diane de Poitiers living just over the road and get to know her. Desmond rejected this out of hand.

'She's gone all quaint and English and planted a hedge nobody else in Brookham wants,' he said dourly. 'She could be dead by the time it's grown. She's got nothing better to do now that the war has grounded her and she can't go jaunting off to Europe.'

The brother and sister were paying him no attention. Edgar was toasting Florence Burnses left eyebrow and decreeing her descended from a rose that had bloomed in the Hanging Gardens of Babylon and been Nebuchadnezzar's favourite wife's favourite flower. Leda was inventing a diet of rose water, rose pudding and rose wine for the old gal.

When Leda came to Brookham this time they were invited to lunch by Florence Burns. If she wasn't settled in after all these years, she was never going to be, was Desmond's reaction as he and Leda walked in. There were flowers in the garden but she'd stuck a bunch of dried up brown twigs in a vase on the hall table. There was zero on the hall floor and just floor again, a mile of it, in the living room. The oriental rug was up on a wall. Her sort must need more than a few years and a platoon of unpackers and decorators to hang a picture. They hadn't advised her about a colour scheme either. There wasn't any. The drapes looked like smoke had drifted in and she'd hung it. Then he saw one bit of decoration if you could call it that, a wire contraption suspended from the ceiling with coloured doodads dangling from it, turning and unturning in the breeze.

'It must be bare for your taste, Mr Guthrie,' said Florence Burns, 'but I was in Japan once? I love their idea of leaving space empty. Besides I've got all the decoration I need out there.'

The living room which was at the back of the house instead of the front had a dense forest up against its glass wall, old gnarled trees whose roots must be buried man-deep, soaring young ones, wild plants madly throwing shoots. She'd be looking at snow-shrouded skeletons all winter but maybe the southern mansion she came from hadn't heard about snow. In a voice like fur being stroked and pleasurably stretching every syllable to make two she invited him and Leda to help themselves to a drink. He was dismayed to be told nobody else was coming. What in Hades could he talk about to a woman who had nothing in the room he could pick up and comment on easylike? Nothing outside it either, not even a view. It was blocked off by the messy forest, good timber going to waste. She'd lived pretty reclusively since moving here, she was saying, and since her good Ezra's death from pneumonia help had been hard to get.

'That butler of yours?'

'A noble soul.'

The drinks were on a wrought iron table at the forest end and paraded every thirst quencher you had heard of and then some but there were no two glasses alike. Leda's choice was long-stemmed, thin and crimson. Desmond picked up a bottle of Bourbon by the neck and thrust it in the direction of the matted branches and wild undergrowth. Aside from all that timber going to waste, he asked, did she realize they'd be icicled skeletons all winter?

'Indeed I do, Mr Guthrie. I can hardly wait. I haven't spent a winter here yet and I'm longing for that snowlight? Snow has highlights, did you know?'

Desmond didn't.

'Snow is so fascinating?' She turned to Leda, 'Did you see the Garbo movie about Napoleon? His army is retreating in all that snow? His soldiers are dying on that icy wasteland and then one of them stands himself eerily upright to salute as Napoleon comes by. I will never forget that scene.'

Desmond stared. 'A corpse does that?'

Mrs Burns already had her drink fizzing in a glass tube within hand's reach on the naked polished floor beside her low chair, and the floorlight was glancing off her fingernails. Desmond picked up and put down several glasses from the jumble before he found a squat heavy rectangular one his hand felt good around. He carried his drink cautiously across the slippery ice underfoot and sank like a stone — no other way to describe it — into the first piece of furniture he reached. How was he to know, he complained huffily to Leda afterward, that the goddam sofa seat practically scraped the floor or what in hell was in the stuffing? It clamped his backside like a trained octopus and when he tried to heave himself into a position of control the raised silver fanciwork of the upholstery bit his skin so viciously he let go and sank to the bottom again. There he had to stay listening to Florence Burnses mania for empty space until her back was turned and he could lever himself out of the undertow with an almighty heave by gripping the huge iron claw of a table leg near him. He was in control by the skin of his teeth when she turned around.

They went through sliding doors into a dining room opening onto a sunny terrace. Desmond said terraces around here were nice for sun-bathing.

'Oh I know it's all the fashion here in the north, Mr Guthrie, but I never did care to look like a baked Virginia ham.'

An overloaded tree had dumped its freight of blossom all over the flagstones. Its petals saturated the dining room with their heavy narcotic perfume. Desmond could have sworn Florence Burns had laid them out there on purpose to muddle her guests' palates and addle their brains. He, for one, had been in too much of a stupor to know what he was eating.

Leda, opposite her hostess at the round table, saw the silk shine of Florence Burns' fingernails, the striped silk wall behind her, and the rose and green Chinese plates upon it with exceptional clarity. At the centre of this subtly ordered harmony Leda saw a woman superbly in command.

∿

It must have been the Sunday after Leda left or the Sunday after that that Desmond's morning went to waste waiting for the weather to clear until it was too late to make ambitious outdoor plans. He took an amble past the church and on an impulse, walked in. It was chockablock but he spotted a pew with an empty seat and squeezed in. 'Ask and ye shall receive!' annouced the preacher ringingly. The authority behind the statement was impressive. No wonder the son of a gun was packing 'em in. He must've been talking out of his own successful experience. Desmond had heard preachers were hell-raisers who sent congregations home with their gizzards fried. He was pleasantly relieved. With no armrests for his elbows he was beginning to wish he hadn't come when a gloved hand on his left caught his eye. The glove was grey and the bold black stitches on it were evidently meant to show unlike the stitches he remembered his mother making that were not supposed to show on the other side. He lost track of the sermon trying to figure out why his mother's threaded needle had bothered to push through cloth to its other side, giving its pusher weak eyesight on the way, if it wasn't going to get the credit for arriving.

When the church emptied he came slap up against Florence Burns on the steps talking to the preacher. She was wearing a bell-shaped hat made out of birds' wings and pushing her Southern-belle syllables as far as they would go. Going down the steps with him she asked if he wouldn't mind the informal invitation and come back with her to lunch? And tell her more about his two wonderful grand-charges?

This time he had steered clear of the furniture after walking back with his drink and stayed standing. He couldn't remember much of what he said except he had no trouble saying it. He opened his mouth and talk came. He was fluent right through lunch. What made him dosey-do like a cowhand up the stairs and into her bedroom after lunch as if he owned the place he didn't know. She was there already as she had a right to be, in her own bed. The room was all cloud and vapour. What he could see of the sky through the big open window looked like jumbled sheeps' brains. Feeling devilish muscular he dived in beside her and started behaving like no man ever had, chimpanzees maybe. When he came to, the pink jewels around the face of her bedside clock were winking in a brighter light. It came on a soft breeze through clear blue window space. Far away across the bare shining floor lay a twisted heap he knew had to be his pants. His jacket sprawled halfway to his pants. His shirt hung on the back of a spindly-legged chair. It was bellying out in the breeze.

He had overslept but he wasn't hung over and he ordered himself to get the hell out of there before she woke, as soon as he could find his underpants. Groping around he located them neatly pressed into a little hollow between him and her. His undervest was on him. The high wide four-poster was more like a rolling prairie than a bed, designed to make the lighter partner roll down to the weightier partner if he so much as took a deep breath. He had to move with the stealth and cunning of a burglar to get out of it, inching his torso one buttock at a time off the mattress. He realized he had his socks on when he skidded getting to his pants. Out and away before he broke a leg became the most fervent short-term ambition of his life and he didn't care who saw him gallop across the road with a shoe in each hand.

He read the Angler till late that evening, listening to the thick hypnotic tick of the grandfather clock coming out of the dark beyond his green lampshade. It grated like a hoary invalid getting ready to hawk up spittle and delivered its gong accurately on the quarter hour. There was a voice in the old wreck yet. He thought about the Checko-slo-vakian for Leda and ways and means of avoiding Florence Burns. He needn't have worried about *her*. When he next met her in the drugstore buying something for bee sting she acted as if nothing had happened.

Could be it hadn't.

∿

Leda had warned Desmond he'd be coming to an artist's studio. She had forgotten to warn him about the raised door ledge. Desmond's toe knocked it. He lifted his other foot over it with exaggerated care, already frowning about just-exactly-what he was doing here, which was his usual attitude toward the unfamiliar, and picked his way stolidly past sculpture. Indoors he tossed his head in the direction of the latticed screen at the sound of bath water being uplugged behind it and its unmistakable gurgle down a drainpipe. Desmond had arrived too early, an eventuality Leda had not foreseen. The bather came out with a towel around his waist, asked Desmond's pardon for not being ready and extended his hard stonebreaker's hand in welcome. Desmond stepped back, aghast. He stood foursquare on the straw matting, shoulders humped, swaying his head from side to side like a bison that had blundered into a trap. The sight before him afflicted him with shortness of breath. Leda could see him struggling for it, only half comprehending what he saw, so profound was his disbelief, so violent his revulsion. In this studio where she had been reborn Desmond's swollen face and clenched fists flatly denied such a possibility, as though by refusing to acknowledge it he could undo what he as yet only scented on the wind. All about Desmond hung the sullen intimations of a savage storm. In other enraging, incomprehensible circumstances, had he been confronted by, say, a deformed or depraved white citizen Leda fancied, his revulsion would have been less physical, less animal. It drained Leda of all will and courage. She could not help Kamei who reappeared, faultlessly attired in cool crisp white. He turned to her for a clue as to how they should deal with this dangerous relative of hers and received none.

They took their drinks to the stone stools in the walled garden. Desmond was not sure, only hideously suspicious about why Leda had asked him here. An inner incredulity kept breaking out in sweat on his forehead, the copious sweat of illness. What held him in check was his doubt. Leda could see him wracking his brains for a reason for his presence and rejecting it fiercely. He was so much the cornered beast, assailed and goaded by tormentors, that it was impossible for them to be natural. Attempts at conversation broke down and jutted up between them like gravestones in a vandalized cemetery. Their planned announcement was never made. It would have been unthinkable to make it when he was desperate for an opposite reassurance.

They took Desmond to their favourite Italian restaurant in the neighbourhood where, as they said nothing about themselves, he must have concluded there was nothing to say. There among convivial diners, in the steamy redolence of olive oil, garlic and herbs, his tension visibly eased as he finally persuaded himself this *Jap* was no intimate of his Leda's. How could he be goddammit?

'Did you plan on making a career of sculpture?' he hazarded.

Kamei considered the question and answered it. He made not the smallest attempt to tailor his remarks to his audience. One does not water down the gospel. Leda had heard him discuss art with a friend's ten-year-old child with the same adult matter-of-factness, making no concession to age or capacity, and the child animatedly responding, but this was Desmond. She listened despairingly to Kamei expand on his approach to sculpture. She need not have. Now that Desmond did not remotely connect the two of them Kamei was just another village weirdie.

Desmond actually livened up. He was an outsider but the kind he had been before, spending an evening with Leda in her peculiar part of New York. He joked about not minding foreign flavours on a night out but it beat him how they could be anybody's daily diet. He didn't care for the taste of Chianti but it lifted his spirits. The heat of the restaurant gave him good reason to sweat. He was willing to try an Eyetalian dessert of fresh peaches in red wine. It was not a success, the wine rough, the peaches raw, but he had not expected it to be. Desmond was back to being himself. Life returned to what is known as normal.

Frighteningly little was said when they had seen Desmond to a taxi. Leda pleaded guilty. She had been prepared to deal with an intractable man, the human being with human quirks and prejudices she knew Desmond to be, not the dangerous beast he had suddenly become. People like Desmond needed time ...

Kamei cut her brutally short. 'Racists have time immemorial. There will always be a racist. You couldn't face up to one and there's a thundering herd behind him.'

Leda did not have to be told. It was a matter of history, a terror of memory. Therefore she had known better than to tackle it. She could not make Kamei understand it was him she was securing against disaster. It was her own temerity in asking Desmond here that appalled her. How had she dared? In a blinding dementing fear she thought she had discarded forever she stumbled out of Kamei's studio, to take refuge in illness at home, leaving his Leda a lump of unfinished clay swaddled in damp cloth. This, the only unforgivable aspect of her defection, had belittled the uncompromising artist in him. When she could summon the courage to get out of bed she went back to the studio, for an artistic project to be harmlessly completed.

The gate was hanging crookedly on loose hinges. Good Riddance Yellow Scum and varieties of abuse had been scratched ferociously into its green paint. The paving stones had been dug up and thrown around. They must have been used to smash the light bulbs and the window glass. Something more massive had reduced the one remaining sculpture to rubble. The studio's straw matting had been sheared to ragged strips, the bath screen's latticework had been knifed and rubbished with wads of crumpled paper that had been lamps of Kamei's design, all of it stamped on in the merry-making. They had partied here. Shards of broken glass mixed with bread crusts, the stink of cheese, rat droppings in scraps of putrefying ham, wine dregs gone rancid testified to drunken celebration.

The stone stools were intact. She sat down shaking uncontrollably. She could picture the herd, horned and shaggy. Their grotesque bison hooves pounded in her ears, obliterating everything in their path. When her head cleared she picked up a page of newspaper flapping against her legs and straightened it. An internment camp in Arizona. A duststorm whirling round its barracks had whipped the Stars and Stripes around its mast. New arrivals were lined up under the flag for army inspection. The caption read: 'Herd 'em up, pack 'em off. Let 'em be pinched, hungry and dead up against it.'

Rosina Mongini had looked in every day of Leda's relapse into fever after her last meeting with Kamei, bearing floury soup, cologne and news of Pearl Harbour and after. Mr Mongini was all for bringing Leda back to their apartment but Rosina could see Leda was immovable, immobile, not registering that America was at war. Rosina understood little of what exactly had made Leda so ill, but had felt in her bones that sooner or later it had been bound to come to this.

'Why don't you go and see him as soon as you feel better?' she had encouraged out of the kindness of her heart, because no practical plea would work in Leda's condition. 'You'll be able to sort it all out. And if he's gone away somewhere he will have left an address for sure.'

About that Rosina had been right. Here was his address.

∽

Florence Burns wrote to say she would be coming to the city and wanted Leda's help shopping for fabric for a very special chair Leda might recall seeing? The slender silver-gilt one with the violin-shaped back?

Leda had been shown it in the course of a tour of the house. Lured from room to room across shining expanses, precious objects she might not have seen on her own had been pointed out to her with their brief histories. At each her comment had been awaited, flatteringly granting her a connoisseurship she was far from possessing.

'It's the boudoir chair in which I peruse Dante, Leda, and it's upholstered in Italian brocade. Brookham wouldn't rise to a replacement even in peacetime, and I haven't been able to find what I want in Boston either. But you'll know where to take me.'

It was no small challenge, and Leda doubted they would find the fabric to suit Florence Burns' stickler's taste, but they discovered a length of suitably faded old rose and violet velvet with a thread of drab silver through the weave.

'I can't abide definite colours, can you, Leda?' she said as they were ushered to a window table in a restaurant she patronized.

A waiter seated her, leaving Leda to seat herself, and holding a waterfall of white linen by its starched corner he flowed it deferentially across her lap. She then received the menu like a lowly offering from his hands. Leda who had dealt less ceremoniously with her own napkin, was not presented with a menu.

'Your gloves must be the only thing you own two alike of, Mrs Burns,' she remarked, not at all sure what manner of conversation the unique creature expected from a lunch partner, but feeling obliged to make some.

'So you've noticed,' Florence Burns approved, 'I see I didn't underestimate you, Leda. There's no need to die of monotony, is there? What can Ernie Pyle *mean* by writing that our boys overseas are all dreaming about the same type medium-voluptuous woman? It makes me seriously concerned about our boys overseas. *Now!*' she said with anticipatory glee, '*what* are we going to eat?' and proceeded to place two different orders without consulting Leda.

Sipping her dry sherry, (Dubonnet for Leda), she thanked her for her invaluable help.

'I would never have located that piece of perfection without you. Don't you think it goes with my violet eyes just as if it had been fabricated to match them?'

Edgar would have had something fulsome to say, Leda could only lamely nod.

'The light from the west window in my bedroom is going to give it the softest opalescent glaze. You know how I treasure my chairs. Have you noticed how some men use a chair, Leda? They back up to it like an automobile going into a parking space, slam their fannies down on it and hunker on down as if they're carving a dugout like a hound settling in for a last hour of sleep. Now chairs are not supposed to be treated like that. Desmond did it the first time he came to my house. I was afraid he was going to bore tunnels through my seating arrangements.'

Her understated sparkle kept Leda entertained with stories of fabric and furniture. The Tudors being the boisterous royalties they were except poor Bloody Mary had had the good judgement to have their furniture built for carousing. Massive oak beds, solid tables and chairs. She herself preferred Queen Anne or Chinese or Japanese. She had a Japanese lamp she could fold away into an envelope when she wasn't using it. She approved the greens glistening with olive oil shown her by the waiter who set the bowl down between them. At an appealing glance from her he helped them both to the salad with solicitous one-handed competence.

Over her sole and Leda's trout she said, 'We must do this more often. I must take you to the Ritz. Too bad they've closed their Japanese Garden for the duration. Plain silly of them. I used to go there for tea.'

'Wartime,' said Leda laconically.

'For some folks it's always wartime. Down where I come from there was a tiny colony of Chinese who had been chased out of California after they finished building the railroad. Our town gave them a hard time to scare them into leaving. One demagogue told a public meeting they had filthy loathsome habits like "niggers". That day a gang wrecked a Chinese curio shop with iron rods and threw dead rats into it.'

Leda recalled a Mark Twain piece she had read at Edgar's about white boys stoning an inoffensive passing 'Chinaman' to death in broad daylight in San Francisco, in front of a cheering crowd.

'But justice fares no better in Dante, Leda. Did you know he puts Mohammed in Hell's eighth circle and has him torn in two from chin to anus through all eternity?'

This raw imagery from the lips of a southern white rose startled Leda — though one more example of jungle justice, designed for humanity beyond Europe's shores, should not have done. All in the day's work men picked up their clubs and came.

'Are you all right, Leda? Take a sip of water. It must be one of those fine trout bones. That's better. You know, Desmond is becoming as boring and fidgety as a hen about you. It's a curious idea people have that a woman's happiness depends on a man when there's all of literature to prove just the opposite.'

She laid her sapphire-ringed hand on her heart and intoned with tragic intensity, '"And death rose clearly and vividly before her mind as the sole means for bringing back love for her in his heart." Now that may be all Mr Tolstoy knew about it but is poor lovesick Anna an example we need to follow? Maybe literature needs Annas but most of us aren't made for taking true love by the horns and getting gored to ribbons. I made up my mind many years ago not to throw myself on the rails for a train to run me over or fling myself down from heaven to Wuthering Heights. I said to myself, Florence Limoges Lamarr Burns —'

'Your middle name is *Limoges?*'

'Why, yes, I resembled a flawless little piece of porcelain when I was born. So I said to myself, Florence, go out and enjoy yourself.'

Leda's mind's eye envisaged the appropriate setting, a high oval-windowed room in a turret on the winding waterway of an old European city, her alluring white rose of a body gliding over, under and around a beautifully synchronized partner. Two dolphins at play, they glided off rumpled sheets to the floor without a break of rhythm, laughing lovingly into each other's eyes.

Before or after Mr Burns, Leda could not ask.

'My marriage wouldn't have ended, Leda,' spoke the witch uncannily, 'if Mr Burns and I had been an old married couple. Whatever it is old folks have — habit, empathy, telepathy — makes matrimony that much easier. But to work your way to old age you have to get past being young. Mr Burns was a fine man and neither of us was to blame. Of course I never could say about him here's a man I will follow to the ends of the earth because that is not where he was going. He was going to board meetings.'

The waiter came to enquire if all was well. It was. Florence Burns ordered miniature tartlets, cherry for Leda, peach for herself. They came set in a teaspoon of confectioner's custard.

Mr Jenner came into her office after lunch to give her Baroness Stretlitz's *Land of Pomp and Pageantry* for translation. P and P was about the Baroness' pre-war stay in a native state in central India. She had made a useful suggestion that they place the verbs at the end of sentences in the English translation as they were in Hindustani. The ADC speaking to the Dowager Maharani would say, 'The betrothal rites about to begin are. Your Highness' presence required is.' It did add to local colour. What did Leda think?

'Is she serious? Are *you* serious?'

Leda referred Mr Jenner to the still popular Jenner edition of *The Book of Ser Marco Polo Covering the Kingdoms and Marvels of the East*. Marco Polo returning home more Tartar than Venetian after a twenty-four year absence and having all but forgotten the Venetian tongue had ripped open the seams of his Tartar garments and spilled out jewels as evidence of where he had been but he had told his story straight with the verbs in their proper place.

Mr Jenner had a civilized slowness to contradict and a genuine regard for Leda's professional judgement. He sat down in the armchair he had provided her with and explained. We of the twentieth century did not have the thirteenth century Venetian's natural propensity to marvel. Our craving for the fabulous must needs find its outlets and found them in far-off places. Remember, Leda, we made our discoveries after difficult and dangerous voyages. What would have been the point of all that adventure had we been content to find human substance no different from our own at the end of it? Mr Jenner's face took on its gently persuasive smile. These places had to be 'else'. The explorers themselves had been way off the accurate mark. Columbus claimed he had discovered China when he landed in Cuba. He thought he was in India when he reached America. Did that in any way diminish the enterprise? But to get back to the Baroness' excellent book, if rearranging verbs could ensure the magic carpet ride readers look for in a Jenner's book, what harm could it do? And he invited Leda to join him and the Baroness for lunch the following day.

'Why do they have to become whirling dervishes and do rope tricks to be noticed? Why can't we take them as they are?' she asked, exasperated.

'Ah, but the voyages put paid to all that,' smiled Mr Jenner, wagging his finger naughtily, not willing to go into all that again.

Punctilious host and brisk businessman that he was he asked Leda not to be late.

Baroness Stretlitz was a regal Austrian of eighty, distantly related to one of the exiled monarchs of Europe. She was fluidly draped in a cobalt blue garment of crepe de chine and wore a matching turban knotted at the front with a crepe de chine rosette.

'Have you travelled, Miss Knox?' she enquired, fixing her soot-rimmed lamplike eyes on Leda.

Leda had not heard the music of the Tartars or scaled the glittering ramparts of the Himalayas or lifted her astounded eyes to the human-headed towers of Angkor Vat, which Edgar classed as travel. And her harrowing excursion through a gallery of Pharoahs would not qualify her in the Baroness' eyes. She admitted she hadn't. The Baroness pointedly addressed herself to Mr Jenner thereafter, detailing the rites attending childbirth in the

Dowager Maharani's domain, where the mother *squatted* to deliver the child and her parts were rubbed with salt after the delivery. Mr Jenner's eyes shone. He salivated. He greeted her every recollection of native custom with entrepreneurial relish. Her hinted participation in a spiritual experience whose details she was not at liberty to divulge (except to sensitive souls) particularly excited him with its saleability and by the end of lunch the Baroness had been persuaded to divulge it. In Chapter Six.

Nine

A loaf of Arnold's white and three cans of Mr Mongini's favourite black bean soup were being delivered from Gristede's when Leda arrived at Rosina Mongini's to tell her she would be moving uptown to Edgar's apartment for a while. The deliveries meant Mr Mongini must have just left for his wartime committee meeting in Washington. He was an old-fashioned husband. He didn't like the neighbourhood knowing Rosina was alone. The only abnormality the war had imposed on Rosina's routine was the grocery order to camouflage Mr Mongini's absences and the unhollowed half of his side of their kingsize bed.

The shoe drawings on Rosina's easel showed her painstaking miniature craftsmanship at its intricate best in lizard, snake and alligator skin fashions for fall and winter. Leda gasped at the height of a jewelled heel.

'Unbelieveable, isn't it?' Rosina agreed. 'Why would any woman want to get up on those stilts? But I'm only the artist, not the designer and the company says the style will sell out before a customer breaks her ankle. I suppose it does something for the leg.' She glanced dubiously down her short leg at her sturdy calf, 'If you have the leg, and the chassis to go with the leg. But let me tell you, Leda, shoes have gone wild before. During the Renaissance they grew out long instead of high. The nobler the wearer's rank was, the longer the toes of his shoes had to be. I've seen pictures in the public library of shoes that were two and a half feet long from heel to toe. The toes had to be chained to the duke's knees to show how noble he was. Now that Mr Mongini has to keep going to Washington I spend quite a bit of time in the library.'

This was venturesome of Rosina for whom Forty-Second Street was another town.

'I never go into the library without thinking of him teasing me when we were courting. "Rosina," he used to say, "Did you know those stone lions at the entrance roar every time a virgin passes?" I would get so embarrassed I wouldn't know where to look. Don't run off, Leda. I'll warm up some black bean soup for supper.'

She emptied the can into cold water, industriously flattening lumps of soup against the sides of the saucepan with a wooden spoon and bringing it to a boil. Her grey-black curls crinkled in the steam, her red cheeks flared a brighter red. The August humidity had added to the kitchen's residual heat. Through the open window she called a timely warning to a child turning cartwheels on the sidewalk too close to a fire hydrant. Whenever Leda defended her own lack of ambition to Edgar, it was the placid untormented Monginis she had in mind.

Conversation lagged, uncharacteristically for Rosina, over Mr Mongini's soup and his white bread, because the ghost of Kamei was unlaid between her and Leda. Rosina was too nervous to revive him knowing how Leda went blank at the mention. Few women were as lucky as Rosina herself in being wooed and won straight out of high school by so ideal a lover, so masterful a protector as Mr Mongini, but Leda's was lucklessness gone crazy. The world over, people stuck to their own kind. Who else could you trust? Even Jews and Gentiles took care not to fall for each other, right here in these United States, never mind Nazi Germany.

∿

The train came in disgorging more servicemen than civilians. Their tan and green uniforms gave them a jungle look of animal vigour. They strode up the platform past the barrier and Grand Central became a carnival of intimacies the war had made public property. Passengers who had no one meeting them were paying no more attention to clinging couples than stagehands dodging cardboard scenery. Leda who had grown up at a time when shattering transitions of emotion had been conveyed on silent screens by no more than the glance of a luminous eye or the twitch of a mobile mouth, and offscreen only behind closed doors, felt a vital ingredient — the privacy of one's most private feelings — had gone out of life, never to return.

She had given up trying to locate a girl in a sari but as the active whole-bodied fighting force thinned out, she saw a legless torso hoist itself down from the train, swinging like a pendulum between crutches. A mummy bandaged from head to foot was lowered after him in a wheelchair and behind the mummy was the girl, looking more like a starveling of twelve than the sixteen-year-old Leda was expecting. She had her suitcase handle clutched in both hands and was kicking a leg free of her sari to step down. The plait of hair down her back swung forward as she managed to plant a foot on terra firma. When the other foot joined it she seemed to be testing solid ground for the first time, like a newly hatched heron or some other starkly vulnerable, still featherless form of fledgling life. An agonizingly thin arm picked up the suitcase it had just put down. Its pair flew out sideways for balance. She looked frighteningly weighted by her load of heavy leather. Leda hurried forward to relieve her with a welcoming smile.

Leda had counted on the soaring glass and concrete towers of New York City as a talking point to get them over the first hurdles of acquaintance, forgetting that the taxi ride home would dwarf the sweltering metropolis to eye level banalities. She had been going to explain that the borough of Manhattan was named for the Manhattan Indians who had traded it to the Dutch for trinkets and other knicknacks but changed her mind. The view from the window made it only too plausible. Conversation was in any case fitful. Shān hadn't slept much sitting up on the train from Los Angeles. Her troopship from Bombay had voyaged circuitously to avoid torpedoes, the Pacific now being safer than the Atlantic, and had landed her at San Pedro harbour instead of New York.

Nearer home the apartment blocks of the East Seventies had never looked more forbiddingly high, grey and featureless than they did today but once they entered Edgar's building the elevator ride brought a flash of pure excitement — Anne Boleyn at her crowning — to the girl's face. Alfred the doorman had brought them up and carried her suitcase in. With a grandfatherly concern Leda had not seen him display before, he advised the girl to have a good rest and she gave him the subdued answering gleam that seemed to serve her for a smile.

The apartment had a prized view of the East River but today it was flat brown water with a barge on it. Edgar's guest room had always lived up to expectations with its batik bedspread and its painting of two golden-brown bare-breasted beauties against breadfruit trees and brilliant tropical flowers inscribed with the Javanese prophecy: 'The continent was split into nine parts, but when three thousand rainy seasons will have elapsed, the Eastern Islands shall again be reunited and the power of the white man shall end.' The girl didn't look at it. She was busy taking a key from a cotton drawstring bag on her wrist. She opened her worn suitcase, burrowed under layers of saris until she found an envelope and presented it to Leda. It was limp and damp. Leaving her to unpack Leda took it into the living room to slit open, then thought it better to let it dry propped against the ashwood Balinese dancer on the cocktail cabinet, and went into the kitchen to see about lunch.

The circumstances being what they were it was safer to stick to practical particulars in the way of talk.

'You're going to need the right clothes for Easthaven,' she said while they were eating, 'twin sets and moccasins and all the things girls will be wearing on campus.'

'Twin sets and moccasins? Are they the uniform at Easthaven, Miss Knox?'

Leda had to smile.

'Dear me, no. Students don't wear uniforms here. They wear whatever they want to wear.'

At Best's next day she waited outside a dressing booth chatting with the saleslady while Shān changed into a skirt and sweater. Leda, all ready to approve, was dumbfounded when Shān held the curtain aside. The girl could have been Edgar's emaciated Balinese dancer without the ashwood figurine's tortured adult grace.

'We'll have to get you a bra,' she said faintly.

Shān said she was wearing one, sewn out of an old silk sari by the tailor at home. Leda wrote bras on the shopping list but a problem she had not anticipated — considering the enormous breasts and buttocks in Edgar's book on Hindu sculpture — was what they were going to be slung on. There was no padding to anchor a girdle either. A garter belt would likewise fall straight down her sides so how was she going to wear stockings? They were not dilemmas Leda could put to the saleslady, a corpulent New Yorker who had never been this close to the bare bones of anatomy.

They bought the skirts and twin sets that every student, to Shān's mild astonishment, had chosen to wear on campus that fall, and the bobbysox and moccasins to go with them. After lingerie they went to accessories and on their way out to the costume jewellery counter for the string of pearls that everybody had also chosen to wear on twin sets that fall. It's fun to wear what others one's age are wearing, said Leda, feeling called on for an explanation.

Milo was expecting them for lunch at the Waldorf Astoria. He rose lithely from his chair in Peacock Alley to kiss Leda on both cheeks and take Shān's hands in his, remarking, '*Come elle est ravissante, la petite,*' to Leda. She had never heard a stranger description of a scrawny child. In reply to Milo's question about the shopping expedition Shān said she was fascinated by the number of clothing layers required to be worn in America and especially by the gloves that must be worn for ladylikeness and not for the weather. The lesson the glove counter lady had given her had made her hands feel like footbinding must have made feet feel in old China. In fairness to western culture, Milo defended gloves. His grandmother had indulged in no less than two dozen pairs, one pair made entirely of lace which had given his grandmother's exposed wrists a heartbreaking vulnerability. He could weep every time he looked at the photograph of her holding him in her arms in his embroidered christening robe.

Shān was visibly taken aback by the portions they were served at lunch. She said she was keeping a notebook of her impressions and as this was her first encounter with normal life in a free country she was especially interested in this island's customs and rituals.

Milo approved.

'The love rituals of this island should make a good contrast with those of, say, the island of Bali, where Edgar tells me there is no word for romantic love, only for desire. He says romantic love only flourishes where there are barriers to free and natural relations between men and women.'

Milo joined their sightseeing after lunch. He and Shān strode ahead, the girl's strapless Indian sandals slapping against her bare childish heels below her sari and Milo a hulk beside her tirelessly deciphering the ways of American islanders. Shān at last craned her neck upward at skyscrapers and exclaimed like any other visitor. The elevator ride up the Empire State Building thrilled her most of all. An hour after Milo had seen them home Leda found her at the refrigerator, gazing into its well-stocked lighted interior like Marco Polo surveying the marvels of the court of Kublai the Grand Khan. And why shouldn't the remains of meat loaf, carrot cake and other wonders figure in a traveller's notebook?

She remembered the envelope she had postponed opening, there being no urgency about a letter six weeks on its way and written long before Shān's voyage. It was dated May first.

'Dear Miss Knox,' she read. 'I am taking this opportunity to write to you from home before I go underground again so that Shān can carry this letter with her. You must know our leaders have been in prison since last August because they demand a share in government and control of our own defence before they can cooperate with the war effort. Those of us who escaped arrest must stay in hiding to be of some service to our leaderless party. It is not only humiliating to be drafted into a war with no control over how or where our men, money and materials are used, the question of defence remains the crucial one. The colonial powers have failed utterly to defend Asia from Japanese aggression. In retreat and defeat they have provided escape routes, protection and evacuation for Europeans only and abandoned Asians to their grim fate. A war we would have fought beside them as their allies has brought ruin to Asia because even in a life-and-death struggle Europe recognizes no other as equal. I don't know how long I can escape arrest, or see the light of day after that, or what the future holds.

So let me thank you and Edgar while I can for all you will be doing for Shān. It is wonderfully generous of you to make yourselves responsible for a girl even he has not met. I hope to repay your kindness one day.

I have spent nearly half of Shān's life in jail and should not panic at one more parting, but many separations have made separation no easier. My most constant memory of Shān's childhood is of myself behind bars watching her trudge away from me through the years and come storming back to cling to me through the bars and beg me not to leave her. I take comfort from what Edgar has told me about you and feel certain she will be in good hands.

I don't know your country but, besides Edgar, I have a few American friends: Elihu Burrit, the blacksmith from Worcester, Massachusetts, who studied Longfellow in Sanskrit and kept a Greek grammar in the crown of his hat to brush up his Greek while he was casting cowbells. Henry Thoreau who believed the barnyard cock was the wild pheasant the poets of the Upanishads knew, and who gave us civil disobedience which we call satyagraha. I could name others who have kept me company. Your proud people, too, defied a distant king and made unparalleled progress once they liberated themselves from British rule. We have great expectations of America. I know Edgar's writings must have made a significant contribution to President Roosevelt's understanding of our cause ...'

It was not the heavy-hearted overcast letter Leda would have expected — in the circumstances. Quite the opposite. Somehow bracing, though she could not understand how or why this should be so.

Mrs Schelling called at breakfast time next morning to invite Edgar to her monthly Wednesday 'evening'. She was desolated to hear he was away and settled for Leda with audible reluctance. The Schelling brothers and their mother were on the rim of Edgar's large amorphous acquaintance and he had taken Leda to their home last month.

'So your dear brother is away again, Miss Knox? Writing another book I very much hope? Such a genius he has for placing far-off people in the room with us.'

Leda who had been introducing Shān to maple syrup in the kitchen, said one such was with her right now. Mrs Schelling's voice sprang into vibrant warmth. She insisted Leda come and bring the guest.

Mrs Schelling, German herself, was an ardent espouser of a United States of Europe excluding Soviet Russia and had spoken feelingly to Edgar at last month's 'evening' of her anxiety that unless Europe sans Russia united, the West would slide into barbarism. Leda suspected it already had but her opinion was not sought. Mrs Schelling's 'evenings' were gatherings of notables and Leda was only the sister of one. Her work was not original, it was translation, and her hobby was fairy tales. A charming work and a charming hobby for a spinster, Leda was sure she had heard Mrs Schelling murmur when Edgar introduced her. A great many things she thought she heard Mrs Schelling say at that party had never been uttered, but they bore a spooky resemblance to what she might have said.

The Schelling apartment was in an old building. The elevator's iron grille needed muscle to drag open and shut. It ascended at a staid dignified tempo very like Mrs Schelling's own, granting the visitor a leisurely view of potted plants and baskets trailing ferns on the second floor, a wildly dejected Greek mask for a door knocker on the third, an ottoman piled with cushions on the fourth and finally the black-and-white check floor that extended into the spacious Schelling salon. The hostess filled the open doorway in a long lace pre-some-war gown which emptied of her would have remained as spheroid and a coiffure that must have bewitched the late Herr Schelling when he spied its baroque splendour through his opera glasses at the turn of the century. Had she never changed it out of wifely devotion or had its swirls and furls, once fashionably ornate, got cast in concrete like her clothes and entertainments? Had Herr Schelling eluded the coiffure, the gown, the 'evenings' and other graver dilemmas by dying before the first Nazi toddler could lisp Seig Heil? Leda could not picture a host here at all.

Mrs Schelling firmly blocked entry, enchanted to learn the young guest was from India. Her face became suffused with incredible happiness.

'An angel from heaven!' she cried, extending a hand each to angel and mortal but continuing to block the doorway.

'There is something quite — Greek — about the face,' she meditated, examining Shan's, 'is it perhaps the nose, or how the nose joins the cheeks?'

She dropped their hands to clasp her own, regretting she had never been to the Orient but she had read a book about Baghdad by Mrs Gertrude Bell. In this book Mrs Gertrude Bell recounted the local custom of eating a bowl of sour curd for lunch every day. However, her most fascinating account concerned her British neighbour whose name Mrs Schelling had forgotten. The British neighbour collected Mesopotamian birds. Now one day he acquired a not yet full-grown eagle which had to be kept in the shade and fed baby bats. His servants used to catch these babies in nets and store them in an ice chest during the night and feed them to the eagle in the morning. But what a pleasure to welcome this young guest of Edgar from the land of the great Tagoray and the Sacred Books of the East, and of course, Miss Knox.

Allowed in at last, Leda wondered why an Indian girl should remind Mrs Schelling of Iraqi bats and eagles. Edgar was right about the blur beyond Europe's shores and Mrs Schelling herself was engagingly candid about her vagueness.

'Once we reach the Persian Gulf we are lost, are we not, Miss Knox?'

Leaving Leda to fend for herself she regained possession of Shan's hand and convoyed her to the other side of the salon much as if Shān were not another guest but a rare long-tailed golden parrot perched on Mrs Schelling's forefinger.

The Schelling salon, spacious though it was, was overladen with the belongings that a far larger residence must have housed in Berlin. Tapestried chairs, mahogany tables bearing handsome family photographs, innumerable little tables covered with lumps of minerals and other curiosities. Velvet curtains fell to the floor from lofty pelmets, exhausted by their own weight. Massively framed Prussian battle scenes of scarlet and gold soldiers on plunging horses took up the walls. Massive, too, the silver candelabra on one of the back-to-back grand pianos. A young severe Mrs Schelling (pre-dating the hairdo) hung in a row of medallions on a vertical brass chain beside the fireplace. Double doors gave on to a terrace wide open to the steamy pressures of August and the strong August light gilded the brass fender and firearms. It was high summer yet in this setting of indestructible winter furnishings where logs lay in the grate waiting to flame forth, it was the summer dresses and sun tans that looked unbelievable.

Leda noted the absence of strain, unusual for European get-togethers these days. The Schellings and their invitees must have agreed never to discuss the war or to wallow in peace nostalgia. They were not a family, after all, who could rejoice either in Germany's victories or defeats. The single exception to the no-war no-peace rule was a topic of current interest after the buffet in the form of 'a few words' by one of the guests. An 'evening' these days could not be devoted entirely to food and drink. Not that Leda had heard any flabby chitchat before or after the 'words'. Conversation was required to be made. She heard Mrs Schelling, still holding Shān by the hand, making it.

'Asia is the Source, is it not? Metternich spoke truly when he said it started at the Landstrasse in Vienna.'

The middle-aged Schelling brothers, one bald, one blond, played masters of ceremony in elegant evening dress, baring their strong white teeth in abrupt laughs. Wolfgang's lynxlike eartips were tufted with short blond fur. Otto's eyes had the glitter and his torso the tighter tauter stance of a Doberman Pinscher. Sparkling Moselle, Leda heard Wolfgang expound, came from the Rheingau along the Rhine's northern bank. Nobody mentioned the east bank where sprawled the new Nazi empire. Mozart music rippled from the further piano. Otto, beside it, exclaimed, 'Beethoven is your favourite composer? Impossible! Women prefer Tchaikovsky.'

An English voice, Hilary Rushmore's of the British Information Service, caught up with her.

'Leda, my dear. I don't see Edgar. I hope he got our Facts About India? We've sent it to the newspapers. And the Viceroy's agent in Washington has advised the White House to do nothing about the Indian question at present.'

'And nothing it's doing,' Leda observed.

'That sounds censorious. Have you any idea, Leda, how serious the disturbances were last year? They're always the work of the turbulent element in the bazaar but they got so out of hand the government had to call in fifty-seven battalions of the army to crush them and the RAF to bomb saboteurs in Bihar.'

'Edgar says if you'd set up a national government none of that need have happened. Those people would have been on our side.'

'Ah, yes. Edgar's pet theory. They're all "people on our side". The Facts should clear up the confusion.'

Like any owner of vast estates, Hilary had attracted a respectful little audience. He turned to a shrunken old prima donna Leda had seen here last time and smiled placatingly at her to indicate he would be with her as soon as tiresome duty permitted. The tiny soprano's black eyes flickered around the room. Her cane tapped restlessly.

'I trust the girl who's staying with you is not going to give us any trouble,' said Hilary, lowering his voice.

Leda looked across at Shān, an animated listener in the group around Otto at the grand piano and said she doubted it.

'I think it's anthropological research she has in mind, Hilary.'

'Really? Into what tribe?'

'Oh, ours, Hilary, we of the island of America, maybe the wider West, I don't know exactly. I get the impression she'll be viewing us like multifarious insects under glass.'

'I'm serious, Leda. Edgar must have told you a military train was wrecked by her father's followers. The wreckers have been sentenced to ten years and he is being held incommunicado as a maximum security prisoner until the authorities decide what to do with him. Edgar is wasting his time trying to get him released.'

He turned away and lowered his head to the prima donna. Leda heard Otto's carrying voice proclaiming he never went to the theatre because theatre voices were terrible. Theatre ruined voices. The vocal chords were the final flower of the human body. Only opera brought them to full bloom. And after all, he expanded, was not opera theatre at its finest? When Borgatti played Siegfried and rushed onto the stage in the first Act leading a young bear, was that not drama? Was there any finer drama than the despair of Desgrieux in the third Act of Manon Lescaut when he sees the ship that will carry his beloved to exile?

'Whatever anyone may say,' Otto concluded devoutly, 'in the end there is only opera.'

On this categorical announcement Leda wandered into the dining room where the table was spread with elaborately decorated galantine and chaudfroid offerings. A side table had fresh fruit, fragrant spiced strudels and wobbling wine jellies with cream cascading down their sides. Leda imagined spun sugar toppings and whorls of whipped cream being individually wrapped, cartoned and crated in Berlin under Mrs Schelling's supervision and lifted to a van for transfer to the docks along with Prussian battlefields and grand pianos. A methodical advance planner she would have had to be to get it all out of harm's way easefully ahead of Armageddon. It was all too gargantuan to be called bag and baggage and the Schellings too superior to be classed as refugees but they, too, had washed up with the wartide and would go their way when the war was over, taking their huge hereditary possessions, their soireées and their bon mots with them. Leda would never discover why women prefer Tchaikovsky.

She helped herself from the buffet and passed through the salon where Mrs Schelling was welcoming a late French arrival. A haggard man detached himself from Hilary Rushmore's audience and followed her to the terrace.

'I saw you here with Edgar last month. You must be his sister.'

Leda admitted she was. It was bound to raise false expectations about her knowledge of world affairs. She hoped she would not be put to the test. She now remembered Mrs Schelling had recommended the man to Edgar and praised his grasp of his subject.

'I told Edgar if he wants to get his viewpoint across and not Hilary Rushmore's, India is going to need packaging and promotion. Like we've done for China.'

'What,' enquired Leda, 'have you done for China?'

'I'll get some food and join you,' he said.

Coming back he informed her his company handled everything from ladies who wanted their names mentioned lunching at The Colony to putting countries on the map. They had done it for China.

'But China is our ally — a known name — which makes all the difference and we have the Kuomintang officials here to help us out with all the information we need. It also helps that Madame Chiang Kai Shek went to school here from age ten to nineteen and bought gum drops at the local store and went hazelnutting with the girls. Now, of course, the lady gets a standing ovation in the House and *Time* magazine is writing she makes tough guys melt. But we put in a lot of work to make it possible. Ask yourself why nobody's heard of India,' he ordered, eating his way through lobster salad.

'Isn't your name Leda? Americans love a great story, Leda, and India is a great story if we can simplify all that confusion of religions and languages for Americans.'

'How can you do that?'

'Identify the people who can do it for us. Like the Kuomintang officials China has here. It wouldn't hurt India to acquire an influential patron like Senator Wherry of Nebraska who made Shanghai a household word when he made his famous pledge "With God's help we will lift Shanghai up, up and ever up until it is just like Kansas City." Edgar knows better than anyone the amount of planning it takes — facts, figures, research — to get through to another culture. How d'you suppose he's been able to do it?'

By looking out of his train window one night, Leda wanted to say.

'He just makes friends,' she said instead.

The man's facial furrows deepened, then relaxed into a broad smile.

'The loving sister,' he nodded. 'You tell Edgar from me I'm packaging a United States of Europe for Mrs Schelling and he should keep India in mind.'

The stars this 'evening' were Hilary Rushmore and the late arrival who was presented as France's former Minister for the Colonies.

'Stay for their few words, Miss Knox,' insisted Mrs Schelling, 'they could be of importance to your dear brother who sadly is not here so you must convey them to him.'

It was Hilary alone who addressed the gathering from the fireplace. The French dignitary was leaving the job to him, apparently conceding the British knew better the world they had ruled so long. He sat on a sofa beside Mrs Schelling, his ear bent attentively to her lips until she reached the end of her long murmured comment.

'I fully appreciate the American prejudice against empire,' Hilary began humorously after the little patter of applause when he stood up, 'but we are there to liberate, not to enslave.'

He and the Frenchman exchanged courteous nods and Hilary went on.

'All His Majesty's subjects may look forward to self-government, but naturally those who are of British origin are very differently placed from others under the Crown. We must recognize these others are politically *in statu pupillari*. I know there are distinguished minds in this country who want us to speed up the process. But the time to consider demands for self-government will be after the war. We will then have to bring the light of western knowledge and experience to bear on every such demand if we are to do what is right for that race. So there can be no hasty transfers of power and no form of international control over these territories while Europe still has responsibilities to fulfil in India, Indonesia, Indo-China and the East Indies. You would accuse us of bad faith and of inviting the worst sort of confusion if we let our American ally believe otherwise.'

Before closing Hilary paid tribute to the great artist present here this evening who is as revered for her compassionate concerns as she has been for her voice. In answer to a question the famous lady had raised about Europe's imperial mission Hilary wished to assure her that the imperial fabric rested on the Christian moral code. Christianity was the keystone of the imperial arch and the bedrock of imperial power.

'If we did not govern according to it, we should have no right to govern at all.'

He bowed toward the wizened soprano.

Finding Shān at her side Leda mimed her grateful thanks to Mrs Schelling whose hand sailed up in startled farewell before it fluttered to her bosom in heartfelt appreciation of their having come.

ᔒ

Shān's first letter from Easthaven said her face was sore from social smiling and she was labouring to project her voice in elocution class. Miss de Selwyn put her abysmal performance down to undernourishment and oriental training for submissiveness in the home but hoped a proper diet would give it body by the semester's end.

She had also made a friend, a kind and caring beauty called Janey Ann Lawrence who had the room next to hers in the dorm, and whose aunt, known as Aunt, had given Shān the surplus curtains, cushions and pictures she had brought for her niece to choose from for her room. Janey Ann, like five other girls, wanted to be a crooner, and hum, sing or mutter songs of love in an undertone for a living. On tea afternoons in the dorm every Monday she linked arms with two other girls to croon Putchorarmsaroundmehoneyholdmetight to the living room piano. In Mrs Maxwell, the House Mother's opinion, Janey Ann would never be a crooner. She had so many telephone calls she would be the first girl in the dorm to get engaged. If a call was for Janey her scream of 'Is it a maa-aa-an?' resounded through the corridor as she ran downstairs to the booth in the hall. Mrs Maxwell was convinced Janey Ann would be a beautiful blonde freshman bride in pure white satin, walking up the aisle on her daddy's arm before the year was through. Aunt was more circumspect. Janey Ann was pretty as a picture, she said, but not a patch on her mother. Now *she* had been a beauty a man could be proud of. Rockwell hadn't been the same since she died.

Dear God, thought Leda, this Lawrence girl was majoring in biology and math, no workload for a moron, so why was she acting like one and why had she dropped on Shān's path like a prize specimen of an American islander?

The letter went on to say Shān had excused herself from attending the campus dance for the girls to get acquainted with the boys from the Easthaven Air Force base. When Mrs Maxwell's puff of pale blue hair had vanished up the road to join the line of chaperones in the gym, Shān had watched the girls leave in a stately procession of tulle and taffeta, scooped, looped and girdled into shapes men could be proud of. Miloji had mentioned it but Shān had had *no* idea how many barriers there actually were to prevent free and natural relations between men and women. Even their hair was hedged into stiff shapes, their hands were bound into gloves and their faces were rigid under Saturday paint ...

Leda put down the letter. Marco Polo, had been a European after all. He had seen, not been, the marvel. Things changed accordingly. Clearly, if I am your thousand and one nights, or your savage, you shall be mine. Whatever strange substance my form of life floats in, so shall yours in your own.

∫

Leda spent Thanksgiving at Easthaven and took Shān and Jane Ann Lawrence to lunch at the village inn. Shorn of her demented cry of 'Is it a maa-aa-aan?' and her gasped ante and post mortems of her countless dates, Jane Ann did not appear unintelligent. A bland artlessness when she spoke to Leda and a china doll stratagem of batting her blue eyes rapidly open and shut were probably her stock-in-trade dating tactics, absentmindedly transferred from their natural habitat to Miss Knox.

When the girls left, Jane Ann to go to Aunt's and Shān to the library, Leda walked along the lake in the twilit autumn afternoon, watching November's crimson-leaved boughs shadowily reflected in it. There was no resemblance between this neat contained campus of classical architecture, gracious lawns and sheltering arches of elms and her own sprawling university campus where Luke Bradford, towering black and godlike on the playing field, had in small accidental encounters helped her find her way around. She must have looked so much the lost alien far from home that he had taken pity on her and told her how to get to her destinations on campus, and on one occasion he had directed her to the reference books she needed in the library. Leda remembered the day he had mockingly challenged rather than invited her to come to Thanksgiving dinner at his home. It was when he gave her careful instructions and imposed strict cautions that she realized they had never met without a library bookshelf or a jutting corner of a building providing a shield between them and others for their brief, and on his part kind and helpful exchanges. She had attributed the shield to his own awkwardness with a white stranger and had had no qualms about accepting his invitation. Following his instructions she had taken a bus and been shocked in spite of his warning at what looked like a dyer's colour chart to her unaccustomed eyes. She was still standing dazed in the aisle when the bus lurched forward dropping her into the nearest seat. Instinct warned her to huddle into her raincoat, pull her hatbrim low over her eyes and sheath her hands in gloves.

Luke had laughingly congratulated her on her safe arrival and led her into a presence for which nothing had prepared her. Majesty sat enthroned in an upright chair in the hands on knees posture of a Rameses, commanding as the statue of Lincoln in his marble memorial, imperious as the pictures Leda had seen of the King of England's consort. Luke Bradford's grandmother must once have been black but age had grayed her to granite, rusted her hair to iron and made a historic monument of her. Leda had humbly wondered what she herself, of no magnificence and less importance, was doing in such a presence.

Nothing had prepared her for their Thanksgiving dinner either. Unfamiliar condiments burned her tongue and seared her palate. Tears sprang to her eyes. Old Mrs Bradford upbraided Luke for not warning their guest that they didn't go in for traditional Pilgrim fare, their forefathers not having come here as pilgrims. Leda swallowed ice water between mouthfuls, glad she wasn't having to say much. She would have had trouble matching the educated international quality of their talk. Mrs Bradford had a warrior's fierce black twinkle in her eyes as she commented acidly on the warlike peace the white peacemakers had made at Versailles.

'But what can we expect of a brotherhood that downgrades a physicist into a football hero so he can get a scholarship to university?'

The physicist piled more fiery food on Leda's plate. Weeping, she ate it hungrily. The atmosphere she had strayed into on an ignominious busride had some heady elixir her own was woefully lacking. She felt herself consuming every aspect of the encounter. It baffled her that intellect denied the light could flower subterraneanly or the virtue she sensed here burn so bright in this austere environment. Far from her origins her self-consciousness fell away from her. She discarded it as she had her layers of wrapping on arrival.

She made her way back to the campus by bus, cloaked and daggered again. By inviting her home for Thanksgiving (never anticipating her acceptance) Luke had returned the courtesy she had done him when she had acknowledged him (time and again) as a human being on campus. And there the matter would have ended. It was Leda with her need of the oxygen his home provided who had wanted friendship, initiated other meetings and entered into complicated intrigues to throw stalkers off the scent for the simple purpose of meeting. She could not believe that daring enterprising young girl had been herself.

ᔑ

They could see the black-branched calligraphy of Florence Burns' skeletal woods through the glass wall of her living room. When darkness blotted them out Mrs Burns got up to draw painted parchment blinds down the glass wall and announced she had made her Will.

'About time,' grumbled Desmond, seated on the highest chair in the room, 'you're not getting any younger.'

She gave Desmond the sidelong smile she conferred on the proletariat, tilting a cheek inlaid with mother-of-pearl toward him and giving her serious attention to Leda.

'You are going to need a setting for a lifestyle of your own,' she said.

'She's got an apartment in New York and my house to come to here,' objected Desmond.

'So what I've done, Leda, is leave you this house. You know how I feel about a bloodline from the fact that I chose not to start one. It's the argument Mr Burns and I parted on. I told him I was not a seed grower and carrier by temperament.'

'Why me, Mrs Burns? I thought Edgar was your favourite.'

'Oh but Edgar is a vagabond. He doesn't belong anywhere special any more. He's at home everywhere. He told me he once met a man in Trincomalee who said if we really *listened*, we'd hear the far-off sounds dogs hear.'

'Meaning,' said Desmond, 'if we try hard enough we can all graduate to bein' as smart as dogs?'

Leda was more than usually at a loss at the extravagant generosity of this self-appointed patron.

'You're the one who needs a home, Leda, not Edgar. Isn't that where they say a woman's place is?'

From Desmond there issued a low caged growl.

'Your comments can be so parsimonious, Desmond, I declare I don't know what they mean.'

Desmond stood up, irascible and irate, saying what he meant was Mr Ebenezer O. Burns the Second must've had a darned sight more sense than she had. Furthermore, what was wrong with his own house across the road, a

house any American would be prouda? And Leda happened
to be *his* relative, not Florence Burnses. He marched to
the drinks table to pour himself a drinkabale drink, not
your hot spiced junk, covering the slippery distance with
a practised assurance he had lamentably lacked earlier.
Florence Burns' myopic gaze — eyeglasses would have
marred the limpid violet beauty of her eyes — rested
midway between him and the drinks. She retorted happily,
'Why Desmond Guthrie, I do believe you're jealous.'

Their sparring had an unmistakably domestic ring.
What other domestic rhythms had they established between
them? There was a satyr's satisfied ease, a suspicion of
goat's ears and budding ivy-wreathed horns about
Desmond. The hot spiced rum in Leda's gold-glazed mug
had grown cold. What could she say about the
overwhelming gift bestowed on her, or make of a gift
intended as a setting for a lifestyle she could never equal?
Leda knew the woman she was she would remain. Years
hence she would be as she was today, sensibly dressed,
studiously occupied. She would trudge through the early
snow of Florence Burns' woods in winters to come, return
to sit by her fireplace and work on endless configurations
of endless translated sentences. In the middle of translation,
she would lean back in her chair to look up at beasts
strewn like flowers in a field on the Persian rug on the
wall. She would drink tea out of eggshell cups, eat off
lustrous plates in a dining room with striped silk walls.
She would read Dante upstairs in the silver gilt boudoir
chair and sleep alone in the high wide four-poster.
Desmond's disappointing spinster would be replanted in

this garden of delights but she would remain the lacklustre spinster he despaired of, living a life, then as now, resembling a deep uninterrupted sleep. Aware that Florence Burns was waiting, Leda bestirred herself to thank her, saying a true successor she could never aspire to be.

'Well that's settled then,' said Mrs Burns gaily and asked how Edgar's young import was doing.

'She's poring over librettos, getting ready to go to the opera when she comes to New York for Christmas vacation.'

'Opera is something she can't afford to miss, Leda, unlike ballet. I never did care for ballet. The way a ballerina gets picked up and put down and twirled and *manipulated* by her partner is just so degrading.'

Desmond said he'd had an overdose of all that crap as a child, and he couldn't stand opera. The guy has a dagger through his solar plexus but he partners a twenty-minute duet before he pegs out. Gilda's in the sack, stabbed practically to death, but she gives out this half hour vibrato farewell to her father. The character with ants in his pants who's supposed to be in a tearing hurry to leave skips around the stage tra-la-la-ing he 'must away and can no longer stay.'

Florence Burns sent an indulgent myopic glance in his general direction.

Ten

On Saturday nights the library stacks were deserted tubelit alleys because of the exodus for the rite known as 'dates'. Shān found a wealth of material, sometimes conveniently placed at eye level. Here she had come across bundling, a custom widely practised among Celtic and German tribes which was obviously a forerunner of today's hectic Saturday night goodnight ceremonies after the date. In bundling the boy and girl lay side by side on a bed once a week. What they did next was not recorded but to make sure they didn't succeed a rope was tied above and below the girl's knees, or little warning bells were attached to the legs of the bed. On actual mating the stacks had only led her to the mating of the mole, a tunnelling frenzy of pursuer and pursued that added nothing to her researches, but about romantic western love in general there was plenty. Shān had only to enter the library to feel warmly, quietly befriended. The librarian, Miss Colvin, gave her a nod of recognition as

she went through to the reading room to take her pick
of its browsing corners. She located the books she needed
for her class assignments and disposed of them under her
armchair, roamed the stacks researching western love rites,
and spent the rest of the evening bringing her Notebook
up-to-date:

In America all hopes are so centred on the 'date' that
Aunt came from Boston to get Janey Ann panty-girdled,
bra-ed, stockinged and pancaked for an important date.
I helped her put Janey Ann into all these obstacles. It took
an hour and a half from start to finish to make Janey Ann
the shape a man can be proud of. Aunt was very tense
but calm. She said the correct way to put on a bra, girls,
so it flatters your figure, is to lean over the cups and let
your breasts fall into them. A bra has to be the kind that
helps your upper curve to match your lower one. Good
dressing starts from the inside out, girls, and foundation
garments are the secret of it. You can't feel confident if
you don't look right. At the very end Aunt made sure the
seams of Janey Ann's stockings were straight — it is very
shameful, involving loss of face, if they are crooked —
and every washed pincurled hair was trained into its exact
place. Aunt couldn't relax until Janey Ann had left with
the date but then she lit a cigarette and blew smoke
through her nostrils, an elegant accomplishment Janey
Ann also has.

'I must say, Shān,' Aunt said, crossing her stockinged
legs, 'your costume is so complicated. It's hard for we
Americans to understand why anyone would want to wear
such a complicated costume. We American women got

used to freedom of movement in the days of the covered wagon when women took up guns and axes alongside the men to fight Indians.'

Aunt gave me the heroic example of Mrs Experience Bozarth who had brained two Indians with an axe and disembowelled a third. I did not like to ask Aunt if Saturday night goodnight ceremonies had been practised in Mrs Experience Bozarth's time. In these, the American woman must confront her date's passion. The rule requires her to egg him on above the neck and fight him back below the neck. Attack and retreat are both necessary, the one to make sure of being telephoned for another date, the other to save the American woman for wedlock. The skills and strategies of this Mahabharata have to be kept sharpened, the body scooped and looped and locked into obstacles, until wedlock. Thermopylae would be a better comparison. Locked into stifling barriers the American woman must make as if to surrender but on no account surrender, with scarcely any room for manoeuvre. At Thermopylae, Leonidas and three hundred comrades fell dead before the Persians could advance. The American woman is under no less a siege, which, however, must end in stalemate. The intolerable strain of goodnight ceremonies can affect an entire semester. The songs on the radio add to the strain.

Aunt has given me a radio. It is better than the library for research on western love. In radio songs love is fallen into and out of, lost and found like an umbrella. The American old and the American young all hanker to stay in the mood for it, nerve-wracking though it is, and the songs make certain that they do. The American masses never get a rest from being in the mood for love. As soon as they start getting into the mood for thought, the songs pull them right back. Love in Bali must be a heaven of calm in comparison. So must Dadaji's fated love have been when he arrived at Dadi's house on his caparisoned chestnut horse to marry her and they saw each other for the first time. Kalidas said true lovers recognize each other because of a knowledge built up through their past lives in other countries and centuries so that when they meet again in India Beata it is not by accident. This method of knowing would take too long for the people of this island. Dating is their exhausting national way.

Radio songs make Janey Ann go weak and woolly on weekends. Not until Monday morning does she start longing for the smell of formaldehyde and itching to dissect the genito-urinary system of a frog. Once she gets back into the mood for work all the flounces Aunt has done her room up with look as pointless as a panty-girdle and a garter belt.

I spent last weekend at Aunt's house in Boston with Janey Ann. We found a pile of old magazines in the attic and got hilarious over women with tufted bottoms and tops sticking straight out like shelves, but Aunt said it had been the height of fashion at the time to have a profile like a zee. Now with the war on, fashions wouldn't be changing till it was over. We'd have to go on wearing knee-length skirts and padded shoulders until styles changed. But she certainly hoped hips would be back after the war. I asked her who would decide about hips.

'Why, designers will, of course. No, Shãn women don't *have* to obey these men. Whatever put that funny idea into your head?'

Aunt's drawing room has brown velvet chairs with lace headrests. When we got there on Saturday morning the room was being aired and feather-dusted for a party and decked out with flowers from a florist shop. In the evening, Mr Rockwell Lawrence, the reason for the room's revival, was there in person. His was the highest handsomest head in it and he had a woman clinging to his coat sleeve. She was wearing a strapless gown but she didn't look at all confident in spite of her bra making her upper curve magnificently match her lower one. She kept touching her fingertips to her throat to apologize for her laryingitis and the little squeak she came out with gave her a headless as well as a helpless look, but Janey Ann's daddy was having that effect on everyone including Janey Ann and even Aunt. It must be quite natural for Mr Lawrence to think he owns everything he lays eyes on, virile example of accumulated capital that he is. It is my great good fortune to meet in the flesh a man like the men who came After Columbus for whom no strait was too narrow, no sea too wide. But direct descendant though he may be of those fearless adventurers, Janey Ann says he's just a babe-in-arms when it comes to love. He keeps on falling madly into it. This time it's with the clinger and this is their engagement party. (The American old have the same desires as the American young.)

At the party I pulled my palla round my shoulders and kept near the bar at the back of the room from where I could see everybody and wouldn't be seen but Mr Lawrence spotted me from his towering height.

'C'mon over, young lady. This is my friend Milton. Milton, this young lady is a friend of my Janey Ann. She is East Indian.'

Milton said 'Is that right!' with hearty indifference and asked me if I spoke English. I tried to say something but Mr Lawrence was having his decapitating effect on me. Janey Ann had told me he was the easiest person to talk to because he had so many interests, from his pineapple plantation down in the Dominican Republic to the feeding habits of hogs, but she had warned me not to mention President Roosevelt on any account, or Edgar Knox, or Clark Gable because her daddy couldn't stand moustaches, and I kept thinking of them. It didn't matter because Milton hadn't waited to hear my English. He was telling Mr Lawrence that Japanese pilots did not have normal side vision like white folks owing to the way Japanese eye sockets are placed in their skulls. The clinger kept smiling and clinging which I took to be the custom as love in America has to keep on being shown and, if possible, heard, but I could see no trace of the legacy of Mrs Experience Bozarth in all this. Mr Lawrence took the clinger to the dance floor when a three-piece band started playing. I saw her pressed against his powerful chest. Both her arms were lifted high around his neck and Mr Lawrence was crooning 'I'm gonna buy a paper doll to call my own' to the music of the band.

Janey Ann and I lounged late in bed on Sunday morning when Aunt went to church. Janey Ann told me her daddy's wife after her mother had been boring but nice and she hadn't minded the one after Loretta, or his girlfriends after Louise. The clinger was a pain in the neck, always showing off her big boobs just because some men are big babies about big boobs. The unscrupulous clinger was not as hoarse as she was making out either. It's one of the tricks in her bagful of tricks because she knows just how susceptible Mr Lawrence is to helpless women with baby voices and great big boobs.

In western love some men go for boobs and some for legs or rumps like preferring juicy breast or crispy tender things on their restaurant menus. But Janey Ann says women just go for the men and not for the measurements of their body parts. Men's organs and body parts don't have to be tape-measured to make sure they're the right size for women to fall into love with them. The way a woman tells if a man is her one and only is if he makes her feel like a helpless speck of nothing in his arms.

Janey Ann doesn't blame her daddy for falling into love with the clinger. He gets so lonely. (When the Americans get lonely they don't just have a chat with someone or take up a hobby or read a book. They fall into the mood for love and marry.)

Professor Orbach gave us a general survey in his first lecture on American history. It has made the character of Mr Rockwell Lawrence clear to me. He has the combined qualities of the colonists and the pioneers. Professor Orbach said the colonists found a wilderness and Indians and it was a tossup which was wilder, but they did not turn back. Later the conquest of the prairie called for even greater hardihood. The Indians had been friendly so long as the pioneers were content to hunt, fish and trap, but they began waging ferocious wars without any regard for the rules of combat when Indian land was taken. They were just out to exterminate. But did the pioneers turn back? No sir, the covered wagons rolled right on and after years of war there was peace at last. The Indians left alive were sent to reservations, and once they were out of the way, little towns with little churches came up in the wilds until civilization stretched from sea to shining sea. At the end of his lecture Professor Orbach summed it up. America's past had set the pattern for America's future. This, he said, is what we call 'the American way of life'. I haven't slept a wink since that summing up, knowing Mr Lawrence has the frontier spirit with no frontier to roll on to. Naturally the clinger must know it's safer not to be on his path. Janey Ann says she has an advanced degree in botany but no one's supposed to know. Clinging to Mr Lawrence has to be her only ambition, and she has to make him feel big and strong though he's already big and strong. I've seen her gazing up at him as if he were an oak, with all her frustrated ardour for botany in her yearning glance.

Mrs Maxwell was so sure Janey Ann who has the most dates would be the first girl in the dorm to get engaged but a lanky spectacled girl called Eunice is the first. I heard the commotion of engagement rites as I walked up the cobbled path. Every girl in the dorm, except Janey Ann who was in the biology lab, was on the living room floor showing enthusiasm and emotion as is the custom. Mrs

Maxwell was showing it less noisily at the tea urn. Eunie and her navy fiancé were holding all four hands on the sofa and Eunie was laughing away between soft screams and sobs. On popular request she held up her left hand for everyone to see the solitaire on her engagement finger, the one directly connected to the heart. There was a loud reverent howl. Mrs Maxwell wiped her eyes. It was a picturesque ceremony. Now Mrs Maxwell is predicting Janey Ann will be the second girl in the dorm to get engaged.

The most sensational line of love lore I have heard so far (under my window on Saturday night) is 'Get those gorgeous boobs outa my way so I can get close ta ya'.

⸱⸱⸱

The girl on telephone duty had come to tell Shān she had a caller downstairs but the last person Shān had expected to see was Otto Schelling, holding his hat to his heart. He strode forward, extracted a cellophane-wrapped box from under his arm and presented her with it. In her skirt and sweater she felt as exposed as a wafer in the wind. Her voice failed to rise to the occasion though Miss de Selwyn had hoped it would by the semester's end. To hide her panic she peeled off the cellophane, opened the box of glazed cherries and thanked him in a cracked whisper.

They stood facing each other to the jumpy tune of I betcha that I getcha that Eunie was banging out on the piano. Eunie stopped to stare fixedly at Otto Schelling before closing the lid and strolling out of the room. At the door she turned around to examine him again. That left two Air Corps boys from the Easthaven Air Force base, lolling in their chairs blowing bubbles of pink chewing gum while they waited for their double date. Both were gaping at Mr Schelling who looked like no one the Easthaven campus had ever seen. Compared with the Air Corps boys' crew cuts, upturned noses and lazily moving jaws, Mr Schelling's jaw was severely still, his nose was nose length and his cratered cheeks could have been crosssections of the moon in a face that started at the dome of his head. The cut of his clothes and his ramrod straightness announced him as irredeemably foreign. Two pancaked and panty-girdled girls came in and the double date departed into battle.

'Shall we sit down?' he prompted, used as he was to playing master of ceremonies at his mother's parties.

He put his hat on the piano, guided Shān to a chair, established her in it and stood in front of her with his hands behind his back. In the pindrop silence Shān understood the importance of social smiling. She smiled.

'You are, of course, surprised to see me,' he informed her, and seated himself so erectly that the upper half of him did not appear to have sat, 'I should have written first. It is many years since I was in a young ladies' establishment. But you may remember I did tell you I had business in Boston and I would take the opportunity to bring you some librettos.'

Now she remembered. Theatre ruins voices, he had asserted, in the end there is only opera. And when Shān said she had never been to the opera he had told her nothing would please him more than to introduce a novice to it and to escort her to the operas of her choice when she came to New York for Christmas.

Shān took the folder of librettos from him, picked up each one and read the title out loud in a methodical manner that delighted him. He had never seen such orderliness in one so young. With the same habitual discipline she replaced them neatly in their folder and thanked him.

Shān could think of nothing more to say to Otto Schelling who wore the keen expectant look of more to come.

'If the rules permit,' said Mr Schelling with a mischievous smile, 'I will take you to dinner in the Village and make you some suggestions about the librettos. There is here such an intensity of human emotion that it will be confusing for a young novice to make her choices.'

But it was Sunday. Nothing would be open at this hour except The Greasy Spoon and Shān could not picture Otto Schelling sitting cheek by jowl with taxi drivers to the accompaniment of Chattanooga Choo Choo on the jukebox, hot fat spluttering in a frying pan, the door swinging open and shut and new arrivals straddling stools to yell ham on rye. Anyway she had had supper at six and had to get on with the Monroe Doctrine.

'Ah well,' he conceded. 'No matter. You will write to me when you have decided what to see. We meet again in New York.'

Shān looked at the librettos again in her room. The first one opened with 'My Lords, if you would hear a high tale of love and death.' She read on, staggered by its trueness to life, and on and on after the tale of the love potion. Rodolfo, enchanted by Mimi, searches the floor with her for her lost key, their hands meet and love is born! The heartless Duke gets ardent with Maddalena, and Gilda watching through a crack gives bitter cries of pain. Lucy marries Arthur but Edgar appears dramatically at the wedding feast. Walls of fire, the white dove of the Holy Grail, visions of love eternal, madness and tender farewells, the librettos had them all and never before had language so literally expressed life. She trembled to think how the music would affect her. Shān put her head down on her desk and wept.

∫

Just before the Christmas vacation Leda got Shān's letter asking permission to bring the Lawrence girl to New York with her. She had found her friend face down on her bed hysterically crying 'Poor Daddy' in such a distraught manner she had thought Mr Rockwell Lawrence was dead. When Janey Ann could control her tears she said it would just about kill him when she was thrown out of school in disgrace because she was pregnant. In her relief that Mr Lawrence was alive Shān had only been able to stammer, 'But I thought he didn't care about your becoming a biologist' before the purport of the disaster hit her.

Miss Knox would understand, she wrote, that though Mr Lawrence was well and happy it was important to keep him in this condition. Fine example of After Columbus that he was, a man who judged himself by the things he owned, Shãn foresaw the terrible consequences of letting his pride of possession, his masculine inventory-taking glance alight on a pregnant Janey Ann. Shãn and Janey Ann had thought frantically about who could help but had dismissed every name that came to mind. Mrs Maxwell. Aunt. The clinger. Even the learned librarian. Nor could Mr Lawrence's wedding date be brought forward and the pair speeded on their honeymoon to the Dominican Republic to give more time for a solution because Mr Lawrence had not set a date yet and he was not the man to be hustled. The obvious solution was for Janey Ann to marry the culprit who had not abided by the rules of combat, but she had forthrightly rejected the idea. 'Don't be such a dope, Shãn. Sure he's cute but good grief I don't want to *marry* him.' Janey Ann was under an intolerable strain and need never have been if America had been more like Bali. And now Miss Knox was their only hope of finding a way to keep Mr Lawrence well and happy.

Shãn's entreaty horrified Leda. A tougher woman than herself would have tackled Rockwell Lawrence over a lunch (paid for by him) and forced him to face his responsibility like a rational human being. Leda recoiled from thrusting herself into someone else's crisis, still more from confronting the After Columbus specimen Shãn's earlier letters had described. A vivid image of the virile Mr Lawrence crooning I'm gonna buy a paper doll came sinisterly back to her. She wished Professor Orbach's encapsulation of American history had not made the saga sound so much like Mr Lawrence. She forbade herself to think about the Lawrence girl. Edgar would have to handle it. He was back in the United States and had gone to Washington. Even as the President's unofficial emissary in India he had not been allowed to see Shān's father and he was now working on a direct appeal to Churchill by the President for the prisoner's release.

Leda longed for her own familiar surroundings, to be able to walk over to Rosina Mongini's apartment to sup on black bean soup, admire a spike-heeled glass slipper and appreciate the wit and wisdom of Mr Mongini. She called Rosina and asked her to lunch, hoping she would be free.

'Yes, I'm free, Leda,' Rosina sounded sorrowful. 'He's away but he'll make it up to me. He isn't going to let anything interfere with our Christmas, war or no war. I'd love to come to lunch. I haven't seen you since I delivered my last drawings uptown.'

She looked small and solid in Edgar's living room, her cheeks bright from the icy wind. She untied her red wool headscarf letting her grey-black hair spring free.

'So this is where your brother lives? My, my! Give me a tour.'

In the study she said, 'All these books! And not one of them bound in showy leather with fancy lettering. You can tell he reads them. A man Mr Mongini knows called Mr Leroy keeps a parade of licures on his bar. What can I tempt you with, he says, but it turns out nearly every one of them's empty, he's only keeping them for decoration, except that awful green peppermint stuff.'

The tour ended in the kitchen and Rosina, clearly more at home with linoleum than with Asian exotica suggested, 'Why don't we eat here? It's silly for just us two women to sit in the dining room.'

Leda poured Dubonnet and in an outburst of pent-up irritation she told Rosina about Jane Ann Lawrence.

'Oh dear God,' whispered Rosina.

She put her glass down with a shaking hand, reached for the back of a kitchen chair and slowly lowered herself into it, planting her elbows on the table for support. Her fingertips groped for her burning cheeks and dug deep into them.

'Whatever is the poor little girl going to do?' she asked in horror.

'Don't worry about it, it's not our problem, Rosina.'

Rosina wasn't listening.

'My cousin Antonella got pregnant when I was a child but can I ever forget it? She had to drop out of sight for a whole year. I can't tell you all the planning it took for the family to smuggle her out to California to have the baby there and give it out for adoption. Antonella was never the same again. She went simple.'

Between forkfuls of chicken á lá king which she could hardly swallow Rosina brooded about the female predicament, few being so lucky as herself. And Mr Mongini was right when he said, 'Nobody's embarrassed about anything nowadays. Back in the old days women used to blush. Whole audiences used to blush when they saw the soles of Isadora Duncan's feet. A blush is a beautiful thing, Rosina.'

Her favourite pecan ice cream and angel cake did not restore her equilibrium. She was busy grappling with Jane Ann's problem.

'When morals were strict and sex was secret there were underground channels to go to for help. Now, with behaviour all out in the open there's no place to go. This little girl is going to need all the help she can get.'

'It's really not our business,' repeated Leda, aware that Rosina's palpitating anxiety made nonsense of this statement.

Wasn't there some loving elder in the family or some distant relative out west Jane Ann could turn to?

'If there had been, Shān wouldn't have written to me. The Lawrence man sounds like an ogre. This serves him right.'

Rosina turned pale and shivered. 'It would serve him right if *he* was in a mess, Leda, but what's the poor little *girl* going to do?'

Edgar returned from Washington that evening, distracted by the failure of his efforts. Leda handed him Shān's letter before he started opening his own mail and he read it quickly standing in the hall.

'Mrs Burns,' he snapped his fingers, 'call her right now and ask her what to do.'

Florence Burns displayed Edgar's and Rosina Mongini's talent for plunging headlong into a crisis that had nothing to do with her. She promised to be in touch soon. Two days later she called to say she had made an arrangement.

She also wanted Christmas dinner transferred from her house in Brookham to Edgar's apartment.

'We can't cancel Christmas, Leda. Desmond would want to know why. And he's so sentimental about family get-togethers.'

She explained why the abortion had to take place on Christmas Day. The fine gynaecologist who was her lifelong personal friend and a great humanitarian did not have a blank space on his appointment calendar from now until the end of January except Christmas Day and only on her fervent confidential plea was he taking the case at all. She had begged him to understand their combined responsibility for the girl — he was one of Edgar's devoted readers — and she had left him in no doubt at all about the impressive personality of Mr Lawrence, without of course mentioning Mr Lawrence's name.

'I don't think Jane Ann Lawrence has the least idea the trouble she is causing,' said Leda primly. 'She certainly doesn't deserve all you are doing for her, Mrs Burns.'

'Ah, Leda, there are times when all we womenfolk deserve all the protection we can get from our loving menfolk. The heartbroken royal lover who built the Taj Mahal in his dearly beloved's memory need never have had to create that outstanding mausoleum if he hadn't killed her off giving birth to his fourteenth child. His Light of the Palace could have lived on into a healthy old age right beside him on the Peacock Throne. Now don't you fret yourself about the turkey and trimmings. It's my party and I'll take care of everything.'

A week before Christmas Leda opened the door to admit Shān and called 'She's here, Edgar' over her shoulder.

He appeared at the door of his study, pulled out of a late afternoon nap, passed a hand over his eyes and stared uncomprehending at the bulky enveloping winter coat until it dawned on him there was a girl in it. They moved toward each other to shake hands formally, each with a legend. Then Edgar, fully awake, flung his impetuous arms around the girl and Leda was strangely moved as though a tumultuous epic had narrowed down to two people in her own life. Behind Shān a shrinking Jane Ann Lawrence hung back, unsure of her welcome, tremulous tears on her eyelashes, her famous gold curls out of sight under her hat. Edgar reached out and pulled her into a three-cornered embrace and she broke into frantic sobs, blowing her nose into the handkerchief he handed her. Leda waited her turn to greet Shān with a kiss and Jane Ann with cordial reserve.

Leda was not hostile to Jane Ann, but she hadn't been able to work up any sympathy for her and thought it better to leave the foolish girl and Shān to their own devices. Soon they were treating her with the consideration visitors show outside the intensive care ward of a hospital, and the hallowed precincts of Edgar's study as their happy hunting ground. Jane Ann had fits of terror as the dreaded event approached and as no member of the household knew in precise actual terms what the ordeal would involve, they — or rather, Edgar and Shān — could only pacify her as they would a child having a nightmare. Two nightmares, amended Leda, the event itself and what it would do to Daddy if he ever heard about it. The After Columbus spirit of Mr Rockwell Lawrence loomed over the countdown to Christmas, ruining the tempting breakfasts Leda cooked, invading the carols on the radio and Alfred's cheerful interminable comments on the weather every time they left or entered the building. On Christmas morning Leda woke with a throbbing head to see a red-eyed, wretched but bravely controlled Jane Ann off to her appointment.

Florence Burns arrived mid-morning in a snow flurry followed by Desmond and Alfred carrying a hamper and an assortment of parcels. Soon after them came an Indian student who Edgar had met by chance in Washington and for no good reason invited to join the Christmas party. Leda took an instant dislike to him.

By twelve o'clock when Christianity should have been uppermost in their minds, Edgar and Shān's 'boyfriend' as Desmond insisted on referring to the diminutive, slightly pompous Indian out of nowhere, were talking Hinduism. Desmond, nothing daunted, was doggedly talking lobster to Shān. This large marine crustacean, Leda heard, is the juiciest and most succulent of all the creatures of the sea, Indian nationalism was purely Hindu at the start, a glorious blue when alive, bright red when boiled, and its rallying cry was Vande Mataram meaning Hail Motherland. Leda's head buzzed with the droning discord of it. She was not sure when the student's sermon on Hinduism began, queerly, to prevail. Next to Desmond's lung power Chandrabhan's shallow monotone should have made no more impression than the soft-lipped bite of a snapdragon yet she herself was succumbing to it. Everyone turned to Chandrabhan (partly to tone down Desmond's last guffaw) and gave in to his sermon's chloroforming calm. Chandrabhan had a knack of turning landscape into scripture and India into Hindus who had waited centuries to reclaim the land from Mongol, Turk, Moghul and Briton. Edgar, normally argumentative, did not argue as Leda had known him to, that India had no need to slide backward into Europe's religion-ruled Dark Ages. No one had a word to say when Chandrabhan demanded: Could Hindus forget the hoofbeats of Islam's hordes or other ransackers who had come by land and sea to suck her blood and leave her humbled, impoverished and dazed? His listeners scarcely drew breath till he drew his, and then only to wait for him to go on. His expressionless litany had a compelling power, giving his monomania the stamp of eternity and there was no interrupting his riverine eloquence. It occurred to Leda this stranger, sipping eggnog and munching salted crackers, was the ally Mrs Schelling's packager and promoter of countries needed to simplify India for Americans. Chandrabhan had come with flowers for her, not a bouquet but a bunch of hothouse violets cupped in his moist palms, which he had presented to her in a gesture of sublime offering. Here in New York's East Seventies, on the threshold of Edgar's apartment, with a holly wreath gracing the door and a Christmas turkey roasting aromatically in the oven, his 'I have brought you flowers, Mother' had made her skin crawl with gooseflesh and eerily transformed her cashmere wool-clad figure into a four-armed symbol with hair of swirling blue lilies and skin of burnished gold.

Leda felt chilled and menaced in the warm room with its festively lit Christmas tree. There was a bloodcurdling sameness about all messages of racial purity, and the swords and scimitars their upholders kept sharpened for their holy wars. The clock had a way of going forward and then back. There would always be a fanatic at the fair. She stopped listening and retreated into the profound pessimism that had sustained her all her adult life.

Desmond was by now paying closer attention to Chandrabhan than any of them, intrigued by this oddfish out of deeper, different water. The boy, having finished presenting the Hindu India of his dreams was saying linear progress was a western concept. According to the Hindus, progress came and went. Right now the universe was in a cycle of dissolution and decay when men delighted in evil doings but this phase had only a few hundred thousand years of mundane time to go. Accepting this statement with a sober nod Desmond clapped Chandrabhan on the back and passed him a cheese cracker.

'You hear that, sweetheart?' he yelled to Leda who had left the room to replenish the nuts, 'blue skies are just around the corner.'

Chandrabhan's universe might be dissolving but he looked super-humanly integrated and more confident than the rest of them, a wavering white blur in their world of uneasy progress. Anybody who could successfully compete with lobster for Desmond's interest was no ordinary being. Desmond broke the spell of India's Hindu destiny by peevishly demanding, 'Hey Leda, where's that frienda yours and Edgar from Checkoslovakia? Why didn't you ask him to join our family get-together?' Leda struggled out of Chandrabhan's narrative as out of a strangler's throttlehold, to say, 'Milo? He's doing his war job, Des, I don't know where.'

Desmond became temporarily violently gloomy. Helping himself to more eggnog he declared Leda's Checkoslovakian friend was a man any woman could be prouda. How did she say he got his hand bones broken? The difficulties of being a foster parent to two such as Edgar and herself, born to fulfil heaven alone knew what yearnings of incurably romantic young parents, came over Leda as it never had before. She had had the best that Desmond was capable of giving. She had no right to expect the Crock of Gold. She went to sit beside him, slipping an arm through his, and explained about Milo's hand yet again.

'When did you say he's heading back?' growled Desmond, aggressive and unappeased, and in the same breath, 'how much longer's this war going on, Edgar?'

Edgar's succinct reply followed, unnecessarily, Desmond having lost interest. But Edgar, now launched, gave it as his discouraging opinion that if India fell to the Japanese, Japan and Germany would meet and join forces in the Persian Gulf. Yet the British obdurately refused to put India's independence on the war agenda to ensure the Indian people's support.

'Well!' said Florence Burns gleefully, coming in from the dining room, 'I think we're ready to eat!'

Thankfully everyone rose. It was two o'clock and snowing hard. In the dining room they sat down to her candlelit feast in a traditional Christmas setting (except for the Kathakali mask on one wall and Indonesian papier-maché puppets on another) in an atmosphere approaching Christmas at last but not quite yet in its spirit of revelry. The clock struck three by the time Edgar lit the pudding and Leda got up to answer the doorbell to let Jane Ann Lawrence in. The Lawrence girl was white to the roots of her straggling hair. A snow blast between her taxi and the canopy at the entrance had blanched and drained her of all living colour. She could have been the disinterred corpse of a Fra Angelico Virgin. She stood drooping until Leda helped her out of her coat and Shān came running out to hug her and take her to the table. Edgar seated her with a gallant flourish and served her with a flaming portion of pudding. Suddenly laughter rang out and long delayed festivity blossomed — except for Desmond who was slightly drunk and belligerently demanding to be told why Jane Ann Lawrence hadn't been invited to the party from the start — and Leda realized they were celebrating an abortion and not a birth.

Four days later Jane Ann boarded the train home to Aunt and on the evening of January first Leda was taken aback at the sight of Otto Schelling in opera cape and cylindrical opera hat at the front door. Her greeting was high-pitched with surprise. She had forgotten he was taking Shān to the opera. She fetched her own fur coat for Shān on whom it was ankle-length and voluminous but the girl went off excitedly in it. Leda closed the door on the worthy Otto and his charge. Edgar was out for the evening. She spent it peacefully, contemplating her return to the Village after Shān's holiday.

She had made plans to entertain Shān during her vacation but apart from selected operas Shān was leading the life of a New York socialite, hobnobbing with New York's musical nobility under the benign aegis of Mrs Schelling. All this soignée coming and going in shimmering saris under Leda's engulfing brown beaver was centred, Leda gathered, on floods of music within and outside the Schelling fortress. One of these occasions was to be a string quartet recital at the Schellings' in honour of Wolfgang Schelling's engagement.

'Mr Wolfgang Schelling is engaged to a Walloon,' Shān importantly informed Leda and was disappointed to learn the Walloons were not a rare Indian tribe, only the first white colonists of New York descended from Protestants who had fled Belgium. However, this was a wealthy Walloon, apparently a feather in Wolfgang's cap.

The engagement party was reported to be a fashionable success except that Mrs Schelling, grievously agitated by news that the Bolsheviks were victoriously rolling the Nazis back over a two thousand mile front, had broken her sacrosanct no war, no peace, rule and the headlines had been discussed.

Leda spent her own vacation from the office at Edgar's, contentedly sealed in from blizzard weather. The day it cleared she ventured out for a walk. The streets were slushy with dirty snow but the sky glowed glacially amber between high buildings. The afternoon's frozen clarity had the stimulating effect on her of uncurtaining fresh views and vistas and reacquainting her with the city. She walked all the way to the Plaza, braced by the exercise, and turned into Central Park South. With a cup of tea in mind she went into Rumpelmeyer's, thawing quickly in the heat of a restaurant that always reminded her of a rouged and ruffled doll. Tales from the Vienna Woods and three-tiered silver stands of pastries completed the illusion of froth and bubble.

The custom of three meals a day had gone out with the bustle. At any hour anywhere in the city one could find New Yorkers eating. The woman facing her from a table for two close by was spooning an intricately layered confection oozing syrup into her mouth with obvious enjoyment. A plate of triangular tea sandwiches and cream rolls waited between her and her escort to be consumed and soon were. The woman had shrugged her blond fur coat off her shoulders. It nestled in a careless sensuous heap around her hips. Her skin and hair emanated a richness distilled of the afternoon's translucent light. Leda had a feeling that her flushed gold and rose opulence was appetizingly repeated through honeyed layers like the pastry's down to the succulence of her own flesh. She was an unbearably luscious sight, flirtatiously engaged with the man opposite her, but with a confidence that showed she had been in long possession of him.

They ate their cream cakes and sandwiches ravenously, thirstily drank their pot of tea and yet they made a remarkably restful picture. The woman's voice was loud enough to be heard but devoid of the grating edge of uncouth loudness. The man's replies were not audible but to judge by her expression he was enamoured and she satisfactorily caressed. She teased him about their New Year resolutions. They talked about where to go for a few lazy days in spring. They would age into Florence Burns' ideal couple, partners who had weathered youth and embarked on the perfect companionship. Old age would find them empathically bonded by hints and nuances, never needing more than a glance or a touch to convey volumes.

As soon as they got up to go their table was taken by an overweight pair. The woman's rasping voice demanded hot chocolate. Her escort, hunched over his menu, acknowledged this with a grunt. Leda's eyes followed her couple nostalgically to the door and out. Through the plate glass window lined with massed bronze chrysanthemums she saw them close together on the sidewalk. The man signalled a cab and handed his princess in. Instead of getting in after her he straightened up and settled his square shoulders more comfortably into his overcoat with a characteristic shrugging movement Leda had seen him make many a time and crooked his finger for another taxi, back to hearth and home in the Village. Leda felt shabbily betrayed.

On her drive home in a drearier light she mourned the Mongini marriage and laid it to rest, aching with her own loss of a nurture she had long taken for granted. Rosina Mongini was not a woman to whom one could, however obliquely, hint at betrayal. That red-cheeked crusty outer valour hid a trusting tremulous heart. She paid off her taxi and set careful feet on the treacherous icebound sidewalk outside Edgar's apartment.

Otto Schelling elevated the hand Leda held out for him to shake and brushed his lips to his own thumb.

'As you see, I am here,' he said, and apologized for coming without an appointment.

Leda offered tea, coffee, spirits but he consulted his watch and confirmed it was a time at which he took nothing. He had come merely to thank Leda for allowing him to take Shān to the opera. Music, he must tell Leda, was his passion but opera was his religion. On this subject, in all sincerity, he knew best. His family and friends joked that dissent on this subject was to him as Martin Luther was to a Catholic. He laughed abruptly at his own sally and then began pontifically to tell her of Shān's response to the great experience. Simply to enter the portals and pass into the lobby of massed flowers, then into the grand interior was itself a sensation unlike any other. He, a seasoned opera-goer, had known the interior to blossom before his eyes as he raised them to the tiers of balconies, the chandeliers, the magnificence. How would it not affect a young novitiate? Yet, that first evening when music surged from the well of darkness beneath the stage, he who was accustomed to the veritable onslaught of music on the senses, had been unprepared for Shān's reaction, the only possible response to music made of hopes too great for earth.

'I have taken debutantes from the best families to the opera, Miss Knox. They have woken up with a start on a piercing high note or when the hunter's horn sounded in the middle of an Act. I have escorted Mrs Van Huesen who is a trustee and has a box. Time and again I have gone with the Giacosa family, all celebrated musicians themselves. Shãn was different. She was as Eve in the garden of Eden. But I see I have disturbed you at a busy moment.'

Leda said she was packing to go back to her own apartment, but no matter, he must stay.

'I asked myself,' continued Otto, 'if her reaction could be the result of hearing an orchestra play. The East knows nothing of Europe's great tradition of symphonic sound so she has never heard strings, wood, winds and brasses played together. The combination makes so powerful an assault on the senses, Miss Knox, that the church forbade instrumental music during the Dark Ages. What then, I asked myself, could such a surge of orchestral sound do to a primitive ear?'

Leda was disconcerted by the glitter in Otto's eyes. Try as she might to concentrate on what he was saying, she heard — instead of strings, wood, winds and brasses — the drummed repetitive chant of Seig Heil! *Seig Heil!* SEIG HEIL! which Edgar had called 'stentorian lungs usurping the functions of the brain'. He had shown her the movie of the Carlsbad rally he had covered in Czechoslovakia in 1938. Swastika badges were everywhere, on people, doors, windows, rooftops. The invading army was trooping its colours in terrifyingly precise goose step. The Führer in long military coat had his hand raised in salute to a screaming crescendo of 'Weir danken unserem Führer'. He switched off the crescendo by a flick of his raised hand, hit the balcony in front of him and said 'Dass ich hier ein Tag stehen wurde, das hab'ich gewusst —

That I would be standing here one day, that I knew.'
Women fainted in ecstasy at this prophecy fulfilled and
were carried out of the square on stretchers. Others wept
for joy.

'Then it came to me,' Otto was saying, 'the orchestra
alone was not the reason for Shān's reaction. There is a
handful of the elect among listeners for whom opera finds
its echo in the soul. For them, Miss Knox, it is life, death,
rebirth. But it is life, Miss Knox, as we have forgotten how
to live it, when frenzy is natural, the world is well lost
for love, and people die of commitment, yes, singing as
they die.'

He paused for a triumphant moment to let this sink
in as Leda did her best to rally.

'Verdi offers us such a life, Miss Knox. Look for a
minute at Rigoletto, at the two Leonoras of II Trovatore
and La Forza del destino. Hear Violetta's agonized cry of
love "Amami Alfredo" at the instant of their farewell
embrace. Who can forget Battisti who saw him in Maria
di Rohan when he drags his wife savagely by the hair
toward the door, the very door through which her lover
is about to enter? Who can forget the fury with which he
tears the bandage from his wounded hand with his teeth
as he learns of his betrayal?'

All this, Otto concluded, which others would consider
improbable melodramatic excess, *she* — how should he
put it? — *recognized*, Miss Knox, as life's truth. A girl of
Shān's refined sensibilities belonged in the West. He looked
forward, with Miss Knox's permission — to continuing
her musical education on her next vacation.

Leda could see Otto back in his mother's apartment, crossing the black and white floor to the record player to play an operatic aria and stand bowed over it, light from the terrace glancing off the dome of his skull, lost in contemplation of the girl who had caught fire with Carmen, pined with Butterfly and been entombed with Aïda.

Eleven

During Christmas vacation Shān wrote in her Notebook: I have given up trying to sort out Otto's peculiar behaviour. I am used to a fanatic light leaping into his eyes but it has been connected with Gilda's sacrifice for the Duke or Rodolfo's besottedness with Mimi or the 'Chi mi frena?' sextet of Lucy, Henry, Arthur, Edgar, Raymond and Alice. I also saw it at the singing of 'Agnel son bianco e vo' (A lamb so white, I bleating go) at the engagement party for Wolfgang and the Walloon, *and* during La Traviata's devil-may-careness the next night. But what on earth can it have to do with Guy Lombardo's band playing 'Dontcha know it's more romantic when a dance is slow' at the Roosevelt Hotel? His leaping light has nothing to do with this kind of music, his voice has got more guttural, and I wish I knew why.

Otto must be in love, but it's not the grand opera love Europeans feel for each other because he doesn't look haunted or uplifted. Otto is twitchy. But just *in case* he's

fallen into love, who with? *Me?* Out of the question. I
haven't got the body parts — the boobs, the rump or the
thighs for post-pioneer love in America. Of course Otto
isn't American. And he did once say that breasts are of
no importance in an elegant woman. For elegance, he said,
the hip bones must be prominent and pointed, the hair
must be abundant, and no expression need be present in
the eyes. Even if I'm more or less all this it still doesn't
explain his feverish oddness. He keeps saying, 'There is
nothing to be afraid of, Ev'chen' whenever he takes me
out, and he's got into the habit of continuing a hint where
he left it the last time. The night after the Roosevelt Hotel
he took me to the Russian Bear and *again* he said, 'Do
not be afraid, Ev'chen.'

'What *of?*' I asked.

I had to say it loudly and lean towards him so that
he would hear me above the yell of the Cossack rising
from his haunches after doing a triumphant piourette on
his left heel and my closeness threw Otto into a trance.
Then he got emotional and covered my hand with his
which he has done before but this time he gave my hand
back to me like a reverent offering and said although he
was not a man of philosophy, Kant's 'What may I hope?'
had come to have a poignant meaning for him. If Otto
has fallen into love he is not behaving like Wolfgang does
with the Walloon or the fiancés at their thrilling
announcement ceremonies in the dorm. He's not behaving
like I've seen men behave with women. Every time he
takes me out I get the funny feeling that the table between
us in restaurants is not a table. It's an ocean and he's the

horde After Columbus sighting an undiscovered shore. The glint of Aztec gold in Spanish eyes is glinting all over again in Otto's. Or else he's Gauguin going gaga over the Tahitians.

'Do not be afraid I will take advantage of you, Ev'chen,' he said at the Russian Bear, 'you may be sure I will not.'

And then he started cutting up and voraciously devouring the shashlik we had just been served on flaming swords.

'Let me give you an example, Ev'chen. Many years ago I was in love with a beautiful Jewish girl.' He wiped his mouth with his napkin as if he was apologizing for a faux pas. 'Her name was Leah. And with Leah I went no further than to kiss her breasts because her father was dead.'

My mind was in a whirl. I know there is an order of events in the goodnight ceremonies. Janey Ann explained it to me step by step before her abortion, very mathematically with a diagram and a long lead statuette called The Bagpiper, donated to the dorm by a 1910 alumna of Scottish ancestry. (The goodnight struggle results from keeping The Bagpiper from shooting out of your date's pants. This must not happen before wedlock. The militant behaviour of The Bagpiper is something I would never have guessed at, there being not a nudging suspicion of it inside trousers.) But even Janey Ann wouldn't know how Leah's breasts would be connected with her dead father. Anyway, if Otto's is the form that western love takes toward Tahitians etc., I'm glad I know the order of events just in case.

I get home from these outings with Otto and let myself in and go to Mr Knox's study to say I'm back. He sits at his typewriter with his sleeves rolled up and his books and papers all over the floor. Mr Knox is writing a book but the way he goes about it is like a construction labourer lifting, carting and dumping heavy loads. He always looks up, smiles his loving smile, asks me, 'Well then, how's Otto the Faithful?' (or Otto the Chivalrous) and goes back to work. Miss Knox asks me if I want a glass of milk before I go to bed. I've broached the subject of Otto's queer condition with both of them and Mr Knox said there was no accounting for the mental stability of these Seig Heil temperaments.

∿

Unlike Edgar, Leda who was steeped in Jenner travel lore and well versed in its dementia, diagnosed Otto Schelling's as an older malaise. She was so familiar with the paths it took she could have been in Otto's skin, felt and spoken for him when he took Shān out for supper after that first opera on January first.

'So! Happy New Year, Ev'chen,' he greeted Shān, lifting his wine glass in salutation to draw her out of her intense immersion in Verdi's grand harmonies. 'Tell me how you like my name for you.'

He would have liked to point out to her the technical brilliance and purity of the high notes, the exquisitely expressed heartbeats and alarms of Violetta. He had saved stories to tell her about Verdi in his garret across the road from the theatre in Milan, with his frail alabaster girl-wife and his dying baby boy. But he had no desire to break the spell. He guessed the opera had been a somehow autobiographical experience for her, recalling lives around her if not her own still fledgling one, and he also surmised this recall had nothing to do with actual episodes she had seen enacted on the stage but with the heart-wringing they had thrust on her, the heights and depths they had flung her to so visibly.

Otto had selected a sparkling Burgundy. He urged her to try it and waited, keen and concentrated, until she raised the glass to her lips and lowered it again. Everything about this occasion had the solemnity of a ceremony, himself a high priest conducting it. He did not miss the waiter's discreet appraisal of this weightless sprite so unlike the female flesh a man usually entertains at supper. Her dark troubled eyes brightened with a few sips of wine. In a few minutes she was entirely animated, taking in the room, the diners and the hauteur of the waiters with a child's rapid change of mood. Appealingly she asked him why a race that had made such sublime music as the Europeans had, had wasted its time seizing other people's lands and oil and gold and timber, time it could have spent creating more masterpieces.

Otto felt his own sharp intake of breath, and then for the first time since leaving his beloved Berlin, possibly for the first time in his forty years, he burst into an uncontrolled and colossally satisfying laugh. He held his napkin to his mouth, then wiped his eyes with it. That this infant also had wit, and an infant's careless way with history, rejoiced him as vastly as her helplessness when Violetta died of consumption in Alfredo's arms had entranced him. He was quite simply in a season of amazement. If he tried to analyse it he melted down into weak rejoicing.

With the permission of that bloodless woman, Leda Knox, her guardian, he took Shān out again and again, never sure how to assess his state of mind. It was not following its usual course in pursuit of women, but his earlier pursuits had never been of the genre celebrated as lyrical, and this present absorption had little to do with 'women' as the Palm Court or the Persian Room at the Plaza decreed them, but with a collector's item of which there is only one, a prize with whom a man does not necessarily behave as he does with a woman though naturally along the same general lines.

With this One there could be endless expert variations on and perhaps even excluding the rather boring main theme. He felt out of sympathy with Wolfgang who harped constantly on the main theme with anecdotes about the brazen heiresses he had dated and now would be doomed to with the Walloon. The intoxication of this experience lay for the moment in thinking about it. Otto allowed himself to contemplate in tantalizing miserly doses the charm of a seduction that would in truth be as much of him as of her, for his bouts of weak rejoicing had revealed an unsuspected virginal streak in himself, showing he was not quite in command.

Even the mechanics this time would not proceed on the usual pattern. In his student days he and Hansjürgen, a bordello enthusiast like himself, had debated whether the order of female disrobing — stockings off first, büstenhalter last — a procedure which here in America striptease had so tastelessly exaggerated with bumps and grinds — was in fact the natural order. But in this case the question was irrelevant. In this case there was (as he thought) only one garment, a single length of it merely to be unwound. The total lack of resistant button, bone or loop, metal or elastic, the absence of pleat or pocket, the stark defencelessness of this unwinding aroused a surge of spiritual angst in Otto. Some little obstacle he had always encountered while undressing a woman, be it a row of buttons down a bodice, a sash or ribbons to undo, lace knickers only half covering a provocative bottom. But this time, without a single obstacle he would be an explorer without a compass. Only at seventeen had he felt so overwhelmed by what awaited him. Only in Carlsbad where he had been holidaying in 1938 had he been possessed of such mystical excitement, when flower-festooned German army lorries filled with infantrymen and machine gunners rolled into the beautiful Bohemian countryside under maypole arches to the joyful thunder of thousands cheering Seig Heil.

Otto did not know Asia but Hansjürgen had travelled widely after leaving the university and spent time in the Orient. The amorous passion of an oriental, he had told Otto, was in startling contrast to the passivity of a European, and nor was it tainted by a Parisian cocotte's lively calculatedness. These women of the tropics, Otto, including the crossbreeds among them, exhale love like a fatal perfume. It is a hallmark of their race. Man is not merely their master, he is their destiny. Why do you think, Otto, Balinese women were in such demand, fetching as much as one hundred and fifty florins each in slave markets in the early seventeenth century? These creatures have an ardour stored up from the heat of their sun, a sun that burns and shines in the splendour of their flesh.

One woman I had, Otto, was of the islands. She must have been thirteen and when I saw the two not yet swelling buds of her little breasts through the thin cloth she wore I hesitated. But my hesitation was all unnecessary. Their thirteen is the equivalent of twenty at home in Europe. Let me tell you these child-women's contractions are famous for bringing a succession of lovers to their graves. With a child-woman of this island breed all the dangers of the adventure will be yours, not hers. However many women you have had until then, she will be your first, your most unique. There is something of the unspoiled eternal virgin in the very instincts of the race.

Hansjürgen, spurred by recollections of pleasures unsurpassed, fulsomely described his island coitions. He had seen no fold of flesh on a single one of those tight-knit tight-bottomed bodies. They retained their grace and there was no corpulent hag among their old women. His stay there had made him an addict of thirteen-year-old breasts and orifices. When he got back into his European stride the maturer home-grown product had been loose-fitting and bulbous in comparison.

Otto had been skeptical of Hansjürgen's tales. Hansjürgen exaggerated. After all, who didn't about sexual exploits? But here, across the table from him eating shashlik, was a tropical wildflower that might have sprung from one of Hansjürgen's known or unknown Indies. Black silk hair flowed down an astonishing slenderness, two breasts that were honeysuckle on a vine, the sway and slightness of a reed. She was a mixture of childlike frivolity and adult gravity which made her not one but many women, succeeding each other capriciously. He feared she was a mirage to which he was steadily advancing and she receding until there was only light and air where she had been.

Her slowness to take a hint, grasp his intention, captivated him, reminding him she was not just a virgin but a virgin of distant exotic origin, not to be carelessly plucked. He got used to the prolonged rigidity of his vital organ in its state of perpetual arousal. He conducted himself at a peak of energy and efficiency at the Stock Exchange. He felt like a sultan who has a harem to command and lives in a condition of actual or anticipated spasm. He considered himself part of a unique experiment. Coitus now struck Otto as a crude and vulgar substitute for this unbearably taut elevated bodymind condition, so erotic that a feather flicked on any inch of his skin would have made him cry out. In all his sexual adventures he had never forborne, yet paradoxically his forbearance now made him feel voluptuously abandoned and depraved. All the same he hinted regularly. Once or twice a flicker passed over her features that convinced him the spark had caught. Then it would vanish. But he deftly slipped his playfully tender hints into his remarks, hoping they would find their mark over coq au vin or a glass of chilled foaming beer. He went no further, realizing he must hasten slowly. Sometimes in her company he heard nothing but the beating of his heart. The feelings of the new man he had become he could only describe as now brook, now tempestuous torrent. He hoped his ardour would not be prematurely conveyed to that bloodless woman, Leda Knox, but if it was, it was.

The world's treasures, he said to Shān, belong in the West where there are connoisseurs. You must stay in the West. A country, Ev'chen? What is a country? Have I not left mine? he demanded. When this war is over I would like to show you the realm of light and learning that is Europe, and its incomparable refinements. And there were his mother's rubies. It had not been necessary to give them to Wolfgang's Walloon whose dowry in vulgar American parlance would be lousy with jewellery. It was his dearest wish, Otto would hint, to see the Bordeaux red of his mother's rubies against the sheen of Shān's throat the like of which Otto had not seen in New York or any European city of his amorous acquaintance. He would be rewarded by the brief spark in her dark troubled eyes before it went out again.

'Well then, how about Otto the Chivalrous and his mother's Bordeaux-red rubies?' Edgar Knox would enquire from the chaotic arena of his study before going back to his strenuous mental activity.

∿

The safe chosen limits of Leda's vision had been greatly extended by her sojourn at Edgar's. When she went back to work in the middle of January the room where she had been cosily cubbyholed for years had the aspect of an expensively curtained and carpeted coffin. Twelve floors below her Madison Avenue traffic glutted Forty-Ninth Street. In the soaring grey antheap opposite ants like herself bent over desks or hurried in and out of offices, conferring busily.

A letter from Shãn said Janey Ann had resumed her dating cry of 'Is it a maaa-a-a-aan?' when she raced down to answer the telephone, as well as her panted post and ante mortems of her dates, but she didn't have her pre-abortion zest and Mrs Maxwell was proved wrong again. Another girl, Trudy, was the second in the dorm to get engaged. She and her Army Air Corps fiancé held all four hands in customary fashion on the living room sofa, Mrs Maxwell wiped the corners of her eyes at the tea urn and Janey Ann gamely did her sister act with two others, crooning Putchorarmsaround-mehoneyholdmetight to wind up the whole emotional ceremony. The strain of all the obstacles the American woman laboured under made Shãn fear for her friend's chances of ever becoming a biologist. (The men must be under a strain, too. To be loved they have to be big and strong.) On the island of Bali, Janey Ann could have roamed bare to the waist, rapturously free of obstacles among orchids, hibiscus and humming birds under a perfumed sky, with a man of any size.

Mr Rockwell Lawrence and the clinger had taken them both to lunch at the Copley Plaza in Boston. They must be waiting till Janey Ann gets engaged before they set their own date because nothing was said about it. The clinger's humble subservience to Mr Lawrence is continuing in spite of her bosom's spectacular contours in her boned bra and her knowledge of botany. The pianist had played a song whose sentiments would have appalled Mrs Experience Bozarth in pioneer times: A doll I can carreee, the girl that I marreee must be.

Rosina had relapsed into moroseness since Mr Mongini's departure from her life and Leda made it a point to see more of her.

'Shān could do worse than accept Mr Otto Schelling's suggestion of staying on,' said Rosina tonelessly.

They had met for coffee at the Brevoort. Rosina ordered cocoa with cream on the side. She floated a blob of cream on the cocoa and swallowed it before relapsing into her somnolent state. Leda had hoped Otto Schelling's courtship would make her laugh.

'Otto Schelling thinks courtship is a European art,' said Leda. 'He thinks the lower culture of America has ruined it. He says it's given kissing a boisterous mass appeal and made it as common as baseball, and as rough and ready.'

'I would say the man is correct,' said Rosina comatosely.

'Mr Jenner once told me,' Leda persisted, 'that Verdi used to kiss his wife's hand even if he was only taking leave of her for an hour.'

'The man knew what he was doing,' muttered Rosina, 'I can see why any woman would fall for Mr Mongini. Don't ask me what he saw in *her*.'

Not one but layered fountains of milk and honey, Leda wanted to say, enough to stun a battalion of hornets. Rosina was moodily contemplating the thick dark dregs of cocoa in her cup.

'What's the matter with Shān anyway?' she muttered. 'How's she going to get to stay on in the USA after she graduates if she passes up an opportunity like that?'

She'll have done with this quaint island by then, I expect, Leda told Rosina, where victuals are sectioned and served for giant, not human appetites, where the sexes meet in combat at Thermoplyae, where men fall in love with butcher cuts of women and the plight of the American woman arouses the traveller's heart to pity. But Rosina was determined not to be diverted.

∿

Wolfgang was wed during spring vacation and the reception was held in the Schelling home. The honeymoon couple left for Maine, the guests departed, the grand pianos fell silent. Mrs Schelling took the train to Long Island for the weekend. Canapé crumbs and the warm flat remains of champagne were cleared away by the maid and her helpers and they too were gone, leaving Otto and Shān in the salon.

Suddenly Otto fell (but more systematically than Janey Ann's dates) into the order of events. He gravely unwrapped Shān from her Conjeevaram sari and deposited it with infinite care in a heap on a piano. Next he laid her like a perishable cobweb on an elephantine Schelling sofa. Himself he positioned on its edge facing the Prussians, to sheath his Bagpiper, and got caught in a version of her agonizing struggle with gloves. Otto was clearly in pain and too agitated to pull the floppy bit of sheath down over his red, swollen, hugely extended Bagpiper. Did sheaths come in different sizes? Shān was much better practised with her gloves. When at last he succeeded he forgot all about the order of events, hovered over her straightaway in the push-up pose Janey Ann had accurately described, and that was the end of his admirable control. He was plunging, heaving and sweating, his contorted face was the glaring scarlet of his Bagpiper and of the Prussians' uniforms. His body was tossing and rearing like the Prussians' horses. Framed he would have been them all. In seconds he came crashing down against the stone wall of her and collapsed. Shān gave him a smile of maternal concern when he came back after tidying up. He looked quite worn out.

During the week of her spring vacation he made progress. On his fifth try he appeared to lose his identity and became a helpless speck of nothing, for which Janey Ann had not prepared her. He moaned and writhed and surrendered himself to cries of clinging dependence. He was worse than any post-pioneer woman of this island. His ecstasies utterly dissolved him like the women in the Schmuckplatz in Carlsbad who fainted dead away after Sieg-heiling the Führer. Shān felt extremely guilty about continuing the experiment seeing what it was doing to him but the week was soon over. Otto was not as despondent about her return to Easthaven as he might have been, saying a young girl must have a break from a mature lover's overmastering passion in order to make the major decision of her life. She must be given time. An awakened sensuality could only turn to its awakener, in this case, the worldly wise lover and musical guide who was Otto Schelling. So said Otto, while Shān no longer felt responsible for him. He would soon be Mrs Schelling's full-time son again and now the only master of ceremonies at her 'evenings'. She only hoped the experience had not scarred Otto for life.

After spring vacation she noted: I am seventeen and nothing of importance has happened to me on this island. Naturally she did not count Otto's exertions which had only altered Otto.

∿

Leda met Florence Burns for a champagne cocktail at the Ritz in the first week of June. It was Mrs Burns' choice of drink and venue. She had a sense of occasion and a flair for celebration and wanted to savour the excitement of General Eisenhower's Normandy landing. In a stirring message to the Allied army the general had said, 'The hopes and prayers of liberty-loving people everywhere march with you.' But everywhere still excluded the blur beyond Europe's shores and Leda's global approach tempered her joy at France's coming liberation with a hardened resignation that older occupations were not going to be vacated as well. All the same she was happy to be sharing the war's exhilarating tidings with this evergreen companion. The cocktail lounge was full to bursting. An atmosphere of thrilled camaraderie crackled through the sedateness of the Ritz.

Florence Burns toasted France and Eisenhower and exchanged congratulations with the French head waiter in her Southern-belle French. Cigarette smoke veiled the room and drifted between them, making the tracery of fine wrinkles on Florence Burns' enamelled cheeks look like gauzy lace.

'Does it ever strike you, Leda, the lives we live for others to see don't count for much?' she said, 'it's the gaps we disappear into until the next social round that matter.'

On that weighty poseur she ordered a second round of champagne cocktails and when they came, clinked glasses with Leda, saying with more than a touch of sly Mona Lisa in her sidelong smile, 'Here's to the gaps!'

'I'm sorry Edgar couldn't join us. What's the word on Shān's father's release?' she asked.

Leda said they were hoping to hear any day now and Edgar had plans to get him over as soon as the war situation allowed.

But it was months after D-Day when Hilary Rushmore telephoned. He apologized for not having been in touch earlier, knowing Edgar's personal involvement in the case but wartime regulations had not permitted and he had not been at liberty to convey the news any earlier. This much Leda gathered, standing by, while Edgar waited impatiently for him to get on with it. She could make little sense of it when Edgar began shouting, 'I want you to repeat that' every few seconds as if he had not heard it the first time, and interrupting every repetition to repeat Hilary Rushmore's words back to him again as in a dialogue of the deaf.

'You are telling me the prisoner had no part in derailing and wrecking the military train ... the train was wrecked by his followers ... You're saying the authorities can't make a fine distinction between actual and moral responsibility in wartime. In cases of sabotage an example has to be made, is that what you are telling me, Hilary? ... No, Hilary, I was not mentally prepared. I was in no way prepared. *When did you do this, Hilary?*'

Edgar replaced the telephone and staring vacantly past Leda into space said the prisoner had been hanged in jail. Leda had a madwoman's urge to scream obscenities on Edgar's behalf, to revive him to life and rage or companion him in mourning his murdered friend. None of this was possible. Edgar was sucked into the blankness that signifies irreparable loss. She had not imagined a single encounter could do this — he and Nikhil had met only that once. It was Leda who sat down and wept, for Edgar and the murdered man, recalling all that Edgar had said of him, the adventure toward freedom Edgar had described, the knight who rode out in search of the Grail, the bar of light and shadow on a prison wall, the perilous ecstatic journey to the stars. She, above all, should have known the tale would end with death for no offence. Jungle justice was justice enough for all that was not Europe, where punishment need never fit the crime, or wait for crime to be committed.

It was Leda, too, who met Shān's train and took her to her own apartment where Rosina Mongini, still reeling from her abandonment by Mr Mongini, was waiting for them. The grief of her condition was stamped all over Rosina as once she had faithfully borne the stamp of Mr Mongini's husbandly protection and care. She had a key to Leda's apartment and came over whenever she needed to, to spend a morose and stupefied hour alone or in Leda's company. The door closed on the three women.

The question of fitting into Leda's scant space resolved itself. Like refugees fleeing death and devastation they fitted in, huddling close, sleeping little, eating less, expecting nothing. They spoke hardly at all and spent their waking hours on small steadying household tasks, darning socks that had long lain folded in Leda's sewing basket, washing tea stains from embroidered cambric tea napkins, oiling door hinges and devoting themselves to other industry of the monotonous miniature time-consuming mould. Rosina snipped numerous tiny pearls from a grey wool blouse of Leda's with minute care and sewed a crystal bead in each pearl's place. Leda, long benumbed by losses of her own, mended pillow lace, sorted and separated snarled threads and rewound reels of them. After her frenzies of weeping, which the older women left her to, Shān mutely copied them, ministering with aching eyes to the ripped lining of her winter coat and the frayed edges of saris. Between chores they sat with mugs of tea. They took turns to slice and butter bread for frugal meals and ate it with lettuce leaves. They washed and dried each other's hair. At bedtime they sat in dumb desolate communion before they went to their makeshift beds. They spent the winter in — for Leda, long delayed — mourning. In spring when Europe's war ended Shān went home.

ᔰ

Mr Jenner was concerned to find Leda looking so extinguished after her long absence. He suspected she had taken the time off because she had lost someone dear to her, a lover maybe, killed in Okinawa or another of the Pacific's final battlefields. A woman of her abnormal reticence would never refer to it so he could not openly condole. He sat down with her on the day of her return in an unobtrusively supportive manner, nothing said, before he dealt with the publishing issue she had raised. She had a valid point. It would have to be thought about, but not quite yet. Americans had been through a world war and were just coming home. The harsh realities of the world out there could wait. Hadn't everyone had their fill of those? Who could blame readers if they craved a little sugar and spice? Movie-makers knew it. Fashion designers knew it. Take a walk down Fifth Avenue, Leda. Look in at Bergdorf Goodman's and the other stores. He patted Leda's listless hand as if she were still the frightened girl with a genius for languages who had walked in years ago.

'It's the oriental look, Leda,' Rosina wearily confirmed, 'that's what they want now. I'm doing these see-through harem pants outfits and these transparent sari-loungers that high caste Hindu ladies are supposed to relax in.'

Bergdorf Goodman displayed diaphanous gem-encrusted sari-negligées in their windows, brocaded rajah coats and filmy sari-nightgowns for dreams like a maharanee's. A sequinned sari-purse of cloth of silver reposed on blue velvet. A cardboard Sinbad the Sailor hung suspended over it all. Rosina's drawing board bloomed with like visions of synthetic enchantment sprinkled with stars and crescent moons, mid-twentieth century excrescences that made the Renaissance duke's shoes look austere in comparison.

Rosina had become heavy-bottomed and broad in the hip. She wore her grey hair in neat earphones. She didn't care how she looked and she remained determinedly morose. What's there to live for, Leda? she kept asking. On a victorious postwar scene of more hectic than ever pairing and mating Rosina drowned in self-pity. The 'plight of the post-pioneer woman' and no mistake, Leda was driven to conclude. Rosina exasperated her as much as the maharanee nightgowns. She came to brief riotous life when Japan's war ended.

Crowds jammed Times Square and hysteria roared through the city as if the ghastly glare of Hiroshima had erupted over New York and driven New Yorkers raving mad. Leda watched the spectacle outside her apartment, standing arm-in-arm on the sidewalk with Rosina to prevent their being pushed off it by the tumult around them, but arms reached out, pulled them apart into the delirious dancing throng. Leda was carried helplessly on the tide to Washington Square where she heard herself singing with the rest in wild rejoicing that the war was over, and

Hiroshima joined the horrors — too inconceivable for comprehension, too vast for private grief or guilt or penance — that must be buried in forgetting. A redheaded red-bearded giant beside her in the singing multitude seized her by the waist, lifted her off her feet and kissed her passionately on the lips.

Hiroshima was a glittering grand finale worthy of the grandest opera. In the end, Otto Schelling had presciently declared, there is only opera. The war inspired by a fairy tale had come to an end surpassing all happy endings. Leda was certain Hiroshima's destruction, and then Nagasaki's, appeased Desmond and quietly propitiated him. Desmond did not lick his chops but he got his own back. An epochal calamity that had exterminated a population had taken care of an unforgivable insult to his self-esteem as well. No, Desmond did not put it in those words. But who did? No one betrayed by so much as a wink or a nudge that the bomb bred for Hiroshima was the most scientific solution ever devised — the ultimate solution — for disposing of detested pigment.

There was no possible expiation for Hiroshima but Leda did live to see New York pay homage to one of its dishonoured and despised. Years later the art gallery on Ninety-Second Street celebrated Kamei's genius. Sculpture lovers queued respectfully as churchgoers along Fifth Avenue. Inside the gallery a thick batter of them spread as fast as it was poured. The glass-roofed interior of the first room had stainless steel compositions placed great distances apart. Clusters of spectators stood rooted or moved silently from piece to piece in the foreordained

motions of an inexpressibly slow dance. It was years since
Leda had been to an exhibition. Gradually she adapted
herself to her environs as to a long neglected language
whose vocabulary does not spring automatically to mind.
The huge hushed flow of marble encircled her in the
second room. A snowbound silence reigned. A narrow
corridor leading off it was intimately lighted for aluminium,
string, bone and wood creations. Some made of cork and
paper opened and closed under scrutiny like witches'
flowers. Viewers walked in single file, conferring in
delighted whispers. An old woman stood leaning her
bejewelled arthritic hand on her cane in solemn
contemplation of a crystalline totem figure.

Leda entered a realm of brass and bronze, polished
to resemble strokes of lightning. A rendering of torture
dragged deep collective sighs from the procession as it
passed and coming up to it she saw Kamei's crucified
Negro in burning blazing bronze. Beside it, when the
clutch of devotees she was following moved on, she saw
revealed — all shining swirling brass, all naked joyful
elation — Kamei's Leda as Kamei alone had known her.
She stopped in front of it. The line of viewers assembled
behind her waited, then parted and met ahead of her and
was gone.

An arrow out of the gallery led into a stone forest
unfurling giant brutish blossoms. In a clearing at the heart
of it black pythons of granite gyrated above her in the
sunlight. Stone flexed and breathed around her in a silence
unbroken by the reveille of human affairs. She smelled the
stone dust of sculpture that Kamei had called his incense.

She saw him, chisel in hand, austerely alone, furiously active in his immobility. The fittest survive was flawed and faulty wisdom. Only the persecuted are indestructible, unless they are killed outright. She had not had the courage, the stamina, the inner iron to stay the course.

✎

Desmond died soon after the war, soothed by the lullabye of the atom bomb, but he had gone to his grave disappointed in Leda. In fairness to him she had let him down. The war that had spawned child marriages to pubescent pleas of Putchorarmsaroundmehoneyholdmetight, the war that had peopled the United States with babyfaced parents — not to mention able and disabled, licit and illicit lovers — had not bestirred poor Leda to land herself one, just *one* whole or truncated male. The ignominy of it! In his poor Leda's life, according to Desmond, there had not been one single goddam man. What the hell was she saving herself for? The answer to what the cypress told the rose? What a goddam waste of a woman, he had gone on fuming to Florence Burns, what a helluva tragedy.

But Leda knew that hell and tragedy had more to do with outer rhythms that pumped your blood up to perform actions you would never, left to yourself, have performed — the war cries and war lust of Chink-Chink-Chinaman that stoned a Chinese boy to death in peaceful San Francisco, the drunken celebration that made a Crystalnacht of a sculptor's studio in New York, the pleas of Putchorarmsaroundmehoney that drove children to collective mating. How close she herself had been to falling in what passed for love as she danced the tribal dances at university pressed to a tuxedoed chest, pulsing to the crooner's June moon and other nursery rhymes. How easily she might have been pressured into hallucinating, trivializing, dwarfing the sublime experience if a sinuous black body unaccompanied by any such artifice had not come her way and taught her all she needed to know of love's glory. It had been a feast so sating and renewing that Leda had lost the appetite she might afterwards have had for the pastel hues of permitted love.

Desmond, of course, knew nothing about the black beloved of her amputated university career. She had kept Luke Bradford her secret. Two animals hiding from the hunter and certain death they could not risk raising their voices above a whisper even when they were alone with each other, or leave a smudged hand or foot or bodyprint on mud or grass where they had lain. One thing we cannot do is forget ourselves, Leda, not for a second. Our thoughts and longings, our legs and arms and tongues must not entwine so enduringly that we can't cut loose and run. Stay ready for action, we don't have time. It's not safe enough to be invisible, we must leave invisibility behind us. Schooled in terror himself Luke had schooled her to eradicate signs of love like signs of heinous crime.

One spring night he was waylaid coming to her. Leda's pencilpoint flashlight fell on his body stretched naked on a wooded path they had used only once before. Something had been done to it. Its skin was scrabbled apart in patches like what rabid dog fangs do to meat. His arms and legs were wrenched apart in four directions and roped to crossed iron poles. His face was pulp. A hole gaped bloodily open in his groin. They had left a posy of his shrivelled genitals on his stomach, tied with satin ribbon. Leda hung over him, crippled by screams that made no sound. She was too weak to rise from her knees until his urgent warning whisper in her inner ear forced her to struggle to her feet.

Back in her room Luke's voice ordered her to pack and lie open-eyed on her bed waiting for dawn. Leda obeyed. He had abundantly warned her but she had not let well alone. She was part of the terror that had brought this about, accessory to this crime. This is lynching, hanging, burning country, his grandmother had taught her. This is where they trained nigger dogs to track down runaway slaves, where men still come in faceless packs on horses or in cars to kill, where slave owners used to say if a mule or a nigger dies you buy another, where their descendants still think so. Armed white volunteers patrolled these parts for two hundred years to ambush niggers and scourge them or hang them in irons. Tradition counts here, Mrs Bradford had said. A hallowed tradition had been observed here this night. No good nigger prowls a campus after dark. By morning there would be no trace of barbaric mutilation on the springtime beauty of this campus. Only a missing student and a scholarship withdrawn.

In the drugstore near the railway station an aproned man was frying bacon behind the counter for his lone customer. He drained it on a paper towel, put it on a plate beside two fried eggs sunny side up and served up the plate. Heeding Luke's voice, Leda asked for coffee and aspirin. A Negro child had come to stand on strenuous tiptoe between two counter stools, resting a spidery arm on each for support and speaking in a mumble. The counter man poured Leda's coffee, whistling tunelessly and wiped the counter clean from end to end.

'Well, look who's here!' he drawled in feigned surprise, looking down. 'What was that again? *I* got it, it's butterscotch walnut you want.'

He lifted the lid off an ice cream bin, scooped vanilla into a cone and thrust his fist forward to halt the cone between her eyes. The girl gave her tightly braided head a vigorous shake, lost her balance and shrank below the counter. Luke's hand stopped Leda's from helping her up. The fisted cone stayed where it was until a spidery arm reached for it, put down a nickel and the child backed out.

'You gotta nother customer out there, Eddie?'

'Nah. Jes that same pesky nigra. Darned if she doesn't come crawlin' in same time every day asking for some downright sassy flavour. Yesterday it was cinnamon cherry. Today it was butterscotch walnut. Keeps right on crawlin' in.'

Two years later Leda had gone to work for Jenner's with lasting lessons learned. What had possessed her to imagine Kamei would arouse a less bestial reaction? The very sight of Kamei had incensed Desmond. Years after that misbegotten evening she had caught Desmond straining for a chance remark that would reveal a clot of lingering contamination in her. He had not come to terms with that encounter until the atom bomb obliterated it.

ᘉ

Mr Jenner assumed Leda was leaving Jenner's because she had come into a legacy. She didn't tell him she could not go on translating varieties of quaintness, or that she had not expected him to publish Shān's Notebook or her letters and his refusal had not upset her. She had no idea what she was going to do for a living the day she went to Brookham to become owner of the mansion she had inherited.

She paid off her taxi at the tall prickly hedge that guarded the property from inquisitive neighbours. She walked through the garden's murmurous summer stillness and summer scents and let herself in. No odour of death or desertion haunted the entrance hall. She walked into rooms that had depended, like paintings, on space and light for effect and found their peaceful smiling complacency undisturbed. The forest glowed emerald through sunlit glass at the far end of the living room's long light expanse. She went upstairs to Florence Burns' bedroom and opened a window. The sky surged in with the leap and sparkle of water. Its brightness occupied the room. It flashed off the gold-topped crystal jars on the dressing table, streamed over the plum blossoms of the Chinese bedspread and flooded Leda with a sense of illimitable freedom, setting her blood free to flow dazzlingly unimpeded through her veins. So *this* is how we come into our inheritance, she exulted, not through pieces of paper informing us we are owners.

As inheritor of a mansion whose smallest accessory had been handpicked to contribute to its own former owner's seductive aura, from the frivolous array of cosmetics on her dressing table to the slender violin-backed boudoir chair assigned to cultivating a grace of mind, Leda found that her benefactress had scorned no artifice known to man, woman or magic. She had emancipated herself like a woman of the Renaissance, cleverly and in secret, without a brawl or a bruise. In this civilized sanctuary she had perfected the art of underground living, never risking the killer's livid eye, the lynch mob or the insanity that lurks under the skin.

'I really don't see why the only secrets left in life should be military or industrial ones, do you, Leda?' she had said, by way of passing on the torch which Leda had not been quick-witted enough to grasp.

Florence Burns had fled the south for sinuous black reasons, Leda now knew. Here she had lived in love with Ezra disguising him as her butler. Gliding out of her skin she had lain on this high fourposter revelling in her black Zeus' shower of liquid gold between her thighs, his forbidden breath upon her breath. There were no letters but there was a photo album of their European holidays. One set of pictures was recognizably Paris. In one of them they sat at their idle ease, Florence and Ezra, at a café table on the Left Bank. Two well-dressed women were at the table beside theirs with their prosperous husbands and on their other side a peasant family with a howling baby. The picture captured fresh bread and wine, hair oil, garlic and cigar smoke in a pageant of pleasures built to last. So must it have been in other cities they had chosen where after a morning's wandering they had returned to the turret room on the winding waterway of Leda's fancy.

In Brookham the front hedge hiding the property and the woods behind the house had secluded the lovers so successfully that Florence Burn's life with Ezra had been as private as a letter to herself. And if there had been lovers after Ezra (though surely she was too old by then, thought Leda) she must have conducted it with the instincts of a migrating wild goose that scans the ground for danger before it lands and keeps its strong hard bill and beating wings ready for attack. Like a goose she must have led her flock to water and to pasture, staying mistress of herself.

'In spite of Dante's sacred love for Beatrice,' she had once said to Leda, 'he had a Mrs Dante and four baby Dantes. And Petrarch never married because his heart and soul were given to Laura but that didn't stop him having an affair and two brats by a lady friend. No Wuthering Heights about those enjoyers of life.'

Or about her either, thought Leda, remembering Desmond.

'I am a friend of your brother,' a papery voice she identified as old, frail and Japanese said on the telephone a week after she had moved in. 'Your brother has told me you are a collector of unusual tales. He wanted me to show you mine.'

Leda was not ready for visitors but no messenger from Edgar had ever been turned away. She invited him to bring his tale to Brookham. The flaying alive at Hiroshima and its rousing encore at Nagasaki had made her think of Japan as a mass graveyard and she expected a visitor who would look unwound from grave cloths, bathed, dried and dressed for this visit, to be bandaged and laid back in his grave when it was over. So she was ready for the deathlike pallor of incurable illness but not for his comparative youth. He bowed politely at the door. A useless leg dragged in after him.

At lunch he savoured his small helping and remarked on the flavours of her casserole with genuine appreciation, not formal courtesy. While he ate he talked about his arrival in the country and his impressions of it as men do who are not dying of the war's most diabolic bomb. He took a second tinier helping. They drank jasmine tea in the living room. He complimented her on the forest view, bringing home to her that it was hers. He pointed to a raspberry red finch on a bough. They watched it fan its pleated wings and fly away.

At night Leda read his tale. He was a construction engineer who had happened to be in Hiroshima on a job when the bomb fell. The house he was staying in lifted off the ground. Its roof and walls exploded in flames and crushed him under their deadweight of fallen timber, breaking bones in his body but securing him from the more calamitous effects of the blast. The day was pitch dark when he lost consciousness. He regained it in a ray of foggy light. Birds lay dead in the debris. There was a live crawling one he could have caught by hand. No wall or building was left standing in the street. Thick black ash billowed up blackening the sky and ghostly apparitions floated out of the fog drifting soundlessly past him. Their mouths gaped open. Some had empty sockets for eyes. They were trailing ragged scarves. It was their flesh torn thickly from bone, hanging loose and blowing in the wind like tattered pennants. An inhuman wail issued from one whose vocal chords were still intact.

Leda cowered between her sheets. The luminous dial of Florence Burns' bedside clock was circled with pink jewels. Its friendly twinkle in the night piloted her back from Hiroshima to her guest's sane behaviour at lunch, his miniature second helping of her casserole, his gladness at the finch's flight.

Was he planning to write more, she asked him, making tea and toast for his breakfast. Alas no, he regretted. As with the crawling bird, radiation had only delayed his death, and he was going blind with A-bomb cataract. He could offer her just this one contemporary tale.

In one of the pieces of information Florence Burns gleaned while 'perusing' Dante and other favourites in her boudoir chair, she had discovered it was Petrarch's first unforgettable sight of Laura in the church of St. Clare Avignon in the year 1327 that had inspired him to sonnetry. The guest from Hiroshima was an unlikely Laura but he started Leda collecting sonnets of another kind, contemporary tales told her by sufferers of the orgiastic operatic punishments designed for the lesser breeds outside Europe. Had anyone told her the subject was immense, that it would cover non-Europe's land, seas and air, experiment on its people, and bring sudden death to meddlers in the design, she might never have embarked on it.

'Did you know, Leda,' Florence Burns had remarked, 'that the Pope used to bestow an exquisitely wrought cluster of golden roses and rosebuds every year on the royal lady whose zeal for the Church had singled her out for the honour?'

Leda had neither known nor cared, but the flawless craftsmanship of the Pope's rose cluster seemed to shine through the punishments that came her way and there was no disentangling the holy alliances that had brought them to pass. They made instruments of individual torture look like kindergarten toys. Whenever she read profoundly moving Churchillian prose about 'all mankind' and 'one world' she threw up quite violently in her bathroom basin.

She had regarded her first collection of tales as a personal enterprise but it found an interested publisher, a latter-day Mr Jenner who viewed it as just right for the market now. Mrs Roosevelt herself had championed human rights and they were on the UN agenda, he said, not rubbing his hands with anticipation but seeming to. At Armando's, with cocktail smoke fashionably thick between them, he told her the collection would earn her a reputation as a champion of human rights, and there could be a follow-up.

'I don't think I know what you mean,' she said, 'by human rights.'

'Come now, Leda, let's not get into dialectics,' he grinned, ordering two more Manhattans. 'The time is ripe for the subject and you do know perfectly well what I mean. You've done a brilliant job.'

Up until now, she doggedly explained, there'd been no such thing. She, personally, had never heard of human rights. For her entire life it had been hard enough for most people to be recognized as human. Rights had waited on some remote star.

'Well, we're in the market for it now, Leda. Salud!'

∿

She went to call on Otto Schelling to condole his mother's death. She said New York would miss Mrs Schelling's distinguished 'evenings'. Otto Schelling bared his teeth in an abbreviation of his abrupt laugh appropriate to her condolence visit.

'It is kind of you to say so but for my mother they were a discipline. Europe was destroying itself. We survivors held grimly to our traditions, pretending to be good hosts on moonlight nights when Cologne and Hamburg were being flattened under bombs. On those terrible nights, Miss Knox, we here were being bombarded with the idiot words of popular songs. "Moonlight becomes you, *it goes with your hair!*" Then came Dresden and Leipzig, after which they started singing "There'll be a hot time in the town of Berlin when the Yanks go marching in" — but who should go marching in, Miss Knox, but the Russians. Is *this* why we waited for the end of the war?'

His accusing glare drove Leda to say the war must have been a traumatic time for the Schellings.

'It was, Miss Knox. You can understand why in all the madness I guarded the flame, the joy of a young girl in the music of Europe. A girl of her unusual sensitivity and her refined response belonged in the West. She could have made a fine match here with old wealth.'

To go home instead to her poor backward country must have entailed a tremendous sacrifice — the sacrifice of all possibility of personal flowering and fulfilment. Europe, he had said to her, had originated and ennobled the I, the me, the mine, around which life necessarily revolves. It had been his greatest wish to introduce her to the culture and the pleasures of Europe once the war was over.

'How about yourself, Mr Schelling? Do you have plans to go back to Berlin?'

'I had plans to go back to Berlin, yes. To half of it, no.'

Still, there's always opera so he's not entirely bereft, thought Leda, not feeling like being held responsible for the Russian occupation of Berlin. And he's got his memories. He can look back on taking Shãn to Figaro and hearing Cherubino sing 'Voi che sapete che cose e amor!' And on the whole it had been a comfortable war for Otto.

ᔕ

'What became of Edgar Knox?' Pete Ryder asks me.

'The Senate Sub Committee on Internal Security branded him dangerous and virtually disappeared him.'

I show Pete Ryder the transcript, or Edgar's

reconstruction of it, which Leda Knox sent me of his appearance before the Committee during the summer of 1951.

SSC: 'This old man you saw out of your train window, Mr Knox, what does he have to do with what we're talking about?'

EK: 'He made a vivid impression on me, of purity.'

SSC: 'Not long after you saw this pure old man, people from his party derailed and looted a military train further up the track. They were saboteurs, aiding the enemy, and sabotaging the Allied cause.'

EK: 'They would have been our allies if we had backed their demand for independence. They kept beseeching the United States for support.' He read from the paper before him, '"We believe in the sanctity of the principles for which the world is shedding so much blood ... We beseech the Great Powers, and particularly the United States, to give aid and assistance in our fight for national liberation ... We will back the Allied cause, welcome Allied arms, give all needed aid ..."'

SSC: 'We have copies of that Vietnamese proclamation right here, Mr Knox. It was released by Ho Chi Minh's League for Independence in Luchow in 1942. It has nothing to do with the train derailment we're talking about.'

EK: 'It's part of the larger problem. All these people kept hoping for a last-minute American intervention on their behalf. They went against us only after their justified demands were turned down.'

SSC: 'But you were still calling them "people on our side".'

EK: 'They looked upon America as a beacon light. What they did after you failed to support them, they felt they had to do. You were not dealing with common saboteurs then, and you are not dealing with obscure museum relics now, called India or Indonesia or Indo-China. You are dealing with leaders who quote Santayana and Dewey, men who are moved and inspired by the ideas that inspire us. One of them used to keep a brass mould of Abraham Lincoln's hand on his desk. They are at least as convinced of their mission as you are of yours. You will not stop them from running their own affairs. Leap on them with stones or batter them with bombs, you'll still lose.'

I have wondered since if it was Edgar Knox's fatal futile anger that sealed his own fate. Some famous Americans asked pardon for their un-Americanness, recanted, ratted, and were let off. At the very least they kept their tempers. Edgar was condemned to professional ruin and oblivion and deprived of his passport for ten years. He had not cared to make a comeback when Senator Joe McCarthy's other victims were rejoining the ranks of the respectable. It was not a scene he cared to come back to. He hated watching America take up the white man's burden and become the new Colonial Power. But his unwise outburst on that occasion may have had nothing to do with the committee's wrath. He had earlier called the atom bomb a new undeclared war. He had said it would look like the latest capitalist trick to the Russians. He had predicted it would lead to endless war. And before all that his book Empire *had prophesied events that seemed, uncannily, to be coming about, suspiciously like his forecasts of them.*

The year of the Committee was the year Iran decided to nationalize her oil and the British Government threatened 'unforeseeable consequences' if Iran failed to negotiate a settlement. 'Britain cannot frighten us with a few paratroopers,' Iran's Deputy Prime Minister told the Majlis. 'They would make a small morsel for our frontier tribes ...' Edgar Knox was there, lending a sympathetic ear and, as usual, the power of his pen, though he had no more influence at home. Roosevelt was dead. Truman was supporting Britain who had agreed to nationalization 'in principle' provided she kept control of oil supplies. Iran wasn't having any of it. Nor was Edgar. It doesn't really matter whether Edgar helped Prime Minister Mossadeq draft the reply he sent to President Truman. Edgar was on the wrong side in the oil crisis. The reply might as well have been his:

Iran is anxious to protect her cordial relations with the British Government. Had we been given outside help like other countries which have suffered from the war, we could have soon revived our economy. Even without that help we could have succeeded in our efforts had we not been hampered by the greed of the Anglo-Iranian Oil Company and the activities of its agents. I ask you, Mr President, whether the tolerant Iranian people had any alternative but recourse to nationalization of the oil industry, which will enable them to utilize the natural wealth of their country and put an end to the unfair activities of the Company?

Talks with the British Government collapsed and the Iranians took over the Anglo-Iranian Oil Company's vast refinery in Abadan. British forces stood at the ready with British warships near the Persian Gulf. I'm not sure if Edgar was still in Teheran the day Mossadeq, an old man in his seventies, broadcast to his nation from his sickbed, 'Fifty years of imperialism in Persia ended today ...'

And that was not all. In August that year the Egyptian Prime Minister, Nahas Pasha, said British troops stationed in the Suez Canal zone had become 'a nightmare' to Egyptians. Britain must remove its forces and recognize Egypt's complete independence. If Edgar hadn't written the script he might as well have done. He was with them, one of them. To him as to them foreign armies in Asia spelled empire again. By the time an American coup overthrew Mossadeq in Iran no national newspaper or magazine was publishing Edgar, but in Empire he had already predicted the West would stop at nothing to ensure a westward flow of oil.

'And Mossadeq was killed in the coup?' asks Pete Ryder.

'No, only jailed and tortured and then kept under house arrest until he died of cancer, weakened by radium treatment. But Edgar Knox had a theory that no one who opposes the Companies stays healthy.'

He had another theory, I tell Pete Ryder. He believed the Americans were more affected by their popular music than any people on earth and the 'dimpled blond syrup' that was being served up as daily doses — 'I'm gonna buy a paper doll', 'Boohoo, you got me cryin' for you' — would vaporize the country's intelligence. He worried about what it would do to America's foreign policy after the war. The three baby atom bombs America kept ready for the

French to use at Dien Bien Phu — though Vietnam won that war too fast for their use — convinced him of worse misjudgements to come. All things considered, the Senate Committee for Internal Security, being short on vocabulary, labelled Edgar Knox a Communist.

'What do you think he was?' asks Pete Ryder.

'A lover of mankind. And of jazz.'

∽

When Leda first met Nurullah three years after the war she was afraid she was looking at someone like the woman she had once been, or one or two visitors who had crossed her threshold with their grisly tales. There are none so depressing as people who look as if they've abdicated from the rest of life. But he was not a case of protracted grief. Some faces at some angles just give that fleeting impression. He was an easy attractive guest, charmed by his surroundings. He amused himself the morning of his arrival from New York and by lunchtime he seemed to have inhabited the spaces of her house and garden for years. She knew he taught English literature at the University of Akbarabad and Edgar had told her he was here to teach in a summer programme at Princeton. He had been Shān's tutor — apart from being an adoptive member of her family — so she did not think of him as a total stranger.

She laid out a cold lunch on the patio scented with its scattering of lilac blossom at this time of year, poured him a glass of wine without asking what he would like and settled down with her own. In answer to her question he admitted it was bewildering to have fallen out of the skies into America. It was the first time he had left his country and he would have preferred a sea voyage to prepare him for the forms and substance of unknown life at the end of it. All he had by way of preparation was Shān's Notebook, now out of date. The broad-shouldered straight-skirted women of wartime were now wearing full graceful skirts and hips were back as Aunt had fervently hoped. Was he right in thinking that hair was less ruthlessly regimented than Shān had described?

Leda's reservations vanished in their laughing reminiscences of Shān's unpublishable observations, judged outlandish by Mr Jenner. The perfect poise Leda had grown into since inheriting this house wavered ever so slightly. She wondered what was the new element here that had not come her way before. Exactly what it was eluded her.

Would Leda believe it, he said, at a dinner Edgar had taken him to last night in New York, he had met a lady who could well have been Aunt. When she heard he was from India she declared India was so *complicated*, it was hard to figure out if it was Hindoo or Moslem, capitalist or communist.

'Even I, an Indian, can't figure out which of those I am,' he had said, sympathizing with her confusion, 'or whether I'm all of them.'

This had created alarm.

'Am I to understand you don't see communism as out to capture the world, sir?' a man asked, his startling use of 'sir' apparently just a mode of speaking.

Nurullah, never good at pat replies, had come out with a thoughtful one, 'Well, capitalism did, and I am certain communism will have a try. The West has always voyaged far and wide with its brands.'

Aunt's and the man's reaction to his wrong replies had made him realize how 'complicated' it was going to be travelling abroad, if one was unsqueezable into a one-book, one-theme-song category. He had had no idea the world outside India was so cubby-holed and cubicled. He had a friend in India's new Foreign Service who was going to be facing Aunts all over the map. Eknath was an impatient sort of chap and it was going to drive him to drink.

Leda had no particular belief in anything. She saw he had, both in the present and in the future. She began to connect this optimism with new nationhood when he remarked that arrival into freedom was an incredible experience. He did not need to elaborate on it. Leda distinctly remembered the day she had come into her inheritance — and how dazzlingly — in Florence Burns' bedroom upstairs. Lunch was over too quickly though they sat over it a couple of hours.

Conversation on afternoon walks through her woods was, in Leda's experience, wider ranging than in rooms. Theirs closed into intimacy of a poignant kind when he spoke of Nikhil's hanging which even his mother had not been permitted to attend. Hearing it was over she had gone to her room in shock, lain down on her bed and died. Nurullah was left alone in the house with the family's fragile oldest surviving member who then guarded them both against misspent mourning. Or was it that Pyare Chacha had reached an age beyond grief? Too feeble to climb the step ladder in the library, or to read fading print, he directed Nurullah to a publication on a top shelf that chronicled hangings, from the same defunct national press that had produced *Palashi*, and had also been authored by him. In Pyare Chacha's youth there had been revolutionary secret societies pledged to drive out the British. He had belonged to one himself called Young India Society after Mazzini's Young Italy. Seditious writings and lesser crimes were punished by long years of transportation or prison sentences, but executions by hanging took place when English blood was shed in the fight for liberty, and there had been a spate of these. He requested Nurullah to read aloud to him the drills he had described of the fettered prisoner mounting the gallows, having his fetters unlocked, his face masked, the rope fixed round his neck and the jerk up from the wooden plank.

'It is certain,' spoke Pyare Chacha dreamily, 'that an expert hangman places a noose precisely and that a precisely executed jerk kills instantly. There is no hanging by the neck until dead. A professional hangman knows his job.'

That, anyway, was Pyare Chacha's grim consolation, Nurullah said to Leda. Who but the hanged could vouch for its truth? And hadn't the same been said of an axe's beheading blade and of execution by guillotine? They walked without speaking for a while after that but in such close communion that Nurullah could tell her what he had done next. Left to grieve alone he had locked his door and thrown himself into the aggressive rituals of prescribed mourning, wailed long and eerily, banged and bruised his head on the ground and still kneeling, beaten his breast with his fists. He had driven his nails into the skin of his arms to draw blood — all to no avail since it was he who had delivered the friend of his heart to the hangman by merely being there at the railway station.

'I'm sorry,' he apologized to Leda, 'you must think I am a madman.'

He had been of little use to Bhai's lawyer and former cell-mate, or to Nina and Jeroo when they came from Bombay to take charge of Bhai's affairs, until Jeroo said harshly, 'Stop snivelling, Nurullah, for God's sake. You're getting on my nerves. Would you have wanted him to die of old age and senile decay?'

Leda had not known until she heard his story that there was a guilt as haunting as her own. She didn't make the mistake of telling him not to blame himself.

She had been planning an elaborate dinner with Gateau Marie Louise for dessert and saw it would be a sickening waste of time when it was vital they should spend time talking. It was suddenly of urgent importance to her to discover where they stood on a variety of issues. But a large part of the evening was spent watching her forest darken through the living room's glass wall, sipping wine. With an effort Leda reluctantly broke the spell. If they were going to live together as she now knew they must, it was right that they should know each others' minds. The process brought an answering light to Nurullah's eyes and took on the exhilaration of joining forces on issues that mattered, which her lone fight from her lone corner had lacked. She could now envisage him and herself joined in worthwhile endeavour through the years to come, living here in the idyllic beauty of Brookham, Massachusetts. She had been heart-whole for so long that it disturbed her to realize she no longer was, nor would be again. She had already made love to him in the room upstairs with its windows open to the sky and he had returned her rapture with his own. None of this had happened yet but 'it is written' as all scriptures say, and she knew it would from all that had happened so far.

While they were eating leftovers from lunch she discovered they would not be living together in the serene haven of New England, in the home Florence Burns had created for making love. Nurullah was describing a haven called Akbarabad and she was discovering an eloquence in him that no other subject had brought forth. His attachment to his teaching job appeared to affect him the same way, lifting him up into a transcendence that was — emotional? spiritual? *oriental*? She was not familiar with this bursting fullness of heart and mind. In its presence she could hardly say literature was also taught in New England and he could teach it here. As he spoke she began to understand that the birth of his nation was an open sesame to all kinds of possibilities and some impossibilities. Therefore it was not a time when one could desert one's post or even wish to, since all other shores and skies looked bleak in comparison. He was telling her the very teaching of literature had changed. Literature as a secret weapon, as ulterior motive, as sabotage, had been put away and now it could be indulged in, cherished for its own pleasure and pain. He talked along these lines with devotion but without vehemence, and entirely without country-ardour of the kill-or-die-for variety, merely as if what they had left of India when they tore her in pieces and quit was nevertheless the best he knew of civilization. The last thing Leda would have looked for in a war-weary world in the year 1948 was this surge of adult idealism.

After dinner, groping her way to solution, it occurred to her that his attachment to Akbarabad need not ring alarm bells for their living here together or to making future plans. Lovers could live continents apart and meet on each others' terrain. That night — another night of amazing joy that had also not yet happened — this solution gave her hope.

A few days later, as a rest from their mutual intense absorption, and because she really should do something to entertain him, she suggested a movie. The one at the local Brookham theatre was within walking distance and had been recommended by Rosina. Rosina's aesthetic sense could be relied on in the cinematic and other arts. The actress is no beauty, Leda, she had said, but she's got what it takes. I read in *Photoplay* she's half Eye-ranian and half Hungarian. The producer who discovered her is that famous man, Sir Algernon Dunster. He's divorced his wife and married her so, lucky girl, she's Lady Dunster now and the sky's the limit with a movie career ahead of her. She's too skinny for Mr Aretino's taste — (Rosina's new husband who had a successful line in lingerie) — he prefers a bust size that fills a medium to large cup, but you know men, Leda, they never think of anything else.

The oriental look lived up to Rosina's promise. The actress had extraordinary appeal. It must be that mixture of Iranian and Hungarian, Leda remarked on their way home. But the mixture, she learned, was pure Akbarabad. She learned more about Lily Hulbert from her jilted lover that night after they had made actual love. Late next morning, at their ease and leisure, they drew up plans for making it forever more, here on her continent and in his India Beata.

III

Trade Wind

'Britain is not maintaining fifty thousand troops in Suez for her own glory. We are in Suez as servants and guardians of the commerce of the whole world.'

Winston Churchill, 17 January 1952

'The 1953 coup had its roots in a British showdown with Iran, restive under decades of near-colonial British domination. The prize was Iran's oil fields.'

New York Times Special Report: The CIA in Iran,
The New York Times on the Web, 2000

Twelve

They were driving over a bridge called Pont Du Mont Blanc when the ambassador saw the bifurcation in the road ahead and road signs reading Nyon and Meyrin. He asked the chauffeur to let him and his guest down at the signpost and drive on a few furlongs where they would meet him.

'A little walk after a big dinner, Gaston,' he explained. 'Good for the digestion after that excellent meal.'

The diamond numerals on the chauffeur's Patek Phillipe shone a quarter to eleven in the lights along the bridge. The watch was a gift from the Indian embassy in Switzerland for his long and valued service. The sky was moonless and it was not the time of a cold spring night, in his opinion, for a little walk but Gaston was accustomed to the eccentricity of the breed. Last year the Indian President's wife had carried her own tin box of rice and curried mishmash to a luncheon in her honour at Geneva's most elegant restaurant. One of their millionaire industrialists was said to travel with his cow. Gaston shrugged mentally and made amiable chitchat till they reached the signpost where he let the two of them down. The Mercedes purred on.

'So, how about it, Nurullah?' challenged the ambassador.

Nurullah took a deep preparatory breath, half squatted and braced his shoulders. The ambassador, who was as agile as he had been in his youth, hoisted himself onto them and balancing with confidence he switched the road signs, pointing Nyon left and Meyrin right. Climbing down he dusted his hands off instinctively as if there was dust in Geneva — old habits died hard — and surveyed his handiwork in the light from the end of the bridge. Hands in their overcoat pockets, he and Nurullah strolled toward the car, convulsed at their own silliness.

'They are such worthy people, the Swiss,' said Eknath contentedly. 'They have everything that anyone could want, except a mite of harmless confusion. What wouldn't I give to see the policeman's face on his beat tomorrow morning and the motorists who find themselves where they weren't going. I've been wanting to do something like this for ages, yaar. I never would've if you hadn't shown up.'

'I'll be on my way home tomorrow,' said Nurullah, 'but your antics could get you thrown out. They would from Sweden where I'm told it's an offence to pull the flush after ten p.m. and there's strong objection to murmurs at the cinema.'

Eknath's hotel lobby slumbered. A majestic staircase curved up three floors under a vaulted ceiling frescoed with pearly clouds, fat cupids and airborne angels. They laid their feet softly on the stair carpet and talked in hushed voices like civic-conscious citizens, not Indians. In Eknath's suite where Nurullah was to spend the night they sank into velvet chairs, neither of them ready to go to bed. For Nurullah it was six p.m. in New York from where he had come and Eknath had never needed more sleep than Akbar the Great.

'How did the disarmament proposal go?' Nurullah asked of the initiative Eknath had come to Geneva from Bern to take part in earlier in the day.

'As disarmament does. Not at all,' said Eknath. 'We and the other seven of our group set out a proposal for a comprehensive test ban, a freeze on missile materials, a ban on the use of nuclear weapons and a steady reduction of weapon stocks. It was turned down flat. Why wouldn't it be? Who knows what they'll use next in Vietnam? I'm going to make some tea.'

In the kitchenette Eknath poured boiling water onto the pale delicate fragrance of Flowery Orange Pekoe, so different from the strong sugary ginger-spiced brew Robinda had served. They carried their cups back to their velvet chairs recalling the scald and sparkle of talk at his teas.

'The West is still The World, yaar, makes the rules, calls the shots, not in the old way — you keep this mountain, I'll take that sea — but nevertheless. It's 1966 but nothing's changed.'

Eknath rubbed his face briskly with both hands and rotated his tired shoulders to relax them.

'When I opted for the Foreign Service after independence, little did I know I'd be answering the same questions for the rest of my career. "Why haven't you joined our military pacts against Communism?" "Because we don't want cold war, hot war, holy or unholy war." "When are you going to get off the fence and get into line?" Ya Allah, as you would say, Nurullah, did you ever know an Indian to get into line? "Why haven't you thrown open your markets to our manufactures?" "Because we're manufacturing our own, from nothing to everything at long last." I tell you it's a bellyache representing India. I never get time off from explaining. I'm a schoolmaster stuck with retarded children, or a heretic being simmered in boiling oil by inquisitors or whatever it is inquisitors do.'

'What is an Indian, Nurullah?' he went on. 'A specimen to gawk at, not a normal chap who joins military pacts and lets his markets get flooded with advanced tomato ketchup. We don't have jolly golfing Generals heading our governments and Colonels overthrowing them with coups. Dammit, Nurullah, we're not even a theocracy. Rank outsiders is what we are, unlovable as halitosis. But do the world's rulers pat our little bottoms and say Never mind if you're god-awful freaks, at least you've got democracy? Not at all. Every few years their think-tanks predict we're about to fall apart. It's so affronting when we don't. Hell hath no fury like a think-tank scorned. I keep telling them, look here, chaps, we had no national preparation for the military mentality. We couldn't even get violent enough to overthrow our occupier because we got trained in non-violence. Ha! About as much use it was as the Pope's balls.'

A generalization typical of Eknath though he well knew that many a lusty wily Pope had made good use of his balls.

'Speaking of tomato ketchup,' said Nurullah, 'this coming Asian trade conference at home should put ketchup and other matters into perspective. I heard the Minister explain the Asia Doctrine in New York. I don't know how the European capitals she toured reacted to it but in New York it could have been anarchy she was proposing. One unfriendly analyst called it a hemispheric policy that looked hostile to the West and would disrupt time-honoured patterns of commerce worldwide.'

'And what did the Commerce Minister say to that?'

'She said it's your wisdom we've turned to for an autonomous hemisphere. We're putting our words to your music. We're so disappointed, she said, that you are reacting like the mighty Metternich did to your Monroe Doctrine. The man sitting in the row in front of me got a chuckle out of that. He told the man sitting next to him she'd have outwitted Metternich any day. The neighbour asked my man, how do these Asian women do it? There was Madam Chiang Kai Shek, in school here, a perfectly ordinary American-educated schoolgirl until she goes home to become the symbol of China and signs death warrants with her own hand. And now there's this female flood of Ministers, Ambassadors, Prime Ministers in saris and sarongs. Must be something in the soil. My man wisecracked, long tradition of intrepid women, old boy, mother of God on.'

Nurullah had found himself standing next to his man at the reception afterwards. He had the lantern jaw and elongated face of the third-last Viceroy which made him familiar in a company of strangers. There was also, of course, his recognizable English. Incontestably an Englishman. Nurullah who could have been enlarging his acquaintance stayed where he was heaven knew why, comfortable where he was. We know each other, it dawned on him in mild astonishment. We are having a conversation whose undertones, irony and a humour subtler than crass humour, makes allies of us. We are sharing the unsaid, too, in the calm relationship of old age that cultures enter when aggressive youth is past. The question of you killed my brother so I must kill yours has been cancelled out. We're past all that. The palimpsest!

'Well, well,' said Eknath adopting his dry diplomatic tone. 'You were having your usual attack of "Soft! What light through yonder window breaks!" But it's a pity this trade cooperation has been so long coming. The heroes are gone. Mossadeq was thrown out and now he's dead. Ho Chi Minh is dying and his peasants are fighting for their land, their grain and their lives.'

'The Minister is a hero in her own right,' affirmed Nurullah.

'Who would have thought the brat had it in her?' Eknath agreed, and congratulated Nurullah on his handiwork.

Nurullah, never modest about his reputation as a teacher, denied himself the credit for once. He had known her since the age of six and she had had strength of purpose even then. It had been her own decision to return to India after her father's execution, and later stand for election to the country's first Parliament and make her triumphant way in politics. He had only freed her from her convent textbooks and pointed her to a new way of seeing. But yes, he had watched her performance in New York with a teacher's love and pride.

The carping critics aside, her supporters in the gathering had been elated. The room breathed that air of hope which marks new beginnings. At the very least it would be that, a beginning. *'Ah, Love! could thou and I with Fate conspire To grasp this sorry Scheme of things entire.'*

Nurullah wished he had stayed back to fly home with her and Edgar and the impressive American brains Edgar had included as observers and advisers at the conference but it would have meant missing his overnight stop with Eknath, and the Nyon and Meyren signs would never have got turned around. A question of priorities.

Otto Schelling was recovering from a stroke and had not been able to attend the reception at Asia House. Leda had gone with Shān to see him the day before. There he had sat, folded into himself, his music and his thoughts, reminding Shān of rishis of old whose eyelashes grew down their hoary cheeks during decades of profound meditation and had to be lifted like curtains with the backs of their hands before they could open again on mundane affairs. Otto Schelling lived in the past, his own and Europe's before the rise of Soviet Russia. He bemoaned the muddy tide of popular songs in every bar and café and recalled the abiding values of opera. As musicians when they meet go to the keyboard and play an exuberant mazurka — it is how they converse — Otto and Shān had looked back on Cherubino in Figaro singing 'Voi che sapete che cose e amor!' By the time coffee was brought in Mrs Schelling's Meissen cups on a traycloth of her Dresden lace, Otto was rosily invigorated and could brush aside Shān's concern for his health, saying he felt as young as Verdi who composed Falstaff when he was a whitehead of eighty.

When Nurullah and Eknath retired for what remained of the night, Nurullah fell deeply asleep and dreamed of Akbarabad during India's vivisection. Instead of wagonloads of refugees fleeing unspeakable butchery, instead of fear-maddened hundreds fighting for space on a train to Pakistan, only wagonloads of Nawab Sahib Vazirabad's luggage had rolled onto the railway platform. Half the town showed up to see him off, except old Zenobia Framjee who having long outlived her Nusli had suddenly died. There were speeches and bouquets at the station. Gosiben presented an Address in a silver frame to Bibijan from the 'ben' khadi workers. The station master had decked out the Nawab's first class compartment with garlands and Khurram had lugged in enough donated Vimto to quench a regiment's thirst. Asghar Ali barber's son's brass band was there braying and trumpeting Loch Lomond. Nurullah, though dreaming, knew all this had been true.

The Vazirabad brats, left to finish their studies in India, had chosen to stay on, so that their mother, who felt thoroughly unsettled away from Akbarabad, could keep coming back to shop to her heart's content for silk saris, Banarsi paans and bananas. Murad, the youngest brat, had made a fortune as a heartthrob in films, while Barkat and Salim had converted the family property into an exclusive exorbitant hotel for rich foreigners where they served food sensations like canaries dipped in honey and roasted with sesame seed. The jaded appetites of the world-travelled wealthy needed titillating. Barkat had just discovered the demoiselle crane. This bird spent nights in jheels or on open riverbeds and fed on young crops. Its diet of tender shoots and grain made its flesh delicious eating, and farmers were glad to be rid of the creatures.

You lie, accuse Eknath's inquisitors. Furnish proof, they order Nurullah, that what you say is true, that no riot took place at Partition. The picture we have here shows millions migrating to flee terror. It shows mass murder, rape abounding.

It's the wrong picture you have, another town far west and north of Akbarabad, Nurullah says.

One town is no different from another, they intone, producing towns on fire. Why would the same thing not have happened in yours?

Who knows why, Nurullah responds, lacking Eknath's diplomatic experience in reply and retort, but there is such a thing as influence, Your Honours. This was the soil of Din Ilahi, Akbar-e-Azam's Divine Faith. If you had read Badauni's history of his reign you would remember the passage that says: 'Thus a faith based on some elementary principles traced itself on the mirror of his heart, and as a result of all influences brought to bear on His Majesty, there grew, gradually as the outline of a stone, the conviction in his heart that there were sensible men in all religions, abstemious thinkers, and men endowed with miraculous powers, among all nations. If some true knowledge were thus everywhere to be found, why should truth be confined to one religion?' Near Akbarabad, Your Honours, Akbar propounded the oneness of religions in that century when religious tolerance was odious heresy among you, Your Honours. And since Akbar the Great we have had other powerfully gentling influences: the voice of a naked fakir from his hut, the words of an English poet, the inspiration of a New England philosophy. All these made Thou shalt not kill a habit hard to break.

Who can measure, Your Honours, the long reach and exact nature of influence, yet who can doubt that the radiance of a smile can outlive the grave, or that a man done to death by imperial decree nearly two thousand or only twenty-four years ago still holds his hand uplifted over hate? Had you read Sa'adi, Your Honours, you would know that such men live on and on to 'guide an elephant with a hair' by their sheer honey-tongued gentleness.

Now it is Christmas in Nurullah's dream and the time has come to open the gift-wrapped Christmas parcel that has been waiting for this day. The time has come to put aside the sad and sordid history of all nations and begin again as equals. A plane silvered by the moonlit Alps is soaring high above their peaks and crests through Europe's night skies to Asia. Sunrise will flush the snowpeaks hours later. When it is light gemlike lakes will sparkle in their valleys. Alpine flowers will turn their faces to the sun. The dew on irises, crocuses and cosmos will evaporate. Sun rays will strike black walls of smoke and bursting flame. The dream blazes out of Nurullah's control as morning sunlight glints on a chaos of mangled flesh and metal smouldering in a Swiss meadow.

Eknath is standing overwrought beside his bed, shaking him awake to tell him of the wreckage. There are no survivors. But why would there be? When had the god of trade not exacted the blood of human sacrifice?

ᔑ

Pete Ryder's hour is up. He thanks me for my time and I walk him to the gate of my small house, left to me by Mrs Shona Tiwari. For a young man the researcher is remarkably equable, a quality I have seen in others of non-violent commitment. Once I was on that high precipice of commitment myself, convinced there was no other path, that it was the path all people would have to take, of battle fatigue and exhaustion, if not wisdom. But the plane crash over the Alps and the warning blow it dealt to the trade wind of a new order put that fantasy to rest. The roughest chapter of trade is about to begin. Oil and allied treasure will exact a more terrifying price than pepper, gold and nutmeg, or teak and diamonds ever did. Asia, and who knows, Africa, will be the battlefields of war immemorial.

At the single small mirror in my room I console myself with gangsterspeak, snarling 'You ain't seen nothin' yet' into my haggard features with a brutishness that fits the future and carries no reminder of the paradise forever lost.